5/07
Hayner 10-08

WHEN GODS DIE

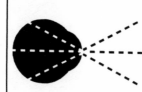

This Large Print Book carries the
Seal of Approval of N.A.V.H.

A SEBASTIAN ST. CYR MYSTERY

When Gods Die

C. S. Harris

THORNDIKE PRESS
An imprint of Thomson Gale, a part of The Thomson Corporation

THOMSON
™
GALE

Detroit • New York • San Francisco • New Haven, Conn. • Waterville, Maine • London

THOMSON

TM

GALE

Thorndike Press® Large Print Historical Fiction.

The text of this Large Print edition is unabridged.

Other aspects of the book may vary from the original edition.

Set in 16 pt. Plantin.

LIBRARY OF CONGRESS CATALOGING-IN-PUBLICATION DATA

Harris, C. S.
  When gods die : a Sebastian St. Cyr mystery / by C.S. Harris.
    p. cm. — (Thorndike Press large print historical fiction)
  ISBN-13: 978-0-7862-9390-2 (lg. print: alk. paper)
  ISBN-10: 0-7862-9390-X (lg. print : alk. paper)
  1. Great Britain — History — George III, 1760–1820 — Fiction. 2. Nobility — Crimes against — Fiction. 3. London (England) — Fiction. 4. Regency fiction. gsafd 5. Large type books. I. Title.
  PS3566.R5877W475 2007
  813'.6—dc22

2006039821

Published in 2007 by arrangement with NAL Signet, a member of Penguin Group (USA) Inc.

Printed in the United States of America on permanent paper
10 9 8 7 6 5 4 3 2 1

For Jon Stebbins, with thanks

ACKNOWLEDGMENTS

A writer always has many people to thank, and this is especially true for me with this book, which wound its way to publication in the aftermath of Hurricane Katrina's destruction of my New Orleans–area home. I am especially grateful to:

My editor, Ellen Edwards, who has been incredibly understanding and cooperative in working with me through all the disruptions of hurricane, evacuation, and rebuilding, as well as providing me, as always, with her wise and thoughtful suggestions. This book would have been less without your input. Thank you.

My daughter Samantha, who handled with aplomb the descent of three generations of family members and five cats upon her tiny Baton Rouge student apartment, and my daughter Danielle, who spent weeks sleeping on a wooden bench and rarely complained. You're both troopers.

My mother, Bernadine Wegmann Proctor, who allowed us to take over her unflooded Metairie bungalow for what began to seem like forever, and my sister, Penelope Williamson, who was there for us when she was so desperately needed. Thank you.

Emily and Bruce Toth (and Beauregard and Mr. Fussy), who generously opened their Baton Rouge home to various members of my family and two of our cats, and my agent, Helen Breitwiezer, friends Ed and Lynn Lindahl, and Paula and Adriel Woodman, who offered us temporary houses from Beverly Hills to Arizona to Alabama. Your generosity overwhelms me. Thank you.

All the friends and relatives who contacted me in the dark and crazy days after the deluge and offered their friendship and support. Thanks especially to old friends Tom Hudson, Nick Fielder, and Tony Lutfi; my Aussie friends Virginia Taylor, Trish Mullin, and Gill Cooper; and my cousin Greg Whitlock. You helped more than you'll ever know.

Ben Woodman, who gave up part of his Christmas vacation to rip out moldy insulation and two-by-fours, and Jon Stebbins, who not only devoted his free time week after week to helping gut and rebuild our house, but also provided a cheerful boost to our morale when we needed it the most.

Friends such as these are rare.

The Monday Night Wordsmiths, Kathleen Davis, Elora Fink, Charles Gramlich, Laura Joh Rowland, and Emily Toth, who kept meeting, even if at first it was only by e-mail. Your friendship, conversation, and support have never been more appreciated. Thank you.

And finally, my husband, Steve Harris, who is not only a great plotting partner, but a whiz with power tools. I couldn't have made it through Katrina or this long, terrible aftermath without you at my side. Thank you.

CHAPTER 1

The Royal Pavilion, Brighton, England.
Wednesday, 12 June 1811.

He knew she'd come to him. They always did.

His Royal Highness George, Prince of Wales and for some four months now Regent of Great Britain and Ireland, closed the cabinet door behind him and let his gaze rove over the swelling curves and exposed flesh of the woman before him. "So you've had a change of heart, have you, madame? A reappraisal of your hasty rejection of my offer of friendship?"

She said nothing, the flickering candlelight throwing the features of her face into shadow so that he couldn't read her expression. She lay with one pale wrist curling provocatively over the gilded carving of the settee beside the fire. Most people complained about the warm temperatures at which George habitually kept his rooms, even on such a mild summer night. But this woman seemed to relish the heat, her gown slipping artfully from her shoulders, her feet bare and seductive. George licked his lips.

From the far side of the closed doors came the strains of a Bach concerto mingling with the murmur of his numerous guests' well-bred voices and, from somewhere in the distance, the faint trill of a woman's high-pitched laughter. At the sound of the laughter, George felt his stomach twist with a spasm of uncertainty.

Tonight's reception had held a special lure, for the guest of honor was none other than the dethroned French King Louis XVIII. But they came here every night, all the snide, contemptuous ladies and gentlemen of the ton. They drank his wine and ate his food and listened to his music, but he knew what they really thought of him. They were always laughing at him, calling him a buffoon. Whispering that he was as mad as his father. They thought he didn't know, but he knew. Just as he knew how they would laugh if he allowed this woman to make a fool of him again.

Why wasn't she saying anything?

Warily, George drew himself up tall, his chest swelling. "What is this, madame? Have you lured me here simply to toy with me? To try to play me for a fool?"

He took a step toward her only to stagger, one plump hand flinging out to grasp the curving back of a nearby chair. It was his ankle, of course. The thing was always giving way beneath him like this. He could hold his wine. Better than most men half his age. Everyone said so.

The candles in the gilded wall sconces flared golden bright, then dimmed. He didn't remember sitting down. But when he opened his eyes he found himself slumped in the chair beside the fire, his chin sunk deep into the elaborate white folds of his cravat. He could feel a line of spittle trickling from one corner of his mouth. Swiping the back of his hand across his jaw, George raised his head.

She lay as before, one bare foot dangling off the edge of the settee's yellow velvet cushion, the shimmering emerald green of her gown sliding seductively from naked shoulders. But she was staring at him with wide, curiously blank eyes.

She was such a beautiful woman, Guinevere Anglessey, the gently molded curves of her half-exposed breasts as white as Devonshire cream, her hair shining blue-black in the candlelight. George slid from the chair

13

to his knees, his voice catching on a sob as he took her cold hand in his. "My lady?"

George knew a tingle of alarm. He hated scenes, and if she'd had some sort of fit there would be a hideous scene. Slipping his hands beneath her bare shoulders, he drew her up to give her a gentle shake. "Are you — oh, my goodness, are you ill?" This new and even more horrifying possibility sent a shudder coursing through him. He was very susceptible to infections. "Shall I call Dr. Heberden?"

He wanted to move away from her immediately, but she lay at such an awkward angle, half on her side, that he had a hard time maneuvering her. "Here, let me make you more comfortable, and I'll have someone send for —"

He broke off, his head jerking around as the double doors to the salon were thrown open. A woman's gay voice said, "Perhaps the Prince is hiding in here."

Caught with the Marquis of Anglessey's beautiful, insensible young wife clasped clumsily in his arms, George froze. Hideously conscious of his ludicrous pose, he licked his suddenly dry lips. "She's fainted, I daresay."

Lady Jersey stood with one hand clenched around the doorknob, her cheeks going white beneath their rouge, her eyes wide and staring. "Oh, my God," she said with a gasp.

The doorway filled with shrieking women and stern-faced men. He recognized his cousin, Jarvis, and Lord Hendon's murderous son, Viscount Devlin. They were all staring. It was a moment before George realized they were staring not at him but at the jeweled hilt of a dagger protruding from the Marchioness of Anglessey's bare back.

George screamed, a high-pitched, feminine scream that echoed strangely as the candles dimmed again and went out.

CHAPTER 2

A cooling breeze skimmed across the Steyne, bringing with it the salty scent of the sea. Sebastian Alistair St. Cyr, Viscount Devlin, paused on the flagging outside the Pavilion and drew the sweet air deep into his lungs.

All around him, the dark streets echoed with panicked shouts for carriages and the running feet of sedan-chair bearers as bejeweled ladies and gentlemen in evening breeches streamed from the Pavilion's open doors into the night. A few threw Sebastian frightened, speculative glances. All gave him a conspicuously wide berth.

"The fools," said a harsh, angry voice from behind him. "What do they think? That *you* killed that woman?"

Sebastian swung around to look into the heavy, troubled features of his father, Alistair St. Cyr, the Fifth Earl of Hendon. Sebastian gave a wry smile. "Presumably they find that a more comforting explanation than the alternative, which is that their regent just stabbed a beautiful young woman in the back."

"Prinny's incapable of that kind of violence, and you know it," snapped Hendon.

"Well, someone certainly killed her. And I, at least, know it wasn't me."

"Let's walk," said Hendon, waving away his carriage. "I need the air."

They turned together toward their hotel on the Marine Parade. Neither spoke, their footsteps echoing softly in the darkness. The familiar scents of sea-bathed rocks and wet sand hung heavy in the warm night air, and the moon-flooded streets were haunted by shared memories neither father nor son cared to confront. For years now they had both avoided Brighton whenever possible. But Hendon's position as Chancellor of the Exchequer combined with the present visit to England by the dispossessed French royal family had made the Earl's presence here in Brighton unavoidable. Sebastian himself had driven down only for the occasion of Hendon's sixty-sixth birthday. The Earl's other living child, Amanda, had stayed away for reasons that were not discussed.

"That woman . . ." Hendon began, only to pause, his jaw working back and forth as it did when he was thoughtful or concerned. In the faint glow of the nearby streetlamp, his face was pale, his hair a shock of white in the moonlight. He cleared his throat and tried again. "She looked oddly like Guinevere Anglessey."

"It was the Marchioness of Anglessey," said Sebastian.

"Good God." Hendon wiped a splayed hand across his grief-slackened face. "This could be the death of Anglessey."

For a moment, Sebastian kept his silence. It was a common enough occurrence in their world, beautiful young women marrying wealthy and titled older men. But even amongst the ton, the forty-five year difference in age between the Marquis and his young wife was considered excessive. "I must admit," said Sebastian, treading carefully in deference to the long-standing friendship between Hendon and Anglessey, "I wouldn't have thought her the type to join the ranks of Prinny's paramours."

Hendon's eyes flashed. "Don't think it for an instant. She was no easy tumble. Not Guinevere."

"Then what the devil was she doing in his cabinet?"

Hendon expelled a harsh breath. "I don't know. But this isn't good. Not for Anglessey or for Prinny — or for you, either," he added. "The last thing you need is to have your name linked with another murdered woman."

Sebastian frowned, his gaze caught by the royal crest emblazoning the panel of a carriage drawn up before their hotel. "Believe me, I have no intention of taking the fall for this one."

Hendon looked at him in surprise. "What makes you even suspect such a thing?"

Wordlessly, Sebastian lifted his chin in the direction of the liveried servant standing beside the carriage's restless team.

"What is this?" said Hendon.

The footman stepped forward and bowed. His livery was unmistakable; the man, like the carriage, came from the Prince's household. "My lord Devlin? Lord Jarvis would like a word with you, my lord. In his chambers at the Pavilion."

Officially, Lord Jarvis was no more than a distant cousin of the King, a wealthy nobleman with a ruthless reputation for shrewdness and a legendary omniscience that came from his wide network of private spies. But in practice, Jarvis was the royal family's brains, a Machiavellian intriguer fiercely devoted to both England and the monarchy with which he identified it. "At this hour?"

said Sebastian.

"He says it's most urgent, my lord."

Given his previous interactions with Jarvis, Sebastian at first wanted to send the servant back to his master with the curtest of messages. Then he thought about Guinevere Anglessey lying pale and lifeless in the Prince's candlelit cabinet, and he hesitated.

"Tell your master Lord Devlin will receive him in the morning," snapped Hendon, his jaw working back and forth in annoyance.

Sebastian shook his head. "No. I leave for London at first light." Wary but intrigued, he leapt into the carriage before the steps were let down. "Don't bother waiting up for me," he told his father, and sank back into the plushly upholstered seat as the footman closed the door.

CHAPTER 3

Charles, Lord Jarvis, occupied a suite of rooms at the Pavilion reserved specifically for his use by his cousin, the Prince Regent.

The Prince's love of the small coastal town of Brighton stretched back thirty years or more, to the days when he'd been young and handsome and even — although it bemused Jarvis to remember it now — popular with the people. The Prince still came here whenever he could, to bathe his bloated body in seawater and host an endless round of musical evenings and card parties, and plan a new series of extravagant extensions and decorating schemes for his Pavilion.

At the moment, Jarvis's rooms were fitted out with dragon-encrusted chandeliers, faux bamboo furniture, and peacock blue wallpaper decorated with gold-leafed exotic beasts. But before the end of the summer, the look might well have changed, perhaps taking on the lush aura of a sultan's harem or a maharaja's temple. Jarvis himself had little affection for the oriental styles with which the Prince was so enamored. But Jarvis understood better than most that the Pavilion — like Carlton House, the Prince's residence in London — was the equivalent of an ornate set of building blocks in the hands of a fat, overindulged child. The endless rebuilding projects might be expensive, but they amused the Prince and kept him safely occupied so that wiser, saner men could get on with the business of running the country.

Standing well over six feet tall and now, in his fifty-eighth year, comfortably fleshy, Jarvis was an imposing man. His size alone would have been impressive. But it was the power of Jarvis's intellect that intimidated most men — his intellect, and the amoral ruthlessness of his dedication to king and country. The position of prime minister could have been his in an instant, had he wanted it. He did not. He knew well that power was far more effective and satisfying when wielded from the shadows. The current Prime Minister, Spencer Perceval, understood precisely how things stood, as did most of the other members of the cabinet. Only two men in the government ever dared to stand against Jarvis. One was the Earl of Hendon, the Chancellor of the Exchequer. The other was this man, the Earl of Portland.

Drawing a delicately carved ivory snuffbox from his pocket, Lord Jarvis eyed the nobleman now pacing back and forth across the chamber's green-and-gold Turkey carpet. A tall, loose-limbed man with an abundance of nervous energy, Portland had been Home Secretary for the past two years. He was generally considered a clever man. Nowhere near as clever as Jarvis, of course, but clever enough to be difficult.

"Why are you doing this?" demanded Portland, the candles in the wall sconces gleaming on his auburn head as his long-legged stride carried him across the room again. "The magistrate has cleared the Prince of all involvement. Let that be the end of it! The longer this thing drags out, the harder it will be on the Prince. The doctors have already had to sedate him."

Jarvis lifted a delicate pinch of snuff to one nostril and sniffed. The Prime Minister, Perceval, had taken himself off to the chapel to pray, content to leave the sordid affair in Jarvis's hands. But not Portland. The man was becoming more than a nuisance; he was becoming a problem.

"The magistrate is an imbecile," said Jarvis, closing his snuffbox with a snap. "As is anyone who seriously thinks the people will believe Lady Anglessey committed suicide by stabbing herself in her back."

Portland had unusually fair skin, nearly as fair as a woman's, with a faint dusting of cinnamon-colored freckles across his high cheekbones. His skin often betrayed him as it did now, flushing with annoyance. "It is theoretically possible. If she positioned the dagger just so and then fell on it —"

"Oh, please," Jarvis shot back. "Half the people out there tonight already believe the Prince killed that woman. If we let the magistrate release this finding, all we'll do is convince the other half."

"Don't be ridiculous. No one could actually believe the Regent capable of . . ." Portland's eyes widened as if on a sudden thought, and his voice trailed away.

"Precisely," said Jarvis. "Everyone will be reminded of Cumberland's valet. The inquest on his death returned a verdict of suicide as well, if you'll remember. Only how many people do you suppose actually believe the poor sod slit his own throat? From left to right. When he was left-handed."

"Cumberland is a dangerous man with a

violent temper. No one could deny that. But whatever else you can say about Prinny, he's nothing like his brother."

Jarvis lifted one eyebrow in silent incredulity.

Again, that faint flush of color showed beneath Portland's pale skin. "Very well. Your point is taken. But why send for Devlin? He was cleared of all suspicion in those ghastly murders last winter."

"Officially," said Jarvis, turning as his footman appeared in the doorway and bowed.

"Viscount Devlin, my lord."

Jarvis could see him now: a tall, lean young man with dark hair and strange, almost animalistic eyes that reputedly had the power to see in the night with the uncanny penetration of a cat. Jarvis knew a moment of quiet satisfaction. He'd half expected Devlin not to come. He was a most unpredictable man, this Viscount; wild and dangerous and utterly, intriguingly brilliant.

Jarvis cast a meaningful glance at the Home Secretary. "If you will excuse us, Lord Portland?"

Portland hesitated, as if tempted to insist he stay. Then he bowed and said curtly, "Of course."

He strode toward the door, his lips pressed

together into a thin line. But Jarvis caught the unexpected, speculative gleam in the man's eyes before he nodded his head and said curtly, "Lord Devlin."

Chapter 4

"Do come in, my lord," said Jarvis, sweeping one arm through the air in an expansive gesture. He'd been blessed with a charming smile that was both disarming and often amazingly effective, and he used that smile now as the Viscount paused just inside the chamber's doorway. "You're surprised, doubtless, by the invitation. If I remember correctly, the last time we met, you held a gun to my head. And abducted my daughter."

Devlin stood very still, his face inscrutable. "I trust she suffered no lasting ill effects."

"Hero? Hardly. The maid, however, has never been the same since." Lifting the crystal decanter from its tray, Jarvis held it aloft. "Brandy?"

Devlin's eyes narrowed. He had inhuman eyes, this young Viscount: as yellow and feral as a wolf's. "I think we can dispense with the civilities."

Jarvis set aside the decanter. "Very well, then. Let's not skirt around the issue. We've asked you here because the Regent needs your help."

"My help."

"That's right. He'd like you to discover exactly what happened in the Pavilion to-night."

The Viscount laughed, his amusement short and sharp and faintly bitter.

Jarvis kept his voice pleasant. "It's not our intention to see you framed for this murder, if that's what you fear."

"How reassuring. Mind you, it would be rather difficult, given that I never left the music room this evening."

"Yet there are those who whisper that your presence at tonight's soiree was . . . shall we say, suggestive?"

"Ah, I see. It's in my own best interest to find this killer — is that what you're say-ing?"

"Something like that."

The Viscount wandered the room, paus-ing for a moment to inspect one of the mythical creatures rendered in gold on the wall cloth. "If I cared what people thought of me, I might be tempted," he said without looking around. "Fortunately, I don't."

Jarvis smoothly shifted tactics, the smile

fading, his voice becoming stentorian and grave. "I fear this murder comes at a critical moment in our nation's history. Our armies are not doing as well as one might wish on the Peninsula, and there are distressing signs that this year's harvest may fail. The people are restless. Have you any idea what a scandal of this nature might do to the country?"

Devlin swung around, a disconcerting gleam in his strange yellow eyes. "I certainly have some personal knowledge of what it might do to Prinny's already faltering popularity."

Reaching for the decanter again, Jarvis poured himself a brandy, then took a long, thoughtful sip. "I'm afraid this isn't just about the Prince. You've heard what people are saying? That it isn't only the King who's mad? They're saying the entire House of Hanover is tainted."

Jarvis had no intention of mentioning it, of course, but there was more to it than that. There'd been disturbing reports lately, of dangerous murmurs and furtive whisperings. Some people were suggesting the House of Hanover was more than mad, that it was cursed — and that England would be cursed, too, as long as the House of Hanover sat upon her throne.

The Viscount was looking faintly bored. "Then I suggest you direct the local magistrate to lose no time in tracking down tonight's killer."

"According to our most estimable local magistrate, the young Marchioness of Anglessey committed suicide."

Devlin was silent for a moment before saying, "Quite a feat, from what I saw."

"Exactly." Jarvis took another sip of his brandy. "Unfortunately, the kinds of people who normally deal with these matters are simply too afraid of giving offense to their betters to be of any real use. What we need is someone who's both intelligent and resourceful, and who isn't afraid to follow the truth wherever it might lead."

He was no fool, Devlin. A faint, contemptuous smile curved his lips. "So bring in a Bow Street Runner. Hell, hire the entire force."

"If we were dealing with some murderous thug who'd come in off the streets, that might suffice. But you know as well as I do that something far more serious is afoot here. We need someone who is a part of our world. Someone who understands it, yet also knows how to track a killer." Jarvis paused significantly. "You did it before. Why not do it again?"

Devlin turned toward the door. "Sorry. I only traveled down to Brighton to spend a few days with my father. I'm expected back in London tomorrow."

Jarvis waited until the Viscount's hand tightened around the knob, then said, "Before you walk away, there's something you should see. Something that actually involves your family directly."

That stopped him, as Jarvis had known it would. The Viscount swung back around. "What?"

Jarvis set aside his glass. "I'll show you."

Sebastian was no stranger to death. Six years of cavalry charges, of slashing sabers and stealthy missions behind enemy lines had left him with searing memories of incidents and images that still haunted his dreams. He had to force himself to follow Jarvis through the door to the Prince's cabinet.

The fire on the hearth had burned down to glowing embers but the room was still warm, the stale air thick with the sweet scent of death. His footsteps echoing hollowly, Sebastian crossed the gaily patterned carpet. Guinevere Anglessey lay on her side, half sliding off the settee where the Prince had dropped her in his agitation. Sebastian stood before her, his gaze traveling the smooth line of her forehead and cheek, the delicate bow of her lips.

She was very young, no more than one- or two-and-twenty. He had met her once, in the company of her husband at a dinner party given by Hendon. He recalled a beautiful woman with a quick wit and dark, sad eyes. Her husband, the Marquis of Anglessey, was close to seventy.

Sebastian glanced back at Jarvis, who had paused, watchful, just inside the door. "The death of anyone so young is tragic," said Sebastian, his voice even. "But it's still none of my affair."

"Take a closer look at her, my lord."

Reluctantly, Sebastian stared down at the woman before him. The shimmering emerald green satin of her evening gown lay loose about her shoulders, its tapes undone, the bodice shoved down nearly to the tips of her full, smooth breasts. From this angle he could only just see the ornate pommel of the jeweled dagger imbedded in her back. But he had a clear view of the necklace that lay nestled in the shadows near the base of her neck.

His eyes narrowed, his breath catching in his throat as he hunkered down beside her. His hand reached out as if to touch the necklace, only to curl back into a fist that he pressed against his lips.

It was an ancient piece, wrought of silver in the shape of a closed triskelion and set against a smooth disk of the same darkly mysterious bluestone found so often in the enigmatic old stone circles of Wales. There was a legend that this necklace had once been worn by the Druid priestesses of Cronwyn. They said it had been passed down through the ages, from one woman to the other, the necklace itself choosing its next caretaker by growing warm and vibrating when the right woman held the old stone in her hand.

Sebastian had been fascinated by this necklace as a child. He used to climb up beside his mother and listen to her soft, melodious voice reciting the old tale. He could remember holding the curiously wrought piece in his hand, willing it to turn warm and vibrate for him. He'd last seen the necklace at his mother's throat, its burnished silver shining brilliantly in the sun as she waved good-bye to him from the deck of the neat little two-masted yacht a friend had hired for a lark one summer's day when Sebastian was eleven.

The afternoon had been unusually hot, the sea breeze a gentle breath of fresh air.

But then the day had turned rough, dark clouds scuttling across the sun, the wind kicking up strong. The two-masted craft had floundered in heavy seas and gone down with all on board.

The body of the Countess of Hendon — and the necklace she'd worn that day — had never been recovered.

CHAPTER 5

"It can't be the same necklace," said Sebastian.

He didn't realize he'd spoken aloud until Lord Jarvis answered him. "But it is," said Jarvis, coming to stand beside him. "Look at the back."

Moving carefully, Sebastian flipped the triskelion, his fingertips just brushing the woman's cold flesh. In the flickering light from the wall sconces he could see where the initials A. C. had been artfully entwined with a second set of initials. J. S.

The engraving was old — not as old as the necklace itself, but still worn with the passage of the years. It had been well over a century and a half since Addiena Cadel had marked the necklace with her initials and those of her lover, James Stuart — the same James Stuart who later assumed the British throne as James II.

Sebastian sat back on his heels, his splayed

hands gripping his thighs. "How did you know?" he asked after a moment. "How did you know my mother once owned this necklace?"

"She showed it to me one day when I happened to admire it. Its story is an intriguing one. Not the sort of thing you forget."

"And did you know she was wearing it the day she died?"

A faint widening of the eyes was Jarvis's only sign of reaction. "No. No, I didn't. How . . . curious."

The memory of that cold brush of dead flesh against his hand nagged at Sebastian. Curious, he leaned forward to study the woman before him. Her fingertips were already turning blue, the muscles of her neck stiff with the rigor of death. Yet the skin of her face seemed unnaturally pink. "How long has it been?" he asked Jarvis.

"How long since what?"

"Since the Prince was found with the Marchioness in his arms. Two hours, would you say? Less?"

"Less, I'd say. Why?"

Reaching out, Sebastian rested his palm against Lady Anglessey's smooth young cheek. It was cool to the touch. "She's cold," said Sebastian. "She shouldn't be this cold."

He glanced over at the glowing coals on the hearth. His years in the army had taught him only too well what the passage of time does to a dead body. Heat could accelerate the processes of death, he knew. But it should at least have kept the body warm.

Jarvis took a step closer. "What are you suggesting?"

Sebastian frowned. "I'm not certain. Have either of the Prince's physicians seen her?" The Regent had two personal physicians, Dr. Heberden and Dr. Carlyle. They were rarely far from his side.

"Naturally."

"And?"

A derisive smile twisted the other man's full lips. "Both supported the magistrate's conclusion that she committed suicide."

Sebastian let out a humorless huff that was not quite a laugh. "Of course."

He rose to his feet. She still lay as he had found her, awkwardly curled on one side. Reaching out, he gently rolled her body toward him.

The disarrangement of her satin gown had left her back essentially bare. There was something violently sexual, almost intimate, about the way the dagger's blade disappeared into her dark, livid flesh. Sebastian drew a quick breath.

Beside him, Jarvis was silent for a moment. Then he said, "Good God. She appears to have been badly beaten."

Sebastian shook his head. "That's not bruising. I've seen it happen before, with soldiers left on the battlefield. It's as if all the blood in a body collects at its lowest points after death."

"But she was lying on her side, not her back."

"It would be difficult to do anything else with that dagger in her," said Sebastian. Gently lifting the blue-black hair that tumbled around her neck, Sebastian released the necklace's clasp and eased the thick, intricate chain away from her throat. "There's a surgeon of my acquaintance who has made a study of these things — an Irishman by the name of Paul Gibson. He has a surgery near the base of Tower Hill. I want him sent for right away."

"You want to bring a surgeon all the way down from London?" Jarvis laughed. "But it'll be ten hours or more before he gets here. Surely we can find someone locally."

Sebastian glanced at the man beside him. "To give us the same opinion as His Highness's personal physicians?"

Jarvis said nothing.

"It's important that no one else be allowed

to enter this room until Gibson arrives. Can you arrange that?"

"Naturally."

Sebastian turned in a slow circle, his gaze covering the chamber. "Do you notice something else strange?"

Jarvis regarded him with vague animosity. The earlier winning smile was long gone. "Should I?"

"That dagger was well aimed. It would have pierced her heart. Wounds of that nature typically bleed profusely."

"Good God," said Jarvis, his gaze lifting from the young Marchioness's livid bare back to Sebastian's face. "You're right. There's no blood."

CHAPTER 6

Half an hour later, Sebastian walked into the private parlor of his father's rooms at the Anchor on the Marine Parade. In a tapestry-covered chair beside the empty hearth, the Earl of Hendon sat with an open book on his lap, his head nodding to one side as he dozed.

"You shouldn't have waited up," said Sebastian.

His head jerking, Hendon quietly closed his book and set it aside. "I couldn't sleep."

Sebastian leaned against the doorframe, one hand absently fingering the bluestone necklace in his pocket. "Tell me about the Marquis of Anglessey."

Hendon rubbed his eyes with a spread thumb and index finger. "He's a good man. Steady. Honorable. He does his duty in the House of Lords, although he has no special interest in government." He paused. "Surely you don't think Anglessey had anything to do with what happened tonight?"

"I don't know what to think. How well did you know Lady Anglessey?"

Hendon let out his breath in a long sigh. "Such a beautiful young woman, Guinevere. They married three — maybe four years ago now. There was considerable talk at the time, of course, given the difference in their ages. Some considered it a scandal, a sick old man taking such a young woman to wife. But the marriage was understandable."

"How's that?"

"Anglessey is desperate for an heir."

"Ah. And was he successful in getting one?"

"I heard just last week that Lady Anglessey was with child."

"Jesus." Sebastian pushed away from the door and walked into the room. "She was discovered in a decidedly compromising position this evening. Yet you say such behavior was not typical of her?"

"No. There has never been a whisper of scandal attached to her name."

"What do you know of her family?"

"Nothing reprehensible there. Her father was the Earl of Athelstone. From Wales. I believe her brother, the new Earl, is still a child." Hendon let his head fall back against the tapestry of the chair as he looked up at his son. "What has any of this to do with you?"

"Jarvis thought I might find the circumstances of Lady Anglessey's death interesting."

"Interesting?" Hendon shook his head. "You? But . . . why?"

Sebastian drew the silver-and-bluestone necklace from his pocket and dangled it in the air between them. "Because she was wearing this around her neck when she died."

Hendon's face went suddenly, completely white. But he made no move to take the necklace or even touch it. "That's impossible."

Bringing up his other hand, Sebastian dropped the necklace neatly into his palm. "I would have said so, yes."

Hendon sat quite still, his hands gripping the upholstered arms of his chair. "Surely they don't mean to accuse you of any involvement in this death."

A slow smile curled Sebastian's lips. "Not this one." He went to stand with one arm braced against the mantel, his head bowed as he stared down at the empty grate. "It has occurred to me that an eleven-year-old's memories of his mother's death might easily be distorted," he said slowly. It was not

42

something they had ever spoken of, that long-ago summer day. Not that day, or the endless, pain-filled days that followed. "Her body was never found, was it?" Sebastian looked around.

"No. Never." Hendon worked his jaw back and forth in that way he had. "She wore the necklace often. But I honestly couldn't say if she had it on the day she died."

"She was wearing it. Of that I am certain."

Hendon pushed up from his chair and went to where a tea service and cups rested on a nearby table. But made no move to pour the tea. "There is a logical explanation. Her body must have washed up somewhere along the coast."

"To be found by some desperate soul who stripped the corpse of everything valuable and sold the necklace for his next meal?" Sebastian kept his gaze on his father's broad, tight back. "That's one explanation."

Hendon swung around again, his fleshy face dark with emotion. "Good God. What other explanation could there be?"

Their gazes met across the room, father and son, startling blue eyes clashing with strange yellow ones. It was Hendon who looked away first.

"What do you mean to do?" he asked, his voice oddly strained.

Sebastian's fist tightened around the necklace. "Talk to Anglessey, for one thing. See if he knows how his wife came by this. Although that hardly seems the most important issue at the moment, now does it?"

Hendon's mouth went slack. "You're not seriously taking it upon yourself to uncover this killer?"

"Yes."

Hendon digested this in silence. Then he said, "What does Prinny say happened?"

"He's been sedated. I intend to talk to him first thing in the morning."

Hendon let out a derisive grunt. "Jarvis won't let you anywhere near the Prince. Not if you're intending to ask something he might potentially find disturbing."

"I think he will."

"Why should he?"

Sebastian pushed away from the hearth and turned. "Because this dynasty is one step away from disaster, and Jarvis knows it."

CHAPTER 7

Jarvis was annoyed.

He wasn't entirely certain how Devlin had managed to coerce him into agreeing to this early-morning meeting with the Prince, but somehow the Viscount had succeeded. Even under the best of circumstances, the Regent was rarely coherent before noon. As it was, last night's shock had come close to over-setting him entirely.

The Prince lay sprawled in silk-dressing-gowned splendor against the tufted velvet cushions of a sofa placed close to his bed-chamber's roaring fire, his pupils narrowed down to pinpoints by laudanum, his lower lip trembling with petulance. The heavy satin drapes at the windows were drawn fast against the morning sun.

"You think I don't hear what people are saying, but I do. I do! They're actually sug-gesting that I might have killed Lady An-glessey. *Me.*" The fat princely fingers tightened around his vial of smelling salts. "You must do something, Jarvis. Make them understand they're wrong. Wrong!"

Jarvis kept his voice soothing but firm. "We're trying, sir. Which is what makes it vital that you tell Lord Devlin precisely what happened last night."

Swallowing hard, the Prince glanced over to where the Viscount stood with his flawlessly tailored shoulders resting negligently against the Chinese papered wall, his arms folded at his chest, his attention seemingly focused on the highly polished toes of his Hessians. George might not understand precisely why Devlin had agreed to be drawn into this nasty little affair; he might even half believe the young Viscount to be guilty of murder himself. But Jarvis knew the Prince was shrewd enough to understand that the attempts by his doctors and the magistrate to portray the Marchioness's death as suicide had done him more harm than good. George needed help, and he recognized it.

Covering his eyes with one hand, the Prince let go a shaky breath. "God help me, I don't know."

Devlin looked up, his expression one of mild interest rather than the irritation Jarvis had expected. "Think back to earlier in the

46

evening, sir," said the Viscount, pushing away from the wall. "How did you happen to be in the cabinet with the Marchioness?"

George let his hand fall limply to his side. "She sent me a note, suggesting I meet her."

Jarvis knew a quiet flare of surprise, but Devlin — unaware of the implications of this statement — simply asked, "Do you still have the note?"

The Prince's face went blank. He shook his head. "I don't think so, no. Why would I keep it?"

"Do you remember precisely what it said?"

The Regent had a reputation for telling tall tales, for boasting of imagined feats on the hunting field and entertaining guests at his table with fanciful accounts of leading troops into battle when the only uniforms he'd ever worn were ceremonial ones. But for all his practice, George remained an appallingly bad liar. Now, his lips threatening to curve into a betraying smile, the Prince stared back at Devlin and said baldly, "Not precisely, no. Only that she wished to meet me in the Yellow Cabinet."

Impossible for Jarvis to tell whether Devlin read the lie or not. The young man had a rare ability to keep his thoughts and feelings to himself. He said, "So you found her there? In the Yellow Cabinet?"

"Yes. She was lying on the sofa before the fire." The Prince sat forward almost eagerly. "I'm certain of that. I remember admiring the gleam of the firelight over her bare shoulders."

"Did you speak to her?"

"Yes. Of course." A note of regal impatience crept into the Prince's voice. "Surely you don't expect me to remember precisely what I said?"

"Do you remember if she answered you?"

The Prince opened his mouth, then closed it. "I'm not certain," he said after a moment. "I mean, I don't *remember* her answering me. But she must have done so."

"One would think so," said Devlin. "Unless she were already dead when you entered the room."

The Prince's normally ruddy cheeks paled. "Good God. Is that what you think? But . . . how is that possible? I mean, surely I would have noticed. Wouldn't I?"

Devlin had his keen gaze fixed on the Prince's face. And for one sliver of a moment Jarvis knew a rare whisper of misgiving, a brief questioning of the wisdom of his decision to draw the Viscount into this investigation.

"How long between the time you entered the chamber and when Lady Jersey threw open the door from the music room?" said Devlin, his voice deceptively casual.

The Prince plucked peevishly at the edge of his dressing gown. "I think . . . I rather think I might have fallen asleep."

The implications were damning. A flicker of something showed in the younger man's eyes. "Then you do have reason to be quite certain that the lady was not already dead when you first entered the room."

The Prince's cheeks flushed from unnaturally pale to sudden dark crimson as he realized the conclusion Devlin had inevitably drawn. "No, no," he said in a rush. "It's not what you think. I never touched her. I'm certain I didn't. My ankle gave way as I was crossing the room toward her, and I sat down on one of the chairs."

"And fell asleep?"

"Yes. I do sometimes. After a heavy meal."

Devlin chose — wisely, Jarvis thought — not to respond to that. Pausing before a faux bamboo étagère tucked inside an arched niche, the Viscount ran his gaze over the artfully displayed collection of delicate ivory carvings. "How well acquainted were you with the Marchioness?" he asked, his attention all seemingly for the carvings.

George's jaw jutted out mulishly. "I barely knew the woman."

Devlin glanced over at the Prince. "Yet you weren't surprised to receive a note from her, asking to meet you privately?"

The Prince's massive torso jerked with his suddenly agitated breathing. "What are you suggesting? It's *Anglessey* people should be suspecting, not me! I mean, it is usually the husband who's found to be the culprit in this sort of thing, is it not?" His moist lips parted, his nostrils flaring as one beringed hand fluttered up to clutch at his chest. "Good heavens. I'm having palpitations. Where is Dr. Heberden?"

Jarvis took a hasty step forward as the doctor appeared suddenly from a curtained embrasure. "That's enough questions for now, Lord Devlin. If you'll excuse us, please?"

For one sharply tense moment, Devlin hesitated. Then he bowed curtly and swung away.

"You will, of course, be looking into the Marquis's possible involvement in all of this?" Jarvis asked in an undervoice as he walked with Devlin to the door.

Devlin kept his expression bland. "It had occurred to me to do so," he said, then added, "In the meantime, you might ask the Prince's man to go through the pockets of the coat the Prince was wearing last night.

It would help if that note could be found."

"Of course," said Jarvis.

Pausing at the entrance to the library that served as an antechamber to the Regent's bedroom, the Viscount looked around. A tight smile curled his lips, a smile that told Jarvis he knew bloody well the note would never be found. "And perhaps when the Prince has recovered sufficiently, you might ask if he remembers exactly who handed him the note from the Marchioness?"

"When and if Dr. Heberden considers it safe to bring up the subject again, yes. You understand, of course, that protecting the Prince's delicate sensibilities is of paramount importance."

"More important than discovering the truth about who killed Lady Anglessey?"

Jarvis held the younger man's hard stare. "Don't ever doubt it for a moment."

Leaving the Prince's suite, Sebastian paused in the overheated corridor, one hand idly fingering the necklace in his pocket. Some of what the Prince had told him, Sebastian knew, was probably the truth. The trick would be to separate the reality from the layers of invention and sheer obstreperousness.

He was about to turn toward the stables

when someone nervously cleared his throat and said, "My lord?"

Sebastian looked around to find a young, pale-skinned man with dark bushy eyebrows and gaunt cheeks hovering nearby, a man Sebastian recognized as one of Jarvis's secretaries. "Yes?"

The man bowed. "The surgeon has arrived from London, my lord. He's been shown directly to the Yellow Cabinet, as you requested."

Chapter 8

Sebastian found Paul Gibson on the floor beside the couch in the Yellow Cabinet, his wooden leg thrust out awkwardly to one side.

"Ah, there you are, Sebastian me lad," he said, his eyes creasing into a smile as he glanced around at Sebastian's entrance.

They were old friends, Sebastian and this dark-haired Irishman with the merry green eyes and a roguish dimple in one cheek. Theirs was a bond forged in blood and mud, and tested by suffering and want and the threat of death. Once, Gibson had been a surgeon in the British Army, a man whose fierce determination to help those in need often took him into harm's way. Even after a French cannonball took off the lower part of his left leg, Gibson had remained in the field. But continuing ill health — and an accompanying weakness for the sweet relief to be found in poppies — had forced him to leave the army two years ago and set up a small surgery in the City, where he devoted much of his energy to research and the teaching of medical students, and to providing the authorities with his expert opinion in criminal cases.

"You made good time," said Sebastian.

"Dead bodies don't share their secrets for long," said Gibson, returning his attention to what was left of Lord Anglessey's beautiful young wife, Guinevere. "And this one has some interesting stories to tell."

He had rolled the body so that it lay fully facedown on the floor. In the harsh light of day, the skin at the back of her neck could now be seen to have turned a greenish red. A faint odor like that of rotting meat permeated the chamber, although the heavy drapes had been pulled back and the long windows thrown open to flood the room with enough fresh air and sunlight to give the Prince Regent an apoplexy.

Sebastian went to stand beside the open windows, his gaze on the gulls wheeling and calling against the vivid blue sky above the Strand. "When would you say she died?"

"It's difficult to be precise, but I think early yesterday afternoon is more likely than yesterday morning."

Sebastian swung around. "Not last night?"

"No. Of that there is no doubt."

"You know what this means, don't you? The servants would have come in this room to build up the fire before last night's performance. There's no way the body could have lain here undiscovered for so long. She must have been killed someplace else and brought here just before the Prince discovered her."

Gibson settled back on his sound heel and frowned. "You think this was set up to deliberately cast suspicion upon the Prince?"

"It looks that way, doesn't it?" Sebastian wandered the room, searching for something — anything — that he might have missed. The cabinet's walls were hung with linen painted with a tracery of apple green foliage against a delicate yellow background. A series of giant arches, each containing a life-sized gilt figure of a Chinese woman, encircled the room. The oriental motif here was strong, with tables and chairs of a pale wood carved to resemble bamboo, and a large lacquered chest decorated with painted dragons that stood between two of the arches. "The Prince claims to have received a note from Lady Guinevere," said Sebastian, inspecting one of the gilded ladies. "A note arranging a rendezvous with him here.

Only, how could she have sent him a note if she was already dead?"

"She could have written the note earlier in the day."

"I suppose it's possible. Unfortunately, His Royal Highness doesn't recall precisely when or how the note came into his hands."

"In his cups again, was he?"

"From the sounds of things, yes." Sebastian went to check the locks on the long windows. All were intact. But then, if someone had access to the Pavilion, it would have been easy enough to open one of the windows from the inside. How many people had attended last night's musical evening? he wondered. The presence of the dispossessed French royal family had attracted even those who normally avoided the Pavilion; the reception rooms had been packed.

His eyes narrowing against the sun's bright glare, Sebastian stared off across the park. It would take an extraordinary amount of sangfroid to carry a dead body across the Pavilion's open grounds in the midst of one of the Prince's musical evenings. Unless . . .

Unless, of course, the body had been moved to the Yellow Cabinet from someplace else *inside* the Pavilion.

"From the pattern of lividity," Gibson said

56

thoughtfully, "the body was obviously left lying on its back for several hours before someone slipped that blade into her."

"What?" Sebastian looked around in surprise. He'd noticed the lack of blood in the room and simply assumed it was because the actual murder had taken place somewhere else. It had never occurred to him that Guinevere Anglessey had already been dead when she was stabbed. "But if the dagger didn't kill her, then what did?"

"There's no way to tell. Not without a proper autopsy." Gibson looked up. "Any chance of it?"

Sebastian let out his breath in an ironic huff. "You certainly won't get the local magistrate to commission one. He's already decreed the lady's death a suicide."

"Suicide? How on earth did he come up with that?"

"The Regent's physicians have concurred."

Gibson was silent for a moment. Then he said, "I see. Anything to avoid casting suspicion on the Prince. Do you think her husband could be persuaded to order a postmortem?"

"I suppose that depends on whether or not the Marquis of Anglessey had something to do with her murder."

Gibson reached to draw a white sheet over the body at his feet. "He does seem a likely suspect, does he not? What do you know of him?"

"Anglessey? He's generally considered a sober enough man — keeps his estates in good order, and divides his time between them and affairs at the House of Lords. Or at least," Sebastian added, "he was considered sober until his latest marriage."

Paul Gibson glanced over at him in surprise. "Was she so unsuitable?"

"By birth, no. Only by age. Anglessey is a year or two older than my father."

"Good God."

"It would give Anglessey a motive both to kill his wife and to attempt to implicate the Prince in her murder, if Anglessey discovered the Prince was cuckolding him."

"*Was* she one of the Prince's paramours?"

"I honestly don't know. The Prince claims they were barely acquainted."

"But you don't believe him."

"He's lying about something. I just don't know what."

Gibson began collecting his scattered instruments to stow them in his black leather bag. "Did you actually see this note the Prince says he received?"

"No. It's gone missing."

"By accident, or by design, I wonder." Gibson pushed up to a stand, staggering slightly as his weight shifted to his wooden leg. "More's the pity. I should think if you could discover the origins of that note, you'd likely have your killer."

"Perhaps. Although I suspect our killer is much too clever to be caught so easily."

Sebastian became aware of Paul Gibson's intense green eyes studying him. "What's any of this to do with you, Sebastian?"

With anyone else, Sebastian might have dissembled. But the friendship between him and the Irishman ran deep. Sebastian drew his mother's necklace from his pocket. "Lady Guinevere was wearing this when she died."

"A curious piece." Gibson's brows twitched. "But again, what has it to do with you?"

Sebastian held the necklace cradled in his palm. It had always seemed to him that the stones grew faintly warm against his skin. But in his mother's hand, he'd seen the stones pulse with so much energy as to become almost hot to the touch. . . . Or at least, so it had seemed to him as a child.

"The necklace belonged to my mother," he said simply.

Paul Gibson raised his gaze to his friend's

face. "Something strange is going on here, Sebastian. Something that could be dangerous. For anyone involved."

"If you want to have nothing further to do with it, I'll understand."

Gibson made a swift, impatient gesture with one hand. "Don't be ridiculous. You're the one I'm worried about. Who brought you into this?"

"Ostensibly, the Prince. In reality? Jarvis."

"And you trust him?"

Sebastian gazed down at the still, ravaged body of the woman hidden beneath the sheet. "Not at all. But someone killed Guinevere Anglessey. Someone slipped that dagger into the livid flesh of her bare back and brought her body here to drape it across that couch in a deliberately suggestive posture. Lord Jarvis's sole intent in all this is to protect the Prince. But mine is different. I'm going to find out who killed this woman, and I'm going to see that he pays for it."

"Because of the necklace?"

Sebastian shook his head. "Because if I don't, no one else will."

"What does it matter to you?"

One of Guinevere's slim white hands peeked out from beneath the sheet, its fingers curled lightly in death. Seeing it, Sebastian was reminded of another woman, left to die on an altar's steps, her throat viciously slashed, her body obscenely violated; and another, hunted down like an unwary quarry and subjected to the same hideous end.

He had few illusions about the world in which he lived. He knew the shocking inequality between its privileged and its poor; he recognized the savage injustice of a legal system that could hang an eight-year-old boy for stealing a loaf of bread and yet let a king's son get away with murder. Once, he'd been so repulsed by the raw barbarism and senseless cruelty of the wars his people fought in the name of liberty and justice that he'd been content simply to let himself drift, aimless and alone. Now that struck him as a reaction that was both self-indulgent and faintly cowardly.

Crouching down beside what was left of the young woman named Guinevere, Sebastian tucked the sheet over that pale, vulnerable hand and said softly, "It matters."

CHAPTER 9

Sebastian was crossing the yard toward the Pavilion's glass-domed, Xanadu-inspired stables when he heard someoneg calling his name. *"Lord Devlin."*

He turned to find the Home Secretary, Lord Portland, coming toward him across the paving. The midday sun was bright on the nobleman's flaming red hair, but the skin of his face was pale and drawn tight as if with worry.

"Walk with me a ways, my lord," said Portland, turning their steps down a path that angled off across the Pavilion's wide expanse of green lawn. "I understand you've agreed to help sort out the truth about last night's peculiar incident."

Sebastian's acquaintance with the Earl of Portland was slight, although in the year since Sebastian's return from the Continent he'd attended several dinner parties and soirees in the man's company. Like Jarvis and Hendon, Portland was profoundly conservative in his politics, dedicated to continuing the war against France and preserving England's institutions in the face of a rising tide of demands for reform.

Yet whatever his opinion of the reactionary quality of the man's beliefs, Sebastian couldn't help but respect him. The Earl of Portland was one of the few men in the government — or out of it — who refused to play the role of one of Jarvis's pawns. But there was something distasteful, almost sordid about referring to the death of a vital young woman as a *peculiar incident.*

"If you mean Lady Anglessey's murder," said Sebastian, "then yes."

"According to both the magistrate and the Prince's doctors, the death was a suicide."

Sebastian raised one eyebrow. "Is that what you believe?"

Portland expelled a harsh breath and shook his head. "No."

They walked along in silence for a moment, Portland worrying his lower lip with his teeth. At last he said, "I feel somehow as if this were all my fault."

"How is that?"

"If I hadn't given the Prince that note —"

Sebastian swung to face him. "*You* gave the Prince the note from Lady Anglessey?"

"Yes. Although, of course, I'd no notion who she was. She was veiled."

"When was this?"

"Shortly after the Prince's chamber orchestra began playing last night. I was approached by a veiled young woman who handed me a sealed missive and asked that I pass it on to the Prince." Portland hesitated, his fair skin coloring. "It's hardly the first time I've been approached in such a way."

Sebastian kept his thoughts to himself. Over the years, the Prince's paramours had ranged from common opera dancers and actresses such as Mrs. Fitzherbert to some of the grandest dames of the ton — Lady Jersey and Lady Hertford among them. It wasn't uncommon for those close to the Prince to find themselves thrust into the role of procurer.

"I actually know Guinevere Anglessey rather well," Portland was saying. "She is — was — a childhood friend of my wife, Claire. It never occurred to me that's who I was dealing with."

"You weren't."

Sebastian watched the man's light gray eyes widen, watched the first shock give way to some other emotion, something that looked oddly like fear. "I beg your pardon?"

"By the time the Regent's chamber orchestra began playing last night, Lady Anglessey had already been dead perhaps as much as six to eight hours."

Portland stopped short. "*What?* But . . . that's impossible."

"The human body undergoes certain predictable changes after death. Temperature and the manner of one's dying can accelerate or retard the process, but not by that much. I'm afraid there's no mistake."

"But I tell you, *I saw her.* She gave me the note."

"You saw a woman, veiled. Do you remember how she was dressed?"

Portland stood very still, as if drawing into himself with the effort of memory. But in the end he simply shook his head. "No. I'm not certain of anything anymore. I mean, I'd have said she wore a green satin gown like Lady Anglessey. But if what you say is true, then that's not possible, is it?"

"Perhaps. Perhaps not."

The Home Secretary shook his head again, his features pinched with confusion. "I don't understand. Who could she have been?"

"I don't know yet," said Sebastian, his

gaze lifting to the gulls wheeling above the Strand. "But whoever she was, she was obviously involved in Lady Anglessey's murder."

Sebastian sent a footman running for his curricle, then stood on the Pavilion's gravel sweep and watched as his tiger, Tom, brought Sebastian's matched pair of blood chestnuts to a stand.

It wasn't a practice that particularly appealed to Sebastian, this current fashion among the sporting gentlemen of the ton for entrusting prime horseflesh to young boys decked out in the yellow-and-black-striped waistcoats that had earned them the nickname tigers. But Tom had taken to his new profession with an innate talent that had caught Sebastian by surprise. Plus Tom had other talents not normally encountered in a gentleman's tiger, talents Sebastian had at times found particularly useful.

A dark-haired, sharp-faced lad of twelve, Tom looked even younger, his slight frame still wiry and small despite the new bloom of health in his cheeks. Up until four months ago he'd been one of the thousands of nameless urchins scratching out a precarious living on the streets of London, a pickpocket with a murky past and a secret passion for horses. His loyalty to Sebastian now was fierce.

Aware of Sebastian's gaze upon him, the boy drew up with a neat flourish. "They're feeling their oats this mornin' for sure, gov'nor," he said, breaking into a gap-toothed smile.

"I'll be certain to give them their heads for a stretch on my way out to Lord Anglessey's." Sebastian swung up to take the reins. "I want you to hang around here. See if you can find out what they're saying in the kitchen and stables. One of the servants must have seen or heard something last night. I'm particularly interested in anyone who might have been carrying something unusual. Something large."

Tom hopped down, his eyes flashing. "You mean, something big enough to hide a body in?"

There was no doubt about it — the boy was quick. Sebastian smiled. "As a matter of fact, yes."

Tom took a step back, one hand coming up to anchor his cap to his head as a salt-laden breeze gusted up from the Strand. "If'n anybody seen anythin', gov'nor, I'll find 'im, never you fear."

"Oh and, Tom?" Sebastian added as the boy started to dash off. "Don't lift anyone's purse, you hear? Not even just for practice."

Tom drew himself up with a show of wounded dignity and sniffed. "As if I would."

CHAPTER 10

Unlike most members of the ton who hired narrow town houses on the streets of Brighton for the summer months, Oliver Godwin Ellsworth, the Fourth Marquis of Anglessey, possessed an estate of his own on the outskirts of town.

It was one of his lesser properties, and quite small compared to his main seat in Northumberland, but the house was neat and comfortable, and pleasantly situated on a hillside overlooking the clean sweep of the sea a reasonable distance from the noise and bustle of Brighton's streets.

Leaving the chestnuts in the care of a groom, Sebastian found the Marquis in a garden of mossy brick paths and carefully tended roses that thrived in the lee of the high walls sheltering them from the worst of the salty winds blowing up from the sea. At the sound of Sebastian's footsteps, Anglessey turned, an old man with once dark hair heavily laced now with strands of gray. Only a few years Hendon's senior, he seemed older, his body thin, his face drawn with the lines of ill health and visibly weighed down by a heavy burden of recent grief.

"Thank you for agreeing to see me at such a time," said Sebastian, pausing in a bright patch of June sunlight. "I can't tell you how sorry I am about what has happened."

The Marquis went back to clipping the spent blooms of a pale pink rose that twined around a stout pillar at the edge of the path. "But that's not why you're here, is it?"

The directness of the question took Sebastian by surprise. "No," he answered with equal bluntness. "Lord Jarvis has asked me to look into the circumstances surrounding your wife's death."

The Marquis's fist tightened around his secateurs. "To protect the Prince, of course." He said it as a statement, rather than a question.

"That's their motive, yes."

The Marquis looked around, one eyebrow arched. "But not yours?"

"No." Sebastian met the old man's steady, intelligent gaze. "Do you think he did it?"

"The Prince?" Anglessey shook his head and went back to pruning the rose. "Prinny might be a drunken, overindulged, self-coddling idiot, but he's not violent. Not like his brother Cumberland." He paused to subject his handiwork to a critical assessment, his jaw hardening in a way that belied both age and infirmity. "But make no mistake about this: if I'm wrong — if I should discover Prinny did have something to do with Guin's death — I won't let him get away with it. Prince Regent or not."

Sebastian studied that angry, grief-stricken face. The Marquis might be old, but there was nothing weak or feeble about either his determination or his powers of understanding. "So who do you think killed your wife, sir?"

An odd half smile touched the old man's lips. "Do you realize you're the first person who's asked me that? I suppose it's because everyone who doesn't think the Prince killed Guinevere naturally assumes I did it."

The Marquis moved on to the next rose. Sebastian waited, the sun warm on his shoulders, and after a moment the Marquis said, "They've refused to let me have Guinevere's body. Did you know that? They say there's some surgeon coming down from London. Someone they want to take a look at her."

"Paul Gibson. He's very good at this sort

of thing. He'd like your permission to do a complete autopsy."

Anglessey glanced around. "Why?"

Sebastian met the old man's pained, haggard gaze. "Because Lady Anglessey wasn't killed last night. She was killed sometime yesterday afternoon and her body moved to the Yellow Cabinet in time for the Prince to find her."

An angry light flared in the old man's eyes. "What is this? Some trick to throw suspicion away from the Prince?"

"No. As a matter of fact, the Prince's physicians have given it as their opinion that Lady Guinevere committed suicide."

"*Suicide!* With a dagger sticking out of her back?"

"Exactly." Sebastian hesitated, then added, "Except that the dagger isn't what killed her. According to Gibson, she was probably dead several hours before she was stabbed."

"Good God. What are you suggesting?"

Sebastian shook his head. "We don't know how she died, sir. That's why Gibson wants your permission to do a postmortem. Without one, it's going to be difficult to ever understand what happened to your wife."

There was a moment of silence, filled with the *click-click* of the Marquis's secateurs and the distant cry of the gulls. Then he said,

"Very well. Your Dr. Gibson has my permission." He cast Sebastian a fierce glance over one shoulder. "But I want to be informed of everything. Do you hear me? No holding back out of consideration for my age or my health or any of that nonsense."

"No holding back."

Anglessey pressed his lips together, his nostrils flaring as he sucked in a quick, deep breath. "I know what people think of my marriage to Guinevere. An old man like me, taking to wife a woman young enough to be his granddaughter. They act like it was something disgraceful, something sordid. As if the forty-five-year difference in our ages made it somehow impossible for me to love her."

He paused, his hands stilling as he stared off toward the end of the garden, his voice becoming hushed. "But I did love her, you know. Not because she was beautiful — although God knows she was. But she was so much more than that. She was . . . she was like a breath of fresh air that came into my life. So full of energy and passion. So bright, so determined to grasp life with both hands and make of it what she wanted —" He broke off and had to suck in a quick gasp of air before saying more quietly, "I can't believe she's dead."

Sebastian waited a moment, then asked again, quietly, "Who do you think killed her, sir?"

Anglessey went to sink down on the weathered wooden bench sheltered by a nearby arbor, his hands in his lap. "Guinevere was my third wife," he said, his voice once again firm, under control. "The first died within hours of presenting me with a stillborn son. The second was barren."

Sebastian nodded. There was no need for the Marquis to explain further. He and Sebastian belonged to the same world, a world in which everyone understood only too clearly the need for a man in their position to produce a legitimate heir. Even at twenty-eight, Sebastian had already felt that pressure brought to bear upon himself, both by his father and by the weight of his own awareness of what he owed his house, his name.

"Ever since the death of my brother twenty years ago," Anglessey was saying, "my heir has been my nephew. Bevan."

The implications were inescapable. Sebastian studied the old man's closed, angry face. "You think him capable of murder?"

"I think Bevan Ellsworth could kill someone who stood between him and what he considered his, yes. And as far as Bevan is

74

concerned, my estates are essentially his. He took my marriage to Guinevere as a personal affront. He actually threatened to try to have the marriage set aside — as if he could."

"Yet it's been several years since your marriage. Why kill Lady Anglessey now?"

Anglessey let out a pained sigh. "Bevan's expenses have always exceeded his income. Of course, as far as Bevan is concerned, the fault lies entirely with the inadequacy of his income rather than with the extravagance of his habits. He's a very natty dresser, my nephew. He's also sadly addicted to games of chance. As long as he was my heir, his creditors were willing to give him pretty much a free rein. I suspect things must have become rather uncomfortable when it became known that my wife was with child."

"Yet the child might have been a girl," Sebastian felt compelled to note, "in which case Bevan Ellsworth's position as your heir would have remained secure."

"The child might have been a girl," Anglessey agreed. "But, frankly, I don't think Bevan could afford to take that chance."

Sebastian stood with the sun behind him, his own features thrown deliberately into shadow as he studied the older man's face, set now in quiet thoughtfulness. The new lines scoured there by recent grief were easy to read, as was the vacant glaze of pain in the Marquis's pale gray eyes and the heavy burden of sorrow that weighed down his slim, aged shoulders.

There was anger there, too, in the hard set of the jaw and the tight line of the thin lips. Rage at the sudden, unexpected loss of one so loved, at the selfish greed of the nephew he believed had stolen from him one held so dear. And yet . . . and yet Sebastian couldn't shake the conviction that something else was going on here, too; something he was missing.

"When was the last time you saw your wife alive?" he asked suddenly.

Anglessey looked up, his eyes squinting as he stared into the sun. "Nearly ten days ago now."

Sebastian drew a quick, sharp breath. "I don't understand."

"My wife hadn't been well lately. Nothing serious, you understand." A sad, wistful smile played around the old man's lips. "It happens sometimes when a woman is in the family way. She was planning to come down to Brighton with me. She always enjoyed the weeks we spent here each summer. But in the end she decided she couldn't face all those hours in a closed, swaying carriage.

She stayed home."

"Home?"

"That's right." The Marquis's hand tightened around his secateurs as he pushed to his feet again. "The doctors thought the sea air would do me good, so she insisted I come without her. We were hoping she'd feel well enough to follow in a week or two. But until last night, I thought Guinevere was in London."

CHAPTER 11

At first it seemed just one more bizarre twist in a tangled, incomprehensible string of imperfectly understood events, that Anglessey should have believed his wife to be in London at the time of her death. But the more Sebastian thought about it, the more it made sense.

According to Paul Gibson, Lady Guinevere had been killed some six to eight hours before the Regent was discovered clutching her body in the Yellow Cabinet. At some point during that long afternoon, she had lain for hours, faceup, so that the blood had congealed and darkened her flesh to a vivid purple. Only then had a dagger been driven into her bare back and her body positioned enticingly on its side in preparation for the Regent's amorous approach.

All of which meant she might actually have been killed in London, and her body brought down to Brighton.

"That's the most preposterous thing I've ever heard," said Hendon, when Sebastian explained his reasoning to his father that evening over a glass of brandy in their private parlor at the Anchor. "And just how do you suppose this mythical killer managed to slip the lady's corpse into the Yellow Cabinet? He could hardly have strolled through the Pavilion bearing her lifeless body in his arms, now, could he? Or do you imagine he smuggled her inside rolled up in a carpet, like some blackguard straight out of a circulating library romance?"

Sebastian watched his father walk over to the table beside the empty hearth and pour himself another brandy. "What are you suggesting? That she traveled down to Brighton unbeknownst to her husband, simply to commit suicide by some mysterious means after arranging to have her dead body fall on a dagger in the Regent's Yellow Cabinet? Oh yes, and then lay there unnoticed for another six hours or so while the servants built up the fire and cleaned the room around her?"

Hendon set the brandy decanter down with a thump. "Don't be ridiculous. What I'm suggesting is that your Irish friend doesn't know what in the bloody hell he's talking about!"

He broke off, his head turning at the sound of a discreet tap at the door. "Excuse me, my lord," said the Earl's valet, every inch of his body rigid with disapproval as he executed a short bow. "Viscount Devlin's tiger is here to see him. He *says* he's expected."

Sebastian brought up a fist and coughed to hide his smile. Tom was not a favorite with the Earl's staff. "That's right. Please show him in."

Not content to be left cooling his heels in the hall, Tom had already appeared in the open doorway, his face pinched and drawn with disappointment.

"Well?" said Sebastian as the manservant bowed himself out. "What did you discover?"

"Nothin', gov'nor," said the boy, his voice heavy. "Not a blessed thing. Nobody could remember seein' nothin' out of the ordinary. Not till all them nobs started screaming their heads off and running outta there like fleas off a dead dog."

Hendon let out his breath in a self-satisfied *humph* and raised his brandy to his lips.

"Any speculation?" Sebastian asked the boy.

"Oh, aye. Lots o' that. The kitchen maids, they're all atwitter at the thought the Regent done the lady hisself, while the stable lads, they reckon Cumberland's behind it somehow. And they're all talkin' about this Hanover C—"

Tom broke off to cast a quick glance at Hendon.

"Go on," prompted Sebastian.

Tom sniffed and lowered his voice. "It's said in whispers, of course. But there's some as will have it the whole family isn't just barny. They're sayin' the Hanovers is cursed. And that England will be cursed, too, as long as the Hanovers —"

"That's rot nonsense," roared Hendon, surging up from his chair.

The boy stood his ground, his eyes narrowed and wary. "It's what they're saying."

Sebastian rested one hand on the boy's shoulder and gave him a light squeeze. "Thank you, Tom. That will be all for now."

"I'll be damned if I'll ever understand why you brought that boy into your household," said Hendon, after Tom had taken himself off.

"You think my gratitude should have been sufficiently served by a simple thank-you and the gift of perhaps a gold watch? Tom saved my life, remember? Mine and Kat's."

Hendon's jaw tightened in that way it always did whenever Sebastian did something of which Hendon disapproved — or that disappointed him. Once, the Earl of Hendon had boasted of three strong sons to succeed him. But fate had left him with only Sebastian, the youngest and least satisfactory. "I think most would have considered a small pension more than adequate," said Hendon.

"The boy is useful."

"Good God. And in what way might a pickpocket be of use to a gentleman of quality?"

"To survive on the streets requires agility, a talent for keen observation, and quick wits. All abilities I can use." *Besides, the boy always wanted to work with horses,* Sebastian thought, although he didn't say it. Hendon would only have scoffed. "He seems to have managed to control his larcenous activities these last four months."

"Or so you think."

Sebastian drained his brandy and set the glass aside. "I'd best say good night. I plan to start for London at dawn."

"London?" Hendon's lips pursed in disapproval. "I thought the business with this murder would at least keep you away from there for a while." Of course, it wasn't London itself Hendon found objectionable; what troubled the Earl was the beautiful young actress he knew Sebastian would be seeing there.

Refusing to be drawn into an argument on that score, Sebastian turned toward the door. "I don't see what else I can do here. Anglessey has agreed to allow Paul Gibson to transfer the Marchioness's body to his surgery for a postmortem. Even if Lady Guinevere wasn't killed in London, someone there might be able to tell me where she went — and why."

The next morning dawned cool, with a fine mist that drifted in from the sea in heavy, salt-laden patches of white swirling dampness to collect between the rows of tall, stately town houses and in the narrow winding alleyways of the Lanes.

Sebastian held the chestnuts in check until they were clear of the last straggling hamlet. Then he gave the big blood geldings their heads and let them run with the wind before easing them down to an even trot that ate away at the miles. By the time they reached Edburton, the strengthening sun had begun to burn away what was left of the fog. On the far side of the village, the rolling expanses of the South Downs could be seen quite clearly, stretching out in all directions. It was there Sebastian's growing conviction that he was being followed solidified into a certainty.

CHAPTER 12

Even in the thickness of the fog, Sebastian had been aware of a steady drumming of hoofbeats, staying always a comfortable distance behind them. One horse, he decided, ridden at a steady clip, never gaining, but not falling too far behind, either.

Then the mists began to thin to faint wisps of elusive white that hugged the deeply cut road's stone walls and brambly hedgerows while laying bare the surrounding fields of green barley and flax. At that point, the shadowy horseman dropped back. But Sebastian's eyesight was considerably keener than most others'. As the wide vistas of the South Downs opened up beneath a strengthening sun, he began to catch glimpses of a single, dark-clad rider mounted on a big bay, first seen in the distance through a tangle of hazel, then half-hidden by a copse of fine beech.

Thoughtful, Sebastian urged his chestnuts

to a faster trot. The mysterious horseman quickened his pace, too. They continued on that way for a mile, two. Sebastian brought his pair down to a walk.

Their shadow dropped back.

"Don't, whatever you do, look behind us," Sebastian ordered his young tiger. "But I think . . . no, I am quite certain, actually, that we are being followed."

Tom went visibly stiff with the effort of resisting the urge to turn around and look for himself. "Since when?"

"Since we left Brighton, it would seem."

"What we gonna do?"

Sebastian held the chestnuts to a steady pace. They were winding up a gradual incline, the twisting road thrown into deep shade by a stand of poplars. But at the top of the slope the ground evened out, the road running across a broad common of vivid green pastureland dotted with a peacefully grazing herd of black-and-white milk cows.

Without looking behind, Sebastian whipped his team into an easy gallop so that the man behind them was forced to do the same. They streamed across the common, the sun shining on the chestnuts' wet flanks, Sebastian urging his team on ever faster until the road crested a sudden rise and fell away rapidly before them in a long, steady sweep.

Sebastian immediately reined in his horses to a brisk walk. The rush of the wind and the thundering of hoofbeats gave way to a soft crunch of wheels and a relative silence in which Sebastian could hear the rapid soughing of Tom's breath, quickened with excitement. They were only halfway down the slope when the rider on the bay crested the hill behind them at a loping canter.

At the sight of Sebastian, he checked for a moment, then urged his own horse forward at a easy walk.

Sebastian swung over to the verge and pulled up. At his signal, Tom hopped down to run to the horses' heads.

"What's he doing?" Sebastian asked, bending forward as if busying himself with something at his feet. In one hand, he clasped a neat little flintlock pistol.

Again the horseman had checked. But now he had no choice: he must either make his intentions obvious, or continue on and pass them. Pulling his hat low on his forehead, the dark-clad rider set his spurs to his horse's flanks.

"Here he comes," said Tom on a tense exhalation of breath.

The rider charged past them in a dust-swirling rush of creaking saddle leather and sweat-flecked prime horseflesh. Looking up, Sebastian had a quick vision of a bloodred bay, its head up, its eyes wide, and a man of medium build wearing a gentleman's beaver hat and a greatcoat of respectable tailoring. Then the bay disappeared with a clatter around a bend in the road ahead. The hoofbeats retreated into the distance until all was silent except for the rush of the wind through the sweetly scented grass and the gentle lowing of a cow.

Tom stood with a hand on the team's reins, his head twisted around as he stared off up the road. "Who was he, gov'nor?"

"I've no idea," said Sebastian, collecting his whip. "Stand away, Tom."

Tom obediently sprang back, then scrambled to resume his perch as the curricle once again bowled away toward London.

They reached Town just after midday. The greatcoated rider on the big bay was not seen again.

Sebastian's own house lay on Brook Street, just off New Bond Street. But that was not his first destination. Drawing up before an elegant little town house in Harwich Street, Sebastian handed the reins to Tom and said, "Stable them."

The maid who opened the door was a mousy creature with thin bony shoulders and pale, unsmiling features. At the sight of Sebastian, she sniffed and looked as if she'd shut the door in his face if she could. "Miss Boleyn is still abed."

"Good," Sebastian said cheerfully, already taking the steps two at a time. "No need to interrupt whatever you were doing, Elspeth," he added, although she remained rooted in the entry hall, her head tipping back as she continued to glower up at him. "I'll announce myself."

The door to the front bedchamber on the second floor was closed but not latched. Sebastian pushed it open, the painted panels swinging into a room of blue satin hangings and heavy shadows. A woman lay in the bed, a beautiful young woman with rich brown hair that spread out over the pillows in a glossy wave. Her name was Kat Boleyn, and at the age of twenty-three she had already been the toast of the London stage for several years now. She was also the love of Sebastian's life.

As he drew nearer, he saw that she was awake, her blue eyes crinkling lightly at the corners with a subtle smile, her shoulders bare where they showed above the fine linen sheets. "Poor Elspeth," she said.

Shrugging out of his many-caped driving coat, Sebastian swung it onto a nearby chair and tossed his hat, whip, and gloves after it. "Why on earth do you keep such a Friday-faced creature about the place?"

Kat reached long, naked arms over her head in a lazy stretch. "She's not Friday faced with me."

"Then what the devil does she have against me?"

Kat laughed. "You're male."

Sebastian knelt on the edge of the bed, one doeskin-clad knee sinking deep into the feather mattress. "How's the new play?"

"Popular. Or maybe it's just my Cleopatra costume that's popular." She brought her arms down to loop them around his neck and draw him to her. "I expected you yesterday."

From any other woman the words might have been read as an expression of reproach. But not with Kat. With Kat, it was simply a statement, an observation.

She demanded no loverlike commitments from him. She had rebuffed his every attempt to make her his wife and refused even to be considered his mistress. He supposed there were men who might relish such an arrangement as a freedom from the ties that could bind; Sebastian lived with a quietly desperate fear that one day, for some reason he would never quite understand, she would leave him. Again.

He slid his hands down her naked back, heard her breath catch in that way it always did when he touched her. He nuzzled his face against her neck, breathed in the wonderful, heady fragrance of her skin and hair. "Forgive me?"

She bracketed his cheeks with her hands, drawing back so she could see his face. Her lips were smiling, her eyes shining with what looked very much like love. But her words were light, frivolous. "That depends on how good your excuse is."

He took her mouth in a kiss of tender hello and subtle promises of want and need. Then, lifting his head, he brushed the ball of his thumb across her lips and saw her smile fade when he said, "How about murder?"

Chapter 13

She had been born with a different name, to a woman with laughing eyes and warmly whispered words of love who'd died degraded and afraid on a misty Irish morning.

Sometimes, especially in the early hours when darkness was only just giving way to dawn, Kat would imagine she could feel the soldiers' rough hands upon her, feel the fibrous bite of the rope at her own throat, the breath of life slowly squeezing, squeezing from her. She would awake gasping, the terror in her mind dark and fierce. But she was not her mother. She would not die her mother's death. And she would not live her life in fear.

For ten years now she'd been Kat Boleyn. There'd been a time when she'd known poverty and desperation, before the whimsies of fame and adoration had changed all of that. And for seven of those years she had loved this man, Sebastian St. Cyr.

She turned her head, a smile warming her heart at the sight of his familiar, beloved features and darkly disheveled hair framed by the crisp white linen of her pillow. She had loved him since she was sixteen and he was twenty-one, when they were both still young and naive enough to believe that love was more important than anything — anything at all. Before she'd understood that one made choices in life, and that some choices carry a price too grievous to bear.

She knew better now. She knew that love could be selfless as well as greedy. And that sometimes the greatest gift that one can give one's beloved is to let him go.

She realized his eyes were open, watching her. In a few minutes he would leave her bed and she would send him into the afternoon sunshine with a careless caress and light words that asked and gave no promises.

She touched her fingertips to his bare shoulder and he reached for her, strong hands gliding up her back to draw her beneath him. She went to him with a sigh, her eyes closing as she allowed herself to pretend for one shining moment out of time that all those things that matter so much — like honor and loyalty, duty and betrayal — mattered not at all.

The necklace lay cool against Kat's palm. It was an unusual piece, three interlocking, almond-shaped silver ovals set against a smooth bluestone disk.

Once, this necklace had belonged to Sebastian's mother. Kat had heard stories about the beautiful countess with the golden hair and dancing green eyes who'd been lost at sea off the coast of Brighton one summer when Sebastian was a child. Now the necklace had reappeared — around the throat of a murdered woman.

Flipping the pendant over, Kat traced the old entwined initials. A. C. and J. S. As Devlin moved around her bedchamber, assembling his clothes and drawing on his breeches and shirt, he told her the legend he'd grown up hearing, about the mysterious Welshwoman who had once possessed the necklace but had given it away to the handsome, ill-fated prince she loved.

"I don't understand," said Kat. "If the necklace is supposed to choose its next guardian, then why did Addiena give it to James Stuart?"

Devlin looked up from where he sat on the edge of her bed, one gleaming Hessian in his hands. "You need to remember that at the time she knew him, James Stuart was a hunted man. Charles the First — his father, the King — had just been beheaded by Cromwell and the Roundheads, while his brother — the future Charles the Second — was a fugitive in exile." Devlin thrust his foot into his boot and stood up. "According to the legend, the necklace is supposed to bring long life. That's why Addiena gave it to James Stuart — to protect him. They say that when he first rode into London after the restoration of Charles the Second, he had that necklace in a special pouch he always wore around his neck."

"She must have loved him very much," said Kat softly, "to give him something so precious to her."

Devlin went to tie his cravat in front of her dressing table mirror. "I think so, yes. Although he was hardly faithful to her. He went on to marry two different wives and have over a dozen children."

Kat closed her fist around the triskelion. "He was destined to be king. He needed a wife the people would accept, not some wild Welshwoman from the fields of Cronwyn. If she loved him, she would understand that."

His eyes met hers in the mirror. She turned away to pick up his coat of Bath superfine. "Only, it didn't work, did it?" she said over her shoulder. "He didn't know long life. He lost his throne and died in exile."

"Ah, but by then he no longer possessed the necklace. According to the story, James the Second had a child by Addiena Cadel, a girl by the name of Guinevere. Guinevere Stuart."

"Guinevere?" Kat swung around in surprise. "What a strange coincidence."

"It is, isn't it? As I understand it, Guinevere Stuart's father acknowledged her. In addition to giving her his name, he arranged an advantageous marriage for her. And he gave her the necklace as a wedding present."

"So how did your mother come to have it?"

Devlin shrugged his shoulders into the coat she held out for him. "It was given to her by an old crone she met in Wales one summer. The woman claimed to be the granddaughter of James the Second — said she was one hundred and one years old, and that her mother had given *her* the necklace shortly before dying at the age of one hundred and two."

Kat studied his face. He seldom spoke of the Countess, although Kat knew the loss of his mother at such an early age had affected Sebastian deeply — particularly coming, as it did, so soon after the death of his last surviving brother. "But why give the necklace to your mother?"

A shadow shifted in the depths of his tawny eyes. He turned away abruptly. "She said it would keep my mother safe."

Kat came to slip her arms around his waist and press her cheek against his broad back, hugging him close. "It didn't keep Guinevere Anglessey safe, either, did it? She was wearing it when she died."

His hands gripped hers where they lay entwined against his satin waistcoat. After a moment, he turned in her arms, and whatever she'd seen earlier in his eyes was gone — or carefully hidden away. "It seems a strange piece for a woman to wear with an evening gown, is it not?"

"I'd have said so, yes." She held the necklace out to him. "What color was the gown?"

"Green." He took the necklace and slipped it into his pocket.

"That makes it even more strange. How does Anglessey say his wife came to have the necklace?"

"Somehow it didn't seem the right time to ask."

Kat nodded. "I remember when she married him. It caused quite a stir. She was so young and beautiful."

Devlin's lips curled up into an ironic smile. "Whereas he was simply very rich. And a Marquis, of course."

"Do you think he killed her . . . or had her killed?"

"If she was playing him false with the Regent, it would seem to give him a motive — not only to murder his wife, but to leave her body in a way that would implicate the man who was cuckolding him."

"*If* she was playing him false with the Regent."

"Or if he thought she was."

"Anglessey didn't need to agree to allow Paul Gibson to perform an autopsy on his wife's body," Kat pointed out. "The fact that he did would seem to suggest that he has nothing to hide."

"Perhaps. We'll know more when Gibson's had a chance to do a thorough postmortem." Devlin went to pick up his driving coat. "Anglessey himself claims to suspect his nephew, Bevan Ellsworth."

"Now, there's a man who's capable of murder."

He glanced at her in surprise. "You know him?"

"He had one of the chorus girls from the

theater in keeping last year. She found him charming — and unpredictably vicious."

"That sounds like Ellsworth, all right." He threw his coat over his arm, then hesitated in a way that was unusual for him.

Kat tipped her head, a smile playing about her lips as she studied his face. "Out with it."

His eyes widened in a parody of innocence. "Out with what?"

She came to take his hat and set it at a rakish angle on his head. "Whatever it is you're circling around to asking me to do."

He smiled and caught her to him to nuzzle her neck in a way that made her laugh. "Well, there is one little thing. . . ."

CHAPTER 14

They were called the Upper Ten Thousand, that small cadre of men and women of birth and fortune who formed the top crust of English society and occupied the manor houses and grand estates that were the sine qua non of English respectability. Bound to each other by ties of blood and marriage, they rode to hounds together, belonged to the same clubs and subscription rooms, and sent their sons to the same schools — to Winchester and Eton, Cambridge and Oxford.

Like Sebastian, the Marquis of Anglessey's nephew and heir presumptive, Bevan Ellsworth, had been sent to Eton. Sebastian had vague memories of a sporting lad with a ready laugh and a well-hidden but savage will to get his own back at anyone he thought had wronged him. But the two years that separated them had been enough to limit their interaction at that age. And whereas Sebastian went to Oxford, Ellsworth had gone to Cambridge. He'd eventually become a barrister, although he was said to spend considerably more time in the gaming hells around Pickering Place than in court.

Being a barrister was considered a respectable occupation for a gentleman. Because barristers could only be engaged by solicitors rather than directly by clients, barristers were not considered to be *in trade,* with all the vulgar associations that entailed. Thus, a barrister's wife could be presented in court, whereas the wife of a solicitor could not — a subtle but important distinction for a man who expected to become the next Earl of Anglessey.

Sebastian ran across the Marquis's nephew sharing a glass of wine with a friend in Brooks's late that afternoon. Pausing just inside the entrance to the club's red drawing room, Sebastian took a moment to study the man Bevan Ellsworth had become.

He had the same open, pleasant countenance Sebastian remembered, his warm brown hair worn in the style of disarray favored by those who followed Beau Brummel's set. Ellsworth had something of a reputation as a dandy himself, his coat of Bath superfine being of a fashionable cut and his cravat intricately tied without falling into the extremes affected by some. But the broad set of his shoulders showed that he also considered himself something of a Corinthian, boxing at Jackson's and fencing at Angelo's and shooting wafers at Menton's.

The gentleman beside him, a fair-skinned man with flaxen hair and an exaggerated neckcloth, looked vaguely familiar, although Sebastian couldn't quite place him. Snagging a glass of Madeira from a passing waiter, Sebastian went to slouch with deliberate insouciance into the empty seat opposite the two men. "I understand congratulations are in order," he said, interrupting their conversation without preamble or apology.

Ellsworth stiffened and swung his head to fix Sebastian with a cold stare. "I beg your pardon?"

Sebastian smiled. "Surely you're not going to pretend you haven't heard about the death of your dear aunt Guinevere? Everything that threatened to stand between you and Anglessey's title and fortune has now been removed. Hence" — Sebastian lifted his glass in a kind of toast — "congratulations."

The unknown gentleman with the flaxen

hair and monstrous neckcloth met Sebastian's steely gaze for one fleeting instant, then slipped quietly away to go stand nervously at the far end of the room.

"That's always assuming, of course," Sebastian added as if in afterthought, "that you were nowhere near Brighton on Wednesday last?"

A faint but discernible line of color touched Ellsworth's cheekbones. "Don't be ridiculous. I spent most of last Wednesday at Gray's Inn."

"In court?"

The man's color darkened. "I'll be damned if I can see what business it is of yours."

Sebastian met his angry stare with a bland smile. "Alibis are always such handy things to have, don't you agree? If you're lucky, it might not even occur to the authorities that you could easily have hired someone to do the dirty deed for you."

Ellsworth brought his own glass to his lips and took a slow, thoughtful swallow before saying with commendable sangfroid, "Very true. But it does rather beg the question, does it not? I mean, why kill the lady in such a flamboyant and decidedly public way? Why not simply hire a couple of footpaths to attack her sedan chair one dark night?"

"Why not indeed?" agreed Sebastian. "Or a highwayman to hold up her carriage on Hampstead Heath? You've obviously given some thought to it."

Ellsworth let out a short, sharp laugh before leaning forward to say, "My debts aren't that pressing." His lips were still smiling, but a hard-edged warning glittered in his gray eyes.

"Rumor has it otherwise."

"Rumor has it wrong."

Sebastian rested his head against the chair's high upholstered back. "So what did you think of her? Your late aunt, I mean." Anyone seeing them from across the room would assume they were having a nice, friendly conversation. "Strange to think of her as your aunt when she was — what? Nearly ten years your junior?"

"Not so strange in our world, is it? London is full of gently bred young ladies panting like bitches in heat after a title or a fortune. Or both."

Bitter, ugly words. But then, the reality was harsh. Firstborn sons — men of wealth and title — were shamelessly pursued and fought over, while younger sons, and sons of younger sons such as Ellsworth, were seen as dangerous pariahs to be shunned, guarded against, despised.

"And the young Lady Guinevere wanted both?" said Sebastian.

"A prime article like her? Why should she settle for anything less?" Ellsworth's lips curled into a sneer. "Surely you don't think she married my uncle for *love?*"

Sebastian studied the brooding, angry lines of the other man's face. He was remembering the time, years ago at Eton, when some baronet's son had eased Ellsworth out of the captainship of his house's football team. Two weeks later, in a rough and confused tumult of play, the boy's arm had been broken so badly he had to be sent home for the rest of the year. There were whispers at the time that Ellsworth had deliberately snapped the boy's arm, although of course nothing could ever be proved. Sebastian heard later that the boy's arm never did heal right.

"And your uncle?" said Sebastian. "Did he have reason to regret his marriage, do you think?"

Ellsworth gave a harsh laugh. "What? Apart from the fact she was playing him false?"

Sebastian had half expected it, and still the words troubled him more than he could have explained. "You mean with the Regent?"

"I wouldn't know about the Regent. But you don't really believe Anglessey fathered that so-called heir his lady wife was carrying, do you?"

"Older men than he have succeeded in siring sons."

"Perhaps." Ellsworth tossed down the dregs of his wine and pushed to his feet. "But not this one."

CHAPTER 15

The breeches were of the finest plush velvet, with a coat of satin-trimmed blue velvet to match. Together with the silk stockings and snowy white shirt, they formed a livery fit for the footman of a duke — or at least for the boards of the Covent Garden Theater, which is where the costume was normally seen.

Twitching uncomfortably in his starched shirt, Tom supposed there were some fellows who might find the ensemble attractive. But as far as he was concerned, the rig made him look like a popinjay.

"Stop fidgeting," said Kat, her normally precise diction slurred by the need to speak around a mouthful of pins.

Tom fell obediently still. His back itched unmercifully, but he didn't move. He had a sneaking suspicion Miss Kat wasn't above sticking one of her pins into him, if he didn't do what he was told.

They were in Miss Kat's dressing room at the theater, and she was busy adapting to his small frame the page's livery she had borrowed from the theater's costume collection. "I don't see why we're doin' this," Tom grumbled. "I got me a bang-up livery already, what the Viscount give me when he made me his tiger."

"Huh." Miss Kat moved around to do something to a seam of the breeches. "One look at that yellow-and-black-striped waistcoat of yours, and Lord Anglessey's servants would mark you down as coming from the household of a sporting gentleman. Those in service have very decided opinions on the subject of young sporting gentleman, and few of those opinions are charitable. You'd be lucky not to find yourself sent off with a flea in your ear."

Tom swallowed the argument he'd been about to make. The humiliation of yesterday's failure to scout out anything of use at the Pavilion still burned within him. He was determined to wheedle the information Devlin needed from Lady Anglessey's servants, and if that meant dressing up like some eighteenth-century fop — well, then, he'd do it.

Tom craned his neck to get a better look at the seam Miss Kat was taking in. "That's crooked."

"I'm an actress, not a seamstress." She bit off her thread and sat back on her heels to survey her handiwork. "And this livery belongs to the theater. You tear it, or spill anything on it, and I'll take the cost of it out of your hide."

Tom stepped off the low box she'd had him standing on. " 'Ow would I tear it?"

She laughed, an open, spontaneous laugh that made him grin. She was bang-up, for being such a famous actress and all. She was also the best pickpocket he'd ever seen, although he supposed most folks didn't know that.

"Tell me about this man, the one who was following his lordship yesterday," she said in an offhand kind of way as she bent to assemble her scattered pins and threads.

"I didn't see 'im afore 'e come up with us. But then, no one's got eyes and ears like his lordship's."

She nodded, not looking around. "Do you think he might have something to do with this murder his lordship is looking into?"

"Don't know what else it could be about. I mean, it stands to reason, don't it? You go pokin' around in a murder, you're liable to stir up some weery desperate people."

Tom thought it was all pretty exciting, but

then he got a look at Miss Kat's face and he suddenly regretted having said so much. He snatched up the ridiculous scrap of satin and velvet that was supposed to serve him as a hat. "Well, I'm off, then."

Her face cleared so suddenly he was left wondering if he'd simply imagined the troubled shadows he thought he'd seen there. "Remember," she told him as he balanced the tricorne on his head and started to dash off. "No scuffling with the linkboys." She raised her voice to shout after him. "And no eating or drinking."

The Marquis of Anglessey's town house was an enormous pile on Mount Street.

Tom stood on the flagged sidewalk, his neck aching as he tipped his head to look up four stories and more to the stately house's pedimented gray slate roof. The Marquis himself was obviously still in Brighton, for the knocker was off the door. But his servants had already draped the house in mourning, festooning the tall, silent windows with crepe and hanging a black wreath on the entrance.

Adjusting his starched stock, Tom marched up the short flight of steps and used his fist to beat a lively tattoo on the shiny, black-painted panels of the front door.

When there was no answer, he pounded harder.

Beside him, an iron railing separated the main front door from the area steps that led down to the service entrance. When Tom knocked a third time, the service door jerked open and a middle-aged woman with a bulbous red nose, plump cheeks, and wiry gray hair covered by an old-fashioned mop cap stuck out her head and peered up at him. "What you doing there, lad? Can't you see the knocker's off the door?"

Tom held up the folded, sealed letter Miss Kat had prepared for him. The letter was empty, of course, but then he had no intention of giving it to anyone. "I got a message here, for Lord Anglessey from Sir James Aston. He says I'm to give it into Lord Anglessey's hand and no one else's. Only, 'ow'm I supposed to get anyone's attention when there's no knocker?"

The woman let out a snorting laugh. "You're new to service, then, aren't you? Don't you know what it means when the knocker's down? It means the family ain't in residence. You'll either have to leave your message or take it back to your Sir James and tell him the Marquis ain't expected till nightfall."

111

Tom blew out a long breath and lifted his page's cap to swipe one forearm across his brow. He didn't need to pretend to sweat: the velvet was fiendishly heavy and the sun was out in earnest now, blazing down unnaturally hot for a June day. "Oh, Lordy," he said, making his voice pregnant with weariness. "I was hopin' to be able to sit a spell and maybe get somethin' to drink while his lordship was writin' his answer."

The woman's pleasant face puckered with motherly concern. "Oh, poor ducky. It is mortal hot today, isn't it?" She hesitated a moment, then said, "Why don't you come down here and have yourself a nice glass of lemonade before going back?"

Tom made a show of hesitating. "Well, I don't know. . . ."

"Come on, then." She swung the door in wide and beckoned him with one hand. "I got a son just about your age, in service with Lord McGowan. I'd hope if he were standing all hot and thirsty on some gentleman's doorstep, that cook'd be kind enough to bring him in and give him somethin' and let him sit a spell."

Tom figured it wouldn't do to give her a chance to change her mind, and clambered quickly down the steps.

He found himself in a white-tiled room

with stone flagged floors and big old wooden dressers laden with massive copper pots. Mrs. Long — as she identified herself — led him to a bench beside the kitchen table and sent one of the scullery maids scurrying to bring him a tall, frosty glass of lemonade. Mindful of Miss Kat's dire warning, Tom thrust his neck out and drank very, very carefully.

"You said the Marquis won't be in till nightfall?" he said, eyeing her over the lip of his glass.

"That's what we're expecting." She heaved a great sigh and swiped at one eye with the corner of her apron. "He's coming to bury that beautiful young wife of his, poor man."

Lined up along the stone windowsill to cool stood three freshly baked pies. Cherry, Tom figured, sniffing longingly at the afternoon breeze, and maybe apple. He jerked his attention back to Mrs. Long's plump face. "She died, did she?"

"You mean to say you haven't heard?" She came to slip onto the bench opposite him, her voice hushed as she leaned forward conspiratorially. "Murdered, she was."

Tom led his mouth go slack with shock. "No!"

"That's a fact. They found her all the way down in Brighton — in the Pavilion, no less

— with a dagger sticking out her back. Although what she was doing there is more than I can understand."

"But I thought you just said his lordship was in Brighton?"

"Aye, so he was. But *she* weren't. Stayed here, she did, this last week and more. Why, she sat up there in the morning room the very day she was murdered, eating the salmon with dill mayonnaise I'd fixed for her nuncheon. Not that she'd had much of an appetite lately, poor thing."

"When was the last time you saw her?"

Mrs. Long propped her elbows on the table, her chin sinking onto her fists as she thought about it. "Why, must have been just an hour or two after that. One of the footmen called her a hackney and she went off."

"A hackney?" Tom had to work excessively hard to keep the thrill of triumphant excitement off his face. Here was exactly the sort of information Devlin needed. "Just goes to show, don't it?" Tom said, keeping his voice slow and casual. "I mean, who'd have thought a lady what lived in a swell establishment like this couldn't afford to keep her own carriage?"

Mrs. Long let out a peel of laughter that rocked her back in her seat. "Get away with you. Lord Anglessey's warm enough he could set up a hundred carriages, if'n he had a mind. Don't you know nothing, lad?" She leaned forward suddenly and dropped her voice to a whisper, as if imparting a secret. "A lady takes a hackney when she don't want her lord to know where she's going."

"Oh." Tom nodded with wide-eyed comprehension, as if this were all new to him. "Did she do that often?"

"Often enough these last few months, that's for sure." Spreading her palms flat on the table, she pushed up from the bench as if she suddenly regretted having said so much. "Now, then, ducky, how about a piece of pie to go with your lemonade?"

Tom wanted that pie so badly his mouth was watering. But he dutifully swallowed and shook his head. "Oh, no, thank you, ma'am."

Reaching down, she patted his cheek with one plump hand. "Your mama taught you real good, ducky. But there's no use you trying to pretend you don't want it, because I seen you eyeing them pies, sure enough. Now, what kind you want? Apple or cherry?"

CHAPTER 16

Sebastian spent what was left of the afternoon at the Inns of Court and the seedy gambling establishments around Pickering Place.

It didn't take him long to discover that Bevan Ellsworth had indeed put in a rare appearance in the legal district on Wednesday. But his activities that day had been erratic, culminating in an evening spent at a hell just off Pickering Place.

In the end Sebastian decided the man could, conceivably, have slipped away from Grey's Court long enough to have killed Guinevere Anglessey somewhere in London. But there was no way he could have hauled her body down to Brighton and still made it back to Pickering Place by ten o'clock, at which time he was deep in a game of faro from which he had not arisen until four the next morning.

Sebastian arrived at his own neatly stuccoed town house at Number 41 Brook Street just as the last streaks of orange and pink were slowly leaching from the sky and the lamplighters were beginning to make their rounds. Changing into evening dress, he directed his carriage to an imposing mansion on Park Street that belonged to his only surviving aunt, the Dowager Duchess of Claiborne. Technically, the house was owned by the eldest of Aunt Henrietta's three sons, the current Duke of Claiborne. But she had the poor sod so thoroughly terrified that he had meekly left her in possession of the place and moved his own growing family into a small house on Half Moon Street.

Sebastian found his aunt descending the house's grand staircase, the famous Claiborne rubies at her throat, a massive lavender turban decorated with red feathers swaddling her gray head. She paused halfway down the steps, one white-gloved hand groping to raise the quizzing glass she always wore on a gold chain around her neck. "Good heavens, Devlin. What are you doing here?"

"Hello, Aunt Henrietta," he said, running lightly up the steps to kiss her cheek with genuine affection. "What a shockingly extravagant hat."

"Yes, it is, isn't it?" she said gaily. "Claiborne would have loathed it."

Hendon's senior by five years, she had been married at the tender age of eighteen to the heir to the Duke of Claiborne. It was considered quite a feat of matrimonial maneuvering at the time, for the former Lady Henrietta St. Cyr had never been a particularly attractive female, even when young. She had Hendon's broad, fleshy face and barrellike body, and the same belligerent habit of staring people out of countenance. She made a grand duchess.

"I was just on my way to the Setons' dinner party," she said, leaning her weight on the silver-headed cane she carried mainly for effect. "As of my last reckoning, Claiborne has been dead two years and six hours. I gave the man four children, fifty-one years of marriage, and two full years of mourning. And now I intend to enjoy myself."

"I wasn't aware of the fact you ever did anything else," said Sebastian, following her into the drawing room.

She gave a delighted chuckle. "Pour me

some wine. No, not that paltry stuff," she directed when he reached for the ratafia. "The port."

She took an enthusiastic sip of her wine and fixed him with a steady stare over the top of her glass. "Now, what's this Hendon tells me about you involving yourself in the death of that poor, unfortunate woman down in Brighton?"

Sebastian nearly choked on his own wine. "When did you see my father?"

"Today, in Pall Mall. They've all come back to London — Perceval and Hendon, Prinny and Jarvis, even that ridiculous Comte de Lille, as he calls himself — although how he can expect anyone to consider him the rightful king of France when he hasn't even got the gumption to call himself Louis XVIII is more than I can see. Anyway, it seems Prinny's taken such a turn over what happened in the Pavilion that his doctors thought it best to remove him from Brighton for a time. Not that he's likely to get much rest at Carlton House, what with all the preparations for this grand fete he's giving next week. Imagine! Giving a grand dinner to celebrate your ascension to the Regency. Might as well celebrate the poor old King's descent into madness. I've a good mind not to go."

It was an idle threat, as Sebastian well knew. The Prince Regent's grand fete was certain to be the most talked-about social event of the decade. Aunt Henrietta would never miss such a spectacle.

She paused to draw breath and take another sip of her wine, which gave Sebastian the opportunity to say, "Tell me, Aunt, what do you know of Lady Guinevere?"

She looked up, a sparkle in her vivid blue eyes. "So that's why you're here, is it? Interested in discovering if the poor child was hiding some nasty little secret?"

"Her or someone close to her."

"Well, let me see. . . ." His aunt went to settle herself in a comfortable chair beside the empty hearth. "She was wellborn on her father's side. He was the Earl of Athelstone, you know. A LeCornu. The family goes back to the Conqueror."

Sebastian smiled. Bright, caustic, and irrepressibly inquisitive, Aunt Henrietta was one of the grandes dames of society. She might have been in mourning for two years, but nothing short of her own death would interfere with her ability to keep abreast of the latest on-dits. "And her mother?"

Aunt Henrietta frowned. "I don't know much about her. She was the Earl's second wife, I believe. Or was it his third? At any rate, she didn't survive long enough for him to bring her to London."

"Good God. How many wives did he have?"

"Five. The man was a regular bluebeard. The first four all died in childbirth. Gave him nothing but girls, too, which is why, I suppose, he kept at it. Managed it in the end, though. The new Earl's about ten, I believe."

Sebastian thought about the vibrant, brilliant young woman he had met at Hendon's dinner table. What must it have been like for her, he wondered, growing up with a succession of stepmothers and a father desperate for a son?

"Lady Guinevere came out the same year as Emily's eldest, you know," his aunt was saying. At the mention of her daughter Emily, Aunt Henrietta's lips pursed into a frown. As far as Aunt Henrietta was concerned, Emily had not married well, an act of folly for which her mother had never forgiven her.

"She was quite the sensation of the Season — I mean Lady Guinevere, of course, *not* Emily's eldest. I'm afraid that poor child takes after Emily far too much to ever have had much of a chance of going off well, even if she had been well dowered, which, of course, she was not. But Guinevere! She was quite the toast of the town. Not much of a fortune there, either, I must admit, but the girl was a regular diamond of the first water, with plenty of spirit. A bit too willful, perhaps, for some, but then I'm not one who's partial to these mealymouthed misses one encounters far too often these days."

"Any scandal attached to her name?"

"None that I ever heard of."

"None? A beautiful, vivacious twenty-one-year-old woman, married to an unwell, sixty-seven-year-old man? No whispers of a young lover?"

The very suggestion seemed to affront his aunt. "I should think not. Headstrong and unorthodox Lady Guinevere might have been, but she was no shameless hussy, however I hear things looked on Wednesday last in the Pavilion. She knew what was expected of a woman of her station, and it's a shabby creature indeed who indulges in that sort of thing before she has managed to present her lord with an heir."

Sebastian took a slow sip of his wine. "You say she has sisters?"

"Two who survived, each from different mothers. The youngest must still be in the schoolroom in Wales. But you may know the eldest, Morgana. She was never the

122

beauty Guinevere was, I'm afraid, and she has the disposition of a Rottweiler. It's amazing she managed to marry at all, let alone do it as well as she did."

Sebastian smiled. "Who'd she catch?"

"Lord Quinlan. Of course, he's a mere baron as opposed to a marquis, and his fortune can't begin to compare to Anglessey's, but *still*. Until Guinevere married so splendidly, Morgana was considered to have done quite well for herself. Athelstone's estates were never particularly extensive, and he didn't manage them as well as he might have. Neither of the girls had much in the way of a dowry. I believe Athelstone settled everything he could on the boy."

Again, her words hinted at a less-than-idyllic childhood. What kind of animosities must have brewed in the schoolroom of that death-haunted estate on the coast of Wales, Sebastian wondered; three girls from three different mothers, the eldest plain and ill natured, the middle one beautiful and appealing? He suddenly wanted very much to hear what Morgana might have to say about her sister.

"Where would I be likely to find her tomorrow?" he asked. "Lady Quinlan, I mean."

Aunt Henrietta drew her chin back against her fleshy neck in a way that made her look more like Hendon than ever. "Well, let's see. Morgana considers herself something of a bluestocking — she's forever attending lectures at the Royal Academy and prosing on about electrical currents and steam engines and such nonsense. I should think she'd be likely to attend this balloon ascension we've been hearing so much about."

"Balloon ascension? Where?"

"Good heavens, as if I would know." Draining her wine, she set the glass aside and pushed to her feet. "Now you must be off. I've a party to attend."

Sebastian stood in the shadows of his empty box at Covent Garden Theater and watched as Kat, splendid in the regal diadem and filmy trappings of Shakespeare's Cleopatra, swept onto the stage below. He knew she couldn't see him. Yet somehow she must have sensed he was there, because for a moment she paused, her head turning toward him, and a brilliant smile flashed across her face. A smile meant just for him.

He stayed some minutes simply for the pleasure of watching her. But before the curtain came down for the entr'acte, he turned to make his way backstage. He was starting to worry about Tom, and he wanted to ask Kat if she'd seen the boy. But as he pushed his way past the Fashionable Impures and the groups of Town bucks ogling them, he spotted a small boy in tiger's livery hovering near the corridor.

"Where the devil have you been?" demanded Sebastian, collaring his tiger. "I was about to send around to the watchhouses to see if you'd been taken up."

Tom tightened his hold on the brown-paper-wrapped package in his arms. "I been waitin' for them to finish cleaning Miss Kat's costume."

"Cleaning?" repeated Sebastian ominously.

"It's as good as new, I promise," he said hastily, then added, "Almost."

"Almost?"

Tom's shoulders drooped. "I should have told her I'd have the apple."

CHAPTER 17

The Public Office at Queen Square didn't have the cachet of Bow Street, with its famous Runners and its Bow Street Patrol and the vicarious glamour that lingered still from the days of the Fieldings. But the position of chief magistrate at Queen Square suited Sir Henry Lovejoy just fine.

He was a serious man, Lovejoy, unimpressed by either fame or glamour. A widower who'd been childless now for more than a decade, he had decided in midlife to devote the remainder of his years to public service. If he'd been a Catholic, Sir Henry probably would have become a priest. Instead, he'd become a magistrate, pursuing his new dedication to justice with a religious zeal that drove him to arrive at his Queen Square office every morning before eight.

The air was cool that Saturday and blessedly clear, thanks to the stiff wind blowing in from the east. Pausing in a slice of sunshine on the corner across from the Public Office, Lovejoy bought a muffin from a baker's boy, then hesitated, his attention caught by a tall young man in an elegant chapeau bras and cape making his way through the crowd of street hawkers and milkmaids.

"You're up early, my lord," said Lovejoy when Viscount Devlin came abreast of him. It was rare to see a resident of Mayfair abroad before midday. But then, judging by the Viscount's evening dress, Lovejoy realized it was unlikely the young Viscount had ever made it to bed last night — or at least, Lovejoy decided after a moment's shocked reflection, it was obvious Devlin had never made it to his own bed.

A faint gleam lightened the younger man's strange amber eyes, as if he had followed the progression of Lovejoy's disapproving thoughts and been amused by it. But the amusement faded quickly. "You've heard about the discovery of the Marchioness of Anglessey's body in the Pavilion?"

"Who has not?" said Lovejoy, the Viscount falling into step beside him as they turned to cut across the square. "I can tell you, I don't like some of the whispers I'm hearing. It's troublesome. Very troublesome. The royal family can ill afford such a scandal at this time."

Lovejoy glanced sideways at his companion, but Devlin's face was impassive. Either he had not heard the rumors about what they had taken to calling the Hanover Curse, or he had decided it was wiser not to comment upon them. Instead he said, "I've discovered Guinevere Anglessey left her house in Mount Street early last Wednesday afternoon, after asking one of her servants to procure a hackney for her."

Lovejoy drew up short. "Do you mean to say she was here? In London?"

"That's right. She could very well have been killed here."

"Good God. Where?"

"I don't know. It would help if I could talk to the hackney driver. The footman can't recall the carriage number, but he thinks the driver was from Yorkshire."

Lovejoy gave a pained sigh. "Do you have any idea how many hackney drivers in this city are from Yorkshire?"

"No. But I would imagine you do."

He studied the young nobleman's lean, handsome face. "Why are you involving yourself in this?"

Devlin widened his eyes in a feigned expression of innocent surprise. "If I remember correctly, you're the one who suggested I might be of assistance in such delicate matters."

"And you told me you were motivated to investigate last January's murderers by pure self-interest. So what is your interest in the death of Lady Anglessey?"

"I have my reasons."

"Huh. That's what worries me."

Ducking his head to hide a smile, the Viscount started to turn away, then paused to glance back and say, "You take an interest in scientific inquiries, do you not?"

It was something Lovejoy prided himself upon, his diligent determination to stay abreast of current scientific developments. But he wasn't sure how Devlin had come to know of it. "Yes. Why?"

"You wouldn't happen to know where there's to be a balloon ascension today, would you?"

The balloon ascension was scheduled for eleven o'clock that morning in St. George's Fields on the south side of the Thames.

"It's unnatural, it is," said Tom as they neared the fields, and the rippling sheets of red and yellow silk could be seen taking shape just above the treetops. "Men weren't meant to sail through the clouds."

Sebastian laughed and handed the chestnuts' reins to the boy. "Keep the curricle well back from the crowd. I've heard tales of these things catching fire and causing a panic."

Tom nodded solemnly. "No need to worry about that, yer lordship. I've no intention of gettin' anywhere near that contraption."

Continuing on foot, Sebastian pushed his way onto the field. A motley throng had assembled to watch the balloon ascension, gentlemen in top hats and ladies with parasols mingling with tradesmen in their Sunday best and the usual assortment of thieves and cutthroats and pickpockets. The cool morning breeze had withered away, leaving the day still and hot. The beer peddlers were doing a brisk trade, the rich malty odor from their barrels rising up to mingle with the scents of grass and hot gas and warm, closely pressed bodies.

He found Guinevere Anglessey's half sister, Morgana, not far from where a roaring furnace was slowly filling the silk sheath with gas. A tall, angular woman with a long, sharp-featured face and skin that was inclined to freckle, she had none of her sister's soft curves or winning ways. She'd brought along a hatchet-faced abigail as a nod to the proprieties, although Morgana Quinlan struck Sebastian as the type of woman who was more than capable of taking care of herself.

"Excuse me, but it's Lady Quinlan, isn't it?" Sebastian said, lifting his hat. "I was wondering if you could tell me the name of the gentleman undertaking today's ascension."

"The 'gentleman' is actually a woman," said Lady Quinlan, indicating the tiny bird-like creature in a feathered cap and narrow skirts who was darting about the balloon's wicker cage and inspecting the cables that held the apparatus moored to the ground. "The famous French aeronaut Madeleine-Sophie Blanchard. But you've no need to dissemble, my lord. I know you're looking into the circumstances surrounding my half sister's death." She smiled with a grim kind of satisfaction at his temporary discomfiture before adding, "Lady Portland told me."

Sebastian tipped back his head, his eyes narrowing against the sun as he watched the balloon swell with hot air from the fire, the red-and-yellow silk brilliant against a deep blue sky. *Guinevere was a childhood friend of my wife, Claire,* Portland had said. It made sense that Lady Portland would be in contact with Guinevere's sister, as well.

"I can't imagine how you might think I

131

could help," Lady Quinlan continued, her gaze, like Sebastian's, on the billowing silk above them. "Guinevere and I were never close, even as children."

He glanced over at her. "Were there so many years between you?"

She shrugged. "Three. Which can be significant when one is dealing with children. But even if we had been born nearer together, I doubt we would have been close. We had little in common. I was always interested in my studies, whereas Guinevere . . ." She hesitated, then ended dryly, "Guinevere was not."

"What interested Lady Guinevere?"

"The cliffs above the sea. My father's horses. The workings of the abandoned mines in the hills behind Athelstone Hall . . . in short, everything but the information that could be found between the covers of a schoolbook. She roamed the countryside as freely as if she were some cotter's child."

"Or a boy."

Morgana turned her head to meet his gaze. "Or a boy. She was always headstrong. I suppose it was easier for our governesses to simply let her go than to try to fight with her."

Of course it would be easier, Sebastian thought. But what of the Earl of Athelstone, her father? Hadn't he cared that his middle daughter was left to run wild? Or had he been content to delegate the rearing of his daughters to their governesses and to that sad procession of stepmothers doomed to die one after the other in childbirth?

"I'm afraid she grew accustomed to it," Morgana was saying. "Accustomed to doing as she pleased and thinking she could order her life as she chose. Marry as she liked."

"Whom did she wish to marry?"

Morgana let out a huff of scornful laughter. "Someone most unsuitable. Such a fit she threw, when she learned Papa meant to send her to spend the Season with our aunt here in London. Guinevere swore she'd never speak to him again, and she didn't, either. Even when Papa lay dying and was asking for her, she refused to go to him."

"Because he forced her into marriage with Anglessey?"

"No one forced her. Anglessey was her own choice." Lady Quinlan gave the black skirt of her mantua walking dress a little shake. "She always claimed she couldn't forgive Papa for refusing to allow her to marry where she wished. But if truth were told, I think what she really couldn't forgive him for was favoring Gerard over her."

"Gerard?"

"Our young brother."

Sebastian studied the woman's closed, hard face. "It didn't trouble you?"

A confused frown creased her forehead. "Of course not. Why would it? All men favor their sons. It's the way of the world. But Guinevere could never accept that. She was so naive, so idealistic." Her lips quivered with disdain. "A fool."

Sebastian glanced away again, across the crowded, sun-scorched clearing to where the cooling shimmer of a canal could just be seen in the distance. What had happened, he wondered, to produce such animosity, to make Morgana hate her sister so much that even now, in the aftermath of Guinevere's violent death, there was no softening, no flicker of either affection or regret?

The balloon was nearly full, the silk stretched taut, lifting the wicker cage from the ground and straining at the moorings. The little Frenchwoman, Madame Blanchard, was in the basket, making last-minute adjustments to the flap that would allow some of the gas to be let off and help her control the balloon's ascent.

Sebastian kept his gaze on the balloon. "This man your father refused to allow your sister to marry . . . who was he?"

Sebastian half expected Lady Quinlan to

be reticent, but she answered him readily enough. "Alain, the Chevalier de Varden. He's the son of Lady Audley from her first marriage. To a Frenchman."

Sebastian had heard of the Chevalier, a dashing young man with a quick temper and a ready laugh who was well liked about Town. He turned to look at Morgana in surprise. "Varden was considered unsuitable?"

"Of course. The family's good enough, to be sure. Better, actually, than that of Guinevere's mother. But Varden himself is penniless. Everything he would have inherited was lost in the Revolution."

There was something about the sneering tone of her reference to Guinevere's mother that piqued Sebastian's interest. "Tell me about Lady Anglessey's mother."

Again, that condescending little laugh. "Guinevere herself was quite proud of her mother's family."

"Why shouldn't she be?"

Morgana sucked in her cheeks in a way that made her look older — and more disagreeable — than before. "Her mother, Katherine, was *not* from the best of families. They say her great-grandmother was burned at the stake as a witch."

It was one of the dirty little secrets of

Western Christendom, the witch-burning craze — an outpouring of hatred and suspicion that had twisted itself around until it found a safe target in society's weakest members — women. He'd heard it said that before the witch-hunting frenzy died down, some five million women had been burned at the stake across Europe. There were some villages where the hysteria ran so high that when it was over, not a woman was left alive.

"If it's true," he said, staring out over the perspiring, sun-dappled crowd, hushed now with a mutual breathless anticipation as Madame Blanchard secured the door of her little wicker boat and snuggled into a warm coat, "then it's an indictment of those responsible for her death, rather than of the poor woman herself."

Someone shouted, "Let 'er go!" The balloon's moorings were cut loose and a great cheer arose from the crowd as the silken ball lifted straight up, soaring high above the treetops.

"Perhaps," said Morgana, her gaze, like his, on the rising sphere. "Although *her* grandmother was said to have been a witch, as well. They say she bewitched no less a person than the King's son and contrived to have a child by him."

Some six or seven hundred feet overhead,

136

the balloon caught a current and began to drift rapidly away to the west, the sun bright on its taut silken skin, the basket with its little Frenchwoman growing so small as to become nearly indistinct. Watching it, Sebastian knew a strange sense of dislocation. There was a roaring in his ears and his cheeks suddenly felt flushed, as if he were hot. "Which prince?" he asked, although he knew the truth even before she answered him. Knew it, deep in his gut where all certainty lies.

"James Stuart. The one who later became James the Second."

Chapter 18

"It must be a coincidence," said Paul Gibson some half an hour later. "What can James the Second possibly have to do with that poor young woman's murder?"

They were in the weed-choked yard that stretched between Gibson's house and surgery to the front, and the small stone building at the rear he used for dissections and autopsies. Sebastian sat on a nearby stone bench, a pint of ale in hand, while the surgeon busied himself with something boiling in a large pot of water over an open fire pit.

"When it comes to murder, I'm not sure I believe in coincidences," said Sebastian, dubiously eyeing the contents of that iron cauldron. Gibson gave the pot a brisk turn with a ladle and something surfaced, something that looked suspiciously like a human arm bone. "Please tell me that's not —"

Gibson looked up and laughed. "Good

God, no! This is a sheep's skeleton I'm rendering for a lecture in comparative anatomy. What did you think? That I'm boiling your murder victim? Anglessey came early this morning to claim his wife's body. I think he was planning to bury her today, rather than wait for this evening." Gibson reached to throw another scuttleful of coals on the fire, then wiped his sleeve across his forehead. "And none too soon. It's bloody hot for June. Too bad you didn't get here sooner. There were several things I'd like to have shown you."

Sebastian had seen enough dead bodies during the war. Given a choice, he decided he'd rather try to remember Guinevere Anglessey as the beautiful, vibrant woman she'd once been, without having to reconcile that with images of a dissected cadaver some seventy-two hours dead.

The fire began to smoke and Gibson knelt awkwardly beside it to poke at it with a stick. "If, as you say, the Marchioness left her house in Mount Street by hackney just after nuncheon on Wednesday, then she must have been killed here in London — or someplace very near. There simply wouldn't have been time for her to have driven all the way down to Brighton."

"You're certain she died in the early afternoon?"

Gibson nodded. "Or that morning. No later. My guess is that after she was killed, someone packed her body in ice and loaded it in a cart or carriage and hauled her down to Brighton. After death, the blood in a body responds to the pull of gravity. If a body is left lying on its back for hours immediately after death, then all the blood will pool in the back and on the undersides of the arms and legs, making them appear purple."

"As happened with Guinevere."

"Yes."

Sebastian stared across the yard to where a neglected old rose was blooming its heart out in a sun-spangled froth of delicate pink. The sound of bees could be heard, a low hum that mingled with the whisper of the wind through the chestnut tree overhead. "Was she with child?" he asked.

"I'm afraid so. The child would have been born sometime in November." Gibson sat back on his heels. "It was a boy, incidentally."

Sebastian nodded. "And the dagger in her back?"

"Was placed there some hours after she was poisoned."

Sebastian drew in a quick breath. "Poisoned?"

"I think so. We've no test to detect it after death, but I suspect cyanide. Her skin was very pink, if you'll remember. There is sometimes a lingering bitter-almond scent, but not after so many hours. It acts very quickly — in five or ten minutes with a sufficient dose. The death it produces is quite painful. And very messy."

"You mean it induces vomiting?"

"Yes. Among other things."

"But there was no trace of any of that."

"That's because after she died, her body was bathed and then redressed — in someone else's gown."

Sebastian shook his head, not understanding. "How do you know it wasn't her gown?"

"That's easy. It was too small." Laying aside his stick, Gibson rose with a lurch to disappear into the small stone building. He reappeared again a moment later with the gown in his hands. "Guinevere Anglessey was an unusually tall woman — five-foot-eight at least." He shook out the folds of green satin and held it up. "This dress was made for a slightly smaller woman — still tall, but probably no more than five-foot-five or -six and less buxom. That's why the tapes were undone and the sleeves shoved down on her shoulders. It simply didn't fit."

Sebastian reached to take the evening gown into his hands. "And her undergarments?"

"There weren't any."

Sebastian looked up at his friend. It wasn't unknown for courtesans — or even ladies such as the scandalous Caroline Lamb — to dispense with the light stays and thin chemise typically worn beneath their filmy gowns. But Lady Anglessey was not of that set.

"When you saw the body Wednesday night," said Gibson, "was it barefoot?"

"Yes. Why?"

"Did you notice any evening slippers nearby on the floor? Perhaps pushed beneath the settee?"

Sebastian thought about it a moment, then shook his head. "No. But I didn't look for them."

Gibson nodded, his lips pressed into a thoughtful line. "I did. There weren't any in the room. No shoes. No stockings."

"So what are you saying? Someone poisoned Guinevere with cyanide, waited until she'd succumbed to her death throes, and then bathed her body and dressed it in a green silk evening gown that belonged to someone else?"

"It would seem that way, yes. And they

either failed to bring along the necessary undergarments and stockings and slippers, or the ones they brought were too hopelessly small to use."

"Which would seem to argue either that the murderer was unfamiliar with the size of his victim, or that he failed to think through what he needed."

Paul Gibson made a face. "I'm not sure which I find the most gruesome. Is it possible that poor woman was killed simply to provide her murderer with a body to be used to embarrass the Regent?"

Sebastian hesitated. "I must admit I find it difficult to credit. Yet I suppose it is possible."

"But . . . why? Why kill the wife of a Marquis? Why not simply take some common woman off the streets?"

"Which do you think would cause the greater scandal?"

"There is that, of course."

Sebastian slid the fine satin of the dress between his gloved fingers. "What I don't understand is how the devil did our killer manage to get the body into the Pavilion that night?"

"Aye. That's the rub, isn't it?"

From the narrow street outside came the lilting cry of a costermonger, *Ripe cher-ries!*

Buy my ripe cher-ries. Sebastian folded the green satin gown into a small package to take away with him. "What have you done with the dagger that was in her back?" he asked.

Gibson went to crouch beside his iron pot. "I don't have it."

Sebastian swung around. *"What?"*

The surgeon looked up, his eyes narrowing against the smoke. "By the time I had made arrangements for the transportation of the body and came back to collect it, the dagger was gone."

CHAPTER 19

Upon consideration, it seemed to Sebastian that there were only two likely explanations for the disappearance of the dagger: either Guinevere's murderer had contrived in some inexplicable way and for some unknown purpose to return to the Yellow Cabinet and retrieve a weapon he had deliberately left behind, or else — which seemed far more likely — Lord Jarvis himself had removed the dagger. Sebastian could come up with several reasons why the Regent's unofficial minder might have done so; none reflected well on the man in whose arms Guinevere's body had been found.

Determined to confront Lord Jarvis, Sebastian drove to Carlton House, where Jarvis's frightened, pale-skinned clerk insisted his lordship was at home. But when Sebastian arrived at Grosvenor Square, it was to be told by the fey, half-mad Lady Jarvis that she rather thought her lord might be at Watiers. Watiers was still under the impression his lordship was out of town.

Temporarily balked of his quarry, Sebastian decided to pay a visit to the Chevalier de Varden.

Alain, the Chevalier de Varden, was a young man of twenty-two not long down from Oxford. He was well liked about Town, although his dashing good looks and tragic history were enough to cause considerable trepidation in the breasts of the mothers of young ladies of a marriageable age. A foreign title was all well and good, but only if there were extensive lands to go with it. The vast estates the young Chevalier was to have inherited from his dead father had all been lost in the Revolution.

Lacking an appreciable income of his own, the Chevalier lived with his mother, Isolde, Lady Audley, in Lady Audley's town house on Curzon Street. A widow now for the second time, she spent most of the year in London rather than at the isolated Welsh castle that had passed upon the death of her second husband to their son, the new Lord Audley.

Asking for the Chevalier, Sebastian was shown into a small but elegantly furnished withdrawing room filled with afternoon light. There, a slim, fine-boned woman with fiery auburn hair barely touched with gray knelt on the carpet in a secluded corner. Beside her lay a panting, very pregnant collie bitch that looked to be in the final stages of labor.

"I beg your pardon," Sebastian began, "there must be some mistake —"

"No mistake," said Lady Audley, looking up. Sebastian supposed she must be somewhere in her midforties, although she appeared younger, with clear, translucent skin and the kind of bone structure that ages well. "I asked that you be brought here. You must forgive me for receiving you like this, but poor Cloe is very near her time and I didn't want to leave her. Please, have a seat."

Declining the offer, Sebastian went to stand beside the open windows, his back to the sun.

"I know why you have come," said Lady Audley, her attention all for the laboring collie. "You think my son had something to do with Guinevere's death. But you are wrong."

He watched her slender hands move with gentle compassion over the collie's sweat-darkened shoulders and quivering flanks. "Let me guess," he said, remembering how Guinevere's sister, Morgana, had also known of his interest in the Marchioness's death. "You, too, are an intimate of Lady Portland."

"Lady Portland is my daughter, Claire."

"Ah. I see."

"Are you familiar, I wonder, with Wales?"

"Not especially, no."

The collie let out a soft whimper. Lady Audley rested her hand on the dog's head. "There, there, sweetheart. You're going to do just fine." To Sebastian, she said, "Athelstone Hall lies on the northern coast, not far from Audley Castle. Traveling by road the distance between them is some three or four miles. But if one follows the path along the sea cliffs, it's a journey of only fifteen minutes. Less for a running child."

"You mean, for a girl child who frequently escaped her governess's care to run wild about the countryside?"

Lady Audley nodded. "Guinevere's mother, Katherine, was very kind to me when I first came to live there. When Katherine died . . . the poor child was nearly inconsolable. No one can take a mother's place, of course, but I did what I could."

"I thought Athelstone remarried?"

"Yes. But I'm afraid the new Countess took little interest in her predecessors' daughters."

Sebastian studied the elegant woman on the floor beside the birthing bitch. She had narrow shoulders and fine-boned hands, and an air of fragility that he suspected was entirely misleading. "I must confess," he said, "I expected you to be French."

"Oh, no," she said without looking up. "I was born and raised in Devonshire. When I was eighteen, I went to spend the spring of 1786 with my aunt in Paris. You can't imagine what Paris was like in those days, the endless round of balls and gaiety, music and laughter. I suppose we should have known it couldn't last." She gave a little sigh. "But one never does."

"That was where you met the Chevalier de Varden?"

She sat back on her heels, an unexpectedly soft, sad smile playing about her lips. "Yes. At a banquet at Versailles. We were married within six weeks. I considered myself an extraordinarily fortunate woman — and then, just weeks after the birth of our son, Alain, came the fall of the Bastille."

Sebastian watched as that haunted smile faded. The year 1789 would not have been an easy one for a gently born Englishwoman married to a French aristocrat.

"It was in the autumn that a mob attacked the château. I managed to escape with Alain through the cellars, but Varden was out riding through the vineyards at the time and . . ." She paused to take a deep, soul-shaking sigh. "They pulled him from his horse and tore him to pieces."

A shudder convulsed the collie's swollen belly, her body jackknifing up as the first of her puppies slipped into the world, wet and shining with blood. Lady Audley stared down at it, but Sebastian thought she was seeing something else, a memory she would never forget.

Once, in the Peninsula, Sebastian's colonel had ordered a Portuguese peasant tied between two horses and then had the horses whipped in opposite directions. Just for fun. He blinked away the memory. "You were fortunate to make it back to England."

"Fortunate? Yes, I suppose we were. One does what one must."

At their feet, Cloe went about the task of severing the umbilical cord and cleaning her pup. Lady Audley was silent for a moment, stroking the bitch's head. Then she said, her voice flat, "I married Audley the following year."

Sebastian watched the elegant woman before him help with the collie's birthing. Lady Audley was beautiful even now in middle age. Twenty years ago she must have been stunning as a young, grieving widow. Did marrying the late Lord Audley fall into the category of things one did because one must?

"Tell me about Lady Anglessey's mother," he said aloud.

"Katherine?" The question seemed to surprise her. "She looked much like Guinevere, although she was a tiny thing, whereas Guinevere was tall, like her father. They had the same blue-black hair, and those eyes that made you think of a fern-filled mountain glen in spring." She smiled softly. "And the same passionate, not always wise nature."

"I've heard it said Lord Athelstone lost four wives in childbirth. Is that true?"

"Not exactly. I believe the first died of consumption when her daughter, Morgana, was a year or two old. But the other three died in childbirth, yes. Lord Athelstone was a bear of a man. All three of his daughters were unusually tall, and one assumes the sons would have been even larger. I gave it as my opinion that it was like mating a Yorkie bitch to a Great Dane. His boy babies were so big they were literally killing his wives. And it's certainly true that he only succeeded in getting a son when he finally had enough sense to take to wife a woman nearly as big as he."

Cloe was cleaning her pup now, licking it roughly, nudging it with her muzzle. It would be another hour, perhaps more, before a second pup was born. Sebastian said, "Why did you want to see me?"

Lady Audley wiped her hands on the apron she'd tied over her muslin dress and stood. There was a sudden fierceness about her, the aura of a mother willing to do battle to protect her young. "Varden was here with me, all last Wednesday afternoon. If you seek to deflect suspicion from the Prince Regent onto my son, I will not allow you to succeed."

Sebastian met her hard gaze. "What I seek is the truth."

She gave an unexpectedly bitter laugh. "The truth? How often do you think we ever really know the truth?"

"According to Lady Quinlan, her sister Guinevere grew up expecting to marry Varden."

Lady Audley pressed her lips together, then nodded almost reluctantly. "In some ways it was my fault, I suppose. There was only a year between them. I always thought of them much as brother and sister. I never imagined for a moment that Guinevere saw them as something else entirely. But it was a child's dream, nothing more. They were children. Why, Varden wasn't even up at Oxford yet when Guinevere married."

"That was four years ago. Much has changed since then."

Her head drew back, her eyes sparkling. "I know what you're implying, but you're wrong. Guinevere had a passionate nature, but she was also fiercely loyal. She would never have played Anglessey false. Never."

He wondered if it was significant that her anger flared in defense of Guinevere's honor and not that of her son. Or was she simply reflecting her society's very differing attitudes toward male and female sexual adventuring? "I'd be interested to hear what your son has to say."

Isolde sucked in a deep breath, and for one telling moment, her mask of calm control slipped. He realized that behind this woman's concern for the laboring collie at her feet lay another fear, deeper and far more troubling.

"My son isn't here," she said, suddenly looking tired and much, much older. "I'm afraid he has taken Guinevere's death quite badly. I haven't seen him since Thursday morning, when we heard what had happened to her."

CHAPTER 20

Late that night, sometime after the watch had called out *Two o'clock on a fine night and all is well,* an unexpectedly cool breeze sprang up, carrying with it the promise of rain before morning.

Sebastian lay in Kat Boleyn's silk-hung bed and listened to the wind set the branches of the nearby chestnut tree to tapping against the front of the house. Rolling onto his side, he let his gaze drift over the sleeping woman beside him, following the strong angle of her jaw, the gentle curve of her breast just visible beneath the tumble of her hair.

The wind gusted up again, rattling the windows and setting the bed curtains to shifting in the sudden cold draft. Reaching out, he drew the coverlet over Kat's bare shoulder and smiled. His love for this woman swelled within him, filling him with a warm feeling of peace and the same stunned awe that he'd known for seven years now, ever since the day he'd first held her in his arms and tasted the intimation of heaven that was her kiss.

He wondered where it came from, that comfortable conviction Lady Audley shared with so many in their society, the belief that the passions of the young are insignificant whirlwinds, temporarily intense, perhaps, but never enduring. He'd been one-and-twenty when he and Kat first met, while she had been barely sixteen.

She stirred beside him, as if disturbed by his wakefulness. Moving carefully so as not to rouse her further, he slid from her side and went to stand, naked, at the window overlooking the front of the house. Drawing back the drapes, he stared down at an empty street lit only fitfully by a half-moon already disappearing rapidly behind a scuttling of clouds.

He heard a whisper of movement as she came up behind him. "Why can't you sleep?" she asked, slipping her arms around his waist.

He turned in her embrace, holding her close. "I was thinking about Guinevere Anglessey. About the life she must have known growing up in Wales."

"It can't have been easy," Kat said softly,

"losing her mother so young."

Sebastian drew her closer, his cheek resting against her hair. They were all marked in an unseen but hurtful way, he thought, the motherless children of the world. Guinevere had been little more than a babe when she lost her mother; Sophie Hendon had sailed away to a watery grave the summer Sebastian was eleven, while Kat had been twelve or thirteen when her own mother and stepfather had been killed. He knew some of what had happened on that dark day, but not all of it. "At least she still had a home," said Sebastian, thinking of all Kat herself had lost on that misty Dublin morning. "And her father."

"He doesn't seem to have concerned himself overly much with her."

Sebastian was silent for a moment, remembering his own father's bitter withdrawal on that long-ago summer of death. "Perhaps. Yet he cared enough not to want to see her married to a penniless young man."

Kat tilted her head to look up at him. "Yes. But for her sake? I wonder. Or his?"

"Morgana claims Athelstone didn't force her sister to marry Anglessey. That the Marquis was Guinevere's own choice."

"Perhaps she decided that if she couldn't

have the man she loved, she might as well marry for wealth and a title."

Sebastian felt the shiver that ran through her as she spoke. He rested his hip against the windowsill so that he could circle her with the warmth of his body, the warmth of his love. "I wonder how Varden felt about that?" he said softly.

She rested comfortably against him. "It doesn't seem to have blighted his life. He's often at the theater with a crowd of other young bucks, laughing and eyeing the dancers. Watching him, one would say he hadn't a care in the world."

"He seems to have taken Guinevere's death hard enough."

"Well he would, wouldn't he? They were childhood friends."

He ran his hands up her sides, enjoying the feel of her bare flesh beneath his touch. "They might very well have been more than that. Still."

She rested her arms on his shoulders so that she could look again into his face. "You think Varden is the lover Bevan Ellsworth claims fathered Guinevere's child?"

He threaded his fingers through her hair, combing it back from her forehead. "We don't know for certain she even had a lover. It's not something I'm prepared to take on

Bevan Ellsworth's word."

She was quiet for a moment, thinking, and he watched her. He loved the way her mind worked. In a world where women learned from an early age to affect an air of helpless ignorance, Kat was a strong, intelligent woman and she wasn't afraid to show it.

At least not with him.

Finally, she said, "What I don't understand is, where does the Prince Regent fit into any of this?"

Sebastian blew out a long breath. "I suppose it's possible her murder was completely cold-blooded — that her killer's sole purpose was simply to use her to cast suspicion upon the Prince Regent and increase his unpopularity. But if that were true, then why select Guinevere Anglessey as the victim? Why not Lady Hertford, or one of the other women with whom Prinny has been closely linked?"

"Perhaps she was simply . . . convenient."

Sebastian ran his hands up and down her arms, his gaze on the night-darkened window beside them. Somewhere out there . . . somewhere, in some corner of this sprawling, dangerous city, lay the answer to what had happened to Guinevere Anglessey, and why. If he only knew where to look. "It would help if Lovejoy could find out where she went in that hackney."

"Her abigail might know."

By now the clouds had completely covered the moon, plunging the street below into a gloomy darkness only faintly illuminated by the feeble glow of the streetlamps. A shadow seemed to detach itself from the house at the corner, a phantom of a shape that was there and then gone.

"What is it?" Kat asked when Sebastian leaned forward, his hand tightening on the drapes beside them.

"I thought I saw something. A man watching the house."

"It's just shadows. The trees moving in the wind." She pressed her chilled body close to his. "Come back to bed."

He wrapped his arms around her, lending her the heat of his own body. He nibbled at her neck, breathed softly against her ear. But what he said was "I need to go home. It's late."

"Stay," she whispered, her naked body moving suggestively against his, her hands roving over him with a lover's familiarity. "I like waking up to find you still beside me."

"You could wake up beside me every morning if you'd marry me."

He felt her stiffen in his arms. She drew back to meet his gaze, the playful eroticism fading from her eyes to be replaced with something stark and painful. "You know why I can't do that."

He knew why she thought she couldn't do that. They'd been through it all a thousand times before, yet he still couldn't stop himself from saying, "Why? Because I am a viscount and you are an actress?"

"Yes," she said simply.

He pushed out a harsh, frustrated breath. "You realize, don't you, that if Guinevere had been allowed to marry the man she loved, she'd probably still be alive today."

"You can't know that."

"I know that I —"

She silenced him with her kiss, taking his face between her hands, her fingers digging into his cheeks as she moved her mouth over his in desperate gulps. "Don't," she said, her voice rough, her breath warm against his face.

He knew she loved him. It shone in her eyes, was there with each trembling breath. And it struck him as the cruelest of ironies that if she had loved him less, she would have married him.

Wordlessly, she threaded her fingers through his, drawing him away from the window toward the warm embrace of her bed. And he went with her, because the shadows in the darkened street below were simply the trees moving in the wind, and it was hours still until dawn.

He had time. Time to convince her that she was wrong, that far from ruining his life by marrying him, she was the only thing that could save him. He still had time.

He told himself they had all the time in the world.

His sleep was often troubled by dreams, haunting recurrent images of red-coated phalanxes of soldiers, their faces coated with dust, their lips tightly set as they marched toward death. Of stone walls battered and blackened by the howling shriek of artillery. A child's cry. A woman's scream. The buzzing stench of death. The remains of men and horses so dismembered as to become indistinguishable.

But that night he dreamed of Kat. She lay upon his bed, dressed in her bridal finery. The golden light of the bedside candle cast flickering shadows across the pale perfection of her features, the delicate flesh of her closed eyelids. He knelt beside her, the silken hangings of his bed whispering softly around him. Yet he knew no joy, only the pain of tears that swelled his throat but refused to fall.

Confused, he reached out to close his hand over hers, and then he understood. Because her hands were cold beneath his, and when he kissed her, her lips did not respond; her eyes did not open. Her eyes would never open again. And he knew then that her wedding finery had become her shroud.

He awoke with a jerk, his breath coming hard and fast, his heart pounding uncomfortably in his chest. Turning his head, he found her asleep beside him, her hair spilling dark and beautiful about a cheek flushed with life, her breath sweet against his face. And still he had to touch her, to feel her body warm beneath his hands.

In the hushed light of dawn she stirred, reaching for him even before her eyelids fluttered open. She skimmed her palms down his arms to his bare hips. He buried his face in her hair, breathed in the familiar scents of rose water and the sweet essence of this woman, and felt his love for her like a throbbing ache in his heart.

She was warm with sleep but softly pliant against him, murmuring gentle words as his hand found her breast. She wrapped one leg around him, sliding her foot up his calf in invitation. He rolled on top of her, her hand guiding him inside her.

He closed his eyes, trailed a line of kisses down her neck as he moved gently within her. She was warm and alive and in his arms, and still he knew a deep and abiding fear that would not be stilled.

CHAPTER 21

Sebastian's valet was an earnest, softly rounding man named Sedlow who had been in Sebastian's employ for just over a year. The man was a genius at repairing the ravages a night on the town could wreak upon a gentleman's coat, and could coax an enviable shine from top boots worn hard on the hunting field. But when Sebastian appeared later that morning with a brown-paper-wrapped package containing a pair of badly cut trousers and an old-fashioned greatcoat such as a Bow Street Runner might wear, Sedlow paled and recoiled with horror.

"My lord. You can't seriously mean to appear in those rags *in public."*

Pausing in the act of tying an unfashionably dark and coarse neckcloth, Sebastian glanced over at his valet. "They're hardly rags. And I don't intend to drop into White's in this rig, if that's what you fear."

"But . . . someone could still see you."

Sebastian raised one eyebrow. "Do you fear such a sighting might do irreparable damage to my reputation?"

Sedlow sniffed. "*Your* reputation? No, my lord. Noblemen are allowed to be eccentric."

"Ah. I see. It's the repercussions on your reputation that trouble you."

Sedlow started to open his mouth, then closed it.

"Wise," said Sebastian, and shrugged into his badly tailored coat.

The rain had begun early that morning, a steady downpour that brought with it a bite of North Sea air and made the unseasonable heat of the past few days seem like a dim, distorted memory. Hailing a hackney carriage on New Bond Street, Sebastian directed the jarvey toward Mount Street. Then, slumping in one corner, he watched the raindrops chase each other down the windowpane, and slowly allowed himself to sink into the personage he'd chosen to assume.

It was an actor's trick, something Kat had taught him to do in those early, heady days when he'd just come down from Oxford and she was still only beginning to make her mark upon the stage. He'd perfected the technique in the army, where his very survival had at times depended upon his ability to submerge himself in a character until he wore the assumed posture and mannerisms as comfortably and effortlessly as an old coat.

By the time he arrived at the service entrance of the house on Mount Street, the Earl's son was gone and he had become Mr. Simon Taylor, one of Bow Street's finest.

It occurred to Sebastian that you could tell a great deal about a woman by the abigail she chose to employ. Some lady's maids were haughty, affected creatures as fashion conscious and condescending as their mistresses. Some were cheerful, fresh-cheeked country women who'd served their mistresses since they were in the schoolroom, while others were timid and apologetic things, forever quivering in terror of being dismissed.

Lady Anglessey's abigail was a thin, slight woman in her late twenties or early thirties named Tess Bishop. She had straw-colored hair and a sallow complexion, and at first glance one might easily take her for the meek, browbeaten variety of abigail. But her gray eyes were clear and intelligent, her step firm as she entered the housekeeper's room

Sebastian had commandeered for their interview.

She wore black, as befitted the servant of a household in mourning. It was Sunday, her day off, but she had an apron tied over her bombazet dress. She had obviously been working, and it occurred to Sebastian that she might very well be packing up her own things. After all, a widower would have no need for a lady's maid.

She paused in the doorway to eye Sebastian with undisguised suspicion. "I don't see no baton," she said, referring to the emblem of office traditionally carried by Runners.

A real Runner would probably have snapped, "We'll have none of your impertinence, girl," and ordered her to sit down. But in Sebastian's experience, most people cooperated best when their dignity was respected. So he simply said, "Please, have a seat," and steered her toward the ladder-backed chair he had placed beside the window overlooking the rain-drenched rear gardens.

She hesitated a moment, then sat, her hands folded in her lap, her spine as straight and uncompromising as a nun's.

"I'd like to ask you a few questions about Lady Anglessey," said Sebastian, leaning his shoulders against the wall. "We understand her ladyship left the house in a hackney on Wednesday afternoon, and we're hoping you might know where she went."

"No," said the abigail baldly. "I don't."

Sebastian gave her a coaxing smile. "No idea whatsoever?"

There was no answering smile to lighten the woman's pinched, unremarkable features. "No, sir. She didn't say, and it's not my place to pry into the activities of my employers, now, is it?"

Sebastian crossed his arms at his chest and rocked back on his heels. "Very commendable, I'm sure. But a lady's maid often knows things about her employers without needing to be told — and without prying. Are you quite certain, for instance, that Lady Anglessey didn't let drop some sort of a hint? Perhaps when she asked you to get out her gown for the afternoon?"

"She selected the gown herself — a simple walking dress with a matching pelisse, as would be suitable for a lady of fashion going out for the afternoon."

Deciding to take another tack, Sebastian went to sit in the chair opposite her. "Tell me, Miss Bishop, how would you say his lordship and Lady Anglessey got along?"

Tess Bishop gave him a wooden stare.

168

"I'm sure I don't know what you mean."

"I think you do." He rested his forearms on his thighs and leaned forward, as if inviting confidences. "Did they quarrel, for instance?"

"No."

"Never?" Sebastian raised one eyebrow in a show of disbelief. "Man and wife for some four years, and no quarrels? No minor disagreements, even?"

"If they quarreled, sir, it wasn't in my hearing."

"Do you know if she ever met a man named Alain, the Chevalier de Varden?"

Something flared in her eyes, something she hid by staring down at hands now clasped so tightly they showed white. "I never heard the name, no."

Sebastian studied the abigail's stiff, hostile face. He supposed it said something about Guinevere Anglessey, if even after death she could inspire this kind of loyalty in a servant. "How long have you been with her ladyship?" Sebastian asked suddenly.

"Four years," said Tess Bishop, relaxing slightly. "I came to her just before she married his lordship."

Sebastian leaned back in his chair. "I suppose it's natural for a young lady about to make such a brilliant alliance to want to provide herself with a more experienced abigail than the one she'd brought with her from the country."

"That's not the way it was at all. This was my first position."

"Your first?"

"That's right. I used to be a seamstress, while my David was a carpenter. But he was pressed into the navy, right before the bombardment of Copenhagen." She paused. "He was killed."

"I'm sorry," said Sebastian, although it seemed a pathetically lame sop to offer her.

"After that, I supported us as best I could, but . . ." Her voice trailed off as if she regretted having said so much.

"Us?" Sebastian prompted.

"We had a baby. A girl." Tess Bishop turned her face slightly toward the window so that she was no longer looking at him. "I took sick. When I couldn't make my quota, they let me go. And then my baby took sick, too."

Sebastian watched her slim throat work as she swallowed. It was a familiar enough story, a tragedy enacted a thousand times or more a year in London, Paris — in every city across Europe. Women barely eking out a subsistence wage, caught by illness or a downturn in the fashion industry and thrown onto the streets. Most turned to prostitution or theft, or both. They had no choice, but that didn't stop the moralists from condemning them as sinful women and railing against them as the source of all corruption and decadence. As if any woman in her right mind would willingly embark upon a path certain to lead to disease and death and an unmarked grave in some noisome churchyard's poor hole.

"I was desperate," Tess Bishop said in little more than a whisper, a flush of remembered shame coloring her cheeks. "I finally took to begging in the streets. Lady Anglessey . . . she took pity on me. Brought us in and gave us something to eat. Even had in a doctor for my little one."

Sebastian looked at the woman's thin shoulders, at the starched white cap that covered her bowed head. "But it was too late," she said after a moment. "My Sarah died that very night."

Out in the garden, the rain had eased up, although the clouds still hung gray and heavy over the city. From here Sebastian could see the outlines of a large glass-and-frame conservatory, its panes steamy with moisture.

This was a side of Guinevere that no one had showed him before, and one he suspected wasn't exactly typical. He wondered what had moved her to extend the hand of salvation to this woman. A chance meeting of the eyes, perhaps? Some intuitive recognition by the young, heartsick Earl's daughter that this other woman, this widowed mother of a dying baby, knew a despair far, far greater than her own?

"I wanted to die, too," said Tess Bishop, her voice little more than a whisper. "But Lady Guinevere, she said I mustn't. She said if we're given a hard road to walk in life, we just have to fight to find some way to make what we want out of what life has given us."

"And she hired you as her lady's maid? Even though you'd no experience?"

Tess Bishop's head came up, her lips crimped together in stubborn pride. "I worked hard to learn, and I'm quick. I haven't let her ladyship down. I'd do anything for her."

"You're letting her down right now," said Sebastian, pressing his advantage. "If you were really willing to do anything for her, you'd help me figure out who murdered her."

She leaned forward, her small gray eyes flashing with unexpected fire. "I can tell you who killed her. His name is Bevan

Ellsworth. He's Lord Anglessey's nephew and he's wanted her dead ever since the day she married his uncle four years ago."

"Wanting someone dead and actually going so far as to kill them are two very different things."

Tess Bishop shook her head, her nostrils flaring on a hastily indrawn breath. "You didn't hear him. You didn't hear him when he came here —"

"When was this?"

"Just last week. Monday, I think it was. He came storming into the house while her ladyship was at breakfast. Shouting so loud we all heard him, about how his creditors had learned she was with child and that he might not be the next Marquis of Anglessey after all. He said they were threatening him — threatening his life, even. And then he threatened her."

"Threatened her? How was that?"

"He said he'd see her dead before he'd let her foist her bastard in his place."

CHAPTER 22

A sampler hung on the wall just behind the abigail's head, a sampler worked in silk thread against a linen background. Sebastian stared at it, at the neatly stitched flowers intricately entwined around the letters of the alphabet. But he wasn't really seeing it. He was remembering the glitter of hatred in Bevan Ellsworth's eyes, and the sound made by a boy's arm breaking on the playing fields of Eton.

"What did her ladyship do?" Sebastian asked.

"She told him to get out. And when he said he'd go all right and tell everyone who'd listen that she'd been playing the whore, she . . ." The abigail's voice trailed off.

"She what?"

Tess Bishop's color was high. She hesitated, then said in a rush, "She laughed. She said he'd only show himself to be the fool he was, because her son would be the next marquis even if he'd been begotten by a hunchback in the gutters."

It was a legal principle that had come down to them from the Romans, a doctrine known as *Pater est quem nupitae demonstrant.* As far as the law was concerned, a woman's husband was the father of her child, whether the man actually sired the child or not. Guinevere's statement didn't necessarily mean anything, of course. Scornful words flung in anger. But still . . .

"You'll have to excuse me now, sir," said the abigail, pushing to her feet. "His lordship has asked me to help with organizing the staff's mourning clothes."

Sebastian rose with her. "Yes, of course." He kept his voice casual, although deep within his breast, his heart had begun to beat uncommonly fast. "There's just one other thing I wanted to ask. You wouldn't happen to know where her ladyship got the necklace she was wearing the day she died, would you?"

"Necklace?" Tess Bishop wrinkled her forehead in a frown. "What necklace?"

Slipping the bluestone triskelion from his pocket, Sebastian held it out in the palm of his hand. "This one."

She studied it for a moment, then shook

175

her head decisively. "That's not her lady-ship's."

For an instant, Sebastian imagined he could feel the necklace burning his flesh, although the stone was cold in the dreary light of the rainy day. "She died wearing it."

"But that's impossible."

"How is that?"

"Because she was wearing the Pompeian that afternoon."

"I beg your pardon?" said Sebastian, not understanding.

"The walking dress of Pompeian red. It's made high at the neck, with an upstanding collar and raised epaulets, and worn with a goffered lawn fraise."

"A what?"

"A fraise. It's a kind of neck ruff with three tiers," said Tess Bishop, impatient with his ignorance and anxious to be gone. "Her ladyship could never have worn a necklace with that dress."

Bevan Ellsworth, nephew of the Marquis of Anglessey and heir presumptive of all his lands and titles, kept a small suite of rooms two floors above an exclusive shop on St. James's Street.

Using the skills he'd honed over five years in the army doing things no gentleman should ever do, Sebastian let himself in the main door from the hall. He found himself in a small parlor, opulently furnished if untidily kept, with riding boots left lying discarded across the Aubusson rug and a scattering of invitations and unpaid bills spilling off an ornate inlaid desk.

On the far side of the room, the door to the bedroom stood half-ajar. Sebastian went to push it open.

He found himself on the threshold of a room even more untidy than the last. An empty bottle of brandy stood on a side table near the door along with a scattering of dirty glasses; a tangle of dirty cravats and socks, waistcoats, and shirts lay strewn across the floor.

Sebastian wouldn't have been surprised to find a naked Cyprian sprawled beneath the hangings of the silk-draped bed. But Ellsworth slept alone, flat on his back with the tangled sheets and covers shoved down around his hips. A heavy odor of brandy and sweat and stale air permeated the room.

Pulling up a delicate, lyre-backed chair to the side of the bed, Sebastian straddled the seat backward and drew a small French flintlock pistol from his coat pocket. A half-empty glass of brandy set on the bedside table at his elbow. Reaching over, he dipped the fingertips of his free hand into the liquid and calmly flicked a scattering of cold drops onto Bevan Ellsworth's gently snoring face.

Ellsworth wrinkled his nose and shifted position, rolling half onto his side, his eyes still tightly closed.

Sebastian flicked again.

The man's eyes blinked open, closed, then flew open wide as he bolted up, his weight on one outflung hand. *What the hell?*

Sebastian rested the arm with the pistol along the curving back of the chair. "You should stick with Howard and Gibbs," he said pleasantly, as if giving financial advice to a friend. "Their interest rates might be ruinous, but unlike some of their more ruthless brethren on King Street, they don't pollute the Thames with the bodies of those customers who make the mistake of falling behind on their interest payments."

Ellsworth cleared his throat, the back of one hand rubbing across his mouth as he sat up straighter, his gaze on the little flintlock. "How do you know about that?"

"Of course," continued Sebastian conversationally, as if the man hadn't even spoken, "the problem with Howard and Gibbs is that they typically require some sort of surety. Particularly when there's a chance the individual involved might not be the heir to a comfortable estate, after all."

Ellsworth's gaze slipped away to the open door behind Sebastian, then back again. "What are you doing here? And why the hell are you dressed like some bloody Bow Street Runner?"

Sebastian simply smiled. "You said your debts weren't pressing. You lied to me. That was not wise."

His jaw tightening, Ellsworth extended one arm in a wide arc that took in the small room, the bed's dirty hangings. "Look at this place. Look at how I'm forced to live. Spending my days at the Inns of Court. Bloody hell. I'm a heartbeat away from being the next Marquis of Anglessey, and the paltry allowance my uncle grants me isn't even enough to pay my tailors' bills."

"Especially after settling day at Tattersall's."

Ellsworth moistened his lower lip with his tongue. In the harsh light of morning, his skin looked sallow and slack with dissipation, his eyes bloodshot. "I didn't kill her," he said, his voice unexpectedly calm and even.

"But you threatened to."

Ellsworth threw back the sheets and stood up. He was naked to the waist, a pair of drawstring underdrawers slung low on his hips, his feet bare. "Who wouldn't want to kill her, in my position?" he demanded. "She was going to take away what is mine." He leaned forward, his curled knuckles thumping against his bare chest. "*Mine*. And hand it all to some ill-begotten bastard."

"You can't know that."

A tight smile curled the man's lips. "Can't I? Some things are hard to keep a secret. And servants do talk." He swung away to go splash water from the pitcher into the bowl on the washstand.

"So who's the father?"

Ellsworth shrugged, not bothering to turn around. "How should I know? I saw half a dozen or more young bucks at the funeral yesterday. For all I know, Guinevere herself couldn't have told you the father's name."

Sebastian rose to his feet as a sudden thought occurred to him. "Where is she buried?"

"At St. Anne's. Why?"

Sebastian shook his head, his lips curving into a hard smile. "What I don't understand is why you went through all the risk of transporting the Marchioness's body from London down to the Pavilion."

"Jesus." Ellsworth swung around, his face flushing with anger and what may have been a trace of fear. "You still think I did it. You *still* think I killed her."

"I made some discreet inquiries around the Inns of Court. You arrived late that day, and left early."

Sebastian expected the man to deny it. Instead, his eyes narrowed and he leaned forward to say provocatively, "You think I killed her? All right. Then let's see you prove it."

The narrow staircase leading down to the street door was dark in the rainy-day gloom. Halfway down the second flight, Sebastian passed a fleshy young dandy laboring up the steep steps, the man with flaxen hair and a florid complexion he remembered having seen with Ellsworth at Brooks's. Studying the man's protuberant eyes, his molded, almost feminine lips, and weak chin, Sebastian thought the man's sense of familiarity might come from his unfortunate resemblance to the portly, ruddy-faced princes of the House of Hanover. Then as the man reached the first floor and turned, his profile was silhouetted against the gray light above in a way that made Sebastian realize he did know this man, after all. He was Fabian Fitzfrederick, natural son of Frederick, Duke of York, second son of George III and next in line behind Princess

Charlotte to the thrones of England, Scotland, and Wales.

The friendship might mean nothing, of course. Legitimate heirs to the throne were dangerously scarce, but over the years George III's seven sons had sired scores of illegitimate children. If Guinevere Anglessey's body had been found anyplace other than in the private apartments of His Highness the Prince Regent, Bevan Ellsworth's friendship with an illegitimate member of the royal family would have been insignificant. It still might be insignificant, although Sebastian decided it wouldn't hurt to look into Fabian Fitzfrederick's activities on Wednesday last.

But first Sebastian intended to pay a visit to St. Anne's churchyard.

CHAPTER 23

The bells in the church tower were ringing, calling the last stragglers to late-morning service when Sebastian jumped down from a hackney in front of St. Anne's churchyard. The rain still came down hard, in big drops that dripped from the sodden leaves of the gnarled old oak trees overhead, flattened the rank grass between the graves, and darkened the granite headstones to near black.

The churchyard was not large, a collection of tombs and monuments hemmed in by tightly packed buildings that had risen up around the old stone church. Standing at the gate, Sebastian could see only two recent burials, their freshly turned mounds of dark brown earth heaped with funeral lilies and mums beaten and bruised now by the rain.

Winding between rusting iron railings and moss-covered statues, he worked his way toward the only other person in the cemetery, a man who stood beside one of the new graves, his head bowed, his collar turned up against the driving rain. At the sound of Sebastian's footfalls on the flagged path, the man turned and Sebastian recognized Alain, the Chevalier de Varden.

The Chevalier's head was bare, his once fine shirt stained, his face pale and shadowed by some three or four days' growth of dark beard. "Well, if it isn't Lord Devlin," he said, blinking away the rain that ran down his cheeks and plastered his dark hair to his forehead. "Have you come to pay your respects to the dead? I wonder. Or simply to add me to your list of suspects?"

Sebastian paused a few steps away. Around them the rain poured, beating on the leaves of the oaks and chestnuts overhead and shooting in noisy torrents from the slanted roofs of the surrounding tombs. "You've been talking to your sister, Claire."

"That's right." The Chevalier's speech was flawlessly precise, his movements fluid and graceful. Only the icy glitter in his blue eyes betrayed the fact that he was profoundly, dangerously drunk. "She thinks Bevan Ellsworth did it."

"And you?"

Varden threw back his head to let out a

harsh, ringing laugh that ended in teeth-clenching scorn. "Only Prinny could be found with a woman he'd murdered still clasped in his arms and yet manage to set everyone around him to scrambling in an effort to find someone else to blame."

Sebastian shook his head. "You're wrong. The Regent didn't kill her. He couldn't have. She was dead some six or eight hours before he found her in the Yellow Cabinet in the Pavilion."

The wind gusted up, bringing with it the smell of damp earth and wet stone and death. Varden stood very still, only his chest jerking with each indrawn breath. "What are you saying?"

"Guinevere Anglessey was killed Wednesday afternoon — probably someplace here in London, given that she left her home in a hackney just after nuncheon."

"A hackney? Going where?" he demanded with a sharpness Sebastian hadn't expected.

"I don't know." Sebastian kept his gaze on the other man's face. He saw grief there, and anger, and some of the guilt that can so often bedevil those left alive. But there was no sign of subterfuge, none of the consternation and fear one might expect from a murderer watching his elaborate stratagems of concealment beginning to unravel. "I thought perhaps you might be able to tell me."

Varden raked his fingers through his dark, wet hair, his eyes squeezing shut as a spasm of pain contorted handsome features. "I hadn't seen her since last week. Saturday."

On the street behind them, a carriage went by driven fast, its iron-rimmed wheels flying, the sound of its horses' hooves clattering dully in the wet air. The heaviness of the clouds had brought an unnatural darkness to the day, making it seem far later than it actually was.

"Lady Quinlan tells me you and her sister were good friends," said Sebastian.

Varden dropped his hands to his sides, his eyes open and alert, his body tense. "I'd hazard a guess she phrased it somewhat differently."

Sebastian nodded in acknowledgment. "There was no love lost between the two sisters, was there?"

"That's one way of putting it. And if it surprises you, then you must have been an only child," said Varden with a bitterness that spoke volumes about the Chevalier's relationships with his own half brothers and sisters.

"I had two brothers," said Sebastian. Both were long dead, but he saw no need to add that. No need, either, to admit he had a sister who less than five months ago had looked forward to cheerfully watching him hang. The bond between siblings could be close — he knew that; but he also knew something of the fierce jealousies and rivalries, resentments and animosities that could flourish within the tight bonds of a family. Especially when birth order could elevate one to a life of ease and power while consigning the rest to obscurity and relative poverty.

"Athelstone never had anything to do with any of his daughters," Varden was saying. "I think he hated them. It was as if they were nothing more to him than unwanted reminders of the son he couldn't seem to have."

"One might expect that sort of childhood to make sisters close to each other."

"Only if one were unacquainted with Morgana. Up until the day Athelstone died, Morgana was desperate to curry favor with the old bastard — and she usually did it by making Guin look bad." An unexpected, tender smile touched the other man's lips. "Mind you, Morgana didn't need to work too hard. Guin did a good enough job of making herself look bad. She was . . ." He paused, searching for the right word. The smile faded. "Guin was very angry, growing up."

"About what?"

Varden shrugged. "About her mother dying, I suppose. About her father. Who knows?"

He went to stand beside the muddy wound of her grave, his head bowed, his fists clenched at his sides. Around them, the rain poured, splashing into the puddles in the sunken hollows of old graves and drumming on the domed roof of a nearby tomb.

Suddenly, he looked up, his eyes narrowing against the driven rain. "He did it, you know. Prinny. I don't care what you say. There's no doubt in my mind."

"What possible reason could the Prince Regent have for killing the Marchioness of Anglessey?"

"Madness needs no reason. And they are all mad. You know that, don't you? Every last member of that God-rotted family. The King might be the only one actually raving, but the taint is there, in each and every one of them, whether it's Clarence roaring around on imaginary quarterdecks or old one-eyed Cumberland betraying the over-zealous nature of his affection for his sister Sophia."

Sebastian held himself very still, his silent

gaze on the other man.

Varden used the palm of his hand to wipe the rain from his face. "My sister, Claire, is right in one sense: Bevan Ellsworth must bear much of the blame for what happened to Guinevere. None of this would have occurred if it hadn't been for all the nasty lies he's been spreading about Guinevere ever since her marriage. That's what made Prinny think her the kind of woman who would welcome his ridiculous advances."

Sebastian knew a quickening of interest. "The Prince Regent made advances on her? When was this?"

"It began at Carlton House sometime last spring. She and Anglessey were attending a state dinner, and the Regent pressed her to allow him to show her his conservatory."

"Where he became overly familiar? Is that what you're saying?"

Varden's lip curled. "He put his hand down the front of her dress."

Sebastian stared off across the rain-drenched churchyard. It wasn't the first time the Regent had done such a thing, Sebastian knew. A spoiled prince, handsome when young and accustomed to a lifetime of flattery and sycophancy, the Regent frequently overestimated his appeal to women.

Yet he'd claimed, when asked, that he'd barely known the young Marchioness.

Sebastian brought his gaze back to the Chevalier's pale, grief-stricken face. "What did she do?"

"She tried to pull away from him. He laughed. Said he enjoyed a spirited woman. So she took more drastic measures."

"Such as?"

"She slapped his fat, self-satisfied face."

"Was he in his cups?"

"No more than usual. You'd think that sort of reaction would have quenched his desires, but it seemed to have the opposite effect. He wouldn't leave her alone. Kept soliciting her hand at balls, arranging to sit next to her at dinners. And then just last week he sent her a trinket. *A small token of his affection,* he called it. From Rundell and Bridge on Ludgate Hill."

They were the Prince's favorite goldsmiths and jewelers, Rundell and Bridge. It was grumbled in some quarters that he spent enough every year on jewelry to feed and clothe the entire British army. He was always buying *trinkets,* as he called them, to shower upon his favorites and lady friends: ivory snuffboxes and jeweled butterflies, amethyst and diamond bracelets . . . and rare, unusual necklaces.

190

Sebastian squinted up at the rain. Silhouetted against the dark gray sky, the leafy branches of the oaks and chestnuts overhead looked black. "What kind of trinket?"

"I didn't see it. She sent it back to him — along with a note stating in no uncertain terms that his advances were unwelcome."

"And Anglessey? Did he know any of this?"

A strange flush darkened the other man's pale, gaunt cheeks. "It's hardly the sort of thing a woman would tell her husband, now, is it?"

"Yet she told you," said Sebastian, and watched the color drain slowly from the Chevalier's face.

Charles, Lord Jarvis, maintained a fervent respect for the institution of the Church of England.

The Church, like the monarchy, was a valuable bastion of defense against the dangerous alliance of atheistical philosophy with political radicalism. The Bible taught the poorer orders that their lowly path had been allotted to them by the hand of God, and the Church was there to make quite certain they understood that. And so Jarvis took pains to be seen at church every week.

That Sunday, his head bowed in due

respect for his Maker, Jarvis attended services at the Chapel Royal in the company of his aged mother, his half-mad wife, Annabelle, and his tiresome daughter, Hero, whom he believed to be in serious need of remembering what the Bible and St. Paul had to say about a number of things, particularly the role of women in society.

During the second reading, when the clergyman loudly proclaimed, "Let your women keep silence in the churches: for it is not permitted unto them to speak; but they are commanded to be under obedience, as also saith the law," Jarvis emphasized the point by quietly elbowing Hero in the side.

Her gaze fixed oh-so-properly on the pulpit, she leaned toward him to whisper maliciously, "Careful, Papa. You're setting a bad example for the ignorant masses."

She was always saying that sort of thing, as if the canker of social discontent spreading across the country were a subject for jest. Yet he knew she took what she referred to as "the dreadful situation of the nation's poor" very seriously indeed. There were times when he almost suspected his daughter of harboring radical principles herself. But it was an idea too disconcerting to be entertained for long, and he quickly dismissed it.

After the service, they walked out of the palace into a gray day still dripping rain. A man stood across the street; a tall young man whose rough greatcoat and round hat did nothing to disguise his aristocratic bearing or the dangerous glitter in his strange yellow eyes.

Jarvis rested one hand on his daughter's arm. "See your mother and grandmother home in the carriage," he said, keeping his voice low.

He expected her to argue with him. She was always arguing with him. Instead, she followed his gaze across the street. For one oddly intense moment, Hero's frank gray eyes met Devlin's feral stare. Then she deliberately turned her back on him to shepherd her mindlessly babbling mother and frowning grandmother toward the carriage.

Stepping wide to avoid the filthy rushing gutter, Jarvis crossed the street to the waiting Viscount.

CHAPTER 24

Devlin leaned against the low iron railing that fronted the street, his hands in his pockets. "You made a mistake. Two, actually."

Jarvis paused a prudent distance before him. "I rarely make mistakes."

The younger man gazed down at the toes of his boots, a strange smile playing about his lips before his head came up again, his eyes narrowing against the rain. "The trinket Prinny sent to the Marchioness of Anglessey. What was it?"

At Jarvis's continuing silence, the Viscount pushed away from the fence to take a significant step forward. "*What was it, damn it?* And don't even think of pretending you don't know what I'm talking about."

"A brooch of rubies," said Jarvis in a calm, unhurried tone, "pierced by a diamond arrow."

The Viscount's reaction was difficult to

decipher, even for a man skilled in reading the thoughts and emotions of others. "An expensive trifle, surely," said the Viscount, "for a woman His Highness claims he barely knew?"

It had begun to rain harder. Jarvis opened his umbrella and held it aloft. "There are times when His Highness has difficulty with the truth. Particularly when the repercussions from the truth might prove . . . unpleasant."

"So what's your excuse?"

Jarvis maintained a studied silence.

"That's why you had the note destroyed, isn't it? Because whoever wrote it referred to her previous rejections of his advances. Suggested in some way that she'd changed her mind."

Again, Jarvis kept his own counsel.

With a violent oath, the Viscount took a hasty step away, only to swing back again. "He was making advances on her. Rude, unwelcome advances. And he wasn't taking no for an answer."

"Are you so certain they were unwelcome?"

Devlin brought up a warning hand to slash the air between them. "Don't. That woman was poisoned, stabbed, and robbed of her life and the life of her unborn child.

Don't you even think of trying to take away her honor with your lies."

"Poisoned? Really? How interesting."

Devlin stared across the street to where the soot-darkened red-brick gatehouse of St. James's Palace thrust up against the cloud-laden skies. And it came to Jarvis, watching him, that for Devlin, this investigation into the circumstances of Guinevere Anglessey's death was more than an intellectual puzzle, more than just an escape from boredom. The Viscount actually *cared* about what had happened to that young woman. It was an unexpected element of emotion that made him both easier to manipulate and yet, at the same time, unpredictable and dangerous.

"Where was Prinny early Wednesday afternoon?" the Viscount asked suddenly.

"In Brighton, of course." Jarvis let out a low, deliberate laugh. "Good God. You surely aren't entertaining the notion that His Highness actually had something to do with this death, are you?"

"It seems less improbable now than it did."

"Why? Because the woman repulsed his advances? Don't be ridiculous. England is full of women panting for the opportunity to copulate with a future king. He need only

196

look at one and smile."

"Yet what would happen, I wonder, should such a vain, sensitive prince encounter a woman with the courage to rebuff his advances?"

"No woman has ever accused His Highness of forcing himself upon her." The words were crisp, carefully enunciated, just bordering on anger. "Ever."

"Perhaps. Yet his father — a model of domestic fidelity if ever there was one — dropped his breeches and attacked his own daughter-in-law just last year."

Jarvis's hand tightened around the handle of his umbrella, although he managed to keep his voice calm, his face serene. "The Prince Regent is not going mad."

Devlin's lean face remained impassive. Unreadable. "Tell me about the dagger. The one you took from Guinevere Anglessey's body."

Jarvis gave the Viscount a warm, reassuring smile. "Now, why would I do that?"

Devlin's smile was just as calculated and decidedly chilling. "I keep asking myself that same question. You might not like it when I come up with the answer."

Sebastian arrived back at his house on Brook Street to discover Sir Henry Lovejoy there before him.

"Sir Henry," said Sebastian, opening the door to the library, where the chief magistrate of Queen Square was reading the *Morning Gazette* in one of the caned chairs beside the front bow window. "I trust you've not been waiting long?"

Lovejoy folded the *Gazette* into a neat rectangle and stood up. "Not long, no." He was a tiny man, barely five feet tall, with a high-pitched voice, thick eyeglasses, and a serious demeanor. He was also, Sebastian knew, passionately devoted to what he did.

Tossing aside his greatcoat, hat, and gloves, Sebastian crossed to the brandy decanter on the table beside the empty hearth. "A glass of wine with me?"

"Thank you, but no." The little magistrate clasped his hands behind his back, cleared his throat, and said, "I heard the strangest story this morning, about some fellow impersonating a Bow Street Officer. A handsome young man with what were described as almost animalistic eyes."

"How odd." His face deliberately bland, Sebastian flicked an imaginary speck of dust from his rough-cut coat. "Is that why you've come? Did you think this fellow might be a relative of mine?"

The faintest hint of a smile lifted the little

magistrate's thin mouth. "No, actually. I've come because we've discovered your Yorkshire jarvey."

CHAPTER 25

"He remembered the fare quite clearly," said Lovejoy. "It's not often a lady takes a hackney to the East End."

Sebastian lowered his glass in surprise. "The East End?"

"That's right. Giltspur Street, in Smithfield."

"Where exactly on Giltspur?"

"The jarvey couldn't say. It seems Lady Anglessey had the fellow let her off at the top of the lane. The last he saw of her, she was walking toward the market." Lovejoy cleared his throat again. "I sent one of the lads over there. Had him ask around. No one remembers having seen her."

That was hardly likely, Sebastian decided, going to pour himself another drink. The sight of a young lady as beautiful as the Marchioness of Anglessey in a walking dress of Pompeian red was not something to be forgotten so quickly. Yet even the most respectable citizens of London were often reluctant to be overly cooperative with the constables. An unassuming man asking more subtle questions might well learn something of interest.

By the time Sebastian paid off his hackney at the bottom of Giltspur Street, the rain had stopped again, although the clouds still hung low and oppressive over the open, death-haunted grounds of Smithfield Market.

It was a meat market now. But once, two hundred years before, in the days of the Tudors, they had burned people here at Smithfield. The Catholics had burned the Protestants to save their souls from the everlasting fires of hell, while the Protestants had burned the Catholics because that's what one did with people whose vision of God didn't exactly match one's own. It'd always struck Sebastian as a strange thing to do in the name of a Christ who'd taught his followers to turn the other cheek and love their neighbors as themselves. But then, Christ's followers had frequently been slack in their application of that part of His teachings, massacring in His name everyone from the olive-skinned inhabitants of Jerusalem to the Irish of Dublin.

Clad in the unfashionably cut greatcoat and serviceable leather breeches of a country gentleman of modest means, Sebastian pushed his way through the throngs of people crowding the streets, many of them drovers in town for Market Monday. They came from as far away as the north of England and Scotland, driving the great herds of cattle and oxen needed to feed the million or so inhabitants of the city. But there were local people here, too, journeymen and apprentices, servants and shopkeepers, for Sunday was the only day most people had off work.

The atmosphere was relaxed, jovial, the street filled with glad voices and laughter, the rich aromas of broiling meat and fermenting ale mingling with the ever-present smells of mud and unwashed bodies and urine. At the first cross street, Sebastian paused, his gaze scanning the signs of the various shops fronting the lane: tanners and chandlers mixed in with coal merchants and distillers, button sellers, and woolen drapers. All were humble establishments, not the kind of businesses typically frequented by a marchioness. What was Guinevere Anglessey doing here?

He walked on, past the shuttered windows of a tea dealer and the haberdasher beyond.

All were closed now for the Sabbath. On Monday, he would send Tom to go into each shop in turn. But something told him Lady Anglessey had not come here in search of tea or buttons.

Halfway up the street he came upon an ancient, half-timbered inn called the Norfolk Arms. Tall and well kept, it had somehow survived the Great Fire of 1666. From the looks of it, it had been here since the days of Edward and Mary Tudor and the martyrs' pyres of Smithfield.

Sebastian started toward the inn. A couple of half-grown boys ran past, careening into him before darting off again with a shouted apology. A one-legged soldier, his face hideously deformed by a saber slash across his cheek, leaned on a rag-wrapped stick and rattled his cup with softly murmured pleadings.

Sebastian dropped a coin into the outstretched receptacle. "Where'd you serve?"

Drawing in a deep breath, the beggar squared his shoulders proudly and said, "Antwerp, sir," in a heavy Scots brogue. Beneath his unkempt beard and matted hair and sallow, scarred skin, he was actually quite young, Sebastian realized, probably no more than five-and-twenty.

"You here every day, are you?"

A grin stretched the Scotsman's scarred cheek and deepened the lines prematurely fanning out from his pain-filled gray eyes. "Aye. This be me spot."

"There was a young woman came past here, last Wednesday afternoon. Dark haired. Pretty. A lady, actually. Wearing a red gown and pelisse. Did you see her?"

The man gave a breathy laugh. "There be nothing wrong with me eyes. Very fetching she was, too, to be sure. She gave me five shillings, she did."

"Did you happen to see where she went?"

The soldier jerked his head toward the ancient inn behind him. "Aye. She went in the Norfolk Arms here."

Sebastian knew a rush of triumph and expectation quickly dampened down. "How long was she in there? Do you know?"

The man thought about it a moment, then shook his head. "Can't rightly say. I don't recollect I saw her come out."

Chapter 26

Sebastian stayed talking to the ex-soldier for some time. He bought some beef roasted on a spit and some ale, and they ate it together and discussed in soldierlike detail the Portuguese campaign and the hardships of the last winter and Colonel Trant's daring exploits in Coimbra. It was another ten minutes or more before Sebastian slowly brought the conversation around, again, to the dark-haired beauty in the red pelisse.

The soldier was convinced the lady had been alone. But he still could not remember seeing her leave; nor could he remember any of the other visitors to the inn that day.

Sebastian slipped another coin in the man's cup and turned toward the inn door. Ducking his head to avoid the low lintel, Sebastian pushed into a common room thick with the smell of ale and warm, closely packed bodies. A roar of boisterous male voices mingled with the clatter of platters and the clink of pewter tankards. Then one man's voice, louder than the others, carried clearly. "If you ask me, they ought to let the poor old King out and lock up his son. That's what they ought to do."

There was a moment's hush, as though everyone in the room had paused at once to draw breath. Then another man, this one from the shadowy recesses of the darkly paneled room, grumbled, "Lock up the lot of them, you mean. They're all as daft as me Granny Grimletts. Every blasted one of them."

A chorus of laughter and *Hear, hear*'s, swelled around the room as Sebastian worked his way toward the bar.

As unassuming as a shy young man just up from the country, he ordered a pint. Then he stood with one elbow resting on the bar, his gaze drifting slowly around the crowded room to the wide upward sweep of carpeted stairs just visible through the open doorway. Guinevere would never have come in here to the common room. But the inn had rooms upstairs and doubtless a private parlor, as well. The place might be far from fashionable, but it was nonetheless respectable, at least from the looks of things.

As for what a lady such as the Marchioness of Anglessey was doing here, in Smithfield, it seemed to Sebastian that the number of possible explanations was rapidly narrowing. There was only one reason he could think of for a lady to avoid the smart, fashionable hotels such as Steven's or Limmer's and seek out an inn so hopelessly outré that there could be no danger of her encountering any of her acquaintances here. But it was a reason Sebastian found himself oddly reluctant to credit.

Still sipping his ale, he shifted his attention to the innkeeper. He was a big man, tall and muscle-bound, with a shiny bald head and the broad nose and full lips of an African. But his skin was the palest café au lait, hinting at a heritage that was at least half-white, if not more.

The man was aware of Sebastian in that way all good innkeepers are aware of a stranger. When Sebastian ordered another pint, the big black man brought it over himself. "New to town, are you?" said the innkeeper, slapping the pint on the ancient, scarred boards between them.

The man's accent was a slow drawl that whispered of magnolias and sun-baked fields and the crack of an overseer's whip. Sebastian took a sip of his ale and gave the man a friendly smile. "I'm secretary to Squire Lawrence, up in Leicestershire. But

207

my father spent some time in Georgia as a young man. Is that where you're from?"

The man's eyes narrowed. "South Carolina."

"You're a long ways from home. Do you miss it?"

The black man peeled back his lips in a hard smile that showed his strong ivory teeth. "What do you think? I was born a slave in the summer of 1775, exactly one year before them Yankees come up with what they call their Declaration of Independence. You ever heard o' it?"

"I don't believe so, no."

"Oh, it's a grand-sounding piece o' writin', no gettin' away from that. All about equality and natural rights and liberty. Only, them fine words, they was only meant for white folks, not for black slaves like me."

Sebastian studied the thickness of the man's strong neck, the way the veins stood out on his forehead. It was a long way for one man to have come, from being a slave on a South Carolina plantation to owning an inn on Giltspur Street in Smithfield. "I understand they're a sanctimonious lot, the Americans."

The black man laughed, a deep rumbling laugh that shook his chest. "Sanctimonious? Yeah, that's a good one. They like to think

208

they're a glorious, godly nation, sure enough, like some shining beacon on a hill that's gonna lead all mankind out o' the darkness o' tyranny and into the light. Only, look at what they done. They done killed all the red men and stole their land, and then they brung us black folks from Africa so's we could do all the hard work and them white folks, they don't need to get their lily-white hands dirty. Uh-uh."

"Squire Lawrence always says the Americans really fought their revolution because the King refused to allow them to disavow their treaties with the red men."

"Your Squire Lawrence sounds like a smart man."

Sebastian leaned forward as if imparting a secret. "To be honest with you, the Squire asked me to come here to London to make a few inquiries for him. A few *discreet* inquiries," Sebastian added with emphasis, clearing his throat and glancing hurriedly around, as if to make certain no one could overhear. "It's his sister, you see. She left the protection of her home last week. We believe some folks from the village gave her a ride to Smithfield, and I'm hoping she might have come here. For a room."

The big man's broad African features

remained impassive. "We don't get a lot of ladies around here. You might try the Stanford, over on Snow Hill."

"I checked there already. The thing is, you see, I've discovered that a lady was seen entering the Norfolk Arms, just last Wednesday. A young lady with dark hair and a red pelisse. Now, as far as I know, Miss Eleanor's pelisse is green, but she certainly has dark hair, and she could always have bought herself a new pelisse, couldn't she?" Sebastian paused, as if reluctant to divulge the truth. "I hesitate to say it, but we fear a man may be involved."

The innkeeper wiped a cloth over the ring-marked surface of the bar. "Last Wednesday, you say?"

"Yes," said Sebastian, all effusive eagerness. "Have you seen her?"

"Nah. I don't know who told you such a daft thing, but we've had no ladies here. Must have been some farmer's wife he seen, up for last week's market."

The innkeeper wandered away while Sebastian went back to sipping his ale and regarding his surroundings. The Norfolk Arms might be in Smithfield, but its clientele was not, for the most part, drawn from the likes of drovers and market people. The two Israelites conversing in low voices over near the window could probably buy and sell the King of England several times over, while at a table near the door, a small huddle of men was sharing a bottle of brandy.

Good French brandy, Sebastian noticed, his eyes narrowing. One of the men bore ink-stained fingers that suggested a clerk, while the rest had the look of barristers and solicitors from the nearby Inns of Court. As Sebastian watched, one older gentleman with a shock of graying hair and a powerfully jutting jaw raised his brandy and proposed a toast. "To the King!"

The words were quietly said, so quietly that someone with hearing less acute than Sebastian's would never have heard them. The others at the table likewise raised their brandy, their voices murmuring, "Hear, hear, to the King," as they deliberately waved their glasses above a nearby water pitcher before taking a sip.

Sebastian paused with his own ale halfway to his lips. *To the King over the water.* It was an old toast, dating back a hundred years or more, a ruse by which men could seemingly drink to the health of the reigning Hanoverian monarch while in reality maintaining their allegiance to that *other* king, the dethroned Stuart King James II

211

and his descendants, condemned forever to live in exile.

Over the water.

CHAPTER 27

Leaving the Norfolk Arms, Sebastian had reason to be grateful for what Kat Boleyn liked to call his cat's eyes. At some point within the last hour, the dark afternoon had slid into night, the heavy clouds left over from the day's rain blocking out whatever moon and stars might have hung overhead. Here were no neat rows of streetlamps, their oil receptacles lit at sunset by a ladder-toting lamplighter and his boy, as in Mayfair. The shops were shuttered and the narrow lane, though still thronged with people, had few lanterns.

But whereas the setting sun reduced the world for most people to a palate of grays only vaguely seen, Sebastian never lost his ability to distinguish colors. He could see almost as well at night as during the day — better, in some instances, for there were times when he could find the light of an extremely bright day almost too painful to

213

be borne.

And so he was aware of the shadow of a girl who slipped from the mouth of an alley he passed to fall into step behind him. "Pssst," she whispered. "Sir. About the lady —"

She took a quick, wary step back when Sebastian swung around. She was an exceptionally tall woman, but young. Studying her face, he suspected she was little more than a child, fifteen at the most, maybe fourteen. She had smooth cheeks and a small nose and strangely pale eyes that gave her an almost unearthly quality.

Sebastian's hand snaked out to close around her upper arm and tighten. "What about her?"

The girl let out a gasp. "Don't hurt me, please." Beneath his grip she felt unexpectedly vulnerable. "I heard you askin' about the lady what come to the inn last week. The lady in the red dress."

He searched her eyes for some sign of deceit, but could find only fear and a habitual wariness. "You saw her? Do you know whom she came to meet?"

Throwing an anxious glance over one shoulder, she sucked in a quick breath that shuddered her thin chest. "I can't talk about it here. They might see me."

Sebastian gave a soft laugh. "That's your trick, is it? You think to lure me to a darkened doorway where your friends can roll me?"

Her eyes went wide. "No!"

Around them, the crowd in the streets was thinning. A musician lilting a familiar tune on a flute strolled by, followed by three laughing drovers reeking of gin, their arms linked about each other's shoulders, their voices warbling the ballad's words. *Oh, Father, oh, Father, go dig me grave, go dig it deep and narrow, for Sweet William, he died for me today, and I'll die for him tomorrow.*

One of the drovers, a big redheaded man with a broken nose, kicked up his heels in an ambitious jig that drew hoots of encouragement from his mates, then catcalls of derision when he stumbled over the edge of the lane's kennel. Breathing out heavy fumes of gin and raw onions, he fell against Sebastian, jostling him just enough to allow the girl to slip from his grasp. She darted back up the alley, bare feet flashing, lank blond hair flying loose about her shoulders.

It was a trap of course. He knew that. And still Sebastian followed her.

He found himself in a crooked passageway of packed earth leaking a line of foul water that ran in a trickle between piles of rubbish and broken hogsheads. The buildings here were of red Tudor brick, old and crumbling, the air dank and heavy with the smell of wet mortar and the pervasive stench of blood from a nearby butcher's shop.

A hundred feet or so down the alley, the girl ducked into a low doorway just as three men rose up from behind a pile of crates and ranged across the narrow space.

They were dressed roughly but not, Sebastian noticed, in rags. "Looks like you made a mistake," said one of the men, taller and better dressed than the others. He had a long, patrician-nosed face that seemed vaguely familiar, although Sebastian couldn't fix a name to it. His starched white cravat was flawlessly tied, the tails of his coat black against the dark red of the brick behind him. "Doesn't it, lad?"

Sebastian swung about. The silhouettes of two more men showed against the dim haze of the smoky torch at the mouth of the alley. He was trapped.

CHAPTER 28

The extent of the preparations for Sebastian's reception surprised him. He'd been expecting one man, perhaps two. His questions in the neighborhood had obviously touched a raw nerve. And it occurred to him, as he lowered himself into a crouch, that there was more involved here then the death of one young woman.

He kept a dagger hidden in his boot, its handle cool and smooth against his palm as he slipped it surreptitiously into his hand. He felt no fear. Fear came when one had time to reflect or was helpless to fight back. What he felt now was a heart-pounding flow of energy, a heightening of all senses and skills.

With a speed and competence honed by six years of operating in the mountains of Portugal and Italy, and in the West Indies, Sebastian summed up the danger he faced. He could stay where he was and let the men close on him, forcing him to fight all five at once. Or he could charge one of the two groups of men and try to escape before they joined forces. With three men ahead and only two blocking his return to the lane, the choice was simple.

For the moment, both groups of adversaries seemed content to hold their distance. "Who sent you here?" asked one of the men near the mouth of the alley, a dark-haired man with the thickening waist and heavy jowls of middle age. He held a cudgel, a stout length of wood he tapped threateningly against the palm of his free hand. His redheaded companion — big and broken-nosed and quite sober — had a knife. In the street, earlier, there had been three of them, Sebastian remembered. Which meant that somewhere, one more drover and perhaps a flute player awaited Sebastian.

Licking his lips in a show of nervousness, Sebastian made his voice go high-pitched and quivery. "Squire Lawrence, up in Leicestershire —"

"Uh-uh," said the man with the cudgel. "Think about this: a man can die quickly or he can die by inches, screaming for mercy and ruing the day he was born. The choice is yours."

Sebastian gave the man a grim smile. *"Oh,*

Father, oh, Father, go dig me grave," he said, and hurled himself forward.

He chose the man on his right, the big redhead with the nimble feet and the knife that could kill quicker than a cudgel. Redhead held his ground, his knife low, waiting to absorb Sebastian's attack. But by switching his dagger to his left hand at the last instant, Sebastian was able to circle his right forearm beneath the big man's lunging blade, knocking the freckled hand holding the knife up and away long enough to drive his own dagger through the waistcoat and shirt of the drover's broad chest, deep into the flesh and sinew beneath.

He was close enough that Sebastian could see the pores in the man's skin, the sheen of nervous sweat on his forehead, smell again the reek of the gin with which he'd doused the coarse wool of his coat. The man let out a whooshing gurgle, blood and spittle spewing from his mouth, his eyes rolling back in his head. Wrenching the blade free, Sebastian swung quickly to face the man with the cudgel.

Not quick enough. A blow meant to dash in the back of Sebastian's head fell on his shoulder, bruising hard. Pain exploded across his collarbone, reverberated to his left arm. He went down on one knee, a grunt escaping his clenched teeth. A shadow loomed over him. Twisting, Sebastian had a vision of heavy jowls dark with anger, lips peeling back from yellow crooked teeth gritted in determination as the man raised the cudgel to strike again.

Sebastian drove his dagger up, deep into the man's stomach.

The man screamed, then screamed again when Sebastian tried to jerk the blade free, only to have it catch on the stout cloth of the man's waistcoat. Someone shouted. He heard the pant of breath, the pounding of feet as the men from the other end of the alley drew near.

Abandoning the dagger, Sebastian pushed up. He could see the mouth of the alley, an eddy of movement and shadow framed by the darker shadows of looming brick walls. He took one running step, two, just as the explosive percussion of a pistol reverberated up the narrow passage. He saw the yellow-white flash of the burning powder, smelled the pungent odor of sulfur.

And felt a stinging line of fire plow across the side of his head.

CHAPTER 29

Sebastian's step faltered, but he kept running.

He burst from the mouth of the alley into Giltspur Street. His hat was gone. He could feel a sheet of blood running down the side of his face, its coppery tang heavy in the moist night air. More blood darkened the front of his coat and waistcoat, only that wasn't his blood.

Heads turned toward him. Women in shawls drew back, faces pale, eyes wide with fear. He knew they must have heard the pistol shot, but no one stepped forward to help him. He was a stranger here. The men behind him were not.

A trickle of warm blood ran into his eyes. He stumbled off the narrow footpath. Horses' heads loomed from out of the darkness, their nostrils flaring. He heard the crack of a whip and a shout, and the jingle of harness. He jumped back barely in time to avoid the flashing hooves and rumbling iron-rimmed wheels of a big green-and-red brewer's wagon driven fast up the road.

The wagon was tall, the top edges of its high wooden sides some three feet or more over Sebastian's head. He heard running steps slap the paving stones behind him. Without looking back, Sebastian leapt at the wagon's high back, trying to catch the top of the tailgate with both hands. But the blow to his shoulder had incapacitated his arm more than he'd realized. His left hand slipped off the rough wood, useless. Only his right hand found its purchase and held, jerking his arm in its socket as it took all his weight.

From somewhere behind him came a shout, followed by a hoarse "There he is! Stop him."

Gritting his teeth, his feet kicking in air, Sebastian fought to pull himself up one-handed onto the tailgate. He'd just managed to hike his elbow over the side when one of the men threw himself forward, his arms wrapping around Sebastian's legs.

The jolting weight of the man's body swung Sebastian around, dragged him back down toward the rushing road. Sebastian had a pain-filled vision of a craggy-faced man with thick, straight brows and a thin nose, his lips twisting into a snarl as he said, "I've got you, you son of a bitch."

Freeing one leg, Sebastian drew up his knee and kicked out hard. His foot landed square in the man's face. He heard the crunch of cartilage and bone, saw the spurt of blood as the force of the blow sent the man reeling back.

For one moment, he clutched wildly at Sebastian's booted foot. Then the boot slipped off with a sucking *plop* and the man fell back to land with a breath-robbing thump in the gutter, the rough country boot of Squire Lawrence's secretary still clasped like a trophy in his hands.

"One of these days," said Kat Boleyn, dabbing a cloth dipped in witch hazel against the side of his head, "someone's going to shoot at you and they're not going to miss."

Sebastian drew in his breath in a pained hiss. "They didn't exactly miss this time."

He was sitting on a low stool beside the kitchen table in Kat's house in Harwich Street. Elspeth and the rest of Kat's small staff had withdrawn to spend their evening off in their rooms in the attics high above, leaving the house dark and quiet. In the distance, he could hear the faint, mournful tolling of a death knell.

223

Bringing up one hand, he explored the open gash that parted the hair just above his ear. She batted his hand away. "Don't touch." She was busy for a moment mixing crushed herbs from the apothecary into a salve. Then she said, "You knew it was a trap. Why walk into it?"

"I thought I might learn something. I wasn't expecting five men. Or a pistol."

"So what did you learn? That your questions are making someone uncomfortable? You knew that. Someone's been following you for days."

"I don't think my shadow was amongst the men who attacked me."

"Would you recognize him if you saw him?"

"No. But the men today didn't know who I was. If they had, my friend with the cudgel wouldn't have been so anxious to find out who sent me."

She finished smearing the open wound with the salve and went to pack a clean cloth with a mixture of grated raw potatoes and cold milk. "Are you going to tell Sir Henry about this?"

Sebastian looked up from peeling his shirt off over his head. "Lovejoy? What the devil could he do?"

She came to slap the cold compress on

his bruised shoulder. "He could send some-one to investigate the Norfolk Arms."

"That's just what I need," he said, reaching up to hold the compress in place. "Some thickheaded constable tromping about the place, asking blunt questions and putting up everyone's back. It's the best way I can think of to make sure we never learn anything."

Her gaze met his, her beautiful blue eyes wide and troubled. "You can't go there again yourself."

He touched her face, his fingertips skimming gently across her cheek. "Careful, Miss Boleyn. You're in danger of betraying an almost wifely concern for my health."

He expected her to make some quick rejoinder and then flit away. Instead, she leaned against him, her arms coming around his neck to hold him close. "If these people are involved in a conspiracy against the Regent and they think you're on to them, they won't hesitate to kill you. You know that."

He pressed his face against the softness of her breasts. "We know the men at one table in the common room of the Norfolk Arms have a romantic attachment to a dead exiled king. That doesn't make the entire district guilty of plotting to overthrow the Hanoverian dynasty."

She pushed away from him and went to assemble the various salves and potions she'd been using. The uncharacteristic moment of vulnerability was gone. She was once more in control, her voice teasing as she said, "I thought you didn't believe in coincidences."

Stretching to his feet, he swung his arm in slow circles, working out the stiffness in the muscle. "I don't. But I can't see how it fits with what I know of Guinevere Anglessey's life. Now, if I could find some way to tie my friends from Giltspur Street to Bevan Ellsworth, it might begin to make sense. According to Guinevere's abigail, he came storming into his uncle's town house last Monday and essentially threatened to kill her. He also has one hell of a motive — the birth of Guinevere's son would have disinherited him. With his creditors already pressing him for repayment, Ellsworth could easily have decided he couldn't take a chance on the child being born a girl."

"And you never liked him anyway."

Sebastian looked over at her and smiled. "And I never liked him anyway." Stripping off his bloodied breeches, he went to tip another kettle of hot water into the hip bath they'd drawn beside the kitchen hearth.

"What do you know of Fabian Fitzfrederick?"

"He and Ellsworth are of much the same set, although Fitzfrederick also runs with the Dandies." She frowned. "Why? You think Fitzfrederick might be involved?"

"Hell. I don't know. He does provide a link between Ellsworth and the royal family."

"A tenuous one."

"A tenuous one." Sebastian stepped over the high enameled sides and settled himself in the tub, his knees drawn up close to his chest. "The problem is, while the Inns of Court are suspiciously close to Giltspur Street, Ellsworth himself simply wouldn't have had time to drag Guinevere's body down to Brighton and still make it back to his faro game in Pickering Place by ten o'clock. Apart from which, the man's interests begin and end with the turf and gaming table — and the set of his coat, of course. Why would he go through all the risks involved in attempting to implicate the Regent?"

"To deflect suspicion from himself?" Kat suggested.

"Surely there are easier ways to have done so?"

She was silent in that way she had, carefully thinking things through. "The only one I can see who might have a reason to implicate the Regent is Anglessey himself. If he found out the Prince was pursuing her when she hadn't told him, he might have believed the advances were welcome."

Sebastian leaned his head against the back of the tub and let the moist heat of the water soothe his sore muscles and aching shoulder. After a few moments, he said, "If Anglessey were to implicate anyone in his wife's murder, I think it would be his nephew, not the Regent. Besides, Anglessey's a sick old man. He's simply too frail to have managed the thing. Apart from which, he was in Brighton, remember?"

She came to kneel on the stone flagging beside him, a bar of soap in one hand. "He could have hired someone."

"Hell, they all could have hired someone."

"Sit forward." Kat worked the soap across his shoulders and down his back. "What about Varden? They could have had a lovers' quarrel. A quarrel that turned violent."

"We don't know that they were lovers."

"They were lovers," said Kat.

Sebastian smiled as she rubbed the soap around his side and over his chest. He himself wasn't so sure. "According to his mother, Varden was at home until that evening," he reminded her.

"Well, she would say that, wouldn't she?" Kat pushed to her feet and took a step back as he stood up, water streaming down his torso.

He stepped from the bath, one hand reaching for the thick cotton towel Kat had set on a nearby chair. "I'm obviously missing something. Something I should be seeing."

She came to help him shrug into the silk dressing gown she kept for him. "If it's there, you'll see it," she said simply.

He turned toward her. In the soft light of the kitchen fire, she looked so peaceful, so sure of his abilities, that for a moment, he felt humbled. He reached to comb the loose tangle of her heavy dark hair away from her face. "Sometimes I find myself wondering, what's the point? Even if I do find who killed her — and why — it won't change anything. She'll still be dead."

"I think she would want to know that the man who killed her and her child didn't get away with it."

"Is that what this is all about? Revenge?"

She pressed her cheek against his chest, her arms warm around his waist. "No. I don't think it's simply a matter of avenging her death. It's also about protecting the memory of who she was by not letting people distort the truth to protect themselves. And about making sure that whoever did this won't have a chance to do it again."

He took her face between his hands, felt the pulse in her neck beat against his palm. She seemed so fragile beneath his touch, so vulnerable that for a moment his heart caught with fear and he knew the urge to sweep her into his arms and hold her close — hold her *safe*, forever.

"Marry me, Kat," he said suddenly. "There isn't a reason you can come up with for refusing me that doesn't sound weak and absurd when you think about how quickly death could take either of us."

Her lips parted, her intense blue eyes widening with pain as she looked into his face and shook her head. "We can't live our lives as if we were to die tomorrow."

"Perhaps we should."

"And spend a lifetime in regret?"

"I wouldn't regret it."

A smile touched her lips, then quickly faded. "You think that now."

He touched his forehead to hers and said again, "I wouldn't regret it."

CHAPTER 30

Waking early the next morning, Kat lay for a moment with her eyes closed and listened to the gentle rhythm of Devlin's breathing beside her. A smile touched her lips. He had stayed the night.

Pushing herself up on her elbow, she let her gaze drift over him. She knew every line and sinew of his body, the rare brilliance of his mind and the even rarer nobility of his soul. And she knew, too, what it would eventually do to him if she followed the aching longings of her heart and married him.

The smile faded. She had loved him since she was sixteen, when she was an unknown chorus girl and he a wild young buck not long down from Oxford. He'd asked her to marry him then, too. And because she'd been young and so desperately hungry to keep him in her life forever, she'd said yes. It was only later — after his father and her own conscience had made her realize what such a marriage would mean for him — that she'd sent Devlin away. What she'd seen in his eyes that night — the agonized disbelief of betrayal — had cut her heart in two and ripped out her soul.

She could remember wandering the fog-shrouded streets of the City, tears hot on her cheeks, heartsick with all the grief of youth and looking for death. But death hadn't come, and those who'd told her that time lessens pain had in part been right. Because in time she'd found a reason to live and a cause to fight for. That was part of the problem now. But only part.

She told herself that the choices she'd made these last few years didn't make any difference, that she would still have the strength to resist the treacherous weakness of her heart. It was a wonder to her that despite all Devlin had seen and done in the last seven years, in this way, at least, he hadn't changed. He still believed he could count the world well lost for love. She knew better.

She knew what it would do to him, to find himself cut off from those of his own class, an object of contempt and scorn, pity and ridicule. Marriage to her would be a social solecism for which neither his father nor his sister, Amanda, would ever forgive him. She didn't suppose Devlin would suffer overly much from an estrangement from his only surviving sibling. But the ties binding the Earl and his heir ran strong and deep.

She knew that. And still she was tempted.

That's when she reminded herself that you can't build a marriage on lies, and that while Devlin might know the sordid truth of her childhood years on the streets, he didn't know about the other years, the years after she'd sent him away from her. The years she'd spent seducing important men and passing the secrets they spilled to the French.

In her weaker moments, a treacherous voice whispered that he need never know about those years. She'd had no dealings with the French since Pierrepont's disappearance from London four months ago. And while she'd been told a new spymaster would contact her, the message she'd been dreading — a two-toned bouquet of flowers accompanied only by a biblical quotation — had never come. Besides, her allegiance had never been to France but to Ireland, to the tragic land of her youth and the scene of her mother's death.

Yet in her heart of hearts, she knew that was mere quibbling. If Devlin knew the truth, if he knew she had aided the enemy he spent six long years fighting, he would turn away from her in disgust . . . or condemn her to the ignoble death of a spy.

She realized his eyes were open, watching her. He had the most extraordinary eyes, the color of amber, with an almost inhuman ability to see not only great distances, but also in the dark. His hearing was abnormally acute, as well. She liked to tease him, to tell him he was part wolf. Yet she knew that his preternatural abilities unsettled him, for there was no history of such gifts in either his mother's family or his father's.

"Darling," he said softly, reaching for her. She went into his arms, a smile on her lips when she bent her head to taste his kiss. She loved it when he called her darling.

He tightened his arms around her, rubbed his cheek against her hair. And she pushed aside all her doubts and fears and impossible dreams, and gave herself wholly to the man and the moment.

For as long as Sebastian could remember, the Earl of Hendon had begun each day he was in London with an early-morning ride in Hyde Park.

That Monday morning dawned cool and damp, with a heavy mist that drifted through the trees and showed no sign of lifting. But

Sebastian knew his father: by seven o'clock the Earl would be in the park, trotting his big gray gelding up and down the Row. And so that morning Sebastian mounted the dainty black Arabian mare he kept in London and turned her head toward the park.

"Don't usually see you abroad until mid-afternoon," groused Hendon when Sebastian brought his mare, Leila, into line beside the Earl's big gray. "Or haven't you made it to your bed yet?"

Sebastian smiled softly to himself, because the truth was that as much as Hendon grumbled, he was actually secretly proud of what he called his son's wildness, just as he was proud of Sebastian's skill with sword and pistol, and as a horseman. Drinking, womanizing, and even gambling were just the sort of manly activities a gentleman expected of his son, excesses of youth to be indulged — as long as they weren't carried to an extreme. It was Sebastian's love of books and music, his interest in the radical philosophies of the French and Germans, that Hendon had never been able to abide or understand.

"I wanted to hear your opinion on something," said Sebastian. He trotted beside his father in silence a moment, then asked bluntly, "How much sympathy do you think there would be in this country for a restoration of the Stuarts?"

Hendon's answer was so long in coming that Sebastian began to wonder if his father had even heard the question. But Hendon, like Kat, was given to thoughtful silences before he spoke.

"A year ago I'd have said none whatsoever." He squinted off across the Park to where a flock of ducks could be seen rising up, dark wings outstretched as they took flight into the mist and filled the morning with their plaintive calls. "The Stuarts have always had a certain nostalgic appeal to the likes of Walter Scott and the Highland Tories. But that's the stuff of romance. Beyond the romance lies the reality of a very foolish king who lost his throne because he insisted on trying to thwart the will of a nation."

"And now?"

He threw Sebastian a quick sideways glance. "Now we have a mad king, a licentious, debt-ridden regent who spends more time with his tailors than with his ministers, and a hey-go-mad, fifteen-year-old princess whose own father calls her mother a whore. The other day, I heard someone — I think it was Brougham himself — say that what went on under the Stuarts was nothing compared to what is happening today."

"But there is no Stuart heir. James the Second had two grandsons, Bonnie Prince Charlie and his brother, Henry. Prince Charlie left no legitimate children, while Henry became a Catholic priest who died — when? Four years ago?"

Hendon nodded. "Henry the Ninth, he called himself. The Stuart claim has now passed to the descendants of Charles the First's daughter, Henrietta. Strictly speaking, the throne should have gone to them after the death of James the Second's daughter, Ann, in 1714, rather than to the Hanoverian George the First. But they were Catholics."

"So who is the current pretender?"

"Victor Emmanuel of Savoy."

"A king without a kingdom," said Sebastian thoughtfully. Once the Kings of Sardinia and Piedmont, the men of the House of Savoy had been forced by the armies of the French Revolution to abdicate all their territories on the Italian mainland.

Hendon pressed his lips into a thin smile. "Exactly."

"But Savoy is a Catholic — which is what got James the Second into trouble over a hundred years ago. England won't even allow a Catholic to sit in Parliament. They're hardly likely to accept one on the throne."

"True. But Savoy wouldn't be the first man willing to change his religion for the sake of a throne, now, would he?"

"Is he willing?"

"I don't know. I've been hearing things lately that disturb me. All this talk about a curse, for instance — people saying the House of Hanover is cursed, and that England will be cursed, too, as long as a usurper sits upon her throne. Where do you suppose that came from?"

"You think the Jacobites started it?"

"Who knows how these things start? But it seems to have fallen on very receptive ground. If there is still an organized conspiracy to replace the Hanovers, now would be the time for them to make a move."

Hendon rode in silence for a moment, his gaze fixed on some point beyond his horses' ears. The silence filled with the creak of saddle leather and the rhythmic pattern of their horses' hooves on the soft earth. "I was born the year after the 'Forty-five," he said in a tight voice. "I grew up with the tales of what those times were like. I wouldn't want to see some fool visit such horrors upon us again."

Sebastian studied his father's closed face. It was the stuff of legends, the Highland

Rising of 1745 in support of Bonnie Prince Charlie. Sebastian had heard the stories, too, from his grandmother, Hendon's mother, who had been a Grant from Glenmoriston. Stories of unarmed clansmen dragged out of crofts and slaughtered before their screaming children. Of women and children burned alive, or turned out of their villages to die in the snow. What was done to the Highlanders after Culloden would forever be a dark stain on the English soul. Everything from the pipes to the plaids to the Gaelic language itself had been forbidden, obliterating an entire culture.

"Who would support a restoration now?" Sebastian asked. "The Scots?"

Hendon shook his head. "The chiefs who supported the Stuarts were all killed or exiled years ago, while their clansmen lie in forgotten graves — or were transported to America. Besides, the Risings were always more about Scotland than about the Stuarts. What interest have the Scots in some Italian princeling whose great-great-grandmother happens to have been the daughter of Charles the First, rather than of James the First?"

Hendon was right: apart from the romantic appeal of a lost cause, the Stuart claimant to the throne would no longer inspire enthusiasm in Scotland. Nor would Jacobit-ism have much appeal to the Tories of today. The Hanoverian succession had been a disaster for the old Tories. There was little resemblance between the Tories of the early eighteenth century and the new Toryism that had emerged from the fears inspired by the French Revolution. Far from sympathiz-ing with the Catholics, the Tories had become fierce defenders of the Church of England, opposing religious toleration of both Catholics and nonconforming dissent-ers alike. It was now, ironically, the Whigs who championed the cause of tolerance.

But it would be hard to imagine the Whigs advocating a restoration of the Stuarts. For in this, the Whigs had not changed. While the Tories had turned their backs on reform and embraced the sanctity of property over the defense of individual liberty, the Whigs remained dedicated to limiting the power of the crown and had claimed the objectives and achievements of the Glorious Revolu-tion as their own.

As they rode, the morning mist began to lift, blown away by a cold wind that kept the park deserted except for one or two solitary riders. Hendon posted along in silence for a few moments, his thoughts to himself. Then he said, "It's the necklace, isn't it? That's what's sent you off on this."

Sebastian studied his father's closed, hard profile. They had never been close, even in the golden years of Sebastian's early childhood, when all the people he'd loved — his mother, his brothers, Richard and Cecil — had all lived. Then had come the black summer of Cecil and Sophie's deaths, and at one point it had seemed to Sebastian that the Earl came very close to actually hating him — hating him for living, when all the others had died. With time, Sebastian had seen a reemergence of some signs of Hendon's gruff affection. But things had never been the same, and now it was as if a wall of silence and mistrust had reared up between them anew. Sebastian had no idea how to surmount it.

"Partially," he said simply.

Sebastian had never asked the Marquis of Anglessey how his wife came to be wearing the ancient talisman once given by a Welsh witch to her Stuart lover. It hadn't seemed fitting somehow, when Sebastian's main interest in the necklace had been personal. But he was beginning to realize the triskelion might have played a more important part in Guinevere's death than he'd first realized.

CHAPTER 31

"I'm dying, Egypt, dying. One word, sweet queen: Of Caesar seek your honor, with your safety." Marc Antony looked at his Cleopatra expectantly.

Kat, her theatrical costume covered with a pinafore to protect it during rehearsal, stared off across the darkened pit to where a gentleman stood in the shadows, his hat pulled low on his brow.

The pit was empty in the afternoon light, the theater silent except for a distant hammering and the swish of the cleaning lady's broom sweeping up the orange peels that littered the floor from last night's performance. The gentleman should not be here.

"Of Caesar seek your honor, with your safety," repeated Marc Antony, his voice sharp with exasperation. "Would someone please wake up the sweet Queen of Egypt?"

Kat jerked and swung back to face her Marc Antony. "They do not go together," she said, then mouthed, *Sorry.*

After that, she was careful not to miss any more cues. But she remained aware of the gentleman in the shadows.

She thought she recognized him. He was the Duc de Royan, one of the noblemen who had come to London in the train of the dethroned Louis XVIII, or the Comte de Lille, as he called himself. Royan professed to be a fierce opponent of Napoléon's regime. But then, Leon Pierrepont had also claimed to be an enemy of Napoléon, all the while serving as the French spymaster in London.

"Come, thou mortal wretch," said Kat, applying a papier-mâché asp to her breast. "With thy sharp teeth this knot intrinsicate of life at once untie. . . ." When she turned around, the Duc de Royan was gone.

As soon as rehearsal ended, she hurried down the corridor to her dressing room. Heart beating uncomfortably fast, she thrust open the door. A bouquet stood upon her dressing table, a lavish confection of white lilies and pink roses in a cloud of baby's breath. A two-toned bouquet.

Kat snatched up the note she found balanced amidst the stems and tore open the seal. "His Highness the Comte de Lille presents his compliments and begs you to accept these paltry blossoms as a token of his admiration."

No biblical quotation. No secret message. No appointment for a rendevous with danger.

Kat leaned her forehead against the wall, drew in a shaky breath, and let it out in a soft laugh of relief.

Sebastian spent the next several hours asking some discreet questions about Bevan Ellsworth's boon companion, Fabian Fitzfrederick, illegitimate son to Prince Frederick, the Duke of York. But Fitzfrederick's movements on that fatal Wednesday proved to be as innocuous as Bevan's. After a day spent at Tattersall's, Fitzfrederick had whiled away the evening at the same Pickering Place gaming hell frequented by his friend Ellsworth.

Thoughtful, Sebastian sent Tom off to canvass the shops of Giltspur Street in Smithfield, then turned his own steps toward the Marquis of Anglessey's Mount Street town house.

He found the Marquis in the tile-floored conservatory built onto the back of the house. Pausing beneath a gently drooping tree fern, Sebastian looked at Guinevere's husband and saw an old man, his once-sturdy frame now gaunt, his gray head bowed as he tended a yellow blooming jasmine. Then the Marquis looked up and the impression of age and infirmity was dispelled by the power of the intelligence and sheer force of personality shining in his eyes.

"I was wondering if you would come today," said the Marquis, jerking off his gardening gloves and laying them aside.

Sebastian glanced around the humid room, crowded with ferns and orchids and tender, leafy tropicals. The warm air smelled of moist earth and green growing things and the sweet perfume of the cape gardenia blooming over by the door. He had something of a reputation as a connoisseur of exotic plants, the Marquis. They said that when he was young, he'd sailed on a naval expedition to the South Pacific, collecting botanic specimens.

"Paul Gibson tells me he gave you the results of your wife's autopsy," said Sebastian.

Anglessey nodded. "He thinks Guin was poisoned." He brought one hand to his face and rubbed his closed eyes with a spread thumb and forefinger. "The dagger would have been a far kinder death. Quick. Relatively painless. But cyanide? God help me, how she must have suffered. She'd have had time to know she was dying. I can't imagine what her last thoughts must have been." His hand fell to his side, his eyes open wide and hurting. "Who did this? Who could have done such a thing to her?"

Sebastian held the old man's tortured gaze. "Bevan Ellsworth claims the child Lady Anglessey carried was not yours."

The words were blunt and brutal, but necessary. The Marquis's head snapped back, his jaw going slack with shock and anger. He tried to take a quick step forward, only to stumble over an uneven tile so that he had to fling out one hand and catch the edge of a nearby iron table for balance. "You dare? You dare say such a thing to me? I've called men out for less."

Sebastian kept his own voice calm. "He's not the only one saying it. The assumption on the streets is that she was the Regent's mistress."

The Marquis's face had gone white, his thin chest jerking so hard with each breath that for a moment Sebastian was afraid he might have pushed too far. "It's not true."

Sebastian met the old man's furious gaze and held it. "Then help me. I can't find out what really happened to your wife if I don't know the truth."

Anglessey swung away. He suddenly seemed older, shrunken. Picking up a long-spouted watering can, he went to fill it at the pump. Then he simply stood there, his head bowed.

When he finally spoke, his voice sounded tired. Resigned. "It's no easy thing, facing the final years of your life with the knowledge that everything you've dedicated yourself to preserving will be destroyed after your death by another man's dissipation."

Sebastian was silent, waiting. After a moment, Anglessey took a deep breath and continued. "Guinevere and I both went into marriage with our eyes wide open. She knew I wanted a young wife to give me an heir, and I knew that her heart already belonged to another."

"She told you that?"

"Yes. She thought I deserved to know. I respected her for it. It was my hope that we would at least become friends. And in that, I think we succeeded."

Friends. A lukewarm enough ambition for husband and wife. Yet it was a status achieved by very few married couples of their society.

"My second wife, Charlotte, was never well," said Anglessey, tightening his grip on the watering can. "For the last fifteen years of her life, I essentially lived the life of a monk. Other men in my position would have taken a mistress, but I never did. Perhaps that was a mistake."

It was a common maxim that a man lost his ability to bed a woman when he quit bedding women. An old maxim that probably had a fair amount of truth in it, Sebastian decided.

Anglessey went to tip a careful stream of water along the roots of a line of ferns. "I was never able to consummate my marriage with Guinevere." A faint line of color touched his sharp, high cheekbones and stayed there. "She tried. We both tried very hard. She knew how much it meant to me to have a son. But it eventually became obvious that it wasn't going to happen."

He hesitated, then pushed on. "Two years ago, I suggested she take a lover, someone who could father the heir I couldn't." He swung his head to look back at Sebastian. "You think it a vile thing, for a man to push his wife into infidelity, to seek to disinherit his own nephew by putting another man's bastard in his place?"

"I know Bevan Ellsworth," said Sebastian simply.

"Ah." Anglessey moved on to a shelf of orchids. "It's the only time I can remember

Guinevere ever being truly angry with me. It was too much to ask of her — too much for any man to ask of his wife. She made me feel as if I'd asked her to prostitute herself, which I suppose in a way is precisely what I had done.

"But then, last winter . . ." His voice trailed away as he gazed out over the lush groupings of exotic ferns and jasmines, gardenias and tender China roses. He tried again. "Last winter, she came to me. She said . . ."

"She said she would do it?" Sebastian prompted when it became obvious the old man could not go on.

"Yes." It was little more than a whisper.

Sebastian stood in the center of the conservatory, breathed in the hot, fetid air. From the far corner came the sound of a fountain bubbling into a small pond with flickering goldfish. Beside it, a caged canary filled the morning with a song that should have been cheerful, but instead sounded mournful, despairing.

"The name of her lover. What was it?"

Anglessey emptied his watering can, then simply stood there, staring down at the moist, dark earth before him. "I thought it better never to ask. I didn't want to know."

"Could it have been the man she was in

love with before you married?"

He was silent for a moment. It was obvious the possibility had occurred to him. "Perhaps. But I honestly don't know."

By last winter, Sebastian thought, the Chevalier would have completed his studies at Oxford. Had the two former lovers met again in London and decided to begin a physical relationship? A relationship to which her husband had already consented?

"Do you know where they used to meet?" Sebastian asked.

"No. Of course not." Anglessey paused. "You think this man — the one Guinevere took as her lover — is the one who killed her?"

"It's possible. Can you think of any other reason your wife would go to Giltspur Street in Smithfield?"

"Smithfield? Good heavens, no. Why?"

Sebastian held the old man's gaze. "She took a hackney there the afternoon she was killed."

There was no sign of dissembling, no indication that Anglessey had known of his wife's visit to Smithfield but had hoped to keep it concealed. Sebastian tried another tack. "Did your wife have much interest in the affairs of government?"

"Guin?" A faint smile touched the old

man's lips. "Hardly. Guin was passionate about many things, but government wasn't one of them. As far as she was concerned, one crowned puppet is pretty much the same as the next. It's the sycophants and thieves with which they surround themselves that you need to watch out for." His smile deepened as he studied Sebastian's face. "Does that surprise you?"

Sebastian shook his head, although if truth were told, he was surprised — not so much by the sentiment itself as by who had aired it. It was hardly a typical opinion for a woman who was the gently bred, privileged daughter of an earl and wife to a marquis. More unexpected still was the realization that the Marquis himself found his wife's opinion amusing, even endearing. Such an expression of heresy would have thrown Hendon into an apoplectic fit.

"What about your nephew, Bevan Ellsworth? What are his politics?"

"I would be seriously surprised if Bevan has ever given a thought to politics in his life. His mind is occupied with far weightier matters, the chief amongst them being women and wagers and the set of his coat. Why?"

Sebastian walked over to where the Marquis stood, the watering can hanging empty at his side. "What can you tell me about this necklace?"

Anglessey's gaze dropped from Sebastian's face to the silver-and-bluestone pendant he now held in his hand. "Nothing," said Anglessey, his age-spotted brow wrinkling as if the sudden change of topic confused him. "Why? Where did it come from?"

"Your wife was wearing it when she died. Do you know where she got it?"

Confusion had given way to mild puzzlement and a blank stare of ignorance that was utterly convincing. "No. I've no notion. I've never seen it before in my life."

Sebastian walked the streets of London, from Oxford to Edgeware Road and beyond, to where the neat town houses and paved streets gave way to massive construction sites and, beyond that, the green fields and market gardens of Paddington.

As incredible as it seemed, he'd found no one who'd known Guinevere Anglessey who would admit to ever having seen the triskelion. Not only that, but according to her abigail, Tess Bishop, the gown chosen by the Marchioness on the afternoon of her death had sported a neckline that would have made the wearing of the ancient piece impossible. Obviously, like the satin gown,

252

the necklace had been clasped around Guinevere's neck after her death. But why? And by whom?

Although Sebastian doubted it, he supposed it possible that Charles, Lord Jarvis, had dangled the necklace before Sebastian simply to entice him into the investigation. Yet even if that were so, it still begged the question: how had a necklace that should have been at the bottom of the English Channel suddenly reappeared?

The explanation suggested by Hendon, that the necklace had been sold by some peasant who'd found the Countess's body washed up on a distant beach, remained plausible. But Sebastian could not avoid confronting the more likely explanation, that Sophie Hendon had not died in that long-ago boating accident, but had simply sailed away, leaving a husband, a married daughter, and an eleven-year-old son to mourn her.

Sebastian stared off across a mist-filled meadow to the line of elms that could be seen edging a stream in the distance. Even as a child, he had nourished few illusions about his parents' marriage. It was the way of their world, husbands busy with Parliament and their clubs while their wives were left to amuse themselves with other things.

In Sebastian's memories, Sophie Hendon was a golden presence, her touch soft and loving, her gay laughter still echoing to him down through the years. Yet his school days had been punctuated with fisticuffs, fought to defend his mother's honor. For in a society where infidelity was commonplace, the Countess of Hendon had been known to be particularly promiscuous.

A crow rose from a nearby field, its voice raucous, its wings dark against the cloudy sky. Sebastian paused, then turned his steps toward the New Road. He had never thought of his mother as unhappy, yet he realized now, looking back, that it might well have been unhappiness that drove her restlessness, that brought that brittle edge to her smile. Had she been unhappy enough to simply sail away and leave them all? To leave him?

He remembered the aching loss of that summer. He hadn't believed it when they'd told him of the tragic end to the Countess's pleasure outing. He thought about the endless hot hours he'd spent on the cliffs overlooking the sea. Day after day he had stood there, his eyes dry and hurting as he determinedly scanned the sun-sparkled horizon for sails that would never come. He thought about the possibility that it had all

been a lie, and he knew a surge of bitter
rage and a deep, abiding hurt.

CHAPTER 32

Of the four children born to the Earl of Hendon and his Countess, Sophia, only two still lived: Hendon's youngest and only surviving son and heir, Sebastian, and the couple's eldest child and only daughter, Amanda.

By the time Sebastian was born, Amanda had already been in her twelfth year. In the memories of his childhood she was a distant, sullen presence, disapproving and vaguely hostile. She had grown into a tall, haughty woman, fiercely proud of her noble lineage and forever embittered by the harsh realities of an ancient tradition that handed everything — titles, estates, wealth — to her youngest, most despised brother.

At the age of eighteen, she had married Martin, Lord Wilcox, a man of staid respectability from a suitably ancient and wealthy family. She was now a widow, left financially comfortable by the terms of her marriage settlement as well as being in full control of her children's fortunes. But the circumstances of her husband's death that previous February were cloudy, and served only to deepen the animosity between brother and sister.

He found her that afternoon walking the boxwood-trimmed paths of the iron-railed square before her house. She still wore the heavy black trappings of deep mourning, a state of forced idleness and isolation he knew she must find trying, although she would never show it. She turned at his approach. In her early forties now, Amanda had inherited their mother's fairness and slim, elegant carriage and combined it with Hendon's more blunt, heavy facial features. At the sight of Sebastian, her blue St. Cyr eyes narrowed.

"Well. Dear brother. To what do I owe this unexpected . . ." She paused just long enough to make the word a lie. "Pleasure?"

Sebastian smiled. "Dear Amanda. Walk with me a ways, won't you?"

She hesitated, then inclined her head. "Very well. What is it?"

They turned their steps together toward the statue that stood at the center of the square. "I wanted to ask you a question. Is it possible, do you think, that Mother didn't die in a boating accident that summer? That the accident was simply a hoax, a ruse?"

Amanda continued to walk in silence for so long that he didn't think she planned to answer him. At last, she said, "What makes you ask?"

He studied her taut, controlled profile. "I have my reasons. As I recall, no wreckage was ever found. Is that true?"

An unexpected smile touched her lips. "What are you suggesting? That Hendon had her done away with, then staged the accident to cover up the dirty deed?"

"No. I'm suggesting Sophie Hendon was fiercely unhappy in her marriage, and that staging her own death was one of the few ways open to her in our society to escape it."

Amanda swung to face him. "You mean, you think she ran away."

He searched his sister's face for some betraying flicker of emotion, but found none. "Could she have done it?"

"Why are you asking me? I wasn't even in Brighton that summer, remember? I was already married, with young children of my own."

"You're her daughter."

She glanced up at the lichen-covered statue of an ancient Tudor king beside them.

258

"Have you discussed this with Hendon?"

"Yes. He may not know the truth himself."

"Not all truths are ever known, dear brother," she said, gathering her black skirts. "Now you'll have to excuse me. I'm expecting Lady Jersey this afternoon." She swept past him, her head held high, a tight smile on her lips.

Left alone in the gardens of St. James's Square, Sebastian watched a young nursemaid shepherd her laughing charges down the steps of one of the stately houses fronting the square, and lead them across the street. He turned in a slow circle, his gaze sweeping row after row of imposing mansions around him. How many women, he wondered, lived lives of quiet despair behind those imposing facades? What tales of disappointment and heartache, fear and desperation, did those walls of marble and brick disguise?

Still thoughtful, he drew the triskelion from his pocket and turned it over to study the entwined initials of another pair of doomed lovers. A. C. and J. S. Addiena Cadel and James Stuart. Was the ancient Welsh necklace that had once belonged to Sophie Hendon a clue to what had happened to Guinevere Anglessey, Sebastian wondered, or simply a distraction? What was

259

Guinevere's intention when she left that grand, four-story house on Mount Street in a hackney carriage headed for Smithfield, only to be found some eight hours later, dead and in the arms of the Regent in Brighton? During the intervening hours, someone had poisoned her, exchanged her simple red afternoon walking dress for a slightly smaller woman's green satin evening gown, and used her dead body in an elaborate scheme to further discredit an already unpopular prince. But why? *Why?*

Somewhere in the half-truths and subtle nuances of what Sebastian had discovered about Guinevere's life lay the explanation for her death. And for some reason he couldn't explain, he found himself coming back again and again to that image of the child Guinevere had once been. Grief-stricken, frightened, left alone by her mother's early death, the young Guinevere had known little love from either her father or her older sister, while her governesses had been content to let her roam the countryside with the kind of freedom usually reserved for the males of her class.

And so the cliffs above the wild Welsh coast had become her refuge, the open fields and forests of her father's estate her schoolroom. In a sense she'd been fortunate. Her childhood experiences had nurtured her instinctive independence and resiliency, while the love she'd been denied at home had been found nearby, within the ancient walls of Audley Castle. First from Lady Audley, herself so recently bereaved, and then from her son, the Chevalier de Varden, a young man with a life as tragic in its own way as Guinevere's.

What would have happened, Sebastian wondered, if the old Earl of Athelstone hadn't placed his own greed and ambitions ahead of his daughter's happiness? Sebastian had a brief image of the woman he'd last seen dead in the Yellow Cabinet at Brighton, only in his mind's eye she was alive, with the golden light of the Welsh sun warm on her face as she played with her children on a windy hill overlooking a foam-flecked sea. What if . . . ?

But that was a futile, if beguiling, path to travel, and he closed his mind to it.

Watching the nursemaid chase after her wayward charges, Sebastian found himself remembering what Guinevere had said to the starving, desperate woman she'd made her abigail. *If we're given a hard road to walk in life, we can't give up. We must fight to find some way to make what we want out of what life has given us.*

Faced with such determined opposition from her family, another woman might simply have succumbed to the wishes of her keepers and lived a pale, unhappy life of resignation and acceptance. But not Guinevere. Given no real choice, she had come to London. But she had come determined to find some way to make her life on her own terms.

And so she had taken to husband the Marquis of Anglessey, a man who was not only wealthy and kindly, but also old enough to be nearing the end of his life. As a wealthy widow, Guinevere would have been free to marry to please herself. Had that been her objective? Only, in the end it had been the Marquis of Anglessey who buried his beautiful young wife.

If the murder had been staged in such a way as to implicate Bevan Ellsworth or Lady Anglessey's unknown lover, Sebastian might have believed the Marquis guilty. It wouldn't have been the first time an old, impotent husband had been driven to murder by the discovery that his beautiful young wife was giving her love to a younger man. But Guinevere Anglessey's killer hadn't implicated Bevan Ellsworth. He had targeted the Prince Regent. *Why?*

Leaving the square, Sebastian closed his

fist around the bluestone necklace, a necklace given as a talisman by a Welsh witch to her lover, a fugitive Stuart prince who in turn had presented it to his illegitimate daughter on her wedding day. From there its history was obscure until that day some thirty years ago now when a withered old crone in the wilds of northern Wales had pressed it upon the young Countess of Hendon.

Whatever link existed between the two women must lay there, Sebastian decided, somewhere in the green, misty mountains of northern Wales.

CHAPTER 33

They were referred to as morning calls, that endless round of formal visits that took place daily amongst the members of Society in residence in London. But the truth was that no gentleman or lady with any pretensions to breeding would dream of appearing on the doorstep of any but his or her most intimate of friends before three o'clock.

And so Sebastian spent the next several hours in Jackson's saloon, working the soreness out of his muscles. It wasn't until half past three that he arrived at the home of Guinevere's sister, Morgana, Lady Quinlan. After the thinly veiled hostility of their encounter at the balloon ascension, he half expected to be told she was not at home. Instead, he was shown upstairs to the drawing room, where he found Lady Quinlan in conversation with another caller, a young woman introduced to him as Lady Portland, wife to the Home Secretary and half sister to Guinevere's childhood love, the Chevalier de Varden.

She had much the look of her mother, Isolde, being incredibly small and fine-boned. Only her hair was different, an ashen blond rather than a fiery auburn. She was also very young, no more than twenty at the most. As a child of Lady Audley's second marriage, she was younger than Varden, younger even than Guinevere.

"Lord Devlin," said Claire Portland, offering her hand and looking up at him with that intense interest used to flirtatious effect by so many of her sex. "I've been hearing a great deal to your credit."

The hand in his was a dainty, frail thing, and he found himself thinking that Claire Portland, like her mother, was far too tiny to have been the owner of the green satin gown that had been used as Guinevere's death shroud.

"Portland tells me you've agreed to help discover the truth about what happened to poor Guinevere," Claire was saying. "How gallant of you."

Sebastian adjusted the tails of his coat and sat on a nearby sofa. "I don't recall," he said to Lady Portland. "Were you present at the Prince's musical evening last Wednesday?"

She gave a little shudder. "Thank goodness, no. I had the headache and decided to stay in my room."

"But you were in Brighton."

"Oh yes." She leaned forward as if confiding a secret. "Personally, I find the place rather tedious. But now that Prinny has been named Regent, I fear we shall all be doomed to follow him down there every summer."

Leaning back again, she fixed him with an intense gaze and said, "Is it true what Portland says, that the people on the streets actually believe the Prince killed poor Guin?"

Sebastian glanced at Morgana, who sat quietly beside the empty hearth. "It's been my experience that most people tend to believe what they are led to believe," he said.

Lady Quinlan's features remained inscrutable, while Claire Portland tipped her head sideways, her expression quizzical, as if she were not quite sure how to take that. Looking into her clear, cornflower blue eyes, Sebastian found himself wondering just how much Lord Portland confided in his pretty young wife. She projected an image of innocence and gaiety, of disingenuous superficiality and the mindless helplessness most men found appealing. But Sebastian knew it was an impression deliberately created by many of her sisters, a consciously deceptive facade that often hid a sharp and calculating mind. Claire Portland was, after all, Lady Audley's daughter. And Lady Audley was neither mindless nor helpless.

Lord Portland's pretty young wife stayed chatting a few minutes more, then very correctly rose as required by custom to take her leave. Yet as she made her adieus with sweet effusiveness, Sebastian caught the furtive glance she shared with their hostess. It was a look that spoke of an intention to follow up Sebastian's visit with a private conference, and hinted at the existence of an old, close friendship. A friendship he wouldn't have expected between the plain, intensely serious Morgana and this flirtatious woman who was at least as young, if not younger than, the murdered sister with whom Morgana claimed to have had so little in common.

"Why are you doing this?" Morgana asked, fixing Sebastian with a thoughtful stare as soon as the footman had shown her other guest out. "It's not for love of the Prince Regent, whatever Claire might think."

Sebastian raised his eyebrows in a simulation of surprise. "Does Lady Portland indeed think that?"

An expression he couldn't quite decipher flitted across his hostess's features. She leaned back in her chair, one hand smoothing her gown across her lap. "You came, obviously, to ask me something. What is it?"

It was no easy thing, asking a lady for the name of her sister's lover. Sebastian tried an oblique approach. "Was your sister happy, do you think, in her marriage?"

A knowing gleam shone in her eyes. "You're being discreet, aren't you? What you really mean to ask is, Did Guinevere have a lover and do I know his name? The answer to the first question is, Possibly. To the second question I'm afraid I must answer, No. I don't know his name. It's not the sort of thing she would confide in me. As I told you, Guinevere and I were not close."

"Yet you knew of her childhood attachment to Varden."

"That was hardly a secret. Presumably even Guinevere would be prudent if she were cuckolding a husband."

"Whom might she have confided in? Did she have a close friend?"

"Not that I know of. She was always something of a loner, Guinevere."

To his annoyance, he heard the distant rap of the front knocker, heralding the arrival of yet another round of guests come to offer their condolences to Lady Quinlan on the death of her sister. Sebastian said, "Your sister had a necklace, a necklace with a silver triskelion superimposed on a bluestone disk. Do you know anything about it? It's an ancient piece, from well before the seventeenth century."

Lady Quinlan shook her head, her expression blank. Either she knew nothing of the necklace, or she was even better at hiding her thoughts and feelings than he would expect. "No. As a child she had a pearl necklace and one or two small pins that once belonged to her mother, but nothing else I ever knew of. You say it was silver? It seems a strange thing for Anglessey to have given her. Unless, of course, it was a family piece." A faint smile touched her lips. "Although if that were the case, you wouldn't be asking me about it, now, would you?"

The new visitors were on the stairs. Sebastian could hear the ponderous tread of a matron, along with the lighter step of a younger woman, probably her daughter. "You wouldn't happen to know what took your sister to Smithfield last week, would you?" Sebastian asked, rising to take his leave.

"Smithfield?" She rose with him. "Of all

the unfashionable places. Good heavens, no."

Standing beside her, Sebastian was reminded again of the unusual height that Morgana Quinlan, like her sister, Guinevere, had inherited from their father. If anything, Morgana was even taller — and certainly more robust — than her sister had been.

The green satin evening gown could no more have come from this woman's wardrobe than from that of Claire Portland.

That green satin gown was beginning to bother him.

Returning to his house on Brook Street, Sebastian decided to take the gown to Kat and hear what she might be able to tell him about it. "Have Tom bring the curricle around," said Sebastian, handing his hat and walking stick to Morey, his majordomo.

"I'm sorry, my lord," said Morey. "But young Tom has not yet returned."

Sebastian frowned. The sun was already low in the sky, and he'd warned the tiger not to linger in Smithfield after dusk. Sebastian turned toward the stairs. "Then have Giles bring the curricle round."

Morey gave a stately bow and withdrew.

Some half an hour later, clad in evening

dress and with the groom Giles sitting up behind him, Sebastian stuffed the brown paper package containing the green satin evening gown beneath his curricle's seat and turned the chestnuts' heads toward Covent Garden. Already, the setting sun was painting long streaks of orange and vivid pink across a fading sky. The traffic in the streets was heavy, the ponderous wagons of the carters and coal sellers mingling with the elegant landaus and barouches of the ton as the fashionably idle set out for the opera and theater and endless round of dinner parties, card parties, and soirees with which they filled their evenings. There were single horsemen, too: fashionable bucks in leather breeches and white-topped high boots, their blood mounts stepping high and proud; country gentlemen in old-fashioned frock coats, their horses sturdy and serviceable . . . and one brown-coated gentleman on a nondescript gray who was still trailing a steady distance behind as the more fashionable districts faded away and Sebastian swung the curricle into St. Martin's.

Ignoring the turning that would have taken him to King Street and Covent Garden beyond, Sebastian simply continued on south toward the river. The horse was different, of course: a gray in place of the more noticeable bay. But there was something instantly recognizable about the set of the man's shoulders, his easy seat in the saddle. It was the shadow from South Downs.

Alert now, Sebastian swung left onto Chandos Street. Following at a judicious interval, the brown-coated horseman kept pace with him.

Ahead, the street formed a lopsided Y around the sharply pointed corner of an ancient brick building whose ground floor housed an apothecary, its rotting sign peeling paint, its small windows shuttered now with the coming of night. Most of the traffic here veered left, toward Bedford Street; Sebastian guided the chestnuts into the narrow opening to the right, then turned a second hard right into an even narrower lane that angled off toward the river.

A heavy odor of age and damp closed in around them. High, sagging walls rose up steeply on either side, cutting off the dim light of the dying day. Most of the shops here were shuttered as well, or simply boarded up, the narrow, nearly deserted footpaths edging a lane of old cobbles half lost in a thick, noisome mud.

"Here, take them," said Sebastian, passing the reins to his groom. "Keep going, and wait for me at the theater."

Giles scrambled slack-jawed onto the seat. "My lord?"

"You heard me."

One hand braced against the high seat iron beside him, Sebastian vaulted lightly to the cobbles. He was aware of heads turning. Ignoring them, he sprinted back to the ironmonger's that stood on the corner. Beside it, a pile of scrap metal and old timbers blocked the footpath and spilled out into the lane. Sebastian scrambled to the top, the boards creaking and shifting precariously beneath him.

From the street came the passing whirl of a lightly sprung phaeton, mingling with the ponderous rattle of a heavy wagon's iron-rimmed wheels and the even *clip-clop* of a single approaching horse. Throwing a quick glance toward the bottom of the lane, Sebastian could see his curricle quite clearly, the solitary figure of the blue-coated groom silhouetted against the brick of the ancient Tudor buildings. But for most people the curricle would be a dark blur, the number of men it carried impossible to discern in the gathering darkness.

The clatter of hooves came closer. Sebastian returned his attention to the corner beside him. An old woman walked past, bent nearly double beneath a bundle of what looked like rags.

Sebastian settled himself into a crouch.

A rat, its nose twitching, its eyes shining in the darkness, crept out from beneath the rotting board at Sebastian's feet just as the brown-coated rider turned the corner. The flickering flambeau thrust into a holder fixed high up on the wall of the building opposite revealed a man with a top hat pulled low on his forehead, his gaze narrowed as he studied the curricle at the bottom of the lane. Sebastian could see the man's powerfully jutting nose and sweeping side-whiskers, the rest of his face clean shaven and utterly unfamiliar.

The rat squealed in alarm and scampered off, just as Sebastian leapt.

CHAPTER 34

Startled by the sound of the rat's screech, the rider swung around. His eyes flared wide in alarm, his right arm jerking up instinctively to shield his face and upper body as Sebastian slammed into him.

The impact was enough to unseat the rider. But that blocking sweep of his arm and the shift in the man's seat deflected Sebastian's momentum enough that, rather than crashing down with the man on the horse's far side, Sebastian was flung back. The edge of one of the boards raked his ribs painfully as he fell.

Squealing in terror, the gray reared up between them, its sharp hooves slashing the air. Sebastian scrambled to his feet, dodged the gray's hooves as the horse reared again. But the brown-coated man was already up. Boots slipping in the mud, he bolted around the corner.

Sebastian tore after him, up a street lined

with workshops and small traders closing now for the night. He sidestepped a tailor's apprentice who turned, a green-painted shutter held in his widespread arms, his mouth forming a silent O as Sebastian ran past.

The entrance to an alley yawned ahead. The brown-coated man darted down it, Sebastian hard after him. They were in an old mews, the high, bulging walls propped up by rotting beams that thrust out to trip the unwary, the former yards filled now with a hodgepodge of illegal shacks and grim hovels. A group of ragged children playing with a hoop shouted as they dashed past. One little boy of no more then five or six, his face smeared with filth, ran after them, calling to them and laughing until he could keep up no longer and fell away.

For a moment Sebastian thought the man had misjudged and trapped himself in a cul-de-sac. Then a black mouth opened up before them and Sebastian saw a low archway where the upper stories of the houses on either side of what had once been a narrow lane had extended out to swallow the sky, leaving only a dark tunnel beneath.

Plunging into a shadowy darkness of recessed doorways and sharp corners where a man might lie in wait, Sebastian was forced to slow his pace, listening always for the slap of running feet, the sawing of labored breath up ahead. Then the traboule opened up and he found himself in a court-yard of what must once have been a fine coaching in, its ground floor now filled with dilapidated workshops overhung by rented rooms where ragged laundry hung limp and the still evening air trapped the scent of fry-ing onions and burning dung.

Leaping a puddle left by the previous day's rain, Sebastian ran on. Two women taking down the laundry paused to stare; an old man filling a clay pipe called out some-thing lost in the din. Sebastian followed his quarry through the arch and down a nar-row passageway between two brown brick buildings. Then the pale glow of lamplight shone up ahead and the passageway emptied out into a wide, busy thoroughfare that Se-bastian realized must be the Strand.

The man ahead of him was breathing heavily now, stumbling as he dodged be-tween a hackney and a ponderous old lan-dau sporting a faded crest. Two men on the far footpath, their red waistcoats and blue coats marking them as men from the Bow Street Patrol, turned and shouted.

Brown Coat's head snapped around, his open mouth sucking in air, his eyes going wide. Abandoning the busy, lamplit expanse of the Strand, he careered around the nearest corner, heading now toward the river.

The streets were newer here and straight, the chance of running into a trap diminished. Lungs aching, his breath coming hard and fast, Sebastian pushed himself on. They were halfway across the open square of Hungerford Market when Sebastian caught him.

Reaching out, Sebastian closed his hand on the man's shoulder and spun him around. They lost their balance together, the man pulling back, Sebastian practically running over him as, legs tangling, they sprawled across the pavement.

Brown Coat's back hit the ground hard, driving the wind out of him. "Who are you?" Sebastian demanded. The man heaved up against him once, then lay still, panting, his face ashen with pain.

"Damn you." Sebastian closed his fist on the cloth of the man's coat to draw him up, then slam him back down again. "Who set you after me?"

A heavy hand fell on Sebastian's shoulder, jerking him up. "There, there now, me lads," said a gruff voice. "What's all this, then?"

CHAPTER 35

His hold on Brown Coat broken, Sebastian found himself staring into the broad, whiskered face of one of the men from the Bow Street Patrol.

Sebastian shook his head to fling the sweat from his eyes. "Bloody hell."

"Now then, let's have none of that," chided the second Bow Street man, grabbing Sebastian's other arm.

Scuttling backward, Brown Coat scrambled to his feet and took off at a run.

"You stupid sons of bitches," swore Sebastian, bringing his arm back to drive his elbow, hard, into the plump red waistcoat of the first man who'd grabbed him.

Air gusting out of a painfully pursed mouth, the Runner let go of Sebastian and hunched forward, his hands pressed to his gut.

"I say," began the other Runner, just as Sebastian drove his fist into the man's face and wrenched his left arm free.

By now, Brown Coat had made it to the end of the market. Sebastian pelted after him, the shriek of the Bow Street men's whistles cutting through the night.

Up ahead, he could see the wide-open expanse of the Thames. The riverbank here had been built up into a stone-faced terrace fronted by a low wall. Dodging across the open space, Brown Coat leapt up onto the flat top of the wall, meaning perhaps to avoid the traffic clogging the street fronting the river by running along the wall to the top of the steps.

But the wall was old, the weathered stone damp and crumbling. His feet shot out from beneath him. For a moment the man wavered, his arms windmilling through the air as he sought to regain his balance. With a sharp cry, he toppled backward.

There was a dull thump. Then all was silent except for the insistent blowing of the Runners' whistles and the lapping of the water at the river's edge.

Leaning his outstretched arms against the top of the wall, Sebastian hung his head and gasped for breath. On the rocks far below, the man lay sprawled on his back, his arms outflung, his eyes wide and unseeing.

"Bloody hell," said Sebastian, and pushed

away from the wall to swipe one muddy forearm across his sweat-drenched forehead.

"If your main purpose was to find out who he is," said Sir Henry Lovejoy, staring down at the body at their feet, "then why did you kill him?"

Sebastian grunted. "I didn't kill him. He fell."

"Yes, of course." Moving gingerly across the wet rocks, Lovejoy hunkered down beside the man's still form and peered at the upturned face, ashen now in the moonlight. "Do you know who he is?"

"No. Do you?"

The little magistrate shook his head. "Any idea why he was following you?"

"I was hoping you might be able to help me discover that."

Lovejoy threw him a pained look and stood up. "Have you seen this morning's papers?"

"No. Why?"

Even though he had not touched the body, the little magistrate drew a handkerchief from his pocket and wiped his hands. "A park woman found a body in St. James's Park. Just before dawn."

A wind had kicked up and set a series of small waves to lapping against the rocks at their feet. The air was thick with the smell of the river and mud and ever-pervasive stench of sewage. Sebastian stared out at the dark hull of a wherry cutting through the dark water. In a city crowded with courtesans and prostitutes, the park women were the lowest of the low, pitiful creatures so disfigured by disease that they could only ply their trade in the dark, usually in one of the city's parks.

"Is that so unusual?" said Sebastian.

"It is when the body in question has been butchered." Lovejoy stuffed his handkerchief back in his pocket. In the pale moonlight, his face looked nearly as pallid as the corpse at their feet. "I mean that literally. Carved up like a side of beef."

"Who was he? Do you know?"

Lovejoy nodded for the constables to remove the body and turned away. "That's one of the more troublesome aspects. He was Sir Humphrey Carmichael's eldest son. A young man of but twenty-five."

Sir Humphrey Carmichael was one of the wealthiest men in the city. Born the son of a weaver, he now had a hand in everything from manufacturing and banking to mining and shipping. Until his son's murderer was caught, the city's constables and magistrates would be expected to concentrate on nothing else.

"Incidentally, one of the Bow Street men is talking about laying charges," Lovejoy said, climbing the steps. "You broke his nose."

"He ripped my coat."

Lovejoy turned to run an eye over Sebastian's exquisitely tailored coat of Bath superfine, now muddied and scuffed beyond repair. A faint smile played about one corner of the magistrate's normally tense mouth. "I'll tell him that."

CHAPTER 36

"What happened to you this time?" asked Kat, her gaze meeting Sebastian's in her dressing room mirror. The curtain had only just come down on the final act; around them, the theater rang with shouts and laughter and the tramp of feet hurrying up and down the passage.

Sebastian dropped the paper-wrapped parcel containing the green satin gown on her couch and dabbed the back of his hand at the blood trickling down his cheek from a graze. "I was coming to see what you could tell me about this evening gown when I decided to stop and have a little wresting match in the mud."

She gave him a look that spoke of concern and exasperation and amusement, all carefully held in check. Removing Cleopatra's gilded diadem from her forehead, she pushed back her chair and went to unwrap the gown. In the golden lamplight, the satin shimmered.

"It's exquisite," she said, turning to hold the gown up to the lamplight. "Dashing, but not outrageously so. It looks like something that would be made for a young nobleman's wife. A lady several years past her first season, perhaps, but still young."

She glanced over at him. "Surely the woman who delivered the note for the Prince couldn't have been wearing an identical gown?"

Sebastian stripped off his muddy coat. Not even a valet of Sedlow's genius would be able to repair these ravages. "I doubt it. Probably a gown of a similar cut and hue. A female might have noticed the difference, but not most men." Sebastian surveyed the damage done to his waistcoat. It was as ruined as his coat. "Whoever she was, she obviously had a hand in the Marchioness's death."

"Not necessarily. I know dozens of actresses more than capable of giving a very credible performance as a lady. The killer could simply have hired someone."

"Perhaps. But it seems a risky thing to have done."

Kat turned the gown inside out to inspect the seams. "Look at these tiny stitches. There aren't many mantua makers in Town capable of producing work of this quality."

He came up beside her. "Do you think if we found the maker, she could tell us who ordered it?"

"Certainly she *could.* Whether she actually would or not depends on how she's approached."

Sebastian hooked an elbow behind her neck, drawing her close. "Are you suggesting my approach might be clumsy?"

Kat rubbed her open lips against his. "I'm suggesting she might find the question slightly more appropriate coming from a female."

Grinning, he laced his fingers through her hair and rubbed the pads of his thumbs back and forth across her cheeks. "Then maybe —" He broke off as a knock sounded at her door.

"Flowers fer Miss Boleyn," called a young voice.

"Oh, Lord. Not again," said Kat.

Sebastian let his gaze drift around the buckets of roses and lilies and orchids that covered every conceivable surface of the dressing room, including the floor. "You appear to have a new admirer," he said, as she went to jerk open the door.

Nichols, the young boy who ran errands for the theater, grinned and thrust a small sheaf of flowers into her arms. " 'Ere's another one. This bloke gave me a whole shilling. If this keeps up, I'm gonna be able to set up my own shop soon."

"It wasn't the same man?" asked Kat.

Sebastian lifted the flowers from her arms. "At least this one won't take up half the room. It's a strange bouquet, though, isn't it? One yellow lily and nine white roses? What an odd conceit. So who is your admirer?"

Kat had gone suddenly, oddly pale. "The others were from the Comte de Lille."

"This one's not?"

She looked down at the card in her hand. "No."

He frowned. "What is it? What's wrong? Who are they from?"

"I don't know. It doesn't say."

He lifted the card from her hand. " 'And the king made silver and gold at Jerusalem as plenteous as stones, and cedar trees made he as the sycamore trees that are in the vale of abundance,' " he read aloud, then handed it back to her with a laugh. "What kind of gallant sends a woman a bouquet with a quote from the Bible?"

After Sebastian left, Kat sat for some time staring at the strange bouquet. One yellow lily, nine white roses. *The nineteenth.* The day after tomorrow.

No, it couldn't be. She told herself it was a simple coincidence, that the flowers must have been sent by an admirer. With a shaking hand, she lifted the note and read it again. *And the king made silver and gold. . . .* With each breath, the sweet scent of the lily and roses floated up to engulf her until she thought she might be sick. She crushed the note in her hand and dropped it to the floor.

She kept a Bible tucked away beneath a collection of old costumes and programs in her trunk. It took her some time to locate the reference. She'd been raised a Catholic and her knowledge of the Bible was not extensive, but she found it eventually.

Chronicles, chapter one, verse fifteen.

She closed the Bible, the black leather covers gripped tight between her hands. Her gaze fixed on the crumpled note on the floor. In the soft light, the broken seal looked like drops of bright blood.

It had been so long, over four months now. Somehow she'd almost convinced herself this day wasn't going to come. She'd even begun to delude herself into thinking that she might be able to put it all behind her. God help her, she'd actually begun to dream about building some kind of a future with the man she loved more than life itself.

But Ireland was still not free. The war between England and France still raged long and bloody. And on Wednesday the nineteenth of June, at one fifteen in the afternoon, Pierrepont's successor and Napoléon's new spymaster in London would be looking to meet Kat Boleyn in the Physic Gardens at Chelsea.

CHAPTER 37

Sebastian arrived back at his house on Brook Street that night to be met by his majordomo.

"Young Tom is in the library," said the majordomo in the same carefully colorless voice all senior servants seemed to use when referring to the tiger. "He insisted upon waiting up for you."

"Ah. Thank you, Morey. Good night."

Opening the door to the library, Sebastian expected to find Tom curled up asleep on one of the window seats. Instead, the boy was at the library table, his chin propped on one fist, a flaming branch of candles at his elbow, a slim volume open on the table before him.

He was so engrossed in his reading that at first he wasn't aware of Sebastian's arrival. Then the hinges on the door creaked and he looked up with a start.

"My lord!" He slithered from the chair,

his face flushing hot crimson before fading to pale.

Sebastian smiled. "What are you reading?"

"I — I do beg your pardon, my lord."

"It's all right, Tom. What is it?"

The boy hung his head. "Jason and the Argonauts."

"An interesting choice." Sebastian walked over to pour himself a glass of brandy. "Where did you learn to read?"

"I went to school once, afore me da died."

Sebastian looked around in surprise. It reminded him of how little he knew of the boy's past, beyond the fact that his mother had been transported to Botany Bay, leaving her son to fend for himself on the streets of London.

"I expected you earlier this evening," said Sebastian, splashing brandy in his glass.

"The place really started 'oppin', come evening. I thought I might learn somethin' if I stuck around."

"And did you?"

Tom shook his head. "I checked the shops all up and down the lane, but no one owned up to 'aving seen her ladyship."

Sebastian leaned against the library table and sipped his brandy in thoughtful silence. "The one-legged beggar, was he at his place near the Norfolk Arms?"

"Didn't see 'im. But I spent some time 'anging around the inn. 'E's a weery rum customer, the African what owns the place. Weery rum indeed. They say he was a slave once, on a cotton plantation someplace in America afore he killed his master and run off."

"What's his name? Did you hear?"

Tom nodded. "Carter. Caleb Carter. He come here fifteen years or more ago. Took up with the widow woman what used to own the Norfolk Arms. She had a daughter then, a pretty little redheaded girl named Georgiana. But the girl took sick and died some two years ago, and the mother, she died of grief not long after."

"And left Carter the inn?"

"Aye. From what I gather, they're in the trade, if you know what I mean."

"Smuggling? That doesn't surprise me," said Sebastian, remembering the bottle of fine French brandy on the table in the common room. He pushed away from the table and straightened. "You'd best get some sleep. I'd like you to go there again tomorrow."

"Aye, gov'nor," said Tom, stifling a yawn.

"Here." Sebastian held out the book. "Don't you want to finish it?"

The boy's glance dropped hesitantly from

Sebastian's face to his outstretched hand.

Sebastian smiled. "Go on, take it. You can bring it back when you're done."

Tom turned toward the door, the book clutched to his chest like a rare treasure.

"Oh and, Tom —"

The boy swung around.

"Be back before nightfall this time, you hear? I don't want you taking any chances. These are dangerous people we're dealing with."

"Aye, gov'nor."

Still faintly smiling, Sebastian stood in the doorway to watch the boy dash off across the hall. Then, the smile fading, Sebastian turned back into the library to pour himself another drink.

The next morning, the Dowager Duchess of Claiborne was lying on a chaise in her dressing room and drinking a cup of chocolate when Sebastian strolled into the room.

She let out a soft moan. "Sebastian? What can Humphrey be thinking? He has strict instructions to allow no one past the door before one o'clock."

"So he said." He stooped to plant a kiss on his aunt's cheek. "I want to know what you can tell me about the Countess of Portland."

His aunt sat up straighter. "Claire Portland? Good heavens, whatever for?"

Sebastian simply ignored the question. "What do you think of her?"

Aunt Henrietta gave a genteel sniff. "A pretty little thing, obviously. But all bubble and froth if you ask me."

"She certainly gives that impression. But appearances can be deceiving."

"Sometimes. But not in this case, I'm afraid." His aunt fixed him with a fierce stare. "And now, not another word until you tell me your interest in the lady."

"It appears that at one time, Lady Anglessey thought to marry Claire Portland's brother, the Chevalier de Varden."

"Hmmm. Yes, I can see that. Dashingly handsome man, the Chevalier. And nothing piques a girl's fancy more than a tragic, romantic past."

"Dear Aunt. One might almost suspect you of nourishing a tendre for the fellow yourself."

She made a deep rumbling sound that shook her impressive bosom. "I've no patience with romantic, handsome young men, and well you know it."

Sebastian smiled. "Lady Portland. Tell me about her."

Aunt Henrietta settled herself more comfortably. "Not much to tell, I'm afraid. Her father, the late Lord Audley, left her well dowered. She had a successful season and married the Earl of Portland at the end of it."

"What about Portland himself?"

Again, that genteel sniff. "I've heard him referred to as a handsome man, although personally I've no use for redheads. But there's no denying the old Earl, his father, cut up quite warm. And Portland himself's not one for wasting the ready at the gaming table. Claire did quite well for herself. I wouldn't say Portland's one to sit in his wife's pocket, but then he hasn't set up a mistress, either, that anyone knows of. He seems to spend most of his time at Whitehall."

"And the lady Portland? Has she established herself as something of a political hostess?"

"I doubt she has either the inclination or the intelligence to carry it off."

Sebastian came to take the chair opposite her. "She seems surprisingly close to Morgana Quinlan."

"Well, that's to be expected, isn't it, given the close proximity of their fathers' estates?"

"I would have said the two women were of starkly different temperaments."

"Yes. But sometimes friendships are like marriages: the best couplings are between opposites."

Sebastian was silent for a moment, his thoughts on his own parents' marriage. That was one instance when a coupling of opposite temperaments had definitely not prospered. But all he said was "Lady Quinlan seems to nourish a particularly bitter animosity toward her sister. Do you know why?"

"Hmm. I suspect she had her nose put out of joint when her younger sister succeeded so much better than she in the Marriage Mart. Frankly, I was surprised Lady Morgana went off at all. The woman's not only a shameless bluestocking, but a dead bore to boot, which is far worse. I once made the mistake of attending one of her scientific evenings. Some gentleman lectured us interminably on Leyden jars and copper wires. Then he killed a frog and reanimated it with electric shocks. It was quite revolting."

Sebastian leaned forward. "How did he kill the frog?"

Aunt Henrietta drained her chocolate cup and set it aside. "Poison, I believe."

The Home Secretary, the Earl of Portland,

was sitting in a coffeehouse just off the Mall, a steaming cup on the table before him, when Sebastian slid into the opposite seat.

"I don't recall inviting you to sit," said Portland, regarding Sebastian through narrowed eyes.

"You didn't," said Sebastian cheerfully.

The air filled with the steady beat of a drum and the tramp of feet as a troop of soldiers marched past. Fresh cannon fodder, thought Sebastian, on their way to Portsmouth and the war on the other side of the Channel. No one in the coffee shop even looked up.

Portland leaned back in his seat, a faint smile touching his lips. "My wife tells me she met you in Lady Quinlan's drawing room yesterday."

"You didn't tell me you were brother-in-law to the dead lady's lover."

"You mean Varden?" Portland raised his cup to his lips and took a thoughtful sip. "I know there was an attachment of long standing between them, but I wouldn't care to hazard on its present nature."

"Tell me about him."

Portland shrugged. "A likable enough lad, I suppose, if a bit too hotheaded and impulsive for my taste. But then he's half-French, so I suppose that's to be expected."

"What can you tell me about his politics?"

Portland gave a sharp laugh and took another sip. "The pup is twenty-one years old. He's interested in wine, women, and song. Not the composition of the Prince's cabinet."

"How about dynastic disputes? Might they interest him?"

Portland lowered his cup, his face suddenly drawn and serious. "What are you talking about?"

Sebastian let the question slide past him. "The lady who asked you to convey the note to the Prince, what can you tell me about her?"

Portland glanced down at his cup, his sandy red eyebrows drawing together in a thoughtful frown. "She was young, I would say. At least that's the impression I had. If I could see the color of her hair, I don't recall it."

"Definitely a lady?"

"I would have said so, yes." He hesitated. "I think she was tall, but I can't be certain. Perhaps I simply imagined that afterward, when I assumed it was Lady Anglessey who had handed me the billet-doux."

Sebastian leaned back in his seat, his gaze on the other man's face. It struck him as too much of a coincidence that the note used to lure the Prince to the Yellow Cabinet had been given to the Home Secretary, rather than to one of the sycophants with which the Prince typically surrounded himself. Then again, it was always possible that the woman in green had singled out Portland deliberately.

Aloud, Sebastian said, "Do you remember the dagger that was in Lady Anglessey's back?"

Portland turned his head to stare out the shop's bay window to the street beyond, empty now in the bright sun. His throat worked as if he had to fight to swallow, and his voice, when he spoke, was strained. "It's not something I'm likely to forget, now, is it? The way it stuck out of her like a —"

"Had you ever seen it before?"

"The dagger?" He looked around again, his eyes opening wide as if in surprise. "Of course. It's part of the collection of Stuart memorabilia that was in the possession of Henry Stuart when he died. I believe it belonged to his grandfather, James the Second."

The bell on the shop's door jangled as two soldiers came in, bringing with them the smell of morning air and sun-warmed brick and a whiff of fresh manure. Sebastian kept his gaze on the Scotsman's freckled face.

"What happened to it?"

"You mean after Henry's death? Don't you know? He willed the entire collection to the Prince of Wales — the Regent."

CHAPTER 38

Kat spent a restless night. Her dreams were troubled by marching rows of dead soldiers and a bloodstained guillotine that creaked ominously in the wind.

Rising early, she went to stand at the window overlooking the street below. In the clear dawn light she could see the milkmaids making their rounds, the buckets of fresh milk dangling from the yokes across their shoulders.

She had no regrets for the things she had done. The tyranny the French soldiers had brought to the continent of Europe was nothing compared to the horrors Ireland had suffered under the English for hundreds of years now. She would still do whatever she could to hasten the day of Ireland's liberation. But she could not, in all honesty, accept Sebastian's love and continue to give aid to the enemy he had risked his life to fight.

She had been torn for a while, but by now she had decided to keep tomorrow's rendez-vous in the Chelsea Physic Gardens with Napoléon's new spymaster. She intended to tell him the French could no longer rely upon her as a source of information. Whether they would allow her to withdraw her services so easily remained to be seen.

Too nervous to go back to sleep, she decided to get an early start in her search for the maker of Guinevere Anglessey's death shroud. But in the end, the task was even easier then she expected. Setting out that morning shortly after breakfast, Kat found she had to visit only three fashion-able modistes before hitting upon the establishment responsible for the creation of the green satin gown.

"*Mais oui,* I remember it quite well, thees one," said Madame de Blois, proprietor of an expensive little shop on Bond Street. "Lady Addison Peebles ordered it from me just thees last season."

Kat had to bite her lip to keep from say-ing, *Are you certain?* The young lady in question was a beautiful but excessively dim-witted heiress who had married Lord Addison Peebles, youngest son of the Duke of Farnham, some two years before. Lord Addison was every bit as vacuous as his bride, to the extent that some members of the ton had taken to calling the couple Lord and Lady Addled and Feeble. It was difficult to imagine either of them having anything to do with what had happened to Guinevere Anglessey.

"Lovely, is it not?" Madame de Blois was saying. "Although hardly the shade of green for a young woman with Lady Addison's coloring, hmm? I tried to discourage, but she would hear none of it." The modiste shook her head and made a little *tsk*ing sound. "For you, I think, we shall do something in sapphire, yes? And a more daring décolleté, of course."

Kat gave the woman a wide smile. "Of course."

Sebastian had never understood the Prince Regent's fascination with the Stuarts.

He was a prince who longed to be popular, who was genuinely troubled by the boos and hisses that greeted him everywhere. Yet despite mounting public fury over his never-ending debts and monstrous extravagance, he made no effort to reform his indulgent ways. While women and children starved in the streets, the Prince gave lavish banquets at which privileged guests had their choice of more than a hundred different hot dishes.

England's soldiers on the Continent shivered in their ragged uniforms, but the Regent continued to order breeches and waistcoats by the score in sizes so small he would never be able to wear them. The poor of England might be groaning under an ever-increasing, onerous weight of taxes, but that didn't stop the Prince from petitioning Parliament to pay his gambling debts.

Some believed the Prince was driven by an evil genius, but Sebastian thought the truth was probably far less flattering. Prinny longed to be loved, but he wanted to be loved as he was, without the need to reform the odious ways that made him hated. Given a choice between popularity and continuing his hedonistic, self-obsessed lifestyle, George the hedonist beat out George the prince every time.

Yet with each passing year, his love affair with the Stuarts seemed only to grow. It was as if he both envied and identified with the Stuarts. Once so despised that they had lost the throne of England forever, the Stuarts had nevertheless managed to acquire a patina of romance. Figures of pathos and tragedy, they had become something Prinny himself would never be: the stuff of legends.

But surely the fate of these doomed princes hung over him. Sebastian suspected that mixed in with the fascination and the envy there was also a powerful element of fear: the haunting realization that what had happened to the Stuarts might someday happen to George, as well.

The Prince Regent kept his growing collection of Stuart papers and memorabilia housed in a special room at Carlton House, a room he was only too happy to show off to anyone who happened to ask. Thus it was that Sebastian found himself, later that afternoon, in a room hung in red silk trimmed with gold tassels and carpeted with a rug woven in the Stuart plaid.

"This was carried by Charles the First on his way to the battle of Naseby," said the Prince, reverently lifting a heavy old-fashioned sword from one of the glass cases that lined the walls. The cases were unlocked, Sebastian noticed; anyone with access to the room could have removed any item at will.

"And this," said the Prince, his face glowing with pleasure and pride as he held up a faded collar of the Garter, "was worn by James the Second." His beefy, clumsy fingers trembled as he smoothed the worn material, and for a moment it seemed as if he were lost in some private reverie. Then he roused himself and, padding across the room on his fat legs, he began to talk about the documents he was collecting for a biography of James II he intended to commission.

Sebastian trailed behind him, pausing to admire a display of seventeenth-century jewelry before coming to a halt in front of a case lined with red velvet. There, nestled in a molded depression obviously created especially for it, lay the jeweled Highland dagger Sebastian had last seen embedded in Guinevere Anglessey's back.

"Ah, I see you're admiring the dirk," said the Prince, coming to stand beside him. "It's a lovely piece, isn't it? We know it was carried by James the Second, but some suggest it is much older, that it may even have belonged to his great-grandmother Mary, Queen of Scots."

His gaze lifting from the dagger to the man who owned it, Sebastian studied the Prince's half-averted face. His features were animated but untroubled, his cheeks ruddy, his almost feminine mouth turned up in a half smile.

That night in the Yellow Cabinet at the Pavilion, the Prince had held the limp body of Guinevere Anglessey in his arms. He must have seen the weapon thrust into her back, must surely have known it as one from his own prized collection. Yet there was no indication now that he remembered the incident at all.

He had a talent, Sebastian had heard, for simply putting from his mind all memory of things he found unpleasant. The dirk had been returned to its proper place in his collection; as far as the Regent was concerned, that was all that really mattered.

The Prince had moved on now, to a shelf of calf-bound books that had once belonged to Charles II. Sebastian watched him, watched the animation in that plump, self-satisfied face. And he couldn't help but wonder if the Prince remembered the events of that night in the Yellow Cabinet at all.

The room was stiflingly hot, as were the rooms in all of the Prince's apartments. But at that moment Sebastian felt a chill. Because a man capable of such self-deception, such self-absorbed focus, must surely be capable of almost anything.

CHAPTER 39

"It's a strange ability some have," said Paul Gibson when Sebastian met him later that day for a pint of ale at a pub not far from the Tower. "It's as if they somehow revise their memories of unpleasant or uncomplimentary incidents until they come up with something more self-flattering, or at least more palatable. In a sense you could say they aren't exactly being untruthful when they lie, because they honestly believe their own twisted version of an event. Memories of particularly horrifying episodes can simply be wiped away completely."

Sebastian leaned his shoulders back against the old wooden partition, one hand cradled around his drink where it rested on the table's worn surface. "It's a good thing the Prince was in Brighton that day. Otherwise I'd be inclined to wonder if he hadn't simply wiped away the unpleasant memory of murdering Lady Anglessey."

"At least the discovery of the dagger's origins tells you the murderer must have been someone close to the Prince."

"Not necessarily. Those cases aren't kept locked. Hundreds of people could have had access to that room."

"Perhaps. But I can't see someone like Bevan Ellsworth prowling around Carlton House."

"No. But his good friend Fabian Fitzfrederick could certainly have taken it."

Gibson frowned. "*Is* he good friends with Fabian Fitzfrederick?"

"It would appear so."

"But . . . why would a son of the Duke of York want to bring down the Hanovers?"

Sebastian leaned forward. "Prinny has created a lot of discontent. Perhaps there are two different forces at work here — one aimed at bringing down the Hanovers, and another simply interested in replacing the Regent with his brother, York."

Gibson paused with his pint raised halfway to his lips. "Princess Charlotte stands next in line before York."

"Yes. But Princess Charlotte's own father regularly calls her mother a whore. Charlotte might well be put aside. It's happened before."

Gibson took a long, thoughtful swallow of

his ale. "Have you considered the possibility that the person who killed Guinevere Anglessey might not be the same person or persons as set up that nasty little charade in the Pavilion?"

"Yes." Sebastian shifted his weight to thrust his legs out straight. "I keep thinking that if I could just understand why she went to the Norfolk Arms in Smithfield, then it would all begin to make sense."

"It does seem an unlikely place for a lover's assignation," said Gibson.

Sebastian shook his head. "I don't think it was a lover's assignation."

The tramp of marching feet filled the air as part of the garrison from the Tower paraded past. His face solemn, Gibson turned his head to watch the men filling the street, the sun gleaming on their musket barrels. "I've been hearing a lot of grumbling about this fete the Prince has set for Thursday. Not just about the cost — which I gather is considerable. But it is rather unseemly, is it not, for a prince to celebrate his accession to the Regency when that elevation was necessitated by his father's madness? I hear his mother and sisters are refusing to go."

Sebastian, too, watched the soldiers. They looked so young, some little more than boys. "I doubt they'll be missed. It's been announced that no woman lower in rank than an Earl's daughter will be allowed to attend, which has naturally set every excluded but ambitious lady in London scrambling to be made an exception. They'll never keep the guest list down to two thousand."

"When does the Prince return to Brighton?"

"The day after the fete." Sebastian stared thoughtfully at the passing ranks of red-coated soldiers. "Think about this: if you were to organize a coup, when would you plan to stage it?"

Gibson's gaze met Sebastian's. "For a time when the Prince was out of London."

"Exactly," said Sebastian, and drained his ale.

CHAPTER 40

"Lady Addison Peebles?" said Devlin, staring at Kat. They were in the drawing room of her house on Harwich Street. He could hear the distant shouts of children playing a counting game on the footpath outside, their laughter mingling with the birds' evening song as the shadows lengthened. "What the devil could Lady Addled and Feeble possibly have to do with any of this?"

Kat gave a soft laugh. "Nothing. It seems the modiste tried to talk her out of this particular shade of green satin, but she was so taken with it that in the end the woman could only let her have her way. I understand she was excessively pleased with it — until her mama-in-law, the Duchess, told her it made her look like a sick frog."

Devlin walked over to pour out two glasses of wine. "So what did she do?"

"She gave the gown to her abigail, who sold it to a secondhand clothes dealer. The woman claims she can't remember which one, probably because she actually sold it to her regular fence out of force of habit."

Devlin looked up, one eyebrow raised in incredulity. "The gown came from a second-hand dealer?"

Kat came to lift her glass from his outstretched hand. "Evidently."

He took a long, thoughtful sip of his own wine. "Let me see if I've got this right. Someone kills Guinevere Anglessey by poisoning her with cyanide. The death is violent. So violent that the murderer finds it necessary to bathe the body and dress it in a fresh gown — a gown he buys from a secondhand dealer in someplace like Rosemary Lane. Only, our killer is so unfamiliar with his victim that he buys the wrong size so that it won't close properly around her. Nor does he bother to assemble the underclothing, shoes, or stockings a lady would normally have been wearing. He loads her body in a — what? A cart or a carriage, we've no way of knowing which — and hauls her down to Brighton, where he somehow manages to sneak her body into the Pavilion. He sends his accomplice — wearing a similar green gown and a veil — into the Prince's music room, where she hands a note to the Home Secretary, Lord

Portland, and disappears. A note which for unspecified reasons no one wants me to see. Oh yes, and did I mention that after he has carefully arranged Guinevere's body in the Yellow Cabinet, our killer stabs her with a Highland dirk which once belonged to James the Second, but now forms part of a collection owned by the Prince Regent himself that is normally kept in London?"

"Well, I'm glad you've got it all figured out."

He went to stand at the windows overlooking the street below. The children had gone. "All except for the who and the why part."

She came up behind him, her eyes on his face. "What is it? You keep going to the window."

"I'm worried about Tom. I left instructions with Morey to send the boy here as soon as he gets back."

"It's not even dusk yet."

"I told Tom I wanted him out of Smithfield before nightfall."

Kat slipped her arms around Sebastian's waist and held him close, her breasts pressing against his back. "Tom's a street lad. He knows how to take care of himself."

Sebastian shook his head. "These people are dangerous."

He was aware of Kat's silence. After a moment, she said, "He's a servant."

"He's still only a boy."

"And he loves tending your horses and poking around, asking questions for you. It makes him feel important and useful. He would be both disappointed and insulted if you didn't let him contribute what he can."

Sebastian turned in her arms to draw her close to his chest. "I know." He rested his chin on the top of her head. "But I have a bad feeling about this."

CHAPTER 41

Tom didn't like Smithfield. It wasn't just the inescapable smell of spilled blood and raw meat and hides that got to him. It was as if an invisible but oppressive pall of death had sucked away the very air here, stealing his breath and pressing heavy on his chest.

He'd spent a frustrating day not really knowing what he was looking for and not finding anything. It was with relief that he watched the shadows lengthen with the coming of evening, and turned toward home.

He was passing the narrow alley that curved around to the back of the Norfolk Arms when he glanced sideways and saw a cart drawn up at the slanted double doors of the inn's cellars. Three men worked in silence, unloading the cart. There was none of the bantering one might have expected, the man on the cart simply handing small kegs one at a time to those laboring up and down the cellar steps. Another man, of slim build in a gentleman's greatcoat, stood nearby, his back to the mouth of the alley.

Ducking behind a nearby pile of crates, Tom watched them for a moment. At first he thought it was just a delivery of French wine smuggled in from somewhere over on the coast. Except that these barrels didn't look like wine kegs. They looked more like powder kegs.

They were a common enough sight in London these days. After some twenty years of nearly continuous warfare, there was hardly a child in England who hadn't grown up with the sight of soldiers marching in the roads, of wagon after wagon piled high with kegs of powder and boxes of muskets heading for the wharves where they'd be loaded onto ships bound for the Peninsula and the West Indies, India, and the South Seas.

Only, this powder wasn't heading toward the coast. It was disappearing into the cellar of the inn Lady Anglessey was thought to have visited the very day she died. And that was something Tom — after several moments of quiet argument with himself — decided he couldn't ignore.

He didn't need the echoing memory of Lord Devlin's warnings to tell him these men were dangerous. Tom had spent enough time on the streets — at first with Huey, then alone — to know danger when he saw it. Sometimes he imagined Huey was still with him, a kind of guardian angel watching out for him, warning him of danger. He thought he could feel Huey at his shoulder, now, telling him not to go into that alley.

"I gotta do it, Huey," Tom whispered. "You know I gotta."

He crept closer, his back pressed against the rough brick of the wall beside him, the dank, stale air of the alley thick in his nostrils. Another man had come out of the inn, a big, bald-headed man with African features whom Tom recognized as the innkeeper himself, Caleb Carter.

Carter and the man in the greatcoat were talking. Lowering his body until he was bent almost double, his footfalls soft in the damp earth of the alleyway, Tom ventured even closer.

"There was supposed to be two wagons," said the innkeeper, his bald head shining in the light thrown by the lamp behind him. "What happened?"

Not even daring to breathe, Tom crouched behind a pile of warped old boards and broken window frames.

"This is it. They say it'll be enough."

The innkeeper turned his head sideways and spat. "If there's resistance —"

"There won't be," said the man in the greatcoat, stepping into the rectangular shaft of light thrown by the inn's open doorway.

Tom could see him now. He was a small man, slightly built, with longish, pale yellow hair and a thin face. His clothes were definitely those of a gentleman, and Tom wondered what he was doing, supervising the unloading of a cart like some common workman.

"This is just a precaution," said the blond man. "It'll be 1688 all over again."

Carter grunted. "From what I hear, they mighta called that the Bloodless Revolution, but you know it really wasn't. Not by a long shot."

From someplace out in the street came a sudden popping explosion followed by children's laughter, as if someone had set off a firecracker. It was so unexpected, and Tom's nerves so raw, that he startled, his foot involuntarily shifting sideways to crunch on a piece of broken glass.

The blond gentleman swung around, one hand flying to his greatcoat pocket. "What was that?"

The innkeeper took a step forward. Tom

imagined he could hear Huey screaming, *Run, Tom!* But Tom didn't need to be told. Pushing off from the wall, he ran.

He took off for the eddy of noise and movement that was Giltspur Street, his feet slipping and sliding in the slimy mud of the alleyway. Bursting out the mouth of the passage, he nearly collided with a dogcart. He heard the blond man's voice behind him, raised in anger. "Stop him! Stop, thief!"

Oh, Jesus, thought Tom, his heart beating so hard in his chest it hurt. *Oh, Jesus, no.* He darted down a narrow street, heard a whistle blowing shrill and insistent behind him. His breath soughing in his throat, Tom leapt over the smoldering barrow in his path and kept running.

It was nearly dark now. He could see the looming, shadowy stalls of the marketplace up ahead. If he could make it to the open ground, lose himself amongst the deserted stalls, maybe hide beneath one . . .

The whistle blew again. He threw a quick glance over his shoulder and ran straight into the outstretched arms of a market beadle who stepped from behind the nearest stall.

The beadle's big, strong hands closed over Tom's shoulders, holding him fast. "Gotcha, lad."

Tom reared back, his blood pounding in his ears, his breath coming hard and fast. The beadle's face was broad and fleshy, his nose bulbous. In the last light of the dying day, the brass buttons on his coat gleamed like gold.

"Whadjah do then, lad? Hmmm?"

"Nothing," said Tom with a gasp. "I didn't do nothing."

The blond man crossed the open ground, his greatcoat flaring with each step. "The little bugger stole my friend's watch."

Tom squirmed in the beadle's grasp. "I didn't!" He was so scared, his legs were trembling. It was only by concentrating very, very hard that he kept from wetting himself.

"No?" said the blond man, reaching out. "Then what's this?"

It was an old trick. Tom saw the gold watch hidden in the man's palm and tried to flinch away, but the market beadle held him firm. Held him there, while the gentleman slipped his hand into Tom's pocket and seemingly drew the watch out by its chain.

"See. Here it is."

Tom lunged against the beadle's hard grip. "*He palmed it.* You saw it, didn't you? Didn't you?"

"There, there, lad," said the beadle.

"You've been caught red-handed. Best you can do now is take the consequences like a true Englishman."

"I tell you, I didn't steal anybody's bloody watch. I'm Viscount Devlin's tiger and these men —"

The beadle roared with laughter. "Ho. Of course you are. And I'm Henry the Eighth." He looked over at the blond man. "You'll be laying charges?"

The blond man had a queer look on his face, sort of thoughtful and calculating. Tom suddenly regretted having mentioned Lord Devlin's name in his presence.

"My friend will," said the blond man, giving Tom a cold, hard smile. "We aim to see the little bugger hanged."

CHAPTER 42

Sebastian awakened early the next morning to the alarming intelligence that his tiger had not yet returned.

"Send Giles to have the carriage brought around immediately," Sebastian told his valet.

"The carriage, my lord? For Smithfield?"

"That's right." This time, Sebastian decided, there would be no subterfuge. He intended to use the full weight of his wealth and position, stopping at nothing to find out what had happened to the boy.

Sedlow stared straight ahead, his countenance wooden. "And will you be wearing one of your Rosemary Lane coats this morning, my lord?"

Sebastian paused in the act of tying his cravat and glanced over at his valet. "I think not."

Sedlow sniffed, his normally placid features drawn. "Yes, my lord. It's just that . . .

if you were by any chance expecting events of a nature such as you have already encountered twice this week, I wouldn't want to think that you were exposing your wardrobe to destruction merely out of consideration for my sensibilities."

"Rest assured, my consideration of your sensibilities was in no way responsible for the destruction of my coat and waistcoat in Covent Garden the other night."

"And your doeskin breeches," added Sedlow. "I fear they are beyond repair."

"Do what you can, Sedlow," said Sebastian, turning at his majordomo's knock. "Yes? Has he returned?"

"I fear not, my lord. But there is a person here to see you." Morey's inflection of the word *person* precisely conveyed his opinion of the visitor. "She says she was Lady Anglessey's abigail."

Sebastian swore softly to himself. He was half tempted to have Morey tell the woman his lordship had already gone out. Except that whatever had brought Tess Bishop here to see him had to be important. And it would take time to have the horses put to. He shrugged into his coat. "Show her into the morning room and tell her I'll be down in a moment. Oh and, Morey," he added as the man turned to leave, "have some tea and biscuits sent in to her."

Morey kept his face wooden. "Yes, my lord."

Sebastian found Tess Bishop sitting straight-backed in one of the morning room's silk-covered chairs, her hands in her lap, the tea service and plate of biscuits on the table beside her untouched. At the sight of Sebastian, she surged to her feet.

"No, please sit," he said, going to the tea service. "How did you know who I was?"

Sinking back into her seat, she watched him pour a small portion of milk into a cup, then add the tea. "I saw you Monday, when you come to visit Lord Anglessey." She gave a small sniff. "I never thought you was no Bow Street Runner."

Caught in the middle of pouring the tea, Sebastian looked up quickly. Something of his reaction to this pronouncement must have shown on his face, because she hastened to add, "Don't get me wrong. You done the accent and the manner real good. Only, you was too nice."

Sebastian laughed and set aside the teapot. "Sugar?" he asked, holding out the tea.

"Oh, no, thank you, my lord," she said, unexpectedly flustered.

"Take it."

"Yes, my lord." Taking the tea, she gripped

the cup and saucer so tightly Sebastian wondered the fine china didn't crack. She made no move to drink it.

Pouring himself a cup, he asked almost casually, "Why have you come to me now?"

She took a deep breath and said in a rush, "There's some things I didn't tell you. Some things I've decided you ought to know."

"Such as?"

"Last Wednesday — when her ladyship didn't come home — I didn't know what to do. I kept going to her room, checking to see if she'd somehow slipped in unseen. In the end, I fell asleep there."

"In her room?"

"Yes. On the couch. It was hours later when I awoke — two, maybe three in the morning. The candle had burned out so that at first I was confused, not quite knowing where I was. Then I remembered, and I realized that what roused me was someone trying to get in the window. Her ladyship's room overlooks the back garden, you see, and there's a old oak with a sturdy limb what has grown quite close."

Sebastian went to stand with his back to the empty hearth, his cup in his hand. "What did you do?"

"I screamed. William — he's one of the footmen — he heard and came, and whoever it was ran away. I thought at the time it was just housebreakers. Then the next day we received notice of what'd happened to her ladyship, and all thought of the previous night's prowler went out of my head."

She paused in a way that told him there was more to this story. "And?" he prodded.

Tess Bishop brought the tea to her lips and took a small sip. "I slept in my own bed that night, of course. But when I went into her ladyship's room the next morning to open the windows and air things out, I found the latch on one of the windows broken."

Sebastian frowned thoughtfully. "That would have been Friday morning?"

"Yes."

"What was taken?"

"Well, you see, that was the strangest thing. Nothing was taken. At least, not so's I could tell. At first glance, you wouldn't have thought anyone had been in the room at all. But I soon realized things weren't quite right. It was as if someone had gone through everything, then tried to put it back exactly the way it was before."

"You mean, as if they were searching for something?"

"Yes."

Sebastian stared down at the cup in his

hands. He had never sought Anglessey's permission to search his wife's room, an oversight Sebastian now regretted — and intended to rectify.

He looked up to find Tess Bishop watching him. "Did you tell the Marquis?" he asked her.

She shook her head. "He's not well. After what'd just happened to her ladyship, I was afraid something like that might overset him completely. I asked William to fix the lock and made out it must have been broken by the intruder I scared away on Wednesday night."

"You're quite certain it wasn't?"

"Oh yes. I checked the locks very carefully."

Sebastian went to stand at the long window overlooking the street below. The morning had dawned clear and still, promising another hot day.

He had no reason to doubt the abigail's story. Yet if it were true, it suggested that whoever killed the young marchioness had believed he had cause to fear something in her rooms. Something that might have incriminated him.

"There's something else," said the abigail, her voice a frightened whisper.

Sebastian looked around. "What's that?"

Tess Bishop's tongue darted nervously across her lower lip. "You asked if I knew where her ladyship had gone that afternoon. The afternoon she was killed."

"You mean to say you do know?"

"Not exactly, my lord. But I know who she went to see." She hesitated, then swallowed hard. "It was a gentleman."

"Do you know his name?"

Her thin chest jerked with her suddenly labored breathing. "I know what you're thinking, but you're wrong. Her ladyship would never have been untrue to the Marquis. Only . . . his lordship, he was that desperate for an heir. And when it become obvious he couldn't have one . . ." Her voice trailed away in embarrassment.

"I know about their arrangement," said Sebastian. "Do you mean to say she discussed it with you?"

The abigail shook her head. "But she was so upset when his lordship first suggested it, I couldn't help but overhear things."

"Do you know what happened to change her mind?"

A faint tinge of color touched the abigail's pale cheeks. "There was this young gentleman come to town. A gentleman she'd known before, from when she was a girl in Wales."

"What was his name?" Sebastian asked again, knowing already what the answer would be.

Tess Bishop's hands shook so badly her teacup rattled against the saucer and she set it aside. "It couldn't have been him what killed her," she said, hunching forward, her hands clenched together, her head bowed. "It couldn't."

Sebastian looked down at her bowed head, at the bones of her neck showing prominently against the pale flesh. "When her ladyship didn't come home that Wednesday night, did you think she might have run away with this man?"

"No! Of course not." The abigail's head came up, her gray eyes flashing with indignation. "Her ladyship would never have done such a thing to the Marquis."

But then Sebastian saw her eyes slide away, and he knew that at some point in those long, anxious hours as the abigail waited for a mistress who would never return, the thought *had* occurred to her, however briefly.

"You don't understand," she said, leaning forward. "No one understands. They look at a beautiful young woman married to an old man and they see a marriage of convenience." She pushed her thin, colorless hair

330

off her forehead in a distracted gesture. "Oh, it began that way, to be sure. But they were well suited to one another — truly they were. They could spend hours together, just talking and laughing. You don't see many couples like that amongst the nobs."

She hadn't used the word *love,* but it hung there unacknowledged in the air between them.

"Yet even after she conceived the child, she continued to see her young gentleman," said Sebastian softly.

Tess Bishop bit her lip and looked away.

"Is it possible she tried to break off with the young man?" Sebastian suggested. It would hardly be the first time a passionate, rejected young lover had killed the object of his affection.

The abigail shook her head. "No. But they did quarrel."

"When was this?"

"The Saturday before she died."

"Do you know what the quarrel was about?"

"No. But it was . . . it was as if she'd found out something about him. Something that . . ." She hesitated, searching for the right word.

"Something that disappointed her?"

Tess Bishop shook her head. "It was worse

than that. She and the Marquis, they were good friends. But that young gentleman, he was like a god to her."

Sebastian turned to stare out the window. Only, he wasn't seeing the sun-warmed bricks of the houses across the street, or the baker's mule trotting past with a slow *clip-clop* below. He was remembering a time when he had loved like that. When he had known the bitter, soul-destroying shock of disillusionment.

For Sebastian, the disillusionment had been false, a carefully crafted charade played by a woman who loved him enough to want to drive him away from her for his own good — although he hadn't known that at the time.

He was like a god to her. What happens when your god dies? Sebastian wondered. When someone is your sun and moon and stars, and then you discover something, something that reveals a hitherto unknown weakness so fundamental, so shattering that it destroys not only your trust in the other person, but your respect, too.

Some people never recover from that kind of disillusionment. Sebastian had taken up a commission and gone off to war. What would Guinevere Anglessey have done?

Sebastian glanced over to where Tess

Bishop sat watching him with a pale, almost frightened face. "His name," Sebastian asked again, pressing her. He needed to have her say it, needed to have every suspicion confirmed. "What was his name?"

For a moment he thought she meant to keep the man's identity to herself in some final act of loyalty to the mistress who had once loved him. Then she hung her head and said in a torn whisper, "Varden. It was the Chevalier de Varden."

CHAPTER 43

The screams were starting to get to him. The screams and the never-ending *drip, drip, drip* of water.

Tom drew his knees up against his chest and hugged them close, his teeth gritted against the shivers that ripped through his body. Outside, the sun might shine warm and golden from a clear June sky, but here within the dank, filth-encrusted walls of Newgate, all was darkness and damp and the bone-chilling cold of perpetual winter.

"You there. Boy."

The seductive whisper was close. Tom turned his face away and pretended not to hear.

"The offer's still open. Tonight. Five shillings."

The man had never exactly said what he wanted Tom to do for those five shillings, but Tom was no flat. He knew. His empty stomach heaved.

He had no blanket, not even a thin pallet to absorb some of the cold rising up from the stone floor. Here in Newgate, such luxuries as food and bedding had to be purchased. If it weren't for the haphazard charity of benevolent societies and various philanthropically minded individuals, the poorer prisoners would starve. Many did.

Pushing up from the vermin-ridden straw, Tom stood and walked away from the crooning temptation of that voice. The room was no more than twelve by fourteen feet, and crowded with some fifteen to twenty men and boys. One of the boys couldn't have been more than six. He lay curled on his side in a corner, his fair hair matted and dirty, his grimy face streaked with tears. Every once in a while he'd start crying for his mother until one of the men would kick him and tell him to be still.

Tom went to press his face against the bars. For a moment, he squeezed his eyes shut and felt himself sway on his feet.

He hadn't dared close his eyes through all the long, dark hours of the night. Not that he could have slept, anyway, what with the fear and the rustling of the rats and the cold that seemed to sink all the way to his bones. And then there were the screams. The screams of the despairing, the mad, the sick and dying, mingled with the plaintive cries of women being taken by force.

The turnkey rented them out by the hour, one of the other boys had told Tom. Some of the women were probably willing enough — they'd learned long ago to sell their bodies to survive. But even when they weren't willing, they were given no choice.

He'd seen them dragging one girl across the yard. She couldn't have been more than twelve or thirteen, her flailing arms showing pale and thin in the sputtering light of a torch, her dark eyes wild in a small, tight face.

"Psst. Boy . . ."

Tom kept walking.

He'd tried to get the beadle who'd hauled him here to send word of what had happened to Viscount Devlin, but the big man had only laughed at him and called him Captain Bounce. Then the gaoler had emptied Tom's pockets so he couldn't even pay someone to take a message to Brook Street.

He paused again beside the bars looking out onto the yard. He kept trying to imagine what his lordship would think when Tom never showed up. Would he assume Tom had simply run off? He wouldn't really think that, would he?

Surely he would know something had happened to Tom. He'd go looking for him. But he would never think to look here. At least not at first. Tom had heard some of the other prisoners talking. They said there was a session scheduled for tomorrow. A boy could be condemned one day and hanged the next. It didn't happen all that often. Mostly the sentences were commuted to transportation. But it did happen. Tom knew.

He felt the walls begin to close in on him, pressing close and heavy. He sucked in a deep breath and the smells of the place overwhelmed him, the stench of excrement and sweat, sickness, and fear. Fear of gaol fever, fear of the whip and the hulls on the Thames. Fear of the hangman's noose and the surgeon's knife.

"Help me, Huey," Tom said softly, sinking to his knees. It was a kind of a prayer, he supposed, although he wasn't sure Huey was any place he could hear, let alone help. Did all thieves go to hell, even if they were only thirteen years old? "How did you stand it? Oh, God, Huey. I'm so sorry."

And he pressed his face against his knees and wept.

CHAPTER 44

The Physic Garden lay just north of the Thames at Chelsea. It was an old apothecary garden, said to date back to the seventeenth century, if not before. Kat herself had never been there, but she could understand how its gently curving walks and nearly deserted order beds would make an ideal meeting place, where spymaster and spy could come together and linger without arousing suspicion.

Once, she might have looked forward to this rendezvous with a certain flush of anticipation. She'd enjoyed it, that tingling sense of exhilaration that comes from living always on the jagged edge of danger. Once, she'd had nothing to lose but her life. That was no longer true.

She drove herself to the gardens in her phaeton and pair, with her groom, George, sitting up beside her. "It's hot today," she told him as she reined in at the West Gate.

"Do what you can to keep them cool."

Holding a sapphire blue silk parasol aloft to shade her complexion from the sun, she entered through the West Gate and turned toward the pond rock garden. It was cooler here. A faint breeze rustled the leaves of the lime trees overhead, bringing her a medley of sweet scents, of sunbaked rosemary and exotic jasmine and freshly scythed grass.

She wandered for a time between neat beds of roses. At one point she spotted an aged gentleman, his back hunched, his weathered skin darkened by years beneath a tropical sun. But he made no move to approach her, and in the end she lost sight of him admidst a planting of distant shrubs.

She walked on, her sandaled toes kicking out the skirts of her gown with each step. She wondered who he would be, this new spymaster. Would he be a French émigré, like Pierrepont? Or perhaps an Englishman, someone who'd been unwise — or unlucky — enough to enable the French to gain an indestructible hold over him. Or maybe someone who'd become disaffected from his own country, who nourished a determined admiration for the French and what they were doing across the Channel.

Kat herself owed no allegiance to France. As much as the ideology of the Revolution appealed to her, its savagery and excesses repelled her. And in the end the French had betrayed their own ideology, surrendering all to a military dictator who seduced them with visions of world supremacy.

But she accepted that old maxim "My enemy's enemy is my friend." Kat's enemy was England. It always had been, even before that misty morning in Dublin, when her world had been shattered by the tramp of soldiers' boots and a woman's screams and the shadows cast by two bodies swaying in the breeze.

She became aware of another visitor to the gardens, a tall man clad in fawn-colored doeskin breeches and a well-tailored olive coat, his figure lean but powerful. She recognized him, of course. His name was Aiden O'Connell, and he was the younger son of Lord Rathkeale of Tyrawley.

She felt herself stiffen. When the rest of the Irish were being hounded from their lands, the Tyrawley O'Connells had embraced both the conquering English and their religion. As a result, the O'Connells had not only kept their estates, but prospered.

Pausing beside the pond's edge, she waited for him to walk up to her. He was a handsome man, with sparkling green eyes and two dimples that appeared often in his lean, tanned cheeks.

"Top o' the morning to you," he said cheerfully, dimples deepening. "Lovely gardens, don't you think?"

She kept her gaze on the sun-spangled expanse of water before her. She found it difficult to believe that such a man could be Napoléon's new spymaster in London, and she certainly had no desire to encourage his attentions if he were here simply by chance.

"Reminds me of some gardens I saw in Palestine once," he said when she didn't answer, "not far from Jerusalem. The cedars and sycamores were shining like silver and gold in the sunlight, so grand you'd swear they scraped the sky."

She swung slowly to face him. He was older than he looked, she realized, probably more like thirty than twenty-five. And there was a sharp gleam of intelligence to his gaze that the beguiling effect of those dimples tended to disguise.

"I came here to meet you as a courtesy," she said, although that wasn't strictly true. She was here because she knew that if she hadn't shown, he would simply have contacted her again. "I don't want to do this. Not anymore."

Aiden O'Connell's smile widened, crinkling the skin beside his eyes. "It's because of Lord Devlin, is it? I did wonder."

She held his gaze but said nothing, and after a moment he looked away, across the smooth surface of the pond to where a duck waddled through the reeds, a row of ten ducklings strung out behind her. "Does he know about your affection for the French?"

"I have no affection for the French. It's Ireland I work for."

"I doubt he'd see the difference."

Kat knew a spurt of anger fanned by fear. "Is that an observation or a threat?"

He threw her an amused glance. "An observation only, to be sure."

"Because if it's a threat, I'd like to remind you and your masters that I can do as much damage to them as they can to me. And that damage would not be contained by my death."

He was no longer smiling. "The French are not my masters," he said. "And I don't think there is any danger of your premature death."

She let the latter part of that statement go; her point had been made. It remained to be seen whether or not O'Connell — and the French — would take her threat seriously enough to leave her alone in the future. And it came to her in a rush of bitter realization that this was one danger that would always haunt her. One fear from which she'd never truly be free.

She studied the pleasant face of the man beside her. "Why do you do this?" she asked suddenly.

"For the same reason you do. Or should I say, for the same reason you did."

"For *Ireland?*"

He raised one eyebrow. "You find that so difficult to believe?"

"From what I know of the O'Connells, yes."

"We O'Connells, we've always believed that a man who beats his head against a stone wall is a fool."

"Is that how you'd characterize the brave men and women who've fought and died for Ireland over the years? As just so many fools beating their heads against stone walls?"

His dimples peeped. "That's right. The time for Ireland's independence will come, but it won't come until the English have been weakened. And it won't be the Irish who'll be weakening them. It'll be someone else. Someone like the French. Or maybe the Prussians."

"The Prussians and the English have been allies."

"They're not anymore."

They stood in silence for a moment, her gaze, like his, on the mother duck shepherding her brood one by one into the water. The air filled with a happy chorus of *quackquack*s and the soft slap of ever-widening ripples moving out over the surface of the pond.

"There's a lot of disaffection in the streets," O'Connell said after a moment. "Rumors. Whispers. People are ready for a change."

"What kind of change?" she asked, her breath suddenly coming so hard and fast she had to call on all her abilities as an actress to make her voice sound casual, disinterested.

He kept his gaze on the mother duck and her brood. "A different dynasty, perhaps."

"How would that help Ireland?"

"The Stuarts were always more sympathetic to the Catholics."

She swung her head to look directly at him. "There are no Stuarts anymore. Not really. And the English would never accept a Catholic king. Remember what happened to James the Second?"

"James the Second never tried to restore Catholicism to England. All he wanted was tolerance and an end to the debilitating restrictions put on Catholics."

"Yet the people still wouldn't accept him. And if they wouldn't accept James the Second a hundred and twenty years ago, what makes you think they'll accept someone like him now?"

"Because the House of Hanover is tainted by madness and everyone knows it. Because men are out of work by the thousands, and women and children are starving in the streets. Because we've been at war for so long it's all most people can remember. If a new King promised to bring peace and an end to high taxes and the press gangs, I think a lot of people would welcome him."

Kat's eyes narrowed. "Who is pushing this?"

He was regarding her with a studied expression that made her realize she'd said too much, shown too much interest. "That's the funny thing about conspiracies," he said with a smile. "Different men can be attracted to the same conspiracy for altogether different reasons. Reasons that sometimes aren't even compatible. Why does it matter so much who's behind it, as long as it's good for Ireland?"

"You suggest a restoration of the Stuarts might lead to peace with France," she said. The sun slipped out from behind the chestnut trees on the far side of the pond, striking her in the eyes. She tilted her parasol until it once again shaded her face. "But I thought England at war with France was good for Ireland. You said that's what we need, to weaken the English. That it's the only way the Irish will ever win their freedom."

He laughed. "You are quick, aren't you?" He leaned toward her, suddenly more serious than she'd seen him. "But if the English at war with France is good for Ireland, then how much better do you think a new English civil war would be?"

She searched his face, but he was as good at hiding what he really thought as she. "Is that what these people want? Civil war?"

"Hardly. But I suspect it's what they're going to get."

By midmorning, Tom was so hungry his head was spinning. He'd known hunger in the past, in the dark days before fate brought Viscount Devlin into his world. But these last few months he'd grown accustomed to a full belly and a warm bed. He'd even begun to feel safe again, the way he'd felt in the golden, half-forgotten years before his da took sick and his mother —

But Tom slammed his mind shut on that

thought before tears and the clawing blackness of terror could take him again.

He was sitting against the back wall, his forehead resting on his drawn-up knees, when he heard a commotion in the yard, men banging tin cups against iron bars and laughing women calling out soft, obscene suggestions.

The men and boys in his cell crowded up to the bars. Tom pushed to his feet and wiggled his way forward to take a look. "What is it?" he asked.

"Some magistrate," said one of the other boys, a big, half-grown lad from Cheapside who'd been caught pinching pewter tankards from a public house and would probably hang for it. "They say 'e's here on account of the nob's son what got hisself butchered in St. James's Park t'other night."

Tom could see him now, a funny little man with bowed legs and wire-framed glasses he wore pushed down to the tip of his nose. Despite the heat of the day he wore a thick greatcoat, and held a pomander to his nose.

Tom surged forward. *"Sir 'Enry,"* he called, pressing his face against the bars. "Oye, Sir 'Enry. It's me, Tom. *Sir 'Enry —"*

A rough hand thumped Tom in the shoulder, giving him a shove that sent him sprawling back into the filthy straw. "You there," spat the gaoler. "You dirty little filcher, you shut yer mouth. You 'ear?"

Tom scrambled to his feet and threw himself forward again, but by then it was too late. The yard was empty and the little magistrate had gone.

CHAPTER 45

Sebastian spent the morning in Smithfield, looking for Tom.

He made no attempt to disguise who he was. He even brought along a couple of strapping footmen to preclude any possibility of a repeat of what had happened on his last visit to the area. But Tom had obviously followed instructions and taken care to blend into his surroundings. Sebastian found an old woman selling buttons who said she'd seen a boy about his age running through the streets just before sunset, running like the hounds of hell were after him. But she didn't know what had happened to the lad, or even who'd been chasing him.

Sebastian looked for the maimed Scottish soldier who'd been reduced to begging outside the Norfolk Arms, but no one could remember having seen the man for days. Standing in the shade cast by a ribbon shop's awning, Sebastian studied the inn's ancient brick facade, and knew a deep and powerful disquiet.

He'd come back at dusk, Sebastian decided, when the creatures of the night were aprowl. "Andrew, James," he said curtly. The two footmen snapped to attention as he pushed away from the building. "I want you to check every watchhouse in the area, every watchman, every beadle. Do you understand? Someone must have seen him."

"Aye, my lord."

Leaping up into the carriage, Sebastian slammed his own door and sent the coachman flying to Queen Square, only to learn there that Sir Henry Lovejoy was out pursuing leads on his gruesome park murder. Increasingly frustrated, his temper fraying, Sebastian thought about Tess Bishop's early morning visit and knew how he would spend the remaining hours until dusk.

He tracked the Chevalier de Varden to Angelo's Fencing Academy in Bond Street, where Varden was fencing with the master himself. Sebastian stood for a time, watching them. The Chevalier was a good swordsman, with a keen eye and flexible wrists and a quick, light step. Barefoot, stripped down to his shirtsleeves and buckskin breeches, he moved effortlessly across the hardwood floor, foil flashing, his light brown hair tumbling in his eyes.

Sebastian had never heard anything to the man's discredit. The ladies liked him for his charming manner and graceful step on the dance floor, while the men liked him for his ready laugh and easy generosity and courage on the hunting field. True, the Chevalier was known to have a quick temper. But there was nothing to suggest he was the kind of man who could subject the woman he loved to a slow and painful death by poison.

As Sebastian watched, the Chevalier feigned to the left, then slipped past the master's guard to land a hit to his shoulder. The master laughed and the match ended. They stood talking a few moments with the easy camaraderie of two men in love with the same sport. Then Varden headed for the changing room.

Sebastian caught him just inside the door.

Locking onto Varden's right wrist, Sebastian twisted the man's arm in a way that shoved his hand up into the middle of his back and spun him around, throwing Varden off balance. Sebastian slammed him face-first against the wall, Sebastian's left arm coming across the front of Varden's throat to hold him from behind. "You bloody bastard," Sebastian whispered in his ear.

The Chevalier tried to turn his head, his eyes rolling sideways. "*Devlin.* What the devil?"

Sebastian tightened the pressure on the man's throat. "You lied to me," he said, enunciating each word slowly and carefully. "I know about the arrangement the Marquis of Anglessey had with his wife, and I know about your part in it. So don't even think about trying to deny it."

"Of course I lied to you," Varden said, his voice strained. "What gentleman wouldn't?"

Sebastian hesitated, then stepped back and let the man go.

The Chevalier swung around, his dark eyes flashing, his left hand rubbing his other arm. "Touch me again and I'll kill you."

He went to pour water in one of the basins on the washstand and splashed his face with quick, angry motions. "Who told you?" he said after a moment. "Anglessey? I wouldn't have expected that."

"He wants me to find his wife's killer."

Varden looked around. "Are you suggesting I don't?"

Their gazes caught and clashed. Sebastian said, "Where did you and the Marchioness used to meet?"

Varden hesitated, then reached for a towel. "Different inns. Usually not the same place twice. Why?"

"Did you ever meet in Smithfield?"

"Smithfield?" There was surprise in the man's face, but something else, too. Something that looked almost like fear. "Good God, no. Why do you ask?"

"Because Guinevere Anglessey went there the afternoon she was killed. You wouldn't happen to know why, would you?"

His brows drew together. "Where in Smithfield?"

Sebastian simply shook his head. "How did you spend last Wednesday?"

The implications of the questions were obvious. Varden's nostrils flared. "I slept late. I'd been out most of the night before with friends. I didn't even leave the house until around five, maybe six." He paused in the act of pulling on his boots to throw Sebastian a malevolent glare. "You can check with the servants, if you don't believe me."

Sebastian watched him shrug into his coat. "I want to know about Wales."

Varden adjusted the lapels of his coat. Two men walked into the room, the older one slapping the younger man on the shoulder as he said, "Well done, Charles. Well done, indeed."

"Not here," said Varden.

Sebastian nodded. "Let's go for a walk."

CHAPTER 46

"I can't remember a time in my life when I didn't love Guinevere," Varden said as they strolled along the Serpentine. A fine haze was beginning to bleach the color from the sky, turning it white. The air had taken on a sultry quality, the scent of grass hanging heavy in the still air. "She was . . . she was like no one else I've ever known. Proud and courageous and everything that's noble, and yet so tender, so giving."

There was something about the way the flat light fell on the Chevalier's face that reminded Sebastian of just how young Varden still was. He was only twenty-two, his handsome face pale and hollow-eyed with grief. "Guin and I grew up together," he said. "I suppose Claire and Morgana were around some of the time, but I don't remember them. In my memory, it's always just Guin and me."

He stared out over the parkland, to where

two children played with their dog, the dog barking and the children running back and forth and laughing while an aproned nurse-maid called to them. A smile touched his lips, a wistful smile that was there and then gone. "I always knew she loved me. And I don't mean in the way a child might love a brother. From the very beginning there was more to it than that, for both of us. Even when we were too young to understand what it was."

He fell silent. Sebastian waited, and after a moment Varden continued. "We grew up thinking we would always be together. That she was meant for me and I was hers. Guin simply took it for granted we would marry someday."

"And you?"

"I was the same at first. But as I grew older I became aware of . . . the difficulties."

"Such as your lack of fortune?"

He huffed a small, bitter laugh. "That most of all. When Guinevere was seventeen, her father's sister invited her to spend the Season in London. She'd done the same for Morgana. At the time old Athelstone had grumbled, but in the end he'd scraped together the money needed for clothes and sent Morgana off. She succeeded better than anyone expected. Athelstone was convinced Guinevere would do even better." Varden paused. "The old bastard needed her to do better."

"Badly dipped, was he?"

Varden nodded. "Worse than Guinevere realized. She thought he'd leap at the opportunity to be spared the expense of a London season. But when she told him she had no need of a brilliant alliance because she planned to marry me, he laughed. And then, of course, he flew into a rage."

While they'd been talking, a breeze had come up, ruffling the long grass and singing through the high branches of the surrounding elms. In the distance, one of the children brought out a kite, a red confection of paper and bamboo that careened straight to earth each time the boy tried to run with it.

Varden's voice was hard. "Everything my father would have left me, everything that was in my family for generations, has been lost. All I have is a title and a noble pedigree and some impoverished royal relatives who are in nearly as bad straights as I am."

Sebastian watched the little boy pick up the kite and try again. There weren't many noblemen who'd welcome a penniless half-French émigré as a son-in-law.

"Guin tried to argue with him, but Athelstone was ruthless. He threatened to cut her off without a penny and cast her out of the house if she refused to go to London — or if she failed to do what she needed to do while she was there. He meant it, too."

"So she agreed?"

"Not at first. She ran out of the house." Varden swung his head away, his eyes narrowing as he, too, watched the kite. "I'll never forget that night. There was a violent storm blowing in from the sea. She came along the cliffs, the way she always had as a child. It's a wonder she wasn't killed." He sucked in a deep, shaky breath. "I'd been out riding and been caught in the storm. She found me in the stables."

Sebastian pictured Guinevere Anglessey as the young girl she must have been, her wet hair tumbling down her back, her eyes wild with desperation and fear. "What did you tell her?"

The Chevalier kept his face turned away, his throat working as he swallowed. "What could I say? I was eighteen years old. I couldn't support a wife. I couldn't even marry without permission."

"Your mother wouldn't have taken her in?"

The younger man smiled. "My mother was fond of Guinevere, particularly when she was a child. But she would never have agreed to such a marriage."

Sebastian thought about the proud, elegant woman he'd met. Lady Audley must have watched the maturing affection between the young Chevalier and his childhood friend with growing concern. Such a woman's plans for her dispossessed son would not include marriage to the daughter of some impoverished provincial earl. London was full of rich bankers and merchants more than willing to take on a penniless son-in-law, as long as the son-in-law came with a title and a noble lineage and royal connections.

"What did Lady Guinevere do when you told her?"

"She ran back out into the storm. I tried to go after her, but I couldn't find her anywhere. I was afraid she'd thrown herself from the cliffs." He paused, and it seemed to Sebastian, watching him, as if the skin had tightened across his features, making him look suddenly older. "She told me later she almost did. But then she decided she wasn't going to let her father destroy her. She made up her mind to go to her aunt in London and marry a rich old man — the older and richer the better. And then when he died, she'd be free of him."

"And free of her father."

"Yes. That was her plan, at any rate. The problem was, while there were plenty of rich old men to choose from, she found the thought of being married to any of them more than she could bear."

"Until she met Anglessey."

Varden's lips compressed into a thin line. "Yes. She said that at first he seemed much like all the others — old and gray and jowly, and carrying far too much weight around his middle. But as she came to know him, she discovered he had a good heart and a fine mind, and they became friends. I think in many ways he was like the father she never really felt she had."

Sebastian tilted back his head, his gaze on the red kite climbing now with sudden dips and eddies against the clouding sky. What was it Tess Bishop had said about the Marchioness of Anglessey and her lord? *They were well suited to one another. . . . They could spend hours together, just talking and laughing. You don't see many couples like that. . . .* He wondered if Guinevere had ever told the love of her life just how much affection she'd come to develop for her aged husband. Sebastian doubted it.

He turned to study the younger man's troubled face. "The night Lady Anglessey was killed, someone tried to break into her room. The abigail scared them away, but they came back again the next night, searching for something. You wouldn't happen to know what that was, would you?"

Varden stared off across the parklands, as if thinking. But there was something about the way he held his mouth that told Sebastian the man didn't need to think, that he knew right away what Tess Bishop's mysterious housebreaker had been seeking. He shook his head. "I can't imagine."

"No? I understand you and Lady Anglessey had a quarrel recently. A serious quarrel."

Varden's brows drew together in a quick frown. "Who told you that?"

"Does it matter?"

He stopped and swung to face Sebastian, the gravel crunching beneath the soles of his boots. "What do you think? That she tried to break things off with me, so I killed her? It wasn't like that at all."

Sebastian held himself very still. "So how was it?"

Varden hesitated a moment, then said in a rush, "She was going to leave Anglessey. That's why we quarreled. She wanted me to run away with her."

Sebastian stared into the younger man's

tense, anxious face, and didn't believe one word of it. "Why? Why would she even consider doing such a thing?"

"Because she was afraid of him. Oh, I know what you're thinking. He seems so mild mannered: the perfect eighteenth-century gentleman. It's what Guin thought at first. They were married several years before she saw what he's really like."

"How is he really?"

"Jealous. Possessive. It was his idea that she take a lover. But then when she did, he couldn't bear it. In the end, Guin was afraid he might kill her. Kill her and the baby both."

Sebastian shook his head. "Nothing is more important to Anglessey than cutting his nephew out of the inheritance. My God, the man was willing to encourage his wife's adultery in the hopes of conceiving an heir. Why would he turn around and harm her?"

"I don't know. But he did it before, didn't he?"

"What are you talking about?"

"That's how his first wife died. Didn't you know? She was with child, and he knocked her down the stairs. He killed her. Her and the child both."

Sebastian was crossing Bond Street, headed

toward the Marquis of Anglessey's house on Mount Street, when he heard a man's high-pitched, anxious voice calling his name.

"Lord Devlin. I say, Lord Devlin."

Sebastian turned his head to find Sir Henry Lovejoy hailing him from a battered old hackney. "If I might have a word with you, my lord?"

CHAPTER 47

London was different from the country. In the country, traveling judges sat only at the quarterly assizes — if then. In the farthest counties a man could languish in jail for three months to a year, waiting for a trial. In London, a man — or a boy — could be caught, tried, and hanged in less than a week.

Sebastian tried not to think about that as he and Lovejoy followed a porter through grimy prison passages lit by smoking rushes. The air in here was foul, reeking of excrement and urine and rot. Rotting straw, rotting teeth, rotting lives.

They were shown to a cold but relatively clean room, its stone floor bare, the small, high, barred window casting only a dim light on a grouping of plain wooden chairs and an old scarred table.

"What were you doing here?" Sebastian asked Lovejoy when he and the magistrate were left alone to wait.

"The watch picked up a couple of house-breakers near St. James's Park the night Sir Humphrey Carmichael's son was killed. I was hoping they might have seen something."

"And?"

Lovejoy's lips twisted. "Nothing."

Footsteps echoed down the passage, a man's heavy stride and the smaller footfalls of a boy. Sebastian swung toward the door.

Tom entered the room with dragging steps, his head bowed. His coat was muddy and torn, his cap gone, his face pale and drawn. It was as if all the boy's plucky determination and jaunty irreverence had been wiped out in one long, hellish night.

" 'Ere 'e is, gov'nor," said the gaoler grudgingly.

"Thank you." Sebastian's voice came out thick. "That will be all."

Tom's head snapped up, his mouth opening in a gasp. "My lord!"

Lovejoy put out a hand to stop the boy's impetuous forward rush. "There, there now, lad. Remember your place."

"Let him go," said Sebastian as the boy dodged the magistrate and threw himself against Sebastian's chest.

"I didn't do it! I swear I didn't prig that

364

bloke's watch." The boy's shoulders heaved, his entire body shuddering. "They made it up 'cause I seen the gunpowder and 'eard what they was talking about."

"It's all right," said Sebastian, one hand tightening on the boy's shoulder even as his gaze met Lovejoy's over Tom's head. *Gunpowder?* "I've come to take you home."

"They was going to hang me." Tom's voice broke. "Hang me just like they done Huey."

Sebastian looked down at the boy's tortured, tear-streaked face. "Who was Huey?"

"My brother. Huey was my brother."

Leaving the prison, Sebastian bundled Tom into the carriage and gave the coachman orders to take the boy to Paul Gibson.

"Gibson?" said the tiger, bounding up. "I don't need no surgeon. You're going back there, ain't you? To Smithfield? Well, I'm coming, too."

"You will do as you are told," said Sebastian in a voice that had quelled rebellious soldiers still bloody from battle.

The boy sank back and hung his head. "Aye, gov'nor."

Sebastian nodded to his coachman, then turned away to call a hackney.

"Whether you like it or not, I am coming with you," said Lovejoy, scrambling into the hackney behind Sebastian as he leaned forward to give the jarvey directions to Smithfield. "The law does not look kindly on those who make false accusations of theft."

Sebastian threw the magistrate a quizzical glance, but said nothing.

Lovejoy settled in one corner of the carriage, his teeth worrying his lower lip as he sat in a thoughtful silence. After a moment, he said, "All this talk of powder kegs and a repeat of the Glorious Revolution of 1688. You think that's what's afoot here? Revolution?"

Sebastian shook his head. Tom had told them in detail what he'd seen and heard beside the Norfolk Arms's cellars. It had been suggestive, but hardly damning. "More like a palace coup, I'd say, rather than a revolution. But God knows where it might lead. Change can be difficult to control once it's under way. The French Revolution was started by a few noblemen wanting to revive the old National Assembly, remember? They certainly got more than they bargained for."

The steadily thickening clouds had robbed the day of its light, making it seem later than it actually was. Sebastian stared out the window at brick houses streaked with soot, at gin shops spilling drunken laughter into the street. The sultry air smelled of boiling cabbage and horse manure and burning garbage. A boy of ten or twelve, a street sweeper from the looks of him, scrambled to get out of their way, his broom held tight in one fist, his eyes wide as he watched them rattle past. Behind him, a little girl of no more than eight, her clothes a jumble of torn rags, her face pale and bleak, stretched out one grimy hand in the beggar's universal plea for help.

The hackney swept on, the boy and girl lost in a ragged crowd.

Sebastian found himself thinking about two other children, one named Huey, the other Tom. And about their mother, a simple but devout widow, out of work and thrown onto the streets with two children to feed. For her as for untold thousands of women in such a situation, the choices were simple but stark: starvation, theft, or prostitution. Tom's mother had chosen theft and earned herself a one-way voyage to Botany Bay. Prostitution might have brought her disease and an early death, but it wasn't a capital crime. Stealing to feed your starving children was.

From what Tom had told him, Sebastian figured the boy had been nine years old when he and his brother stood on the docks and watched their mother being rowed out to a transport lying at anchor in the Thames. The older by three years, Huey had taken it upon himself to care for his younger brother the best he knew how — until they caught Huey for stealing, too. Huey wasn't as lucky as their mother. They'd hanged him.

Lovejoy's voice broke into Sebastian's thoughts. "We discovered the identity of the man you killed by the river."

Sebastian moved his head against the hackney's cracked leather upholstery. "I didn't kill him. He fell."

Lovejoy's lips twitched, which was about as close as the dour little magistrate ever came to a smile. "His name was Ahearn. Charles Ahearn. Ever hear of him?"

Sebastian shook his head. "What is known of him?"

"Nothing to his discredit. He served as tutor to Lord Cochran's sons until the youngest went off to Eton last fall."

"What's he been doing since then?"

Lovejoy withdrew a large handkerchief from his pocket and held it to his nose. "That we're not sure."

Sebastian had become aware of a heavy stench of raw smoke overlying the other smells of the district, the reeking tannery pits, and the fetid stink of the shambles.

Now, as they turned onto Giltspur Street, they could hear shouts and running feet and the roaring crackle of flames, the hackney struggling to wind its way through a thick crowd. From the distance came the steady *clang, clang, clang* of the fire bell.

"Something's on fire," said Lovejoy, craning his neck to look out the window.

Sebastian could see it now. Flames danced across an ancient pitched roof and shot from windows that yawned like gaping holes in a crumbling brick facade. Thick black smoke billowed up to mingle with the low gray clouds ahead.

"Bloody hell," swore Sebastian, throwing open the door to leap down even before the hackney had rolled to a halt. "It's the Norfolk Arms."

CHAPTER 48

The lane was a confusion of sound, of roaring flames and screaming women and smoke-blackened men, their sweat-slicked faces reflecting the orange glow of the fire as they lined up to form a chain, water sloshing from buckets quickly passed from hand to hand.

Sebastian pushed his way through the crowd, his gaze scanning the flame-licked facade of the old inn. Black ash swirled about him, drifting down like dirty snow. He could feel the heat of the fire against his face, feel it sucking the air from his lungs. As he watched, smoke curled from beneath the door of the little bow-windowed button shop that lay beside the inn. Then the front window exploded and the entire building burst into flames.

A great moan went up from the crowd around him. This was what they all feared, that the fire would spread. It was always a danger in any part of the city. But here, where houses built of dry old timbers leaned toward one another across narrow, twisted streets, one carelessly minded candle could consume an entire district in a night.

Sebastian shifted his attention to the crowd. He expected to find the big black innkeeper at the forefront of the men dashing bucket after bucket on the growing inferno. But Caleb Carter was nowhere to be seen.

Sebastian's gaze stopped on a tall girl with pale gray eyes and lanky blond hair who stood near the curb. For an instant, her gaze met his. He saw her eyes widen with recognition, her mouth going slack.

She whirled to run. Sebastian was on her, his hand closing hard on her upper arm, jerking her around to face him. "Where's Carter?" he demanded, hauling her up close to him.

She stared at him, her eyes huge, her nostrils flaring with fear.

He gripped her other arm and lifted her up until her feet barely touched the ground, her head snapping back and forth as he gave her a shake. "Where is he, damn you?"

"The cellars! He said somethin' about the cellars —"

Sebastian thrust her aside. She stumbled

but was off and running before he even turned away.

The fire had yet to work its way down the alley to the back of the inn, although he could hear its warning hiss, smell the acrid tinge of smoke in the sultry air. He found the thick wooden doors to the cellar closed and bolted from within. There would be another entrance, from inside the inn itself, but time was running out. Sebastian grabbed a nearby length of iron and brought it down hard. The wood cracked and splintered.

Someone shouted. "Hey! What you doin' there —"

Ignoring them, Sebastian kicked in the shattered doors.

The rush of air from the cellars was unexpectedly hot and dry, and already tinged with smoke. For a moment, Sebastian hesitated. If the gunpowder Tom had watched being unloaded was still stored here, Sebastian could be walking into an explosive death. But he didn't think the men he was dealing with were that careless.

Someone had left a lamp lit in the farthest reaches of the cellar. Sebastian could see the distant, steady glow as he plunged down the worn stone steps. The smoke was thicker here, seeping down through the ceiling boards overhead.

At the base of the steps he paused. The cellar itself was earthen floored. Tall racks of oak barrels and row after row of bottles loomed around him, the air heavy with the rich scents of French wine and brandy overlaid with the stench of burning wood. The sounds of the fire were muffled here, but coming closer. He could hear the distant roar and, from somewhere nearer, an ominous sizzling crackle.

From nearer still came a man's wet, hacking cough.

Sebastian turned toward the sound, making his way cautiously amidst the towering racks. He found the innkeeper facedown in the earth, his arms flung wide, his legs sprawled. As Sebastian watched, the big man drew his arms beneath him, his weight on his elbows as he struggled to push himself up. The back of his bald head was dark and shiny with blood that trickled down his neck, soaked the white collar of his shirt.

Groaning again, Carter pressed his palms flat to the earth and gave a mighty heave that sent him rolling onto his back. He lay there, his chest jerking with each breath. The blow to the back of his head had obviously stunned him. But what had laid him

373

low and brought a bloody foam to his mouth was the knife someone had thrust between his ribs.

The African's eyes rolled in his head, his chest heaving again as Sebastian went to kneel beside him.

"*You,*" said Carter, his face contorting with pain. "What the hell —"

He fell into a fit of coughing. Sebastian slipped his hands beneath the man's shoulders, raising his head to help him breathe. "Who did this to you?"

Carter's throat worked as he struggled to force the words out, bloody spittle foaming around his mouth. "F—"

Sebastian leaned closer.

The hot scent of urine filled the air as the black man's bladder let loose. He was almost gone, his chest jerking as he fought to suck in air. "Fu—" His upper lip curled, the light in his dark eyes flickering, fading. "Fuck you," he said with a rattling gasp. And the light in his eyes went out.

Sebastian eased his hands from beneath the big man's shoulders and laid the body on the hard-packed earth. The glow in the cellars had taken on an orange tinge. Looking up, Sebastian saw flames licking across the ceiling.

He pushed to his feet. The kegs of gunpowder might be gone, but the cellar's rich store of brandy would be nearly as inflammable. Sebastian leapt for the stairs, just as the door from the inn's yard exploded and tongues of fire shot down the steps toward him.

CHAPTER 49

A thick pall of smoke stung Sebastian's eyes, tore at his throat. Throwing one crooked arm in front of his face, he took the stairs to the alley two at a time.

He was halfway up the steps when he heard a tearing crack above him. He cast a quick glance over his shoulder in time to see a fiery beam crash onto the stone steps behind him, bringing half the ceiling down with it and unleashing a fierce blast of heat that slapped him in the back, knocking him to his knees.

Coughing badly now, he pushed on, practically crawling the last few steps. Wrapping one hand around the edge of the shattered cellar doors, he heaved himself up and staggered out into the cool of the night.

He stood with his hands braced on his knees, his head bowed as he sucked in great drafts of sweet, life-giving air. Behind him, the inn had become a fiery shell. Lungs aching, he swung around and watched as the walls collapsed inward, sending a torch of flames and fiery embers roaring up toward the cloud-filled sky.

He felt the evening breeze cool against his skin. The breeze, and something else that stung his eyelids and ran down his cheeks as he lifted his face to the sky.

Rain.

Sebastian was sitting on an ancient stone mounting block and wrapping a wet handkerchief around his singed hand when Lovejoy found him.

The little magistrate's hat was gone, his collar crooked, his normally spotless shirtfront smudged with a black stain that was turning gray now in the steady rain. "If your lad was right and there'd been gunpowder in that cellar, the explosion would have taken out half the street," said Lovejoy, removing his spectacles to wipe the lenses.

Sebastian used his teeth to tighten the knot in his handkerchief. "The gunpowder's gone. They probably moved it last night after Tom was taken up. They couldn't run the risk of someone deciding to investigate the boy's story."

Lovejoy's head fell back, the muscles of his face twitching as he stared up at the smoldering facade. "And the fire?"

"Was set to destroy whatever evidence they might have missed, I suppose." Sebastian stretched to his feet. "That and to cover up the murder of Caleb Carter."

Lovejoy shot him a quick look. "You mean the black innkeeper? He's dead?"

"I found him in the cellars. Someone had slipped a knife between his ribs."

"But . . . why?"

"Think about it. Last Wednesday, the Marchioness of Anglessey was seen walking into this inn. As far as we know, no one except her killer ever saw her alive again. A few days later, I show up asking questions about her. Then last night, my tiger watches a shipment of gunpowder being delivered and hears talk of a reversal of the Glorious Revolution of 1688. Something serious is afoot here. But the only link we had to it was Caleb Carter and this inn."

Sebastian paused to stare up at the smoking, crumbling walls of the building before him. "And now they're both gone."

Stopping at Paul Gibson's surgery at the foot of Tower Hill, Sebastian found Tom asleep in Gibson's back bedchamber.

"I thought it best," said Gibson, one cupped hand shielding the flare of his candlestick. "He was exhausted."

Sebastian stared down at the sleeping boy. "Is he all right?"

"He had a bad fright. But nothing worse."

Sebastian nodded. There was no need to elaborate. They both knew what could happen to the boys and girls — and men and women — unlucky enough to find themselves in one of His Majesty's prisons.

"He kept talking about someone named Huey," said Gibson, leading the way to the parlor.

Sebastian nodded. "His brother. I gather the boy was hanged."

Gibson sighed. "These are barbarous times in which we live." He went to pour two glasses of wine. "This conspiracy to depose the Hanovers . . . any idea who might be involved?"

"To have any chance of success it would need the allegiance of prominent men, both in the army and the government. But do they have that support?" Sebastian shrugged. "I don't know. I haven't seen any sign of it. But that doesn't mean it isn't there. The Norfolk Arms was surely only at the periphery."

"Could Anglessey be involved?"

"It's possible, I suppose. Although I'd be surprised." Sebastian took the wine from

Gibson's hand and went to sink into one of the tattered leather armchairs before the empty fireplace. "I haven't found anyone associated with Lady Anglessey's death who's at all in a position of power." He paused. "Except for Portland, of course. And he's such a rabid Tory, he hardly seems a likely candidate to be advocating revolution."

Gibson came to stand before the cold hearth. "Any idea yet how Lady Hendon's necklace fits into all of this?"

Sebastian glanced up into his friend's open, concerned face. Once, years ago in Italy, he and this man had been to hell and back together. Their friendship had nothing to do with rank or birth, but with a shared moral code and the deep, mutual respect of two men who had tested each other's mettle and found courage under fire and a level-headed response to danger.

But even the best of friendships have their limits. Not even to Kat had Sebastian been able to bring himself to say, *I don't want to believe it, but I'm becoming more and more convinced that my mother didn't drown on that long-ago summer day. Because if she had, this triskelion would have spent the last seventeen years buried in silt someplace at the bottom of the Channel. It wouldn't be play-*

ing a part now in what happened to Guine-vere Anglessey.

So Sebastian simply drained his wine and said, "No. It's still a mystery."

Reaching the house in Brook Street, Sebastian intended to go upstairs, face his valet's tears over another ruined coat, and change into evening attire. Instead he wandered into the library, poured himself a brandy, and stood staring down at the empty hearth.

There was a time for subtlety and cleverness, and then there was a time for brute force. Sending Tom to scout out the neighborhood of Giltspur Street had been a mistake, he decided. Not only had he placed the tiger in unconscionable danger, but he'd also missed the chance to go back to the Norfolk Arms himself and directly press Caleb Carter for the truth about the Marchioness's visit to the inn. Now it was too late.

He became aware of a bold hand beating an insistent tattoo at the front door.

"I'm not at home, Morey," Sebastian said as his majordomo moved to open the door.

"Yes, my lord."

Taking a sip of his brandy, Sebastian glanced out the window overlooking the front street. A smart carriage drawn by a pair of beautifully matched dapple grays stood drawn up before the steps. He didn't need to see the coronet on its panels to know its owner.

He could hear Morey's polite, soothing tones, blending with a woman's voice, louder and only too familiar.

"Don't be ridiculous," said his sister, Amanda. "I know perfectly well Devlin is at home. I saw him climb the steps myself just moments ago. Now, you can either announce me, or I shall simply go looking for him. The choice is yours."

Sebastian went to stand in the library's doorway, the brandy glass held lightly in his unbandaged hand as he studied the tall, slim woman in heavy mourning who stood in the marble tiled entry. "Leave off harassing the poor man. He's simply following orders."

Amanda turned her head to look at him. "As I am only too aware." Her eyes widened at the sight of him, her nostrils quivering at the stench of smoke and soot. "Merciful heavens. What have you been doing? Hiring yourself out as a chimney sweep?"

Sebastian laughed and stepped back to sketch her a flourishing bow. "Do come in, my lady."

She swept past him, jerking off her gloves

but making no attempt to remove her bonnet. "You realize, of course, that you have the entire Town talking about you. Again."

"Oh, surely not as bad as the last time."

She swung to face him, her blue eyes blazing. "Is it too much to ask that you have some consideration for your niece?" She waved one hand through the air in a dismissive gesture. "Oh, not for my sake. But for Hendon's. She is his granddaughter, after all."

Sebastian frowned. "Stephanie? What has she to do with anything?"

"She is seventeen. In less than a year she will be making her come out. What do you think will be her chances of contracting a respectable alliance if her uncle is known to make it a hobby of consorting with murderers?"

Sebastian went to pour himself another drink. "Sherry?" he asked.

Amanda shook her head.

"I'm not consorting with Lady Anglessey's murderer," said Sebastian. "I'm simply trying to discover who he is."

"Really, Sebastian. Like some common Bow Street Runner?"

"With rather more finesse than that, I like to think. And, of course, I'm not getting paid, so you needn't worry there's any hint of the stench of trade being attached to the practice."

"I should rather think not."

Sebastian gave her a hard smile. "Offends your delicate sensibilities, does it?"

"It would offend the sensibilities of anyone of breeding and culture."

"Really? Well, murder offends mine."

"You have no sensibilities." She turned away, one hand coming up to shade her eyes before she suddenly moved to face him again. "Why are you doing this?"

Sebastian took a slow swallow of brandy. "I thought I just explained that."

She shook her head. "No. Why you? Why *this* murder?"

Sebastian hesitated a moment, then said, "Do you remember the bluestone necklace Mother always used to wear? The one she said was given to her by some old crone in the mountains of Wales?"

"Yes. Why?"

"Did you know she was wearing it the day she was lost at sea?"

"No. What has the necklace to do with anything?"

"It was around the Marchioness of Anglessey's neck when her body was found in the Pavilion."

Amanda's eyes opened wide with surprise.

"You can't be serious. How extraordinary. Wherever did she get it?"

"No one seems to know. But Jarvis recognized it and suggested I might have my own reasons for looking into the matter."

Amanda searched his face. "Are you so certain the Prince did not kill her?"

Sebastian met her gaze. Whatever else one might say about Amanda, she was a level-headed, intensely unimaginative woman. If even she had come to suspect Prinny of murder, then the Regent was in serious trouble.

Sebastian shook his head. "She was killed earlier that afternoon. Her body was simply moved to the Pavilion and arranged so that he would find her."

She frowned. "How much earlier was she killed?"

"Some six hours or more."

Amanda's lips curled in a contemptuous smile. "Ah. There, you see? No great mystery. Why, I could have told you Prinny didn't do it myself. He wasn't even in Brighton earlier that day."

Sebastian's hand tightened around his brandy glass. "What?"

Amanda laughed. "Did you not know? He was here in London. I saw him myself. Coming out of Lady Benson's."

"Last Wednesday? You're quite certain?"

"Last Wednesday was Lady Sefton's breakfast. I wasn't able to attend myself, of course. But I remember it distinctly." She gave the skirts of her mourning dress an unconscious twitch. "I can quite understand why Prinny kept his visit to Town secret — a lady's reputation and all that. Not that Alice Benson has any reputation left. If her father hadn't tied up her portion the way he did, Benson would have divorced her years ago. As it is, I fear being without Alice's fortune would be even more mortifying for Benson than being cuckolded by the Prince, now, wouldn't it?"

"What time was this?" said Sebastian sharply.

"Shortly before Lady Sefton's breakfast. I'd say sometime in the early afternoon."

Amongst the fashionable set, breakfasts were held in the afternoon, just as morning visits were held after three o'clock. Sebastian knocked back the rest of his brandy and set the glass aside. "Where might I find Lord Jarvis this evening?"

"Jarvis?" She paused a moment, thinking. "Well, there is Lady Crue's ball. But I believe I heard something about the Dowager Lady Jarvis making up a party for Vauxhall. *Sebastian,*" she called after him as he

headed for the stairs. "Where are you going?"

"Vauxhall."

CHAPTER 50

Pressing a coin into the wherryman's callused palm, Sebastian stepped onto the quay at Vauxhall. Beside him, a link torch flared against the dark sky to fill the moist, sultry air with the scent of hot pitch.

The earlier rain had brought little relief from the heat. As he entered the gardens through the Water Gate, he found the gravel of the wide main path still showing wet in the shimmering light cast by row after row of glowing oil lanterns. Around him, the thick expanses of lush vegetation steamed.

At the Grove he paused, his gaze sweeping the colonnades. The sweet strains of Handel's *Water Music* drifted through the trees from the orchestra's pavilion in the center, the melody punctuated with maidenly shrieks from the darker recesses of the gardens.

It didn't take him long to locate Jarvis's party in a supper box near the center of the

Colonnade. The fierce, hawk-nosed old Dowager was there, as was Lady Jarvis, her once pretty face vacant and slack. Sebastian recognized the baron's two stout, middle-aged sisters, one kneading her hands in silent, endless worry, the other as harsh and irascible-looking as her brother. It had all the appearance of a typical family outing, Sebastian thought — until one remembered that the Dowager had once tried to have her daughter-in-law committed to a lunatic asylum, or that Jarvis had several times offered to have the wastrel husband of his sister Agnes quietly killed.

Jarvis himself, however, was absent, as was his daughter, Hero; the presence of two empty chairs suggested they had stepped out for a brief stroll. Glancing at his pocket watch, Sebastian suspected that father and daughter had escaped the family gathering by going to watch the playing of the fountains. Sebastian kept walking.

He came upon them near the Hermitage. They stood half turned away, their attention caught by the spectacle of dancing water so that they remained unaware of Sebastian's approach. He was struck, as before, by the similarity between father and daughter. Sebastian had sometimes heard Miss Hero Jarvis referred to as a handsome woman, for she had large gray eyes and a fine, Junoesque build. But he doubted anyone had ever called her *pretty,* even when she was a child. Her chin was too square, her nose too close an echo of her father's. She was also far too tall. Sebastian himself stood just over six feet, and she could nearly look him in the eye.

It was she who saw Sebastian first, her gaze lighting on him as she turned, laughing at something Jarvis had just said. She froze, the laughter dying on her lips.

Sebastian sketched an easy bow. "Miss Jarvis," he said, smiling sardonically as Jarvis himself swung about. "If you will excuse us?"

She hesitated, and Sebastian thought she meant to refuse. The last time they'd met, he'd broken into her house, held a gun to her head, and essentially kidnapped her. But all she said was "Very well."

She swept past him, pausing only to lean in close and say quietly, "If he fails to return safe and unharmed in five minutes, I shall set the guards after you."

Sebastian watched her walk away, her head held high, her back straight. "Your daughter seems to fear I mean you some harm."

"My daughter thinks you ought to be

locked up."

Sebastian turned his gaze to the King's cousin. "It has recently been brought to my attention that His Royal Highness the Prince Regent was visiting Lady Benson in London the day the Marchioness of Anglessey was murdered. What time did he make it back to Brighton? Four? Six? Or later?"

Jarvis's fleshy face remained impassive. "I beg your pardon? The Prince never left Brighton that day. There must be some mistake."

Sebastian held the baron's hard stare. "The mistake was yours."

It was Jarvis who glanced away, his jaw tightening as he gazed out over the darkened gardens. "Who told you?" he said at last. "Very few people knew."

"He was seen."

They turned to walk together, the gravel crunching beneath their feet, the distant strains of the music drifting to them through the trees. After a moment, Jarvis said, "What, precisely, are you suggesting? That the Prince killed Lady Anglessey in London, and then hauled her lifeless body back to Brighton with him? Don't be absurd."

"Not exactly. But perhaps someone else brought her to the Pavilion, someone who

391

knew what the Prince had done and was determined not to allow the Regent to get away with murder the same way his brother Cumberland did."

Jarvis faced him, the gravel spraying out from under his heels. "You are supposed to be finding a way to scotch these ridiculous rumors. Not start new ones yourself."

Sebastian calmly held his ground. "It's what everyone will be saying when the Prince's presence in London that day becomes known. And it will become known, have no doubt of that. These sorts of things always do."

Wordlessly, Jarvis turned and continued up the walk.

After a moment Sebastian remarked almost conversationally, "Did you know the Stuart dagger is back in its rightful place in His Highness's collection? But, of course, you knew. You're the one who put it there, aren't you?"

Jarvis swiped one hand through the air in a dismissive gesture. "Enough of this. I have decided your assistance in this matter is no longer required. You are to have nothing further to do with it."

Sebastian smiled. "You should have hired the Bow Street Runners after all. Them, you could have dismissed. Not me."

They were passing through a long, arched passage open at the sides and illuminated by dozens of brilliantly hued lanterns. Two young women strolling arm in arm glanced their way in passing, and Jarvis significantly dropped his voice. "If you understood —"

Sebastian cut him off. "How vulnerable the Prince's position is at the moment? Ah, but I rather think I do." A rocket exploded overhead, showering the darkened gardens with a rain of light as the fireworks exhibition began. "Tell me what you know about the Stuart threat to the dynasty."

"There are no more Stuarts," said Jarvis blandly. "They died out with Henry four years ago."

"But there are still those with a better claim to the English throne than King George and his sons. And you'll never convince me you don't know their supporters have become active."

His hands clasped behind his back, Jarvis turned again to walk toward the Colonnade. After a moment, he said, "How did you come to know of this? Has it something to do with Lady Anglessey's death?"

"Possibly. It would help if I knew who is involved."

Sebastian didn't expect an answer. But to his surprise, Jarvis pursed his lips and blew out a long breath. "We don't know who's involved. Oh, we've managed to get our hands on a few individuals, but they've all been at the lowest levels and they've known nothing of any real importance. Whoever these people are, they're very clever, and very well organized." Jarvis dropped his voice even lower. "There are suggestions that they have managed to attract supporters in the army as well as in the highest reaches of the government, but no one seems to know precisely who."

It was disquieting information. "I find it difficult to believe anyone could seriously expect a scheme of this type to succeed," said Sebastian. "It wasn't that long ago that the people of London reacted to the Catholic Relief Act with the Gordon Riots. They'd never accept a Catholic monarch."

"Ah. But you see the current claimant, the King of Savoy, has a daughter, Anne, married to a prince of Denmark. She's a Protestant. If Savoy were to resign his claim to the throne in her favor . . ."

"Is that likely to happen?"

"There has been some suggestion of it, yes. The Prince of Denmark has a claim of his own to the English throne. It's weak, of course, but not much weaker than that of William in 1688."

A second rocket exploded overhead, filling the night sky with a cascade of colored light. Jarvis paused to look up, his head tilting back. "The times are unsettled," he said as another rocket burst into clusters of fire. "One rip in the fabric of tradition and legitimacy, and who knows where it might end? Killing is always much easier to start than it is to stop."

Sebastian watched the colored stream of fire pour back to earth. "If the Prince truly is mad, you would do better to admit it now, while the damage might still be contained and a new Regent named. If you leave it too long, when he does go down, he might very well take the entire monarchy with him."

"The Prince is not mad," said Jarvis in a low, steady tone. Then he said it again, as if by repeating it he might make it so. "He is not mad, and he did not kill that woman."

"Guinevere," said Sebastian. "Her name was Guinevere."

Jarvis brought his gaze to Sebastian's face. "Leave it, my lord. I'm warning you —"

Sebastian took a hasty step toward him, only to draw himself up short. "Don't. Don't even think about threatening me."

Sebastian was crossing the Grove with long

strides when his gaze fell on another party seated at a table snuggled beneath the elms, a party consisting of Lord Portland, his wife, Claire, and his wife's mother, the widowed Lady Audley. Sebastian hesitated, then turned his steps toward them.

As he drew nearer, he could hear Portland complaining about the cost of Vauxhall's famous ham, sliced so thin that some claimed one could read a newspaper through it. "Look at this," he said, hefting a sliver of ham on his fork. "A shilling's worth of sliced ham weighs an ounce here. Which means the proprietors are selling this stuff for sixteen shillings a pound. Now, if you figure a thirty-pound ham can be bought for ten shillings, they're making twenty-four pounds on every ham."

Lady Portland laughed and laid a hand on her husband's arm. "Do give over, Portland. You sound like a merchant in his counting house. When one is out for pleasure, what signifies a few shillings one way or the other?" She smiled at Sebastian as he approached. "Wouldn't you agree, my lord?"

"Undoubtedly," said Sebastian, sketching the ladies a bow. He turned to Lady Audley. "How does your collie bitch?"

A soft smile touched her lips and shone in her eyes. "Well, thank you. She's the proud mother of six fine pups."

"Varden does not accompany you to-night?"

He caught the quickest of exchanged glances between mother and daughter before Lady Portland said laughingly, "I'm afraid there aren't many young men who would choose to make one of a party with their mother and sister, when there are livelier amusements to be had."

It was true, of course. When men of the Chevalier's set came to Vauxhall, it was typically to dance beneath the stars with courtesans and steal kisses and more in the dark, secluded alleys of the gardens. But while that might explain the Chevalier's absence, it did nothing to explain the look Sebastian had intercepted between Lady Audley and the Chevalier's half sister, Lady Portland.

"Do you go to the Prince's fete tomorrow night?" asked Lady Audley, drawing his attention.

"Of course," said Sebastian. "But with two thousand guests expected, I must admit I am tempted to outrage all notions of propriety and simply walk, rather than risk spending an hour or more caught up in a snarl of carriages."

"Perhaps we should do the same," said Lady Portland with another laugh.

"Perhaps we'll start a fashion," said Sebastian, withdrawing with a bow just as the whizzing bang of another rocket split the night with fire.

Chapter 51

Catching a scull from Vauxhall's quay, Sebastian directed the boatman toward the steps near the Westminster Bridge, then settled on the thinly cushioned thwart with his long legs thrust out in front and his arms crossed at his chest.

The night lay heavy and dark around them, the thick cloud cover holding in the day's muggy heat while hiding the light of both moon and stars. He kept thinking about the woman who had handed Portland that note. What if there had been no mysterious woman in green? What if Portland's part in the evening's charade had been less accidental? Less innocent?

A faint breeze skimmed across the prow, carrying with it the sounds of men's laughter. Looking up, Sebastian saw a livery company barge, its lights reflecting in the dark waters of the Thames as it swept past. He could feel the scull rocking gently with the barge's passing, hear its wake slap against the scull's sides, the sound mingling with the gentle splash of his boatman's oars.

In the pale light thrown by the scull's lantern, Sebastian studied the man at the oars. He had a thick shock of dark, almost black hair tucked beneath a beaten felt cap, his broad-featured face weathered and toughened by years of sun and wind and rain. With every thrust of his oars the cords in his thick neck bulged, the muscles of his shoulders and arms straining the worn fustian of his coat. But his movements were slow, almost laconic. Sebastian was about to lean forward and tell the man to put his back into it when he caught the faint slap of another set of oars coming up fast behind them.

Sebastian glanced again at his boatman's closed, lined face. There was something about his posture, something watchful, even anxious, that gave Sebastian pause. It was as if the man were waiting for something. Someone.

The sound of the second set of oars drew nearer. In itself, that was in no way unusual. The river was full of wherries transporting passengers from one bank to the other. Given his boatman's slow progress, a more energetic oarsman could easily overtake them. And yet . . .

Shifting his weight, Sebastian threw a quick glance over one shoulder. He saw the prow of a dinghy appear out of the gloom, its hull painted black, its oarsman a dark shadow. A man with less acute hearing and eyesight would have remained oblivious to its presence. Deliberately, Sebastian turned his back on the approaching boat.

It was the perfect place for an attack, Sebastian thought. Here he had no place to run, no hope of any assistance from chance passersby. His options were strictly limited. The shore was a distant line of black against black. They were just over midway between the banks, in a river that ran a quarter of a mile wide. The livery barge with its gaily reflected lights and laughing crew was long gone. If Sebastian could extinguish the scull's lamp, it might be possible for him to go over the side and strike out for shore beneath the cover of darkness. Yet the tide was running strong, and a lamp could be relit. He decided to take his chances here, now.

The dip and pull of the second set of oars came closer, mingling with the gurgle of the river washing against the approaching dinghy's bow. He could feel the closing boat as a looming presence, a thing of darkness materializing out of the night.

Holding himself tense and still, Sebastian heard the dinghy part the waters directly behind them. He heard its oars slip, heard the telltale shift of timbers as the unknown second boatman rose.

The scull's oarsman paused in his stroke, his jaw clenched as he stared intently straight ahead. Sebastian waited until the last possible instant, until he heard the whistle of wood sweeping through the thick, sultry air. Then he threw himself forward, flattening himself against the wet, mud-smeared bottom of the scull just as the dark-coated man in the dinghy swung the flat edge of his oar at the space where Sebastian's head had been.

The momentum of the oar's weight carried the man's body around and opened up an expanse of black water between the two boats, the dinghy lurching as the boatman struggled to regain his balance.

Rolling onto his back on the scull's wet, grimy planks, Sebastian saw his own boatman ship his oars and rise, his lips pulled back in a grimace, a knife clutched in his left hand. Thrusting up his right arm, Sebastian broke the man's forward lunge and caught his wrist in a hard grip. Beneath them, the scull pitched dangerously. Sebastian lurched up onto his knees.

"Ye bloody bugger," swore the boatman, his breath foul against Sebastian's face.

Struggling up, Sebastian felt the scull shudder as the second boat bumped against its side again. Out of the corner of one eye, he saw the shadow of the dinghy's oar raised to strike. Pivoting quickly, he swung the scull's boatman around, using the man as a shield just as the oar came whistling through the air toward them.

The edge of the oar's blade caught the boatman just below the ear, the impact making a dull *thwunk.* With a sharp cry he pitched sideways. His body hit the water with a splash that sprayed through the air and set the scull to tipping violently.

The sharp movement brought Sebastian to his knees again. He freed one of the scull's oars and brought it up, driving the tip of the handle like a blunt lance into the second boatman's chest, just as he swung again.

The oar's tip caught the man at the junction of his ribs. He was a small man, with longish blond hair and the thin, effete face of a gentleman. For one brief instant, his gaze met Sebastian's. Then his eyes rolled back in his head and he toppled off the scull's prow with a splash.

His breath coming in quick gasps, Sebastian fit the oar back into place. They were near enough by now to Westminster Bridge that he could see its lights reflected in the black waters of the river. He heard the voice of the scull's oarsman, raised in panic. "Help! I cain't swim."

The worn wood of the oars felt smooth beneath his hands as Sebastian settled into place. Pausing, he glanced over at the oarsman's bobbing head. "Who hired you?"

"Bloody 'ell. Throw me a line. I cain't swim."

"Then I suggest you save your breath," said Sebastian, leaning into his oars.

Swearing loudly, the boatman called after him, "The yellow-headed bloke in the greatcoat. 'E 'ired me. I dunno who he is."

Sebastian scanned the gently heaving waters. The blond-headed man in the dark greatcoat had disappeared.

The boatman's voice came again. "Oy. Ye gonna throw me a line?"

"Here." Sebastian nudged the dinghy's floating oar toward the floundering man. "I suggest you use it to remove yourself from the vicinity. The Thames Patrol doesn't tend to look kindly on boatmen who try to murder their fares."

CHAPTER 52

Kat watched Devlin peel off his shirt, the soft light from the brace of candles beside her bedroom washstand glazing the skin of his neck and back with gold as he bowed his head to study the smears of foul-smelling muck on the fine cloth of his evening coat. "Bloody hell. If this keeps up, my valet is going to succumb to a fit of the vapors. Or quit."

Coming up behind him, Kat ran her hand across his bare shoulders, her fingertips gentling as she traced a long bruise there, just beginning to show purple. "It's taking a toll on your body, as well."

Tossing the ruined coat aside, he pivoted to draw her into his arms. "At least nothing vital has been damaged," he said with a hint of laughter.

"They meant to kill you tonight."

He nibbled at the tender flesh behind her ear. "I think the idea was to have my body wash ashore somewhere around Green-wich."

She drew back so that she could look up at him. "But why? Why do these people want you dead?"

He shrugged. "They obviously think I know more about this conspiracy than I do."

"Perhaps. Or perhaps they're simply afraid of what you might learn." She pulled away and went to get him a brandy. "Who's behind it, do you think?"

"Even Jarvis doesn't know." He poured water from the pitcher into the bowl and bent to splash his face. "It's bigger than any one man — or even a score. Something like this needs a broad base of support if it's to have any chance of success."

"Yet someone must be at its core."

He nodded. "The Whigs would seem the most likely candidates. They spent the last twenty years expecting Prinny to sweep them back to power, only now he's been made Regent and the Tory government is still firmly in place. The problem is, I can't see the more radical Whigs risking their lives simply to replace one dynasty of spoiled, crowned fools with another. Why not do away with the monarchy altogether?"

"You mean like the French?" said Kat with a wry smile.

"I was thinking more about the American model." He straightened and reached for a towel. "The Tories would make better suspects, except that they're already in power, and will likely stay there for another twenty years or more. So why would they want to get rid of Prinny?"

"Especially when moving against the Hanovers might very well set in motion precisely the kind of popular movement the Tories fear the most," said Kat, thinking about what Aiden O'Connell had said that morning in Chelsea.

He glanced over at her. "You mean a revolution?"

"Or a civil war."

"I doubt they'd see the danger. Not men with the kind of hubris required to plot to overthrow a dynasty. It's probably never occurred to them just how easily they could lose control of everything."

"But what does any of this have to do with the death of Lady Anglessey?"

"I wish I knew." Devlin tossed the towel aside. "I suppose she might simply have stumbled across something, the way Tom did in the alley behind the Norfolk Arms. Or . . ." He hesitated.

"Or she could have been involved in it herself," said Kat, handing him the brandy.

He took a sip and looked up to meet her gaze. "It's possible, isn't it?"

Kat was thoughtful for a moment, remembering what else Aiden O'Connell had said, about a Stuart restoration leading to peace with France. Alain Varden was half-French.

"The Chevalier de Varden," she said suddenly. "What are his political inclinations?"

"As far as I can tell, he has none — or at least none he's made known. His brother-in-law, Portland, is obviously a Tory, as is Morgana's husband, Lord Quinlan. But then, most men of birth and property are Tories — including Anglessey. And my own father." Devlin went silent for a moment, the glass of brandy held forgotten in his hand.

"What is it?"

"When I saw Varden this afternoon at Angelo's, he told me Guinevere wanted to leave Anglessey. That she was afraid of him."

"*Afraid?* Why?"

"He said Anglessey killed his first wife."

"Is that possible?"

"I'd heard his first wife died in childbirth. I was on my way to Mount Street to ask him about it when Lovejoy caught up with me this afternoon."

"What are you suggesting? That Guinevere somehow found out about her hus-

408

band's involvement with the Stuarts and was afraid he'd kill her to keep her quiet? But . . . surely she wouldn't betray her own husband. Would she?"

Devlin brought up one hand to rub his forehead, and she realized just how tired he was. Tired and frustrated. "Obviously, I'm still missing something. Something important."

Slipping her arms around his waist, Kat pressed her body close to his. She would never be his wife, but she could know the joy of holding him, of loving him and being loved by him. She told herself that was enough. For his sake, it would have to be enough. "You'll find it," she said, her voice low and husky. "If anyone can, you will. Now come to bed."

She awoke before dawn to find the place beside her cold and empty. She turned her head, her gaze searching the room.

He was standing beside the window, one of the heavy drapes pulled back so that he could look out upon the gradually lightening street. He was turned half away from her so that all she could see was his profile, and he had his head bent, as if he gazed not at the street below but at something he held in his hand. It wasn't until she slipped from beneath the covers and went to curl her arms around his shoulders that she realized he held his mother's bluestone necklace, the silver chain threaded through the fingers of one hand.

"What is it?" she asked, nuzzling his neck. "What's wrong?"

He reached back his free hand to cup her head in his palm and draw her around to him. "Amanda came to see me last night."

"Lady Wilcox?" said Kat in surprise. As far as Kat knew, Devlin's sister hadn't spoken to him since February.

"She's concerned that my unusual activities might harm her daughter's chances of contracting a successful alliance. She wanted to know what had possessed me to do something so plebian as to take part in a murder investigation."

"You told her about the necklace?"

"Yes." He held up the necklace so that the triskelion swung slowly on its chain, tracing a short arc through the darkness. "She was puzzled, but not surprised."

Kat studied the shadowed lines and angles of his profile, but he had all his emotions locked away someplace where she couldn't see them. "Perhaps the implications escaped her."

One corner of his mouth lifted in a tight

smile. "Oh, no. Amanda is nothing if not quick. She might have been puzzled that my mother would give up something she'd always held dear, but it never occurred to her to question what happened that day off the coast of Brighton."

Kat drew in a deep breath. "What are you saying, Sebastian?"

He turned his head to look directly at her, and for one unguarded moment she saw it all — the bewildered mingling of anger and hurt, confusion and pain. "Amanda knows. She's always known." He let out a soft huff of laughter that held no humor. "That pleasure outing — the sinking of the yacht — it was all for show. My mother didn't drown that summer. She simply left. She left my father and she left me. But she didn't die."

His hand closed over the necklace, his knuckles showing white in the first light of dawn. "She didn't die."

Chapter 53

Amanda was seated at her breakfast table, the *Morning Post* spread out beside her plate, when her brother strolled unannounced into the room. She didn't look up.

The Countess of Hendon's silver-and-bluestone necklace hit the newsprint beside her, the unexpected slap startling her enough that it was only with effort that she avoided flinching.

Holding herself composed, she lifted her gaze to Devlin's. The blaze of emotion she saw there was so raw and powerful that her gaze veered away again before she could quite stop it.

"She's still alive, isn't she?" he said.

Amanda drew in a deep, steadying breath and defiantly stared into his terrible yellow eyes. "Yes."

"How long have you known?"

"Since that summer."

He nodded, as if she'd only confirmed

what he'd already suspected. "And Hendon?"

"He knows, of course. He has known from the very beginning. He helped to arrange it."

She saw a flicker of — what? Surprise? Pain? — in the depths of those strange, animalistic eyes. "And why wasn't I told?"

Amanda gave him a wide, malicious smile. "I suggest you ask Hendon."

It wasn't often Sebastian allowed his thoughts to drift back to that long-ago summer, the summer before he turned twelve. It had been hot, days of unrelenting blue sky and a sizzling golden sun that turned the crops to dust in the fields. Wells that had never failed in a hundred years or more ran dry.

The Countess of Hendon had spent most of that spring and summer at the family's principal seat in Cornwall. His mother loved London, loved the excitement and mental stimulation of the political salons as much as the endless round of balls, breakfasts, and shopping expeditions that occupied most women. But Hendon considered London an unhealthy place for women and children, especially when the streets turned dry and dusty and the air hung close. His involvement in affairs of state might keep Hendon himself tied to Whitehall and St. James's Palace, but that year he insisted that his wife retire to Cornwall, and that Sebastian and his brother Cecil join her there when they came down from Eton.

Sebastian tried to recall how Sophie had occupied herself that summer, but his memories were of tramping the fields and woods with Cecil and swimming in the forbidden cove below the cliffs. In his recollections, she was an atypically distant figure seen riding out each morning on her neat bay hack. He had one clear image of an afternoon's tea served on the sun-splashed terrace, Sophie's smile bright yet still somehow . . . distant. And then, in July, the family had gone to spend the month in Brighton.

Sophie adored Brighton, reveling in the concerts on the Steyne and the balls at the Castle and Ship. But that year, even Brighton was hot and dusty, and crowded with those anxious to escape from the stifling, unhealthy interior. Hendon grumbled that Brighton had grown as foul and noisome as London, and threatened to send the Countess and their sons back to Cornwall. The Countess alternately stormed and wept, begging to be allowed to stay.

And so they had stayed, until the morning in mid-July when Sebastian's brother Cecil awoke flushed and feverish. By nightfall he had become delirious. The best doctors were called in all the way from London. They shook their heads and prescribed bloodletting and calomel, but Cecil's fever continued to climb. Two days later he was dead, and Sebastian found himself the new Viscount Devlin, his father's only surviving son and heir.

There followed tense weeks filled with loud voices and angry accusations. But whenever he was around Sebastian, Hendon kept a strange, tight silence. It was as if he couldn't comprehend why Fate had taken his first- and second-born sons and left him only the youngest, the one least like their father.

For Sebastian, those days remained a painful blur. But he could remember quite clearly the sunny morning Sophie Hendon sailed away on what was supposed to have been a simple day's outing with friends.

And never came back.

The pain of that summer fueled Sebastian's anger now as he took the steps to his father's house on Grosvenor Square.

He found Hendon in the entrance hall,

headed for the stairs. The Earl was dressed in breeches and top boots, his crop in one hand, and it was obvious he'd only just come in from his morning ride. "What is it?" he asked, his gaze on Sebastian's face.

Sebastian crossed the hall to throw open the door to the library. "This is a conversation we need to have in private."

Hendon hesitated, then came away from the stairs. "Very well." He walked into the room and tossed his crop on the desk as Sebastian closed the door. "Now, what is it?"

"When were you planning to tell me the truth about my mother?"

Hendon swung around, his expression guarded and wary. "Which truth is that?"

"Bloody hell." Sebastian let out his breath in a sharp, humorless laugh. "Are there so many lies? I mean the truth about what happened seventeen years ago in Brighton. Or should I say, what *didn't* happen. Is she still alive today? Or do you even know?"

Hendon held himself very still, as if carefully considering his answer. "Who told you?"

"Does it matter? You should have told me yourself — long before I asked you about the necklace."

Hendon blew out a long, slow breath. "I

was afraid."

"Of what?"

The Earl drew his pipe from a drawer, his movements slow and deliberate as he filled the bowl with tobacco and tamped it down with his thumb. "She's still alive," he said after a moment. "Or at least she was as of last August. Every year she delivers to my banker a letter briefly detailing the major political and military events of the previous twelve months. Once we have proof she still lives, I send her annual stipend."

Sebastian was aware of a fine trembling going on inside him. He couldn't have said if the discovery Sophie still lived, after seventeen years of his thinking her dead, brought him relief or only fueled his rage. "You pay her? Why? To stay away?"

"It's not such an unusual arrangement. Couples who can no longer live together frequently agree to live apart. Look at the Duke and Duchess of York."

"The Duchess of York didn't fake her own death."

Hendon went to kindle a taper and hold it to his pipe. "Your mother . . . she was involved with another man. For her to have lived with him openly here in England would have ruined my standing in the government. She agreed to go abroad in return for my granting her an annual stipend."

Sebastian was silent for a moment. Had there been a man that summer — a special man? Impossible to remember. There were always men around Sophie Hendon. "Why didn't you simply divorce her?" he said aloud, searching his father's heavily featured face. "What does she have on you?"

Hendon met his gaze and held it. "Nothing I intend to tell you."

"My God. And the necklace?"

"I honestly don't know how Guinevere Anglessey came to be wearing that necklace. I suppose it's possible your mother gave it to someone over the years."

Sebastian doubted it. Sophie Hendon had never been a particularly superstitious woman, but she had believed in that necklace and in its power. "Where is she now?"

Hendon sucked on his pipe, kindling the tobacco. "Venice. Or at any rate, that's where I send the money. The acquaintances she went out with that day — the ones who helped coordinate the accident — they were Venetians."

The air filled with the sweet smell of burning tobacco. Sebastian stood at one of the long windows overlooking the square. "All those years," he said, half to himself, "all those years of missing her, of mourning her . . . and it was all a lie." He was aware of his father coming to stand behind him, although he didn't turn his head.

"If she could have taken you with her," said Hendon, his voice gruff, "I think she would have. Of all her children, I always thought her love for you was the most intense."

Sebastian shook his head, his gaze on the scene outside the window. A boy and a girl of ten or twelve were running with a hoop, their laughing voices carrying lightly on the morning breeze. He'd had that sense himself, growing up. Sophie Hendon had loved all her children, but until today Sebastian would have said he'd held a special place in her heart. Yet she had left him.

He was aware of a yawning inner ache that twisted his guts and brought a bitter taste to his mouth. A heavy silence stretched between them, a silence Sebastian ended by slamming one hand down on the sill and swinging away from the window to face his father again. "Why the hell didn't you tell me the truth? You let me think she was dead. Every day, I went up on those cliffs looking for her. Hoping it was all a mistake and I'd see her come sailing home. But in the end I gave up. I believed what you had told me. And it was all a bloody lie!"

Sebastian stared at his father. The Earl's jaw worked back and forth, but he said nothing.

"Why?"

"I thought it for the best."

"For whom? You, me, or her?"

"For all of us."

Sebastian brushed past his father and headed for the door. "Well, you were wrong."

CHAPTER 54

The Dowager Duchess of Claiborne awoke with a start, one hand groping up to catch her nightcap before it slid over her eyes. A tall, shadowy figure moved across the floor of her artificially darkened bedchamber. She gave a faint gasp, then sat up in bed, her cheeks flushing with the heat of indignation when she recognized her only surviving nephew.

"Good heavens, Devlin. You nearly gave me an apoplectic fit. What are you doing here at this ungodly hour? And why are you glaring at me in such a fashion?"

He came to stand beside the carved footboard of her massive Tudor bedstead, his lean figure held taut. "Seventeen years ago, Sophie Hendon did not die in a boating accident. She simply left her husband and surviving children behind and sailed away. Tell me you didn't know."

Henrietta let out a sigh. She wished she

could deny it. Instead, she said, "I knew."

He swung abruptly away, going to jerk open one of the heavy velvet drapes at the window and letting in a stream of bright morning sunshine that made Henrietta groan. She brought up a hand to shade her eyes, and sat up straighter. "I thought at the time you deserved to be told the truth. But it wasn't my decision to make."

"I'm told she left with a man. Is that true?"

She stared at the rigid set of his shoulders. "Yes."

He nodded. "As I recall, there were other men in her life. Had been for years. Why did she decide to leave with this one?"

"The others were distractions — or tools of revenge. I can only assume this one was different somehow."

"Who was he?"

"I don't recollect his name. He was a poet, I believe. A most romantic-looking young man."

"A Venetian?"

"There was some Venetian connection. But the young man himself was French."

"He was younger than she?"

"Yes."

"You met him?"

Henrietta twitched at the high embroidered collar of her nightdress. "He was quite the darling of society that spring. Although, if I remember correctly, he left Town early."

"Where did he go? Cornwall?"

"Evidently."

Devlin brought up one hand to rub his eyes. Looking at him, Henrietta thought he looked older — and more exhausted — than she could remember having seen him. "Do you know where she is now?" he asked.

"Your mother? No. We were never close, and we certainly didn't keep in contact after she left. I don't believe even Hendon knows precisely where she went, although he sends money to her every year."

"Why? He's certainly not doing it out of the goodness of his heart. She obviously knows something. Something he's willing to pay to keep quiet. What is it?"

The Duchess of Claiborne looked into her nephew's troubled eyes, and for the first time that morning told him a blatant lie. "I honestly don't know."

Sir Henry Lovejoy was annoyed. He was making little headway in his attempt to capture the man the press had taken to calling the Butcher of St. James's Park. He had the magistrates from Bow Street interfering in his investigation of the Carmichael murder. And now he was having to take time away from pursuing several promising leads to deal with an irate foreign embassy and a decidedly peeved Foreign Office.

Leaving Whitehall, Lovejoy hailed a hackney and went to see Viscount Devlin.

He found Devlin just preparing to mount his front steps. "I need to speak to you, my lord," said Lovejoy, executing a small bow on the footpath.

The Viscount was looking unusually pale and distracted. He hesitated, then said crisply, "Of course," and led the way into his library. "Please have a seat, Sir Henry. How may I help you?"

"I won't detain you but a moment," said Sir Henry, standing with his round hat held in both hands. "One of the wherrymen pulled a body from the Thames last night."

The Viscount's features sharpened with interest. "Anyone I know?"

"A foreigner," said Lovejoy, watching the young man's face. "From northern Italy."

Devlin's brows twitched together in a frown. "A thin man, with blond hair?"

"Ah. So you do know him."

"He tried to kill me last night."

"And so you killed him?"

"He fell into the Thames," said the Viscount blandly. "What made you think to

424

come to me?"

Lovejoy made a noncommittal sound far back in his throat. "He was a known associate of your previous victim. Charles Ahearn," Sir Henry added, when Sebastian simply stared at him in puzzlement. "The gentleman you killed near Hungerford Market."

"I didn't kill Ahearn, remember? He fell, too," said Devlin with a soft smile. The smile faded quickly. "You're certain the blond man was Italian?"

"Quite." Settling his hat back on his head, Lovejoy turned to take his leave. "He was a cousin of the King of Savoy."

CHAPTER 55

After Lovejoy's departure, Sebastian stood for some time with his gaze fixed on an ancient pair of crossed swords hanging on the library's far wall. The link between the King of Savoy and the effete blond man who had chased Tom through the streets of Smithfield and tried to drown Sebastian in the Thames seemed inevitable; the connection between the conspiracy to depose the Hanovers, Lady Anglessey's murder, and the ancient bluestone necklace that had once belonged to Sophie Hendon remained less clear. But it was a puzzle Sebastian knew he was never going to unravel as long as he allowed himself to dwell on the events of that distant summer and the lies it had spawned.

And so he forced himself to put away the rage and hurt and focus instead on what his new knowledge of his mother's true fate added to his understanding of Guinevere

Anglessey's death. The tie between the Countess of Hendon and an unknown French poet with Venetian connections was troubling, although Sebastian was not yet convinced it was significant. Sifting through all that he had learned in the last few days, he decided it was past time he paid another call on the bereaved Marquis of Anglessey.

Reaching out, Sebastian gave the bell beside the mantel a quick tug. "Have Giles bring round my curricle," he told Morey when the majordomo appeared.

Morey gave a stately bow. "Yes, my lord."

But when Sebastian stepped out of the house some fifteen minutes later, it was to find his tiger, Tom, reining in the chestnuts at the base of the steps.

"What the devil are you doing here?" Sebastian demanded. "I told you to take a couple of days off and rest."

"I don't need no days off," said the boy, his features pinched and set. "This is my job, and I'm doin' it."

Sebastian leapt into the curricle and took the reins. "Your job is to do what you're told. Now get down."

The boy gave a loud sniff and stared straight ahead. "It's on account of I let you down, ain't it? I flubbed it, and because o' me, you almost ended up fish bait."

"No, you didn't let me down. I let *you* down by exposing you to unconscionable peril. These people are dangerous, and I'll be damned if I'm going to be responsible for getting you killed. Now hop off."

The tiger kept staring straight ahead, but Sebastian noticed he blinked several times, and the muscles of his throat worked hard as he swallowed. "There's boys younger'n me servin' as cabin boys in His Majesty's Navy, and goin' to war as drummer boys. I guess you reckon I couldn't do those things, either."

"Bloody hell," said Sebastian, giving his horses the office to start. "Just don't take any more unnecessary risks, you hear? And next time I tell you to do something and you don't obey me, you're fired. Understand that?"

Clapping one hand to his hat to hold it in place, Tom scrambled back to his perch and grinned. "Aye, gov'nor."

The Marquis of Anglessey moved across the floor of his conservatory with slow, painful steps. It seemed to Sebastian, watching him, that the man had aged visibly in the past week.

He looked around at the sound of Sebastian's footfalls, one hand tightening on the edge of the shelf of orchids beside him as if for support. "What is it?"

Sebastian paused in the center of the room, the warm humidity of the place pressing in on him like a blanket, the smell of damp earth and lush foliage heavy in the air. "I want you to tell me how your first wife died."

To his surprise, a wry smile lifted one corner of the old man's lips. He turned away to begin carefully plucking yellowing leaves from a large China rose. "I take it you've heard the rumors about how I pushed her to her death."

"Pushed her?"

Anglessey nodded. "She slipped on the stairs at Anglessey Hall. She was big with child, clumsy. She couldn't catch herself." His hands stilled at their task, his gaze becoming unfocused as he lifted his head to stare away as if into the past. "Perhaps she would have died in childbirth, anyway," he added softly. "She wasn't well those last few months. But there's no way to know."

He brought his gaze back to Sebastian's face. "Who told you I killed her?"

"Does it matter?"

"No. I suppose not." Anglessey plucked another leaf and dropped it into the basket he held slung over one arm. "What are you suggesting? That I have a nasty habit of killing my pregnant wives? What possible reason could I have for killing Guinevere?"

"Jealousy, perhaps."

"Because of the child she carried? You forget how desperately I wanted that child."

"People in the grip of strong emotion often act against their own interest. It could be she discovered something about you. Something you didn't want her to know."

"Guinevere knew about my first wife. I told her of the rumors before we were married."

"I wasn't talking about your first wife's death."

The old man looked around, puzzled. "Then what?"

"Perhaps she learned of your involvement in a conspiracy to restore the Stuart dynasty to the throne."

The Marquis looked unexpectedly pensive, his eyes narrowing. The man's body might be weakening, Sebastian thought, but it would a mistake to assume that his mind was also failing.

"I've heard murmurs — innuendo, disgruntled whispers. But I must admit I never credited them. I assumed it was all just wild talk, wishful thinking. Do you mean to say there's something in it? But . . . what could it possibly have to do with Guinevere's death?"

"That's what I haven't been able to figure out yet." Sebastian paused. "I'd like to take a look around your wife's room, if I may."

The request obviously caught Anglessey by surprise. He drew in a quick breath, but said, "Yes, of course. If you wish. Nothing has been touched. I know I should let Tess gather Guin's things together and give them to the poor, but somehow I haven't been able to bring myself to do it."

Guin. It's what Varden had called her, Sebastian remembered. He let his gaze drift over the aged nobleman before him. If Guinevere had been simply shot or even stabbed, Sebastian might have found it easier to consider the Marquis a suspect. But it was hard to see how this frail old man could have played a part in the complicated charade that had followed her murder.

Sebastian turned toward the house, then paused to look back and say, "Is there any possibility that your wife was planning to leave you?"

The Marquis still stood beside the rose, the basket of yellowing leaves gripped in one hand. "No. Of course not."

"So sure?"

A ragged cough shook the old man's

frame. He turned half away, his hand fisting around a handkerchief he brought to his mouth. When the cough subsided, he tucked the cloth quickly out of sight, but not before Sebastian glimpsed the bright stains of blood against silk.

Anglessey looked up to find Sebastian watching him. A faint band of color touched the old man's pale cheeks. "So. You see. Why should Guinevere consider leaving me when she'd have been a widow soon enough? According to my doctors, I'll be lucky to last out the summer."

"Did your wife know?"

Anglessey nodded. "She knew. It's ironic, isn't it? I keep thinking about the day before I was to leave for Brighton. Normally, she was strong about what was happening to me, but I'd had a difficult night and she took it badly. She tried to hide her face from me, but I knew she was weeping. And she said —"

His voice cracked. He looked away in some embarrassment, his eyes blinking, his lips pressed together for a moment before he was able to go on. "She said she couldn't imagine how she was ever going to live without me."

Sebastian found Guinevere's rooms enveloped in silent darkness, the drapes at the windows drawn closed against the daylight. A light scent hovered in the air, as if the memory of the woman still lingered here, elusive and sad.

He crossed to open the drapes, the thick carpet absorbing his footsteps. The windows overlooked the garden below. From here he could see Anglessey's conservatory, and the limb of the big old oak that thrust out close enough to give access to the bedchamber, just as Tess Bishop had described it.

Sebastian turned back to the room. The bed's hangings, like the drapes at the windows and the upholstery of the chairs beside the hearth, were done in a soft yellow. The morning sun filled the room with a warm, cheerful light. He couldn't have said what he'd been expecting, but it wasn't this, this sense of serenity and calm joy. It didn't seem to fit with what he knew of Guinevere Anglessey, a woman torn between her passion for a lifelong love and her growing affection for her aging, dying husband.

He worked his way methodically through the apartment, starting with the dressing room, not at all certain what he was looking for. The intruder who had come here after Guinevere Anglessey's death had been desperate to get his hands on something.

Had he been successful, Sebastian wondered, or not?

Opening a chest near the largest wardrobe, he found himself looking at tiny caps decorated with delicate tucking and lace, nestled amid stacks of carefully folded miniature gowns and white flannel blankets embroidered with birds and flowers. His chest aching with a strange catch, he searched it quickly and gently closed the lid.

Returning to the bedchamber, he stood in the center of the rug, his thoughtful gaze taking in the sun-filled room. On the mantel above the empty hearth, Guinevere had kept a collection of seashells casually arranged beside an ormolu clock. Mementos from her childhood in Wales?

Intrigued, he was walking over to study them when a flash of white from the rear of the cold grate caught his eye. Crouching down beside the hearth, he reached back to free it from the grate and found himself holding a tightly wadded sheet of paper.

Straightening, he uncrumpled the paper and smoothed it out upon the flat top of the marble mantel. It was a short note, written in a bold masculine hand.

Beloved,
I must see you again. Please, please let

me explain. Meet me Wednesday after-noon at the Norfolk Arms in Giltspur Street, in Smithfield, and bring the letter. Please don't fail me.

The signature was scrawled but still legible.

Varden.

CHAPTER 56

It took some time, but Sebastian eventually tracked the Chevalier de Varden to White's in St. James's.

"There 'e is, gov'nor," said Tom, jumping down from his perch to run to the chestnuts' heads.

The Chevalier was descending the club's front steps in the company of another young buck when Sebastian drew in the curricle close to the footpath. "If I might have a word with you, sir?" he called.

The Chevalier exchanged a few pleasantries with his companion, then strolled over to the curricle's side. "What is it, my lord?" The smile that accompanied the words was pleasant enough, but his eyes were guarded and wary.

Sebastian returned the smile. "Drive with me a ways, won't you? There's something I'd like you to see."

The Chevalier hesitated, then shrugged

and bounded up beside him.

"Stand away from their heads," called Sebastian, bending his hand to give the horses the office to start.

"What is it?" Varden asked as Tom scrambled back up to his perch.

"I was wondering what you might make of this." Without taking his eyes from the road, Sebastian drew the crumpled note from his pocket and held it out.

He was aware of Varden's breath quickening as he took the note and read it through. His hand tightened around the paper, his face fierce when he looked up to meet Sebastian's quizzical gaze. "Where did you get this?"

"It was behind the grate in Lady Anglessey's bedchamber."

"But . . . I don't understand." He thumped the back of one hand against the crumpled page, his voice tight with anger. "I didn't write this."

"That isn't your handwriting?"

"No." Varden shook his head, as much in confusion as in denial. "It looks like it, but it's not. I tell you, I didn't write it."

If it was a lie, it was a very good one. Yet Sebastian had known people who could lie with such ease and apparent sincerity that it would never occur to the unwary to suspect them. Kat could lie like that. It was a gift that served her well on the stage.

"Would you say the writing is similar enough that it could have deceived Lady Anglessey?" Sebastian asked, reserving judgment.

Varden read through the note again. "It must have done so, obviously. This hotel — the Norfolk Arms. Is that where she went? The afternoon she died?"

Sebastian nodded. "And the letter she was supposed to bring with her?"

"I have no idea," said Varden, meeting Sebastian's gaze and holding it unblinkingly.

This time Sebastian thought, *That line was delivered less well, my friend.* Turning the curricle in through the gates to Hyde Park, he said aloud, "Tell me again about your quarrel."

A faint flush darkened the Chevalier's lean cheeks. "What more is there to say? She wanted to leave —"

"No," said Sebastian, anger putting a tight edge on his voice. "That's pitching it too rum by half. Anglessey is dying, and his wife knew it. She had no reason to leave him and every reason not to."

Sebastian thought for a moment that Varden meant to brazen it out. Then he pursed his lips and expelled his breath in an audible gust, as if he'd been holding it. "All right. I admit I made that up."

"The quarrel," pressed Sebastian. "What was it about?"

Varden set his jaw. "What happened that night was between Guin and me. It has nothing to do with her death."

"This note suggests otherwise."

"I tell you, it has nothing to do with her death."

"So certain?"

"Yes!"

Sebastian doubted it, but he decided for the moment to let it go. Whoever had sent that note — whether Varden or someone else — had obviously known about the quarrel. Had known about it, and used it to lure Guinevere Anglessey to her death.

"Tell me," said Sebastian, his attention seemingly all for his driving, "who do you really think killed her?"

Varden fixed his gaze on the horses' heads, their manes tossing lightly with the late-morning breeze and the smooth action of their gait. After a moment, he said, "When I heard she was dead, I naturally assumed Bevan Ellsworth was responsible. Then I heard she'd been found in the Prince's arms, and I thought he'd done it. A part of me still suspects Ellsworth, although you say it couldn't have been him, that he was otherwise occupied that day." He swiped an open hand across his face, rubbing his eyes. "Now? I don't know. I just don't know," he repeated softly.

Sebastian drew the bluestone necklace from his pocket and held it out. "Have you ever seen this before?"

The Chevalier stared at the necklace, his nostrils flaring with a sudden intake of breath, his eyes opening wide with what looked very much like horror. "Good God. Where did you get that?"

Sebastian threaded the silver chain through his gloved fingers. "It was around Lady Anglessey's neck when she was found in the Pavilion."

"What? But that's —" He broke off.

"Impossible? Why? You have seen it before, haven't you? Where?"

Varden stared off across the Park. Even this early in the day, the Park was crowded. The morning had dawned clear, the sun warm in an open blue sky. But dark clouds could be seen building again on the horizon, threatening more rain before nightfall. "The summer when I was twelve or thirteen, my mother took us to the south of France. There was a peace then, if you'll remember. It didn't last long, but my mother missed

France, and she wanted us to see it. We took Guinevere with us."

"Just Lady Guinevere?"

Varden shook his head. "Morgana, too. We stayed with some people who had a château near Cannes. Somehow or another they'd managed to survive the Revolution, although they'd fallen on hard times. We came to know a woman there — an English-woman who was another of their guests. The necklace was hers. She told us a strange story about it, how it had once belonged to a mistress of James the Second, and how the necklace always chose the next person it was to go to by growing warm in their hand."

He leaned back against the curricle's seat, his arms crossed at his chest. "I didn't believe any of it, although it made a wonderful story. But when the woman took the necklace from around her neck and handed it to Guinevere . . ." His voice trailed away.

"It grew warm?"

"Yes. It was practically glowing." He let out a ragged half laugh. "I know it sounds unbelievable. I remember Morgana was so jealous she practically snatched the necklace from her sister's hand. But it immediately went cold again."

Sebastian looked at him sharply. When Sebastian had described the necklace to Morgana, she'd disclaimed all knowledge of it. Had she simply forgotten the incident? Or remembered it all too well? "And this woman . . . she gave Guinevere the necklace?"

"No. That's just it. The last time I saw the necklace, it was still around the Englishwoman's neck. And that was eight or nine years ago."

"What was her name?" The question came out sounding harsher than Sebastian had meant it to. "Do you remember?"

Varden shook his head. "They said she was mistress to a Frenchman — one of Napoléon's generals, I believe. But I don't remember her name. I couldn't even tell you what she looked like."

"Was she fair?" said Sebastian, his chest so tight he found himself scarcely able to breathe. "Fine-boned and fair?"

"I'm sorry," said Varden, the sun golden on his face as he turned to look directly at Sebastian. "I don't remember."

CHAPTER 57

Kat's gowns were made by London's most fashionable modistes, her slippers of the finest silk and kid, her chemises trimmed with delicate Belgian lace. But there had been a time when she had been intimately familiar with London's booming secondhand clothing trade. She'd known who would fence a silk handkerchief, just as she'd known who would give the best price for a stolen watch.

Not all the goods in the secondhand clothing trade were stolen. Men and women fallen on hard times with nothing left to sell could still sell their own clothes, their appearance becoming ever more ragged as they spiraled down into the gutter. Yet such a huge traffic in used items also created a ready market for thieves. Having once been a thief, Kat knew exactly where to go when she decided to track down the dealer who had sold Lady Addison Peebles's green satin ball gown to Guinevere Anglessey's killer.

Many of the secondhand clothing dealers had stalls in the Rag Fair in Rosemary Lane, while others sold their goods from barrows in Whitechapel, with the occasional purloined round of cheese or bacon hidden away beneath the tattered petticoats and breeches. But the finest quality goods could be found in a little shop kept by Mother Keyes in Long Acre.

There, in her elegantly bowed front window, Mother Keyes displayed delicate silk handkerchiefs and nightdresses of linen and lace, snowy white kid gloves and ball gowns fit for a queen. All looked new, although they were not. Some had been sold by their owners or the servants to whom they had been given. Others had come into the shop by more nefarious channels, with any initials or marks carefully removed before the items were put on display.

The bell on the front door jangled pleasantly as Kat entered the shop, bringing with her the warm scents of sun and morning breeze. Mother Keyes looked up from behind her counter, her sharp hazel eyes narrowing as they traveled up the length of Kat's fringed and embroidered poult-de-soie walking gown, assessed the package she carried, and came to rest on her face.

It had been nearly ten years now since a

much younger Kat had slipped through Mother Keyes's door, and she hadn't been wearing soft kid gloves or a chip hat with a delicately curled ostrich feather that cost enough to feed a family for months. But Kat knew the woman recognized her. Remembering faces and reading the subtle, telltale signs of character writ there had kept Mother Keyes out of Newgate for sixty years or more.

Holding the old woman's gaze, Kat spread the green satin gown on the polished counter between them and said, "If I were abigail to a duke's daughter-in-law and my lady gave me a gown such as this that she no longer wanted, I think I'd bring it to you to sell."

Mother Keyes glanced down at the gown, her eyes narrowing, although her face gave nothing away. She was a tiny woman, her frame delicate, the features in her wrinkled face small and even. She looked back up at Kat. "Think me a flat, do you?"

Kat laughed. "I know very well you are not. And this maid I'm talking about — the one who sold you this dress? She spoke the truth. Lady Addison Peebles did give her the gown. Her mother-in-law said the color made her look like a sick frog."

Mother Keyes blinked. "You have the

dress, and you know who sold it. So why are you here?"

Kat laid a guinea on the expanse of shimmering satin. "I want to know who bought it."

Mother Keyes hesitated a moment, then picked up the coin with quick, nimble fingers. "I don't know their names, but I do remember them."

It didn't surprise Kat. People were Mother Keyes's hobby. She amused herself by watching them, studying them, analyzing them. "They were a queer pair," she said. "No doubt about it." She paused expectantly.

Kat placed a second coin on the counter. "There were two of them?"

"That's right. One of them was from the Colonies. The Southern Colonies, from the sound of him." She leaned in close and dropped her voice. "An African, no less. Mind you, 'e was as pale skinned as a Portuguese, but 'e 'ad the features, if you know what I mean. That flat nose, and them full lips. Big, 'e was, too. And bald as a plucked goose."

Kat dutifully deposited another coin. "And the other one? What was he like?"

"Not a man. A girl. A London girl. Young, she was. No more'n fifteen or sixteen, I'd say. Maybe less. Yellow-headed and tall, but otherwise ordinary lookin'. I don't remember much else about her, 'cept for her eyes."

"Her eyes?"

"They were so pale. Reminded me of rainwater on a cloudy day. Nothin' there but a reflection."

"You wouldn't happen to remember anything they said, would you?"

Mother Keyes gazed out the shop's window at the troop of soldiers marching past, her lips pursing with studied thought. "Well, let me see. . . ."

Kat placed another coin on the table.

The coin disappeared beneath Mother Keyes's tiny hand. "They argued a bit about the size of the dress. The girl, she kept insistin' they needed something bigger, but the African, he said no, it'd do just fine. And then he said the queerest thing."

The old woman paused expectantly. Suppressing a sigh of impatience, Kat produced another coin.

Mother Keyes drew back her lips in a smile that displayed a mouthful of unexpectedly sound teeth. "He said that dress, it was just the thing for a lady to wear to the Brighton Pavilion."

CHAPTER 58

"I'd like you to spend some time hanging around Lady Quinlan's house," Sebastian told his tiger after they had returned the Chevalier to St. James's Street. "See if you can find out what her ladyship was doing the day Guinevere Anglessey was killed."

"You think Lady Quinlan offed 'er own sister?" squeaked Tom in surprise.

"I think I'd like to know what she was doing last Wednesday."

"I'll find out, ne'er you fear," promised Tom.

Sebastian grunted. "And do endeavor not to get picked up by the watch this time, do you hear?"

"I never —" Tom began as they turned onto Brook Street, only to break off and say, "Gor! Look there. Ain't that Miss Kat?"

She stood on the footpath before Sebastian's house, the embroidered skirt of her poult-de-soie walking dress clutched in one hand as she prepared to mount his steps. Kat never came to his house. She said it wasn't appropriate, that the time they shared together should be kept separate from the life he lived in Mayfair as the Earl of Hendon's son and Lady Wilcox's brother. She knew it infuriated him, but she wasn't the kind of woman to be intimidated by a man's anger. No matter how much he told her he didn't give a damn about the conventions, that he had only one life and she was a vitally important part of it, she stubbornly stayed away. Only once before had she come here, and then she'd been both unconscious and bleeding.

At the sound of the curricle, her head turned, the brim of her chip hat casting the features of her face into shadow.

"Stable them," he told Tom, handing the boy the reins and jumping lightly from the curricle's high seat. "What is it? What's wrong?" he asked, his hands clasping Kat's shoulders as she came up to him.

She shook her head. "Nothing's wrong. I located the secondhand dealer who sold Lady Addison's green satin evening gown."

He knew better than to ask how out of all the secondhand clothing dealers in London she'd known which one to go to. "And?"

"She says she sold it to an African and a

tall young girl with pale gray eyes."

The girl was easy enough to find.

According to one of the men Sebastian came upon sifting through the still-smoking rubble of the Norfolk Arms on Giltspur Street, her name was Amelia Brennan. The eldest of eight children, she lived with her mother and father in a ramshackle white-washed cottage built into what had once been the garden of a bigger house facing Cock Lane. The larger houses themselves had long since been broken up into lodgings, their gardens disappearing beneath a warren of shanties and hovels threaded by a narrow byway half-filled with heaps of ashes and steaming rubbish piles.

As Sebastian's carriage turned down the lane, ragged children stared from open doorways, their hair tangled and matted, their faces and arms as caked with dirt as newly dug potatoes. Most had probably never seen a lord's carriage, with its well-fed, glossy-coated horses, its liveried and powdered footmen standing up behind. They had certainly never seen such a sight here in Ha'penny Court.

Sebastian waited in the carriage while one of the footmen hopped down and went to rap on the Brennans' warped door. The show of ostentatious power and wealth was deliberate, and Sebastian meant to use it to his advantage.

The Brennans' cottage was better tended than its neighbors, he noticed, its missing windows covered with oiled parchment rather than simply stuffed with rags, the front step freshly swept. But signs of encroaching decay were evident in the rotting eave at one corner, in the shutter that hung drunkenly from a broken hinge.

A woman answered the door, a boy of about two balanced on one hip. She had the worn face and graying hair of an old woman, although considering the age of her children, Sebastian suspected she was only in her midthirties. He watched her gaze travel from the powdered footman to the grand carriage filling the lane outside her cottage, and saw the terrible fear that flooded into her eyes. Her lips parted, her arm tightening around the child so that he let out a whimper of protest.

Sebastian swung open the carriage door and stepped down with an affected, languid pace, a scented handkerchief held to his nostrils. "Your daughter Amelia has been implicated in the murder of the Marchioness of Anglessey," he said, his voice at its most patrician and condescending. "If she

451

cooperates, I can help her. But only if she cooperates. If she doesn't, it will go hard on her." He let his gaze drift with unmistakable meaning over the humble cottage. "On her, and on you and your other children."

"Oh, my lord," gushed the woman, sinking to her knees. "Our Amelia's a good girl — truly she is. She only did what she was told, like a proper servant, when —"

Sebastian cut her off. "Is she here now?"

"No, my lord. She's —"

"Get her."

A crowd of stair-stepped children filled the open doorway behind the woman. She twisted around, her gaze singling out a thin boy of perhaps eleven or twelve. Normally, a lad of that age would be off earning money to help his family. That he was here now suggested that the boy, like his sister, must have worked at the Norfolk Arms. Last night's fire would be hard on this family.

"Nathan," said the woman. "Go. And be quick."

Sebastian watched the boy dash off, then turned back to the woman. "I would like to come in and sit down."

Mrs. Brennan stumbled to her feet, her thin chest jerking with each rapid breath. "Yes. Of course, my lord. Please, come in."

The house was neat and tidy, the dirt floor

swept, the walls scrubbed clean. There were two rooms, one above the other, with a steep set of steps along one wall leading up to the second floor, where the children doubtless slept. It was a luxury for a family to have two rooms. In some parts of London families slept twenty and more to a room.

Shoving the baby into the arms of a girl of about seven, Amelia's mother showed Sebastian to a settle beside the empty hearth. Fronted by a crude trestle table with benches, the hearth took up most of the back wall. A box bed stood in the far corner, where in the dim light Sebastian could make out the huddled shape of a man lying on one side so that he faced the wall.

"He hurt his legs some months back," said the woman, following Sebastian's gaze. "His legs and his head. He hasna been able to work since. He cain't even walk."

Which explained the rotting eave and broken hinge on what had once been a well-tended cottage, Sebastian thought. Without its major wage earner, this was a family sliding toward the edge of disaster. Through the open door at the rear, Sebastian could see a small yard with a washhouse and a big copper kettle steaming over a brassier. According to the man at the Norfolk Arms, Amelia's mother worked as a laundress.

When she brought him a pot of ale, Sebastian's gaze fell on her cracked, raw hands. A woman could scrub clothes until her hands bled, and still she wouldn't be able to earn enough to feed a family of ten.

"Our Amelia's a good girl, truly she is," Mrs. Brennan said again, her red hands twisting in the cloth of her apron. "She was only doin' what she was told."

"Which was?" Sebastian cradled the ale pot in his hands, but he was careful not to taste it. Not after what had happened to Guinevere Anglessey in this neighborhood.

The click of a woman's pattens on the muddy cobbles outside brought Mrs. Brennan around, her face pinched and anxious. Amelia paused on the threshold of the open door, her hands gripping either side of the frame, her pale eyes widening. At the sight of Sebastian, she whirled to run, then let out a soft cry when Andrew, one of the strapping footmen Sebastian had brought with him, stepped forward to grasp her by the arms.

"There, there now, miss," said Andrew. "I believe his lordship was wishing to speak with you."

CHAPTER 59

"Amelia, please," said Mrs. Brennan. She reached out to loop an arm around the neck of one of the younger children and pull him closer to her, as if she might somehow protect him from what was about to happen. *"Please."*

Amelia's pale gray eyes met her mother's darker, troubled gaze. She hesitated, then bent to unstrap her pattens. When she straightened, her face was carefully wiped clean of all expression.

She came to slide onto the bench on the far side of the table. Four of the younger children crowded around her, their faces solemn as they stared at Sebastian. The girl with the baby hung back against the far wall, but her gaze, like her siblings', was fixed on Sebastian. Only Amelia refused to look at him, her gaze on the table before her.

"I want you to tell me precisely what happened at the Norfolk Arms last Wednesday," he said to her. "I already know about the murder. All I need you to do is confirm the details."

She brought up both hands to smooth her lank hair away from the sides of her face. Her expression might be calm, but her hands were shaking. She sucked in a deep breath, her teeth working her lower lip. "I didn't know nothin' about it till it was all over." She glanced up at him once, quickly, then away. "I swear I didn't. We was busy that afternoon and I was workin' the common room. Then Mr. Carter, he comes to me and says he wants me to help him buy a dress for . . . for the lady."

Sebastian waited. A quiver of revulsion bordering on horror passed over the girl's face. "He wanted me to go with him to make sure he bought the right size. He said she was tall, like me. But he made me look at her, so I'd be sure."

"You went with him to Long Acre?"

She nodded. "That green gown, I told him it was too small, but he was that set on buying it. He said it was just the thing for —" She broke off.

"For a lady to wear to the Brighton Pavilion?" Sebastian finished for her.

Her head bowed until he could see

the crooked white line of the part in her hair, her hands clutched together on the worn tabletop. "He said it'd fit, that her ladyship weren't such a strappin' wench as me."

"Only you were right, weren't you? It was too small. Did they make you wash her ladyship's body and dress her, as well?"

Amelia's gaze flew to her mother. Mrs. Brennan pressed her lips together, then gave a barely perceptible nod of her head.

Amelia sucked in another shaky breath. "Mum does most of the laying out round here. While Mr. Carter and I was gone, he had Mum brought in to see to the lady."

Sebastian glanced at the woman who stood beside the empty hearth, her thin shoulders hunched, her hands clutching her elbows close to her sides. "Did he tell you what they intended to do with the body?" Sebastian asked.

It was Amelia who answered. "No. But we heard them talkin'. They was at the other end of the room, arguing, while Mum and I got the lady dressed and finished cleanin' up the mess."

"The mess?"

"In the room where she died."

"And where was that?"

The girl's forehead puckered with confusion, as if she'd expected him to know this, since he knew so much else. "The best upstairs parlor."

Sebastian set aside the untouched pot of ale and pushed to his feet. "Tell me about the necklace," he said. "The silver necklace with the bluestone disk. Was her ladyship wearing it when you first saw her?"

Again, that furtive exchange of glances between mother and daughter. "No. It was on the floor, underneath her," said Amelia. "Mum found it when she was cleanin' her up. The clasp was bent a bit, but I was able to straighten it out enough so's we could get it back on her."

"And then what did you do?"

Amelia swallowed. "We rolled the lady up inside a length of canvas, and Mr. Carter and me carried her down the back steps and out into the alley. They had a cart waitin'."

"What kind of a cart?"

Amelia lifted one shoulder in a shrug. "Just a cart, like the ironmongers use. It was empty 'cept for some canvas bags filled with ice, and a big chest."

"A chest?"

"That's right. One o' them fancy Chinese chests, with black lacquer work all covered with paintings of dragons and trees picked out in yellow and red."

Sebastian gave a wry smile. He remembered noticing the chest when he'd looked around the Yellow Cabinet in the Pavilion. He'd seen the chest, and hadn't given it a second thought. The Prince was always ordering cartfuls of oddities and trifles for the Pavilion. No one would question or even remember the delivery of yet another Chinese lacquered wood chest, while the ice . . .

The ice could very well have come from the inn's own cellars. It wasn't so uncommon these days. The extra cold would have delayed the onset of rigor mortis enough for Guinevere's killers to haul her body down to Brighton in the cart, then stuff her into the chest and carry her into the Pavilion.

Yet all those hours in the cart had left their mark in the pattern of lividity Paul Gibson had identified so accurately on Guinevere's body, just as the passing of the hours had left their own signs, signs that could be read by those who knew how to interpret them. But whoever had killed Guinevere Anglessey and conspired to implicate the Prince Regent in her murder hadn't known about those signs, hadn't known that their victim's very body would betray them.

"Who else came to the inn that afternoon?" Sebastian asked aloud. "Do you remember?"

Amelia shook her head, her face confused as if she couldn't quite understand where he was going with the question. "The usual crowd. The common room was full."

"I'm not talking about the common room. I'm interested in anyone who might have gone upstairs."

"I wouldn't know about that. Like I said, we was busy."

"You didn't see a young gentleman? A handsome gentleman with dark eyes and light brown hair?"

"No. I told you, I didn't see nobody!"

The girl was becoming agitated, her back held tight, her eyes wide. Sebastian eased up on her. "Several nights ago, some men unloaded a cargo into the inn's cellars. One of them was a gentleman, a thin man with longish blond hair. Do you know who he was?"

"No."

Sebastian pressed his hands flat on the tabletop and leaned into them, his arms straight. "The woman whose murder you helped to conceal was a marchioness. The Marchioness of Anglessey. Did you know that?"

Amelia looked up at him, her chest rising and falling with her quick breathing. "But we didn't do nothin'!" She scrambled up from the bench and backed away from him. "We only did what we was told."

"It's enough to get you hanged. You and your mother both." Sebastian's gaze swept the huddled, silent children. "And then what will become of them?"

The woman beside the empty hearth let out a sharp cry. Sebastian didn't even glance her way.

Amelia covered her mouth with one hand, her eyes squeezing shut. Then her hand slipped away and her eyes opened slowly. "I've seen him around the inn a few times," she said, meeting Sebastian's compelling gaze. "But I don't know his name. I swear to God I don't. He usually comes with his lordship."

"His lordship?"

"They was both there that day. I thought you knew. He's the one brought the cart."

Sebastian searched her face, looking for signs of deceit. "You're certain this other man was a lord?"

Her head nodded vigorously up and down. "A tall gentleman, with red hair. Lord . . . I can't remember it exactly. It's like that stone they use. You know the one? They use it for all the grand buildings."

"*Portland?*"

"Yes. That's it. Lord Portland."

Chapter 60

Intent on intercepting the Home Secretary before he left Whitehall for the Regent's fete, Sebastian directed his coachman toward Westminster.

The shadows were only just beginning to lengthen toward evening; the Regent's first guests wouldn't be arriving for hours. But the streets were already packed with crowds surging toward Carlton House in the hopes of catching a glimpse of the exiled French royal family and two thousand noblemen and -women arriving at what was being called the grandest, most extravagant sit-down dinner in the history of the European monarchy. By the time Sebastian's carriage had passed Temple Bar and swung onto the Strand, the horses were barely moving. They sidled nervously in their traces, the lightly sprung coach rocked from side to side by the jostling crowd.

Sebastian threw open the door. "Get the

carriage out of this," he shouted to his coachman. "I'll make better time on foot."

"Yes, my lord."

Leaving the carriage awash in a sea of ragged humanity, Sebastian threaded his way through a crowd that grew increasingly surly as he neared Somerset House. "They say they's gonna let us in tomorrow to look at the place," yelled one man. "Them nobs, they get to eat and drink their fill. All we getta do is look."

"Hear, hear," murmured a score of men near him.

Sebastian pushed on, aware of the sullen looks being cast his way. He found himself regretting the exquisitely cut coat of fine blue cloth, the skintight leather breeches and shining top boots that unmistakably marked him as a gentleman. Prinny had planned this fete as a grand celebration of the inauguration of his Regency. But it occurred to Sebastian as he looked into the sweating, bitter faces around him that the Prince had misjudged his populace. People were angry, resentful. Tomorrow, the Prince would again leave London for Brighton. What better time, thought Sebastian, to stage a coup?

Someone up ahead began to sing, *"Not a fatter fish than he/Flounders round the polar sea. . . ."*

An ugly chorus of jeers swelled through the crowd. A dozen more voices took up the ditty, *"See his blubber and his gills/What a world of drink he swills. . . ."*

"Oy, who ye think yer shovin' there?" growled a voice behind Sebastian.

Sebastian threw a glance over his shoulder. A dark-haired man with a craggy face, lips peeled back and jaw set in determination, was pushing his way through the crowd, his gaze fixed on Sebastian.

The mob surged, hemming in Sebastian. Craggy Face lunged, his right hand fisted around a dagger. Sebastian tried to feint to the left, but the crowd was too close. The searing edge of the blade slid across his ribs, slicing through coat, waistcoat, and shirt to nick the flesh beneath.

"Every fish of generous kind," sang the throng, *"scuds aside or shrinks behind. . . ."*

"Bloody hell," swore Sebastian, bringing the edge of his hand chopping down on the man's wrist. "You've ruined another of my coats!"

Craggy Face yelped. His fist reflexively opened to drop the knife into a scuffle of rough-booted feet.

"But about his presence keep," roared the crowd, *"all the monsters of the deep. . . ."*

465

The man grabbed for Sebastian's arm. Cupping his left hand over his right fist, Sebastian drove his elbow back into Craggy Face's stomach. The man's eyes flared wide, the breath gusting out of his pursed lips as he doubled over. He stumbled back, careening into a carpenter's apprentice in a paper cap.

" 'Ey, what the 'ell?" the apprentice swore, his fists coming up.

Twisting around, Sebastian scanned the sweat-sheened, hostile sea of faces around him, lit now by the rich golden light of a fading day. His head swam with the close-packed odors of sunbaked stone and brick, of hot men and foul breath. He saw a clean-shaven man with dark hair and a patrician nose, and recognized him from the alley near the Norfolk Arms. Then Sebastian's gaze locked with the hard gray stare of a man whose auburn head towered above the ragged crowd.

The Earl of Portland wore the dark, unassuming coat of a man who has dressed with the intent of not calling attention to himself. At his side Sebastian glimpsed a familiar, half-grown lad: Nathan Brennan from Ha'penny Court.

"Bloody hell," Sebastian swore under his breath. How many more were there?

A fat baker with graying whiskers threw back his head and sang, *"Name or title what has he? Is he Regent of the sea?"*

Sebastian cast a quick glance up the Strand. The crowd ahead was too thick, too hostile for Sebastian to have any hope of pushing his way through it. He began to slip sideways, edging his way toward a narrow lane he could see opening up just beyond the alehouse on his right.

"By his bulk and by his size," sang the crowd, their voices swelling toward the punchline, *"by his oily qualities . . ."*

Slipping between a fishmonger and a tattered begger, Sebastian reached the corner. The side streets here lay in shadow, the shops already shuttered out of fear of the restive throng. Without looking back, Sebastian darted down the lane.

"This or else my eyesight fails," roared the mass of voices. *"This should be the Prince of Whales!"*

Sebastian heard a shout go up from behind him, followed by a chorus of angry protests from the crowd as his pursuers pushed their way forward.

CHAPTER 61

The cobbled lane stretched straight before him. Throwing a quick glance over his shoulder, Sebastian took the first alley that opened up to his left. Already he could hear the sound of running feet behind him. He quickly ducked down another byway.

He hoped to lose himself in the warren of mean streets that ran between Bedford Street and St. Martin's Lane. But the area was unfamiliar to him. Dodging the low-hung, swinging sign of a shuttered gin shop, he rounded a corner and found himself in a cul-de-sac. Ancient, soot-stained brick buildings rose around him three and more stories. He was trapped.

He spun around, his breath sawing in and out of his heaving chest. Several doors opened onto the pavement, but all were padlocked from the outside. The slap of running feet grew nearer. Impossible to go back now.

His gaze fell to the arched entrance of the culvert at his feet. Once, the arch had been barred by an iron grill, but now the grill was rusted and broken, the bars twisted apart to make a space wide enough for a man to slip through.

He'd heard tales of men who made their living by scavenging the honeycomb of ancient viaducts and sewers that ran beneath the streets of London. Toshers, they were called. The work was dangerous. The vaults flooded quickly with the rising tide of the river into which they emptied, or even from a heavy storm that could pass unnoticed by those toiling away belowground. There were deadly gasses, too, that could overcome the unwary. Sometimes the floor of one tunnel would collapse into an older vault that ran below it, the sinkhole covered by deceptively flat expanses of silt that only betrayed themselves when a man stepped onto their smooth, deadly surface.

"This way," someone shouted.

"Bloody hell," swore Sebastian.

Rolling into the gutter, he squeezed his way through the grill, the rusted bars scraping his wounded side as he lowered himself into the shaft. He felt his coat catch on one of the bars and pulled it sharply, swearing again when he heard the cloth rip.

Scrabbling around for the iron rings driven into the brickwork of the shaft, he lowered himself into the darkness. Some six or eight feet down, his legs plunged into the void of a vault. He let go, dropping the last four or five feet into a noisome stretch of mud and muck that splashed beneath his feet as he landed.

The close, foul stench of the place pinched at his nostrils, roiled his stomach. Panting heavily, he paused to give his eyes time to adjust to the darkness and heard a voice from the street above say, "Where the devil did he go?"

Sebastian held himself very still.

"There," he heard Portland say. "He's gone down the culvert. See —" There was a dull twang of metal. "He's torn his coat. You, Rory, fetch some lanterns, and be quick about it."

"Sweet bleedin' Jesus," said a man's gruff voice. "I ain't goin' down there. People die down there."

"You fool," spat Portland. "If we don't find him and stop him, we'll all be dead. Now get going!"

Setting his teeth against the stench, Sebastian slipped away from the shaft. He could see better now, his eyes growing accustomed to the dim light that filtered down through the occasional grates. He was in a brickwork tunnel that arched so low over his head he had to stoop to keep from scraping his crown against the curving roof. A slow trickle of water ran down the center of the tunnel, but he suspected it wouldn't be enough to wash away all trace of his footprints. If Portland and his men could find lanterns, the direction Sebastian had taken would be all too easy to see.

The uneven, muck-covered bricks were treacherous beneath his feet. Moving as quickly as he dared, he followed the water downhill, hoping to come across another open grate that would give him access to the streets above. But he'd gone no more than a few hundred feet when he heard the sound of splashing and men's voices behind him, followed by a wavering gleam of light. Rory had found lanterns far quicker than Sebastian would have expected.

"Devlin." Portland's voice echoed through the shadowy tunnel. "Devlin? I know you can hear me."

Sebastian paused, listening.

"You won't get far down here, Devlin. Not without a lantern. It'll be dark soon. Is this what you want? To die in a sewer like a rat? For what? For a shrieking madman of a king and his bloated buffoon of a son?"

A silence fell, filled with the drip of water and the furtive scurrying of unseen rats' feet.

Portland's voice came again. "You know what we're doing is right, Devlin. You saw what it was like up there. The people of England have had enough. They're restless, angry. If we don't act now, the people themselves will bring down the monarchy. Only, they won't just sweep away this king, this regent. It'll be the end of us all. We know what happened in France. Is that what you want? To see England a Republic? With a guillotine in Charing Cross and every man, woman, and child of noble birth a target?"

Sebastian could feel the damp chill of the place seeping up through the soles of his boots and wrapping around him like a fetid embrace. He glanced up at the rough bricks overhead and tried not to think about the crushing weight of the tons of earth above him.

"Join us," Portland was saying. "You want what we want. A strong England, a strong monarchy. It can happen. All it takes is a few selfless, determined men in the right places. Tomorrow the Regent leaves for Brighton. We will simply seize control in his absence. Declare for Anne of Savoy and her husband, and present the world with a fait accompli. What can Prinny do? March on London? It won't happen. What regiment would follow him? It'll be the Bloodless Revolution of 1811. Join us, Devlin. It will be a historic moment."

The Home Secretary fell silent.

"There!" said a man's gruff voice, cutting through the darkness. "See the footprints? He's headed toward the river."

Sebastian splashed forward, heedless now of the noise he made. His feet slipped in the muck, his head brushing the rough bricks above. He could hear Portland and his men behind him, their feet slapping in the mud, their voices breathless. The feeble light from their lanterns bounced and flickered over the tunnel's damp-stained walls, chasing him.

Rounding a long bend, he came upon another tunnel that angled away uphill to his right. This tunnel was both higher roofed and broader than the one he followed, and for a moment he considered taking it.

He'd long ago lost all sense of orientation. But when he hesitated at the junction, the air of the wider tunnel lay still and dead in the darkness, while a faint stirring of air seemed to waft up from below.

He followed the air.

Before he turned away from the intersection, Sebastian was careful to leave the sides of the tunnel and deliberately wade out into the sluggish stream that now trickled down the center. The water was deeper here; it would hide his footprints, mask his choice of direction.

Debris-fouled water swirled around his boots, slowing his steps and growing higher by the minute. He dared not move too quickly now: the least sound would betray the direction he had chosen. He covered another two hundred feet, three. Then the lights behind him wavered and the splashing, scrabbling sounds quieted.

Sebastian immediately drew up, holding himself perfectly still. He could hear his own breath soughing painfully in and out, so loud in his ears he wondered Portland and his men couldn't hear it.

"Son of a bitch!" swore Portland. "Which way did he go?"

Sebastian breathed through his mouth, trying to block the stench of the place. The bloated carcass of a dead dog floated beside him. Glancing around the damp, cramped vault, he became aware of myriad eyes staring at him, glowing pinpricks of light in the darkness. More rats, he realized, scores and scores of rats.

"We'll have to split up," he heard Portland say. "Bledlow, you and Hank keep going ahead. Rory, you come with me."

The splashing started up again. Cautiously, Sebastian pushed on. But he had to move more quietly than before, lest the two men still behind him become alerted to his presence and call the others back.

The tunnel he followed angled downward, becoming both broader and higher as he neared the river. He could move more easily now, walking upright rather than stooping. But the water at his feet was rising, lapping at the tops of his boots, splashing up on his thighs.

He became aware of the sound of rushing water coming from up ahead. A cold draft wafted toward him, carrying a different smell, the salty scent of the river mingling now with the acrid stench of sulfur and decay. Rounding a bend, Sebastian could see that up ahead the tunnel he followed emptied into a larger vault. Wider and flatter than the sewer he followed, the larger tunnel looked old, probably dating back to medieval times. Built of stone rather than brick, its center formed a deep culvert through which rushed a wide stream of water flowing so fast it filled the air with a soft mist.

Just before its junction with the older sewer, the tunnel Sebastian followed opened out into a broad basin so wide the water only ran down the middle, with flat banks of deep mud stretching out to either side. Finding a shallow embrasure in the brick wall beside him, Sebastian drew back into the shadows, eased the dagger from his boot, and waited for the two men following him to come abreast.

He didn't have long to wait. The patrician-nosed gentleman Sebastian had seen in Smithfield passed first. Bledlow, Portland had called him. He carried the lantern thrust out before him at the end of a straight arm that shook so violently the light wobbled drunkenly over the curving walls and ceiling. Sebastian held himself very still and let the first man pass.

The handle of the knife felt smooth and hard against Sebastian's palm, the chill from the dank earth around him seeping through his sweat-dampened clothes. He waited until the second man — the dark-haired, craggy-faced assailant from the Strand — had taken one step, two, beyond the embrasure. The man moved clumsily, the scuffling of his feet on the slimy, uneven brick making enough noise to cover the whisper of sound as Sebastian slipped from the embrasure.

Catching the second man from behind, Sebastian clamped his left hand over the man's mouth and slit his throat, the blade slicing swift and sure.

The man died instantly. Sebastian quietly eased the body down to the muddy bricks at his feet. But something in the man's pocket clunked against the ground loud enough to bring the first man — Bledlow — around.

"Oh, my God," he yelped. Swinging the lantern like a weapon, Bledlow charged.

Ducking the edge of the lantern, Sebastian sidestepped the lunge. His foot slipped on the slimy bricks and he went down on one knee, the knife spinning out of his hand. Whirling around, Bledlow charged again, the lantern still gripped in one fist. Crouching, Sebastian fell back and used the man's own momentum to roll him over one shoulder with a heave that sent Bledlow lurching out into the broad mud of the basin.

The lantern flew through the air and splashed into the water, going out. The tunnel plunged into near darkness. Sebastian heard a deep, subterranean rumbling. The mud heaved, sucking Bledlow down.

"Help!" The man floundered in the mud, sinking deeper, to his hips now in the oozing muck. "For God's sake, help me!"

Sebastian hesitated. He even took an unthinking step off the brick onto the treacherous, sucking muck. But the man had stumbled far out into the muddy basin. Even if Sebastian were to throw himself flat across the unstable silt, his outstretched arms still would not grasp the doomed man's flailing hands. Sebastian felt the earth shift ominously beneath him. He leapt back.

From far down the tunnel came the echo of a shout and the flicker of a lantern. Portland.

"Quit struggling and try to keep still," Sebastian said, although he knew the man was beyond listening, beyond reason. Already the mud had sucked him down to his neck. He was screaming, the shrieks punctuated with quick, gasping sobs.

Sebastian regained his footing on the brick and broke into a run.

Chapter 62

The light filtering down through the gratings had dimmed with the approach of evening. Soon, Sebastian realized, it would be night. And with the fall of night would come the rising tide.

Reaching the main culvert, Sebastian turned left, moving away from the river. The water here was already running deep and swift enough to carry a man away. He kept to the narrow elevated footpath that ran beside the chasm. But the path was treacherous, its stones broken and crumbling, forcing him to slow down. It wasn't long before he saw the flare of a light behind him, heard Portland's loud, angry voice. "Leave him! There's nothing you can do for him. The man's dead."

Sebastian pushed on.

At one point he came upon a broad shaft opening to the street above, with a sturdy iron ladder firmly bolted to the damp stone walls. Taking a chance, Sebastian scrambled up the ladder to find the bars on the culvert above soundly in position. Conscious of the passing of precious seconds, he dropped back down and kept going.

A quarter of a mile or so farther on he came to a place where a side tunnel had collapsed into the main vault, bringing down a heap of rubble and dirt that formed a makeshift dam. Water shot over the lip of the cave-in like a waterfall. But when he scrambled to the top of the tumulus, Sebastian found a broad expanse of water that had backed up behind the debris. A subterranean lake stretched from one side of the vault to the other, submerging the footpaths on either side.

"Well, hell."

The light was fading fast, the dam alive with rats that scuttled, screeching, across the refuse at his feet. Reaching down to pick up a stout branch, he found himself staring at the pale body of a newborn baby mixed up with the carcasses of dead cats and dogs, and the broken chairs and filthy twisted rags that had snagged on the rubble. The stench here was almost overwhelming.

Moving gingerly in the near darkness, Sebastian lowered himself into the cold, murky water on the far side of the dam. His cravat wasn't exactly white anymore, but he tore it off anyway, and buttoned up his dark coat to hide the betraying gleam of his silk waistcoat. Scooping up a fistful of muck, he smeared his face with mud. Then he settled down to wait, the branch held ready.

The glow of the lantern grew closer. He heard a man say, "Oh, God," in a voice half strangled by disgust. "Rats. And look what they're eating."

"Here," snapped Portland. "Give me the lantern."

Sebastian could see him now, the light from the battered tin lantern wobbling over the vaulted ceiling of the sewer as he clambered across the debris. The Home Secretary's hat was gone, his once fine coat torn and muddied. A jagged scrape trickled blood down one cheek. At the top of the dam he paused.

"Mother of God, it's a lake," said the other man, coming up beside him. "We can't get across that."

"Devlin obviously did."

"You don't know that. Maybe he drowned."

"He didn't drown." Perching the lantern on the end of an outthrust slab of rubble, Portland waded into the lake. The water swirled up over his boots until it was lapping at his thighs, then his hips. As he lifted his arms above the dark water, Sebastian could see the pistol stuck in the waistband of his breeches.

Hidden behind a pile of trash, Sebastian sank lower in the water and let him pass.

The other man hesitated, then scampered after him. He was reaching back to grab the lantern when Sebastian rose like a specter from the water, the branch gripped in both hands.

The man's eyes widened, his lips parting in a high-pitched shriek. Sebastian put the entire weight of his body into the swing and sent the wood smashing into the man's legs.

The crack of breaking bone echoed around the shadowy, lamp-lit vault. The man screamed in pain, his legs buckling beneath him. Sebastian swung again as the man splashed into the water, the branch splintering in Sebastian's hands as it shattered against the man's head.

Portland turned, moving awkwardly in the waist-deep water. *"Devlin!"*

The other man's body floated between them, facedown.

Portland surged forward, wading into the shallows. Smiling grimly, he reached to snatch the pistol from his waistband. He held it out in a steady grip, the dark bore of the barrel pointed at Sebastian's chest. "You lose, my friend," he said, and pulled the trigger.

Sebastian listened to the click of the locking mechanism striking steel and smiled. "Powder doesn't like to get wet."

"You son of a bitch." Portland's nostrils flared, his lips pressing together in a tight, grim line. Shifting his grip on the pistol, he swung it over his head like a club and lunged at Sebastian.

Dodging sideways, Sebastian felt the slime-coated rubble shift beneath his feet. He lost his balance and plunged deep, sucking in a quick breath just before the water closed over his head.

He had to fight his way to the surface, the ground beneath his feet still treacherous. Breaking water, he found Portland there before him. The Home Secretary raised the pistol to bring it down on Sebastian's head again, the barrel blue-black in the faint glow of the lantern, the dark, polished wood of the handle dripping water.

Sebastian still gripped the splintered remnants of his cudgel in his fist, and he used it now like a dagger, driving it up into Portland's gut just as the man leapt.

Portland's eyes flew open wide, a gasp coming from the back of his throat as the jagged wood thrust deep into his stomach. Sebastian took a quick step back. The man's legs collapsed beneath him.

He sank quickly, the lake closing over his head, his body sucked along by the current so that Sebastian had to dive into the murky water to find him.

Fisting his hands in Portland's coat, Sebastian hauled the man out of the water and dragged him up onto the pile of rubble. "Why Guinevere Anglessey?" Sebastian said with a gasp, dropping down beside him. "Why did she have to die?"

Portland's eyes were open, his chest jerking with each breath. "Varden was careless," he said, his voice a hoarse whisper. "He let her find the letter. . . ."

Water dripped down Sebastian's cheeks, ran into his eyes. He swiped at his face with one wet sleeve. "*What* letter?"

"A letter from Savoy. Varden . . . he swore she wouldn't tell anyone. But we couldn't take the chance."

"So you lured her to the Norfolk Arms and killed her?"

"No. Not me." Portland shook his head, the movement causing his chest to heave as he fell to coughing. "Carter needed help getting the body out of his inn. It was my idea to use her death to" — his face twisted in a spasm of pain — "to discredit the Prince. It was working, too. Until you interfered."

"What are you saying? That Carter killed her?"

Portland's eyelids flickered closed.

Sebastian gripped the man's shoulders, shaking him. *"Damn you!* Who killed her?"

Portland's jaw had gone slack. Pressing his fingers to the side of the man's neck, Sebastian caught the thread of a pulse. A man could live for hours, even days, with a gut wound.

Sebastian sat back on his heels, his gaze on the man before him. If he tried to haul the Home Secretary out of the sewers by himself, he'd simply kill the man.

Slipping his hands beneath Portland's shoulders, Sebastian dragged the man's limp body to the highest point of the landslide, where he'd hopefully be safe from the rising tide. He left him the lantern, too, in case Portland should come back to consciousness.

Then he retraced his route to the surface.

It was an hour or more before Sebastian and a troop of constables made it back to the ancient, stone-walled sewer, the lights from their lanterns reflecting eerily off the dark walls and high, soaring ceiling. But when they reached the site of the cave-in, the Home Secretary was gone.

Standing at the top of the pile of rubble, Sebastian looked out across the dark expanse of water. The body of the other man he'd killed lay half-submerged at the base of the rubble. But the Home Secretary still floated, his body lying facedown in the subterranean lake.

"I don't understand it," said the Chief Constable, coming to stand beside Sebastian. "The rocks aren't wet here. The tide couldn't 'ave come high enough to carry him off. So what happened?"

Sebastian stared down at the smear of blood that led to the water's edge and said nothing.

CHAPTER 63

Sebastian limped across the black-and-white marble floor of his entry hall, his boots squishing foul-smelling water with each step. His cravat and hat were gone, his breeches and coat ripped and smeared with malodorous muck. His valet would likely succumb to a fit of the vapors at the sight of him.

Morey hovered near the door, careful not to approach too near.

"Send Sedlow to me right away," said Sebastian, moving toward the stairs.

"I regret to have to inform your lordship that Sedlow resigned his post this afternoon," said the majordomo in a wooden voice.

Sebastian paused, then gave a soft laugh. "Of course. I'll have to make do with one of the footmen. I need a hot bath. Quickly."

"Yes, my lord." Morey gave a stately bow and withdrew.

Sebastian, having bathed, was slathering an herb-rich ointment from the apothecary's onto his various cuts and scrapes when Tom knocked at his dressing room door.

"I got what you wanted on that Lady Quinlan," said the boy, giving Andrew the footman a puzzled look.

"Yes?" said Sebastian, not turning around.

"She 'ad a scientific demonstration at her 'ouse on Wednesday last — some gent with a bunch of glass tubes full of queer-colored liquids that foamed and smoked. The downstairs maid said she was afeared they'd blow the place sky-high before they was done. 'Er ladyship was there all afternoon. She even 'elped mix the chemicals 'erself."

Tom paused, his nose wrinkling. "What is that smell?"

"The sewers," said Sebastian, pulling a fine shirt over his head.

Tom accepted this without comment. "You don't look surprised," the boy said, sounding rather disappointed.

"No. I already know who killed Guinevere Anglessey."

Sebastian arrived at Curzon Street to find

Audley House standing dark and quiet in the moonlight. Wearing the elegant knee breeches and long-tailed coat of evening dress, he climbed the shallow steps to the front door and found it unlatched. He hesitated a moment, listening to the stillness. Then he pushed the heavy door open and went inside.

Stepping into the darkened hall, he followed the faint flicker of candlelight that showed from the back of the house. The light came from the library, where a single candelabra had been lit upon the mantelpiece. The Chevalier stood beside it, his back to the door as he worked, assembling papers from the desk.

"Your servants seem to have disappeared," said Sebastian, leaning against the doorjamb.

At the sound of Sebastian's voice, the Chevalier started violently. He swung around, his pale face drawn and tense. "My mother dismissed them all this afternoon."

"Going away, are you?"

Varden turned back to the desk. "I am, yes."

"The Earl of Portland is dead."

"Good," said Varden, shoving the papers into a satchel that lay open upon the desk.

Sebastian pushed away from the door and

walked into the room. "He didn't kill her."

"I know."

Sebastian went to stand before the empty fireplace, his gaze on the flickering candle flames reflected in the mirror above the mantel. "Tell me about the Savoy letter."

"How much do you know?"

"About the plan to oust the Regent? Not much. What concerns me now is what happened to Guinevere Anglessey. How did she end up with the letter?"

He thought for a moment that the Chevalier didn't mean to answer. Then the man turned away from the desk, his hands coming up to press flat against his face, his chest rising as he sucked in a deep breath. "The Saturday before she died, we met at an inn near Richmond."

"I see."

Varden let his hands fall, scrubbing them across his face. "I know what you're thinking, but it wasn't like that. Once she'd conceived the child, we met only as friends. She said anything else would be disloyal to Anglessey. We spent that Saturday wandering through the park, then ordered tea in a private parlor at the local inn. I'd been out late the night before, and what with all the fresh air and the exercise, I fell asleep in the chair. I'd taken off my coat and tossed it aside." His lips quirked up into a soft smile that faded almost instantly. "Guin was always so tidy. She picked up the coat, meaning to straighten it. The letter simply fell out of the pocket."

"She read it?"

"Yes. It wasn't like her, to do something like that. I think she must have been suspicious of some of the things she knew I'd been doing lately. When she saw the Savoy seal — well, she simply couldn't resist."

"She confronted you?"

Varden nodded. "When I awoke."

He went to stand beside the library's long table, one hand fiddling with the tumble of books scattered across the gleaming wood. "She was horrified at the thought of what we were planning to do. I still don't understand it. She never had anything but disdain for the house of Hanover. There was even a family legend that some great-great-grandmother of hers had once been mistress to James the Second. But all she could talk about was the miseries of war we'd be visiting on the people — and the danger to me, of course. I tried to make her see that getting rid of the Prince Regent was the only thing that could save England — keep it from going down the same path of violent revolution as the French."

"She didn't believe it?"

"No." He let out his breath in a long sigh, as if he'd been holding it for a lifetime. "I'll never forget the way she looked at me. As if I were a stranger. Someone she'd never seen before."

"Why did she take the letter?" Sebastian asked softly.

"I honestly don't think she meant to. She'd thrown it away from her when we were arguing, as if it were some vile thing she couldn't bear to touch. The only thing I can figure is it must have fallen into the folds of her cloak. She didn't put the cloak on when she left — just snatched it up and ran out. I didn't realize the letter was missing until after she had gone."

"Surely you didn't think she would betray you?"

"No. But when I tried to contact her, she refused to see me. I had to practically accost her in the street one morning when she was on her way to ride in the park. She swore she'd destroyed the letter as soon as she discovered she still had it." He paused, his throat working as he swallowed. "And then she told me she never wanted to see me again."

Sebastian studied the young man's taut profile. "But when you told your mother the letter had been destroyed, she didn't believe you?"

His face contorted with pain. "No."

"And so your mother wrote Guinevere a note in your hand, asking her to bring the letter to Smithfield. Only, Guinevere didn't bring the letter. She couldn't, because she'd already destroyed it. But your mother killed her, anyway."

"Yes," said Varden in a torn whisper. "She said she couldn't allow Guinevere to live. Not with what she knew."

"When did you put it all together?"

"This afternoon. When I saw the note and you told me about the necklace. I came home and confronted her. She didn't even try to deny it. She said she'd done it for me." He dragged in a ragged breath that shuddered his chest. "God help me. She did it for me."

"Your father was related to the House of Savoy?"

Varden swung his head to look at Sebastian through narrowed eyes. "Yes, although not to the Stuarts. How did you know?"

"Something you said to me once, about impoverished royal relatives. What did they promise you in return for your support? A rich wife?"

A faint touch of color stained the ridges

of his high cheekbones. "Yes."

"No wonder Guinevere never wanted to see you again."

"Well, what the devil was I supposed to do?" demanded Varden, pushing away from the window. "Spend the rest of my life in poverty, waiting for Anglessey to die? The man could live another twenty or thirty years."

"Or he could be dead before the end of the summer."

Varden's head jerked back as if he'd been slapped. "She never told me that. The first I knew of it was from you." He let out a low, harsh laugh. "Do you know what she said to me the last time I saw her? She said she was glad her father had refused to let her marry me. She said . . . she said she'd loved me all her life, but now she realized that the boy she'd loved had grown up to be less of a man than the husband she'd married."

The silence of the house seemed to stretch around them, thick and ominous.

"Your mother," said Sebastian, "where is she?"

"Upstairs."

Sebastian turned toward the door, then paused to look back at the man who still stood beside the desk, one fist clenched around the handles of the satchel. "This conspiracy against the Prince . . . who else was involved besides Portland?"

"I don't know. Portland was the contact between Savoy and the others. He kept their identities secret."

Sebastian nodded. It might be a lie, but he doubted it. Men in positions of power were typically very, very careful about committing themselves to treason. "What will you do?"

Varden twitched one shoulder. "Go to the Continent."

"To Savoy?"

"Perhaps. Or perhaps I'll go to France. Make my peace with Napoléon." He cast Sebastian a penetrating look from beneath dark, heavy brows. "You don't feel it incumbent upon you to attempt to stop me?"

"No. But others will doubtless feel differently." Sebastian turned again toward the stairs. "I suggest you lose no time in reaching the coast."

CHAPTER 64

A gentlewoman never lay upon her bed until it was time to retire for the night. For spells of faintness and periods of rest, a lady of quality had a small daybed in her dressing room.

And so Sebastian found Lady Audley there, on a Grecian-style couch upholstered in green velvet. She wore an evening dress of black silk richly embroidered and trimmed with Chantilly lace, and had loosened her hair so that it spread out on the pillow around her face like a bright flame. Her breathing was already slowed, her cheeks pale. Whining softly on the carpet beside her lay the collie bitch, Cloe.

"What did you take?" asked Sebastian, pausing just inside the doorway. "Cyanide?"

Her gaze flickered toward him. "No. Opiates. I will simply go to sleep and never awake."

"It's a far kinder death than the one you

gave Guinevere."

"With Guinevere, I needed something that would act quickly."

He walked into the room. The collie stretched to her feet and padded up to him, sniffing. He crouched down to stroke her soft coat.

"How did you know it was me?" Isolde asked when he remained silent. "It was the necklace, wasn't it?"

"The necklace and the note." And the certainty that had Claire been the killer, Portland would never have disclaimed responsibility for Guinevere's death.

"The note." Isolde moved her head restlessly against the pillow. "That, I hadn't anticipated. What woman doesn't destroy a note from her lover?"

"Yet you sent someone to search her rooms for it after her death."

"No. He was looking for the Savoy letter."

"That she did destroy."

With a whine, the collie returned to its mistress's side. Isolde reached out to rest one hand on her neck. "Varden confronted me. After you spoke with him. The note I could have denied, but not the necklace." She gave a soft laugh. "How ironic. It was supposed to bring its owner long life. Instead it has brought me death."

Sebastian stretched to his feet. "But it wasn't meant for you, was it? It had once belonged to one of Guinevere's great-grandmothers. That woman you met in the south of France asked you to give it to Guinevere, didn't she? But you kept it instead."

Isolde's voice sharpened. "That necklace has power. I could feel it when I held it in my hand. Power. I didn't often wear it. It was enough for me simply to have it." Her tongue darted out to moisten her dry lips. "Now it's gone, and I am dead."

"So is Guinevere."

For a moment, the serene features of Isolde's face contorted with a quiver of rage and hatred so fierce it took him by surprise. "She would have ruined everything. Everything I worked so hard to bring about."

Sebastian shook his head. "She loved Varden. She would never have destroyed him."

"Yet she did destroy him in the end."

"No." Sebastian turned toward the door. "You've done that. You've destroyed Varden and Claire both."

"Claire knew nothing of this. Nothing."

"And Portland?"

"Portland was a fool."

He heard her suck in a gasping breath

and turned to look back at her. She was almost gone now. "I've never understood why you interfered in all this," she said hoarsely.

"The woman with the necklace," said Sebastian.

Lady Audley's lips parted, her delicately arched brows twitching together in the ghost of a frown. "I don't understand."

"She was my mother."

Dressed in a splendid scarlet uniform with a saber at his side, the Prince Regent was having a rollicking good time. He was a marvelous host; everyone said so. People were always praising him for his generosity and congeniality.

The ballroom was so crowded that no one could actually dance, but that didn't matter. The orchestra played gamely on, while the guests amused themselves by taking in the wonders of his most recent architectural improvements to Carlton House. He'd heard gasps of awe provoked by the grandeur of the Throne Room, with its curtained bays and gilded columns, its rich red brocades and massively carved chairs. The Circular Dining Room, with its mirrored walls reflecting a two-hundred-foot table that stretched out into the Conservatory, was sure to be the talk of the town for weeks to come.

At half past two, supper would be announced, and then everyone would marvel at the real serpentine stream he'd had confected to run down the center of his table and meander around the massive silver tureens and serving dishes. Flowing between banks built up from moss and rocks, with real flowers and miniature bridges, the river featured live gold and silver fish and created an amazing spectacle. He just hoped the fish didn't start dying.

Looking out across a garden filled with flambeaux and Chinese lanterns, George felt a thrill of pride. For those guests not fortunate enough to sit at the Prince's table, there was an enormous supper tent festooned with gilded ropes and flowers. Then his gaze fell on the tall, dark-haired figure working his way through the crowds, and George's smile slipped.

Viscount Devlin was correctly, even exquisitely attired in evening dress, with knee breeches and silver-buckled shoes. But heads still turned his way and conversations lagged when he walked past.

"We need to talk," said the Viscount, coming up to where George's cousin, Jarvis, stood chatting with the Comte de Lille.

"Good God," said Jarvis with a laugh. "Not now."

Devlin's smile never slipped, but his terrible yellow eyes narrowed in a way that sent a shiver up George's spine and had him groping for his smelling salts.

"Now," said Devlin.

"It would have been considerably more convenient," said Jarvis, producing an enameled gold snuffbox from his pocket and flipping it open with one practiced finger, "if you could have discovered Lady Anglessey had been killed by a jealous lover. We can hardly tell people this tale, now, can we?"

Sebastian simply stared at him. They were in a small withdrawing room set apart from the main state apartments in Carlton House. But the voices and laughter of the Prince's two thousand guests, the hurried footsteps of the servants, the clink of fine china and glassware were like a roar around them.

Jarvis lifted a pinch of snuff to one nostril. "We'll have to place the blame on Varden."

Sebastian gave a short laugh. "Why not? It worked with Pierrepont. Whatever would we do without the French?"

Jarvis sniffed. "You didn't, by any chance,

come upon the names of the other conspirators?"

"No. But there are others — you can be certain of that."

"Yes." Jarvis dusted his fingers. "I doubt they'll make a move in the immediate future, however. Not after this. Particularly if we shift the regiments around and keep the Prince here in London."

The Prince wouldn't be happy with the change of plans, Sebastian knew. His Royal Highness was already fretting, anxious to return to Brighton. The people of Brighton didn't tend to boo him when he drove down the street the way they did in London.

"And the necklace?" said Jarvis. "Did you ever discover how Lady Anglessey came to be wearing it?"

There was something in the big man's smile that told Sebastian that Jarvis knew: he knew that Sebastian's mother still lived, even if he didn't quite understand how her necklace had come to be clasped around the throat of a murdered woman in Brighton.

Sebastian slipped the triskelion from his pocket. Just the sight of it stirred within him a well of anger and hurt that was suddenly more than he could bear. He held it for a moment, its smoothly polished stone cool against his palm. What had made his mother change her mind all those years ago in France? he wondered. Why had she decided to give it up to Guinevere after all?

"No," said Sebastian, returning Jarvis's lying smile with one of his own. "But perhaps you can see that it is returned to her."

With a flick of his wrist, he tossed the necklace onto the table at the big man's elbow. Then he turned and walked out of the room.

CHAPTER 65

The churchyard of St. Anne's lay peaceful and quiet, a place of wind-tossed trees and dark shadows trembling over tombstones that loomed pale in the moonlight. But near where he knew Guinevere Anglessey to lie, Sebastian could see a glimmer of light.

Directing his coachman to pull up, Sebastian threaded his way through the trees. The light was too constant to belong to grave robbers. It was a common enough practice for families to hire a watchman to sit through the night beside the grave of a newly buried loved one. In the depths of a cold winter it was sometimes necessary to maintain the vigil for months. The heat of summer usually made a body unusable to the surgeons in a week.

Only, this was no hired guard. The Marquis of Anglessey himself had come to keep watch over the body of his beautiful young wife. He sat beside her tomb in a campaign chair, a rug pulled over his lap despite the warmth of the night. A blunderbuss lay across his knees.

"Devlin here," Sebastian called in a clear, ringing voice. "Don't shoot."

"Devlin?" The old man shifted in his chair, his face contorting as he squinted into the darkness. "What are you doing here?"

Sebastian stepped into the circle of light cast by a brass lantern and hunkered down beside the old man's chair. "I've something to tell you," he said. And there, beside Guinevere Anglessey's grave with the night wind soft against his cheek, Sebastian told Guinevere's husband how she had died, and why.

When Sebastian had finished, the Marquis sat in silence for some moments, his head bowed, his breath coming slow and heavy. Then he lifted his head to fix Sebastian with a fierce stare. "This woman — this Lady Audley. You're certain she's dead?"

"Yes."

He nodded. The wind gusted up, shifting the leaves of the oak tree overhead and bringing them the scents of the place, of long grass and decay and death.

"Do you believe in God?" Anglessey asked suddenly, breaking the silence that had fallen between them.

Sebastian met the old man's anguished

gaze and answered honestly, "Not anymore, no."

Anglessey sighed. "I wish I didn't. If I didn't, I would take this gun and blow Bevan's brains out. It's what I should have done before."

"Perhaps if you can stay alive long enough you'll be lucky and someone else will do it for you."

Anglessey grunted. "The ones who deserve to die rarely do."

He stared off across the graveyard to where the moonlight reflected off the high arched windows of the ancient stone church. "I was sitting here tonight, wondering what it would have been like if I had been born thirty years later — or if Guinevere had been born thirty years earlier. Do you think she would have loved me?"

"She loved you. I think in the end she came to realize you had given her the one thing no one else in her life ever had."

Anglessey shook his head, not understanding. "What was that?"

"Your unselfish love."

The old man's eyes squeezed nearly shut, as if he were wincing at some deep, inner pain. "I was selfish. If I hadn't been so obsessed with getting an heir — if I hadn't pushed her into that young man's arms again — she never would have died."

"You can't know that. I may not believe in God, but I've come to believe that there is a pattern. A pattern that works itself out in ways we can't begin to understand."

"Isn't that just another way of describing God?"

"Perhaps," said Sebastian. He was suddenly very tired. He felt a powerful need to hold Kat in his arms. To hold her safe and close forever. "Perhaps it is."

He came to her in the stillness of the night, when the last carriage had rumbled through the streets and the moon was only a pale memory on the horizon. Moving restlessly in the unnatural heat of the night, Kat awoke and found Devlin beside her.

"Marry me, Kat," he said, his hand shaking as he brushed the hair from her sweat-dampened brow.

She watched his face in the dying moonlight, watched until the hope began to fade and the hurt crept in. And when she could bear it no longer she leaned into him, her forehead pressing against his shoulder so that she couldn't see his face and he couldn't see hers. "I can't. There's something you don't know about me. Something I've done."

"I don't care what you've done." He twisted his fingers through her hair, his thumbs slipping under her chin to force her head up. "There's nothing you could have done that would make me —"

She pressed her fingertips to his lips, stopping his words. "No. You can't say that when you don't know what it is. And I don't have the courage to tell you."

"I know I love you," he said, his lips moving against her fingers.

"Then let that be enough. Please, Sebastian. Let that be enough."

Tossing his chapeau bras and gloves on a table in the darkened hall, Jarvis walked into his library, kindled a small branch of candles, and poured himself a glass of brandy.

Smiling with satisfaction, he carried the brandy to a chair beside the fire. But after a moment, he set the brandy aside untasted and slipped Lady Hendon's silver-and-bluestone necklace from his pocket.

Threading the chain through his fingers, he held it up to the light, the bluestone disk and its superimposed silver triskelion tracing a slow arc as it swung back and forth through the air. It was all nonsense, of course, the legend that had grown up around the thing; intellectually he knew that. And yet it seemed to him that he could feel the pendant's power. Feel it, yet not grasp it.

"Papa?"

Looking around, he found his daughter, Hero, standing in the doorway. His fist closed over the pendant, stilling it.

"Why are you still up?" she asked, coming into the room. In the white satin evening gown she'd chosen for the Prince's fete, with the soft light of the candles golden on her skin and her hair crimped around her face, she almost looked pretty.

He dropped the necklace onto the table and reached for his glass. "I thought I'd have a brandy before going up to bed."

Her gaze fell on the necklace beside him. "What an interesting piece," she said, reaching to pick it up before he could stop her.

She cradled the pendant in her palm. As he watched, her expression slowly altered, her lips parting, her eyebrows twitching together.

"What?" he said more sharply than he'd intended. "What is it?"

"Nothing. It's just . . ." She gave a shaky laugh. "It sounds ridiculous, but it's almost as if I can feel it growing warm in my hand." She looked up at him. "Whose is it?"

Jarvis drained his glass in one long pull and set it aside. "I believe it's yours."

AUTHOR'S NOTE

The Jacobite threat to the Hanoverian dynasty was considered quite real in Georgian England. The Catholic Relief Act of 1778 was contingent upon the swearing of an oath to disavow the Stuarts. But the death in the early nineteenth century of Henry Stuart, brother of Bonny Prince Charlie, effectively ended the Stuart dynasty. Their claim passed to the King of Savoy, who was descended from the daughter of Charles I (the Hanoverians traced their descent from a daughter of Charles I's father, James I).

This much is history. The Prince of Wales did, indeed, hold a grand fete in June of 1811, to celebrate the beginning of his Regency. It was much as I have described it, although sticklers will note that I have moved its date back one day to accommodate my story. The Prince Regent's obsession with all things Stuart was also very real, as was his enormous unpopularity. The song Sebastian hears the crowd singing on the night of the fete was actually part of a poem written by Charles Lamb in 1812. However, the 1811 conspiracy to replace the Hanovers with the House of Savoy is my invention, as is the existence of a daughter Anne married to a Danish prince.

The story of the Welsh mistress of James II and her necklace is based in part on the true story of a woman named Goditha Price. She bore Prince James two children, one of whom, Mary Stuart, married a Scottish laird named McBean. As a wedding present she received from her royal father her mother's necklace. An ancient piece in the form of a silver triskelion set against a bluestone disk, the necklace is said to grow warm in the hands of the one destined to possess it. It is also said to bring long life.

Mary Stuart gave the necklace to her son, Edward McBean, when his participation in a rising against the Hanoverian dynasty on behalf of his uncle, the Old Pretender, led to his exile. McBean sailed for America, where he lived to the ripe old age of 102 and fathered a large family from which the author is descended. The necklace has not, unfortunately, descended along my branch

512

of the family. Its most recent owner, a salty old lady I first met over the Internet, died at the age of 103.

ABOUT THE AUTHOR

C. S. Harris graduated Phi Beta Kappa, summa cum laude, with a degree in classics before earning a PhD in European history. A respected scholar of the French Revolution and nineteenth-century Europe, she is also the author of the nonfiction study *Women, Equality, and the French Revolution,* written under the name of Candice E. Proctor. After years of living in England and various far-flung regions of the old British Empire, she now makes her home in New Orleans with her husband, retired Army intelligence officer Steve Harris, and two daughters. Visit the author at www.csharris .net.